NEW WORLDS

Borgo Press Books by DAMIEN BRODERICK

Adrift in the Noösphere: Science Fiction Stories
Building New Worlds, 1946-1959 (with John Boston)
Chained to the Alien: The Best of ASFR: Australian SF Review (Second Series) [Editor]
Climbing Mount Implausible: The Evolution of a Science Fiction Writer
Embarrass My Dog: The Way We Were, the Things We Thought
Ferocious Minds: Polymathy and the New Enlightenment
Human's Burden: A Science Fiction Novel (with Rory Barnes)
I'm Dying Here: A Comedy of Bad Manners (with Rory Barnes)
New Worlds: Before the New Wave, 1960-1964 (with John Boston)
Post Mortal Syndrome: A Science Fiction Novel (with Barbara Lamar)
Skiffy and Mimesis: More Best of ASFR: Australian SF Review (Second Series) [Editor]
Strange Highways: Reading Science Fantasy, 1950-1967 (with John Boston)
Unleashing the Strange: Twenty-First Century Science Fiction Literature
Warriors of the Tao: The Best of Science Fiction: A Review of Speculative Literature [Editor with Van Ikin]
x, y, z, t: Dimensions of Science Fiction
Zones: A Science Fiction Novel (with Rory Barnes)

Borgo Press Books by JOHN BOSTON

Building New Worlds, 1946-1959 (with Damien Broderick)
New Worlds: Before the New Wave, 1960-1964 (with Damien Broderick)
Strange Highways: Reading Science Fantasy, 1950-1967 (with Damien Broderick)

NEW WORLDS

BEFORE THE NEW WAVE, 1960-1964: THE CARNELL ERA, VOLUME TWO

JOHN BOSTON &

DAMIEN BRODERICK

THE BORGO PRESS
MMXIII

Borgo Literary Guides
ISSN 0891-9623
Number Seventeen

NEW WORLDS

FIRST EDITION

Published by Wildside Press LLC

www.wildsidebooks.com

DEDICATION

As always, for Dori and the guys.
J.B.

These books were first aired in more rudimentary form on the Fictionmags Internet discussion group, and benefited greatly from the robust and erudite commentary and correction customary among its members. In particular we thank Fictionmags members Ned Brooks, William G. Contento, Ian Covell, Steve Holland, Frank Hollander, Rich Horton, David Langford, Dennis Lien, Barry Malzberg, Todd Mason, David Pringle, Robert Silverberg, and Phil Stephensen-Payne, as well as David Ketterer, for the encouragement, insight, and information that they respectively provided.

J.B. and D.B.

CONTENTS

INTRODUCTION

by Damien Broderick

Science fiction (SF) is often regarded as one of the new genres created in America, alongside the Western, "mean streets" *noir* crime fiction, and "chick lit." By the time SF came close to taking over the blockbuster movie slot in the late twentieth century and the start of the new millennium, it could be seen as the pre-eminent form of storytelling in the voice of the technological West. Yet the names still often blurted out when someone expresses an interest in science fiction are not American. "Oh, you mean that Jules Verne, H. G. Wells stuff?" Leaving aside the antiquity of these fabled names, it's revealing that one is French and the other British.

Still, commercial science fiction really did start as a mass commercial genre in the USA. So it can come as some surprise that a parallel universe of SF developed in Britain in the middle of last century, sometimes borrowing stories from the established US writers and magazines but also developing its own distinctive strains of SF narrative. This book looks closely at two magazines that played a key role in this parallel-but-entwined history, the classic British science fiction magazine *New Worlds* from the start of the Sixties and its younger sibling *Science Fiction Adventures*, through to their demise or transformation in the mid-1960s. It follows the first volume, *Building New Worlds*, which carried *New Worlds* from its founding amid the ruins of war into the post-Sputnik era.

As noted in Volume One, John Boston is an occasional

science fiction critic of long standing, and attorney (Director of the Prisoners' Rights Project of the New York City Legal Aid Society and co-author of the *Prisoners' Self-Help Litigation Manual*).[1] Several years ago, Boston read through every issue of *New Worlds*——sometimes with grim disbelief, sometimes with unexpected pleasure, often with gusts of laughter, always with intent interest. That magazine is best remembered today as the fountainhead of the New Wave of audacious experimental SF in the second half of the 1960s, and beyond, under the great helmsman, Michael Moorcock, and his madcap transgressive associates. But these 141 pioneering issues, from 1946 to 1964, were edited by the magazine's founder, Edward John (Ted, or John) Carnell (1912-72). Not to be confused with the prominent Baptist theologian and apologist of the same name, Ted Carnell was a pillar of the old-style UK SF establishment, but gamely supportive of innovators——most famously, of the brilliant J. G. Ballard, whose first work he nurtured.

John Boston, for his own amusement, found himself writing an extensive commentary on those early, foundational years of *New Worlds* and companion magazines *Science Fantasy* and *Science Fiction Adventures*. He posted his ongoing analysis in a long semi-critical series to a closed listserv devoted to enthusiasts of pulp and subsequent popular magazines. The present study, published in three parts (two of them largely focused on *New Worlds*) due to the length of its exacting but entertaining coverage of these fifteen years of publication, is an edited and reorganized version of those electronic posts. This volume covers the late years of *New Worlds*, from the point at which it had become solidly established as the UK's leading SF magazine to its transformation into a quite new kind of SF.

I found Boston's issue-by-issue forensic probing of this history enthralling and amusing, and read it sometimes with shudders and grimaces breaking through, and often with a

---

1. See "The Long Road Toward Reform," http://www.wahmee.com/pln_john_boston.pdf (visited 9/9/2011).

delighted grin at a neatly turned *bon mot*. Don't expect a dry, modishly theorized academic analysis, nor a rah-rah handclapping celebration of the "Good Old Days." This is a candid and astute reader's response to a magazine that, by today's standards, was often not very good—but one that was immensely important in its time, and improved, like the Little Engine (or maybe Starship) That Could. The story of how *New Worlds* got better, achieving and consolidating its position, is an essential piece of the history of the genres of the fantastic in the UK, and indeed the world.

I had the good fortune, as an SF theorist and writer, to read these chapters as they arrived via email. Greatly entertained, often flushed by nostalgia (for this was the literature of my remembered youth), I insisted to John Boston that his work deserved to be read by as many interested people as possible. He was busy on important legal work in defense of those lost in an overburdened US criminal justice (or "justice") system, and had no time for such laborious scutwork. I rapped on his internet door from time to time, insisting that it would be a shame—a crime, even—not to allow this material to be read by the world at large.

At last he buckled, and passed me his large files covering all the issues of Carnell's *New Worlds* and the short-lived *Science Fiction Adventures* (some quarter million words), plus another large book's worth of equivalent reading into *Science Fantasy* (my favorite as an adolescent, in colonial Australia). All three volumes of reading and commentary really comprise one large book of some 350,000 words. This concluding portion carries the saga of *New Worlds* through to the end of the Carnell era and the birth of its scandalous successor.

1: ANYTHING GOES
(1960-61)

New Worlds maintains its groove in 1960 and 1961, staying monthly, price 2/6, 128 pages exclusive of covers.[2] As usual, there's an editorial in every issue (a few of them guest editorials) and "The Literary Line-Up," readers' story ratings and announcements of next issue's contents, appears in all but one, plus another issue where it is combined with the editorial. The letter column "Postmortem" and book reviews appear intermittently, and there's a *New Worlds* Profile on every inside front cover, plus a brief science article by Kenneth Johns in more issues than not. The cover format remains mostly the same: logo, unchanged for years, on a band across the top, contents listed on a band down the left side. The top band doesn't go all the way across the top until **99**, and the clearly demarcated side band

---

2. Bibliographic and historical information not from the magazine itself is from the *Science Fiction, Fantasy, & Weird Fiction Magazine Index* by Stephen T. Miller and William G. Contento; from Contento's *Index to Science Fiction Anthologies and Collections* (both on CD-ROM from Locus Publications); from Ashley's article on *New Worlds* in *Science Fiction, Fantasy and Weird Fiction Magazines*, edited by Marshall B. Tymn and Mike Ashley (Greenwood Press, 1985); from Ashley's recent histories of the SF magazines, *The Time Machines* and *Transformations* (Liverpool University Press, 2000 and 2005); and from Rob Hansen's web site, http://www.fiawol.org.uk/FanStuff/THEN%20Archive/NewWorlds/NewWo.htm (visited 9/9/11).
Occasional references to the *Encyclopedia of Science Fiction* are to the Second Edition by John Clute and Peter Nicholls (St. Martin's Press, 1995), the latest available at time of writing.

disappears on **113**, but overall the changes are minor and the look of the magazine is little altered.[3]

Unfortunately, the quality of the magazine has slipped rather than progressed from the promising issues of 1958-59, both in its content and in its visual presentation. Brian Lewis, who dominated that period, has only a little more than half of the 1960-61 covers, and they tend more towards the deadeningly literal-minded and illustrative than towards the gaudily imaginative and surreal, as witness **91, 92, 101, 103, 106, 107, 108**. These are dominated by human figures, which in Lewis's hands generally appear waxen or (see especially **92**) wooden. It's not until the end of the period (**113**, Dec. 1961) that he comes up with anything comparable to his best earlier Richard Powers-ish efforts; **98** and **104** are the nearest competitors. In between, he manages some decent enough space and planetary scenes (no foregrounded people, just strange landscapes and machines); see **96, 100, 111**.

Jarr provides five of the 1960 covers, which vary widely in quality and approach, the best ones being **93**, with its strange reptilian creatures being ridden over a desert through a racetrack of what look like gigantic wishbones, and **95**, a colorful rendering of Sector General. The others (**94, 97, 99**) are more humdrum and **99** is downright crude. Sydney Jordan contributes three covers of varying quality and attitude, ranging from the stiff and simplistic (**102**) to a striking if hokily melodramatic offering (**105**) that looks like it might belong on a better-than-average Ace Double, with **109** splitting the difference.

In late 1961, Gerard Quinn reappears with two covers, neither among his best: another Sector General illustration for **110** and an extraterrestrial violinist (a trio all by itself) on **112**.[4]

---

3. See these covers at http://www.sfcovers.net/mainnav.htm. That URL takes you to the main page and you'll have to navigate from there, but how to do so is self-explanatory. Among this site's virtues is an artist index. Another handy source—and probably easier to use—is http://www.philsp.com/mags/newworlds.html (both sites visited 9/8/11).

4. Broderick disagrees, finding **110** creepily enticing, and **112** charming.

Carnell commences putting the cover artist's name on the cover along with the story titles with **112**, whether in honor of Quinn's return is not clear—in any case this innovation lasted only a few issues (for that matter, cover illustrations only lasted for another half-year).

The artists get considerable attention in the *New Worlds* Profiles. Brian Lewis is profiled in **104**, where it is said that he wanted to be an artist since childhood, a revelation Carnell is granted while attending Lewis's newest child's christening. After technical school, Lewis spent seven years in the RAF, during which he began reading SF. Then he took up "engineering draughtsmanship," later became a technical artist with Decca Radar, and left that position in the Fall of 1960 for a job drawing "picture strips" for Beaverbrook Newspapers—currently football strips in the Scottish *Daily Express*, aspiring to get one in the London edition shortly. He works in the same studio as Sydney Jordan, who draws the "Jeff Hawke" SF strip in the *Daily Express*.

Jordan is profiled in the next issue, **105**. Born in Dundee in 1928, he reveals his long-standing preoccupation with horror movies. He spent two years at Miles Aircraft Technical School, took up drawing seriously in 1952 and two years later was commissioned to do "Jeff Hawke." He has admired Theodore Sturgeon's work since *Unknown Worlds* and "fulfilled a small ambition when asked to illustrate 'Venus Plus X'." He now lives in Surbiton.

Gerard Quinn is profiled in **110**. Still in Belfast, he has had for some five years a commercial art position with a Belfast business house, leaving him little time for magazine work (plus he now has a wife and three children). However, he is friends with James White, and when he read the draft of White's novelette "Resident Physician" he felt compelled to do a painting for it. "His technique has changed considerably during his five years' absence from our magazine. He now uses coloured inks which almost give an oil painting effect and covers the finished work with a coat of Damar varnish." Carnell hopes for more.

In the event, Quinn did only three more covers for *New Worlds* before the magazine abandoned painted covers entirely. But he also did nine for *Science Fantasy* and three for *Science Fiction Adventures* before work dried up in those magazines.

Interior illustrations make a brief return starting with **100**, the anniversary issue. ATom, a.k.a. Arthur Thomson, provides a number of small sketches—two or three for some of the stories. These continue in **101** but are then dropped, although some of them are recycled as fillers in later issues. Carnell says in his **104** editorial that there was no reaction from fandom, which had been agitating for the return of interior art. "My final summary, therefore, is that you couldn't care one way or the other and as it is easier, editorially, not to have art work in the magazine, I see no reason to belabour the fact."

There are a couple of milestones during this period. One is the "anniversary" 100th issue, which Carnell celebrates by cramming in as many big names with short items as will fit. It's an impressive contents list—Aldiss, Brunner, Kapp, Hynam (Kippax), Rackham (with an article), William F. Temple, Eric Frank Russell (with a guest editorial), Arthur Sellings (a film review), Tubb, White, and Wyndham, and *no* F. G. Rayer or E. R. James—but none of the stories are especially memorable with the possible exception of Aldiss's "Old Hundredth." Ballard's "The Voices of Time," maybe the most celebrated story *New Worlds* has published up to this point, was squeezed out of the special issue because of length.

The other notable event is the US reprint edition of *New Worlds*, which unfortunately turned into a fiasco, and a brief one at that. As Carnell explains in his **99** editorial, "Missing Links," he had arranged North American distribution of his magazines for as early as October 1959, but then held *New Worlds* back from the deal on the promise of a full-fledged US reprint edition. However, when that edition appeared, it almost immediately disappeared. Carnell was notified that it would be discontinued while the first issue was still on the stands, though four more, already in the pipeline, were issued. Along with it went Great American Publications' other magazine titles, one of which was *Fantastic Universe*, in the last phase of the die-back of SF magazines following the late-1950s collapse of magazine distribution in the US. To Carnell's great if stiff-necked annoyance, no credit was given to his editorial role or even to the British origin of the magazine, editorial credit being given to Hans Stefan Santesson. I'm sure this irritation was compounded by Carnell's own scrupulous treatment of the American origins of the first several issues of *Science Fiction Adventures*.

The magazine's major contribution to the American SF scene was what I think were the second and third American appearances of J. G. Ballard: "The Waiting Grounds" in June 1960 and "Manhole 69" in July 1960. ("The Sound-Sweep" was reprinted in Judith Merril's annual "best" anthology published in 1960, and it is possible that that publication technically preceded these magazine appearances, though I doubt many people saw it before the Merril book appeared in paperback.)

Otherwise, the US *New Worlds* gave a pretty good cross-section of what was going on in the UK magazine at the time, from Aldiss, James White, and Colin Kapp to F. G. Rayer and E. R. James—though as it happened, the Rayer and James stories (six of them!) in those issues include some of those authors' better moments. In fact, the latter half of 1959, from which most of the reprinted stories came, represented a high point in the magazine's short fiction.

The US issues did not correspond completely with British issues. They couldn't, since the reprint magazine did not include the serials. In most issues, most of the stories were from one UK issue with supplementation from the same general time period (e.g., the second US issue contained four stories from UK issue **86**, August 1959, and one each from **77** and **78**, the March and April 1959 issues). There were a few stories from older issues, presumably selected on merit, since they all had some: Robert Presslie's "Another Word for Man," Aldiss's "Segregation" (retitled "Planet of Death," which I'm sure impressed him and Carnell), and Ballard's "Manhole 69."

A few filler stories and articles were reprinted from *Fantastic Universe*, and the last couple of issues included a fanzine review column, "Fannotations" by Belle C. Dietz, left homeless by the demise of *Fantastic Universe*.

One final loose end from *New Worlds*'s colonial misadventure is Sam Moskowitz's specially commissioned editorial for the US edition, explaining the magazine's origins, which was killed. Carnell presents it in **99** as a guest editorial, though it's hard to see why. About half of its page and a half of text consists of name-checking prominent British SF through the 1940s. Then there's a potted history of *New Worlds* that makes the following interesting comparison: "...John Carnell repayed [sic] his debt to the writers who helped him by making *New Worlds* to British science fiction what *Story* was to the art of the short story in the United States." Moskowitz's familiar tormented literacy also shows through. Parse this: "After World War II, British writers realizing they did not have a regular market that would develop science fiction talent went into a huddle with John Carnell, whose newly established *New Worlds* had lost its publisher after three issues and subsidized the magazine to keep it alive."

§

The fiction in these two years' issues of *New Worlds* is, overall, surprisingly lackluster, disappointingly so in view of the very noticeable improvement in 1958-59. The best of these years' fiction is as good as Carnell's *New Worlds* ever got, but there's not a lot of it. After Ballard and Aldiss, things fall off pretty quickly.

The most prolific contributor during these two years is J. G. Ballard, with eight appearances, one of them the serial "Storm-Wind," which in a different version became his first US book as *The Wind from Nowhere*. His other contributions include several of his best-known early stories. Ballard is followed by E. C. Tubb, with seven appearances (one as by Alan Guthrie), Philip E. High and John Rackham (six each, with Rackham contributing an article and an editorial as well), and five each by James White, Brian Aldiss (including a serial, plus a guest editorial), Colin Kapp, Kenneth Bulmer (one each under the names Frank Brandon and Rupert Clinton, and including two serials), and A. Bertram Chandler (four under the George Whitley pseudonym). Francis G. Rayer and Alan Barclay have only two appearances each, and E. R. James is entirely missing.

What is striking about the list of prolific contributors is that they are all usual suspects by now, with the exception of John Rackham, and he'd had half a dozen stories in *Science Fantasy* and elsewhere before his *New Worlds* debut. The quality of his work is uneven. The only other new writers to emerge and make a strong showing during this period are Australians David Rome (pseudonym of David Boutland) (four stories), Wynne Whiteford (three), and Lee Harding (two, and two in *Science Fantasy*). Rome contributed another 10 stories to the Nova magazines, and Harding provided 8, but Whiteford (who, like Rackham, had a track record in other magazines anyway) disappeared from the genre for 18 years after his three 1960 stories. So these two years suffer from a dearth of emerging and lasting talent.

What is striking substantively about the fiction in these issues is that the staid *New Worlds*, formerly constrained by Carnell's fear of prosecution for indecency, has now become pretty racy indeed—at least by the standards of the preceding years. As Brian Aldiss put it, the Romans are becoming Italians,[5] in *New Worlds* as in the surrounding society. (Carnell backhandedly acknowledges this point in a comment about Aldiss in the *New Worlds* Profile in **113**: "A penchant for off-trail approaches to various s-f themes makes his work controversial but more than adds lustre to the changing mores of the genre.") The quantity of sexual allusion and in a few cases preoccupation is quite striking, though the quality is, of course, another matter. The most admirable exemplar of this tendency is the serialization of

5. Brian W. Aldiss with David Wingrove, *Trillion Year Spree* (Atheneum, 1986), p. 299.

Sturgeon's *Venus Plus X*, discussed below. At the other pole, as it were, is something like John Rackham's "Blink" (**106**), which I will let speak for itself as far as possible. Unfortunately it will go on for a while.

In "Blink," young journalist Cameron is much put out at his complacent society and also at his present assignment, to track down Petra Dawson, whose father Sir Arthur is believed to have betrayed Earth to the alien Beetles, who have taken over Mars. He finds Petra easily enough, and engages her in a conversation about her father and the advent of the Beetles, during which she displays a passive and fatalistic attitude. Further: "The edge of her gown parted and slid back from her hip, revealing her smoothly naked, rounded rump and thigh, quivering." Cameron's "fingers itched to hit out, to smack that pink and inviting flesh, to jolt some sort of reaction into her."

He restrains himself momentarily. But a bit later, after another "What does it matter?" from Petra:

> This time the sight of her bare rump was too inviting to be resisted. He swept his flat hand down, smartly. The smack echoed, and was caught and drowned by her sudden, full-throated yell. She twisted, sat halfway up, and he thought he saw a momentary flash of fire in her eyes. Then, rubbing her abused flesh with a trembling hand, she said, "What did you do that for?" Her voice was quite loud, and he grinned.
>
> "Made you come alive, didn't it? Now, you just say that to me once more, 'What does it matter?' and you'll get more of the same, understand?" [Etc.]

She shows him Sir Arthur's letter from Mars, which adds up to nothing in particular. He decides he will help her vindicate her father's name. She proceeds to change clothes in front of him ("Pinkly nude, she put a finger to her lip as she decided what to wear. He could see his violent hand-print quite plainly now, and regretted it.") So they are off to the Humaneering Institute.

where her father used to work, after a brief pause to knock out and tie up a meddling civil warden investigating Petra's yell. In Cameron's open air car, from which he has removed the speed governor, she is quite taken by the breeze:

> With a pretty determination, she let go his arm, and her grip on the dashboard. Still blinking, she slid out of the folds of her gown, letting it fall to her waist, and offered her body to the breeze. Unconsciously graceful, she swayed and turned, to let the rushing air press and rush past her skin. The expression on her face was like that of a child with a new treat.

Arriving at the Institute, they are greeted by an Amazonian figure named Margrit: "No slip of a girl, this, but a big, buxom, magnificently shapely young woman." She's got some handshake, too. They've arrived just in time to catch a broadcast of a spaceship arriving from Mars, debarking some brainwashed-looking people plus one Crowther, who announces that he has a message from Sir Arthur, which he has to deliver to his colleagues in person, but doesn't mind saying on TV: "Remember Pavlov's dogs."

The Institute folks look at his old letter again and Petra discerns that the first letters of each sentence spell out "EYE BLINK KEY TO BEETLE HEEL." Margrit says this must refer to the aliens' Achilles heel. Cameron grabs her by the shoulders and says "You're a genius! A big beautiful genius!" "'Go on!' she chuckled. 'You save that for when you mean it,' and she gave him a hearty thump on the shoulder with her fist. He swung away, just in time to surprise a most peculiar look on Petra's face." Meanwhile the TV is showing a subliminally loaded film of the Beetles, who seem to be fairy-like creatures with musical voices.

The folks at the Humaneering Institute decide that they need to get Crowther there without an entourage of journalists and officials. Kidnap him? No one will ever suspect that he was kidnapped by the very people he was on his way to visit! Off they go, including Petra ("she set her little chin, mulishly"), and violently snatch Crowther in front of a crowd, with plenty of kicks, punches, fingers in eyes, etc. ("The shock jarred him all the way up to the elbow, but it felt grand."), from everyone including the diminutive Petra ("'Spitting wildcats,' Stephen muttered admiringly.") As Cameron is rendering moderately intimate first aid to Margrit, Petra speaks to him "with a strange, cool, crisp note in her voice. Funny look in her eyes, too."

Back at the Humaneering Institute, they figure out that Dawson has encoded memories in Crowther with electric shock (the eye blinks have something to do with this too), so they wire him up and it comes out: the Beetles are like the wasps that lay their eggs in living creatures, they've got their eye on us for their nurseries, but they're really very fragile and loud noises will do for them. So the Humaneerers load up with band instruments and head back to greet the aliens when the main body lands, but their horns and cymbals are confiscated. What to do? Engage in another brawl, obviously—they head for the PA tower, wreaking havoc all the way, especially little Petra ("She had blinded one, and used her foot and knee with sickening effect on another")—but there's no power to the PA. All is lost! Except that the Beetles' ship triggers off a thunderstorm and they are all obliterated anyway. Meanwhile, Petra has been conveniently killed during the carnage, so Margrit can stake her claim to Stephen qualm-free.

Whew! There isn't anything else in these issues where the sexual politics are quite so florid, though Bill Spencer's "The Watchtower" (see below) briefly comes close. But it's indicative of the drastically changed atmosphere that it could be published at all—though whether it should have been is another question. Reader F. Haller of Derby ("Postmortem" in **108**) says:

> Science fiction has given us many pictures of Utopia, which may or may not have conformed to the authors' secret wishes; but *New Worlds* has sponsored

one which is quite unique in my reading—one in which a man can walk in off the street into the home of a perfect stranger and proceed to slap her buttocks.... Ah, well. I make no moral judgment on corporal punishment for women and most of us I imagine have our sexual fantasies.

My objection is almost wholly literary. The way sex is stuck on externally to this story, rendering it unpleasing without contributing to the structure—like pebble-dashing on a cheap house. This story justifies up to the hilt all complaints of [Kingsley] Amis, [Angus] Wilson, etc., about the unspeakable quality of the writing in s-f and its treatment of sex in particular. [Etc.]

Lee Harding says more succinctly in **111**: "A better title would have been blank for all the interest this one aroused."

§

The serials continue as before. Carnell remains unable to get a really good novel or serializable novella out of his stable of homegrown writers. Brian Aldiss's "X for Exploitation" **(92-94)**—*The Interpreter* in its UK book version and *Bow Down to Nul* as half an Ace Double—is, if anything, a step backwards from his previous shorter serial "Equator" (*Vanguard from Alpha*). The latter was a flawed novella that was at least interesting, but this is a flawed novel that is pretty much a bore. Aldiss seems to have decided it is time to play it straight as an SF writer, and that's usually a mistake for him.

Earth has been ruled for a thousand years by the twelve-foot tripedal nals (nuls in the Ace version) and now it is under the thumb of a particularly corrupt colonial administrator. A relatively honest one has come to check things out. Gary Towle is an interpreter, a member of the privileged class of humans who work for the nals, who can't be bothered to learn their inferiors' language. He's also covertly working for the underground. The corrupt administrator now offers him freedom off Earth if he will interpret to the inspector so things look good. The underground leader offers him his own estate after the revolution if he will get evidence of the real deal to the inspector. Then his girlfriend disappears; and the whole thing grinds on in a familiar gear of melodrama and conflicting loyalties to an ironic and rather arbitrary happy ending.

About the only interesting scene in the whole thing takes place in a sort of nal pleasure palace, where Towle is socked in the jaw and strapped in to a virtual reality device, in which he is half-immersed in a nal reproductive ritual while the action proceeds around him. The position of Towle, who must present a different face to all the contending parties and who partly controls their perceptions of what is going on, is potentially interesting but not much is done with it. Aldiss himself called the novel "pretty fumbling" and "unsuccessful" (*The Shape of Further Things*, ch. 14).

Leslie Flood says in **97** of the Ace edition: "I did not find this anywhere near Brian's usual standard and doubtless the American reviewers will have some interesting remarks to contribute in view of the good notices he has received for his earlier works." Sure enough, P. Schuyler Miller describes it as "boiling a pot with smoothness but none of his usual originality of viewpoint" (*Analog*, May 1961). Hilary Bailey is more generous in **166** upon its reissue by Ace: "[Towle's] struggle between fear and altruism is well done, and good writing obscures the fact that in most respects this novel could have been set in an imaginary colony of ten years ago," which is about right—aside from their physical form, the aliens are alien only in that they seem to have evolved to be bureaucrats.

Aldiss's own comment, in the *New Worlds* Profile in **92**, is consistent with these observations:

> Science fiction stories featuring galactic empires have always intrigued me, partly because I had the

chance of seeing at first hand the uneasy relationship existing between "imperialists" and subject races in India and Indonesia. So there's a galactic empire in "X for Exploitation," with Earthmen on the receiving end as subject races. The plot hinges on the notion that the further spread your empire is, the greater are the opportunities for graft therein.

So the villains of the piece are not so much the all-conquering *nals*, as the size of the galaxy and the economics involved in its rule. At the same time, the fact that the four central characters each have good reason to mistrust the other three does complicate things.

I hope it doesn't complicate things too much. Van Vogtian complexities of plot and sub-plot are not for me. "X" aims at being a simple study of four pretty hard types each trying to out-think the other. I offer my apologies to the inhabitants of Eastbourne for wrecking their pleasant town in the process.

§

Kenneth Bulmer's "The Fatal Fire" (96-98) is considerably more ambitious than his previous *New Worlds* serials, and consequently more interesting if not really much better. In the future, humanity is divided between the Aristos, a ruling class of cowboy businessmen, and the denizens of the Pool, vast conurbations of the unemployed-and-proud-of-it. In between are a fraction of Pool folk who have signed up or been press-ganged for construction companies, the Assassins' Guild, or other enterprises owned by the Aristos. Julian Justin, a Pool man with a peculiar vague precognitive talent (his "colours" warn him of danger), is shanghaied into a construction job on another planet, where he meets the entrepreneurial Ed and turns his talent to gambling. They try to escape on an Aristo's booby-trapped spaceship, wind up crashing and trekking through the desert and bonding with the Aristo shipowner Hurwitz. There is considerable page-filler talk of Homer and Troy during this interlude. Ed and Justin end by joining with Hurwitz to aid in his business ventures, using Justin's talent to navigate risks, leading to a confrontation with the real economic powers among the Aristos.

In broad outline it's a nice try at a panoramic presentation of a complex future society, with attention to class and economic issues. Unfortunately Bulmer is not able to present his society in convincing detail. Despite a lot of talk of enterprises being "pressured" and the like in the Aristos' economic warfare, there's not much about how that actually works. The big corporate rivalry running through the book is largely an Oedipal family drama, which may be dramatically effective in some contexts (like Alfred Bester's celebrated *The Demolished Man*) but does not much illuminate Bulmer's future society.

Bulmer also falls back on melodramatic clichés: Justin and the daughter of one of the Aristo bigwigs are in love, but both Hurwitz and the Snively Whiplash-model Aristo villain also covet her. The story ends in a confrontation, complete with fist-fight and shootout, over her disposition, and the noble death of Julian, who realizes his love for the Aristo Estelle could never be. The clichés are intellectual too—the Aristos are really a separate breed who have developed their talent of "balancing" (which boils down to knowing what's what really fast, in business, traffic, or whatever) through the evolutionary pressures of the business environment. So does that mean the successful businesspeople out-reproduced the losers? Bulmer doesn't say, and that doesn't tend to be the way things work out in advanced societies. This is another case of SF treating evolution as a sort of disembodied force without any attention to how it does or might actually work.

The novel also contains periodic outbursts of purple prose, though that is not new for Bulmer. ("The space field lay flat and featureless like an eternally frozen sea of concrete over which the mournful blasts of electronic and magnetic guidance systems wailed like the bleak and icy winds forever howling above an arctic barrenness." This accompanies a scene in which a masked and cloaked figure booby-traps a spaceship. The next scene, in which Julian and Ed are contemplating escape, begins, "The space field lay flat and featureless like the vast marble entrance platform to Heaven.") At the end, there is a three-page afterword (or "Footnote" as it is labeled), explaining the story's premises, which by this time are pretty obvious.

This relatively ambitious novel seems to have been less immediately successful than Bulmer's earlier ones. It had no US edition, even as an Ace Double, though in the UK there was an immediate Digit paperback edition and a hardcover in 1969 from Robert Hale. Bulmer also mentions that the same background is "assumed" in his story "Three-Cornered Knife" (*Infinity*, Feb. 1957), one of the handful of stories he sold to the US magazines. He has the *New Worlds* Profile in **97**, and after disclosing that the major recent event in his life is "the volcanic, catastrophic, endearing, sheerly time-consuming irruption" into his life of his daughter, says, *pace* his earlier comments in connection with "The Patient Dark," that "The Fatal Fire" is "more into the category of a novel than a serial. The other remarks still hold true, however, and some of the results of the recent poll mentioned by Editor John Carnell in the editorial in *New Worlds* 96 bear this out." The poll he refers to is Earl Kemp's "Who Killed Science Fiction?" questionnaire,[6] but exactly what point Bulmer is making about "The Fatal Fire," if any, remains obscure.

§

Sturgeon's "Venus Plus X" (**102-105**) comes highly touted. Carnell's editorial in **101** is titled "Sturgeon Serial Next Month," and he explains that the long-promised serial by John Brunner will be put back once again. "Venus Plus X," which he snatched up when he learned it had had no serialization before

6. See Earl Kemp (ed.), *Who Killed Science Fiction?* (Merry Blacksmith Press, 2011).

book publication in the US (it wasn't offered), will run in four parts because "it is too good to cut, and my opinion at this early stage is that it will be the Big Book of 1960; nothing so far published this year is comparable to it in scope, idea, or theme.... This, I feel sure, is the Sturgeon book we have been waiting for since the high promise of *More Than Human* back in 1954." He also says it "takes over where [Farmer's] 'The Lovers' left off, widens, deepens, and improves along philosophical lines the highly combustible and controversial subjects of sex and religion—and comes out honorably."

The plot: Charlie Johns wakes up in a strange place with even stranger people and impossible architecture. They tell him that he's been brought from his time because they want somebody to take a look around and tell them what he *really* thinks of them. If he'll do that for them, they'll send him back to his time (he infers he's been snatched into the future by time machine). So he follows around various members of the Ledom, as they call themselves, and learns that they are hermaphroditic and maintain a stable utopian society that has access to high tech when necessary, but mostly hews to the simple life. Later, he learns that the Ledom are not quite what they seem, and by the end of the novel we learn that Charlie isn't what *he* seems either.

By then, the Ledom have found out what this guinea pig human thinks of them: when he learns that they are not mutants but are surgically created, he detonates in an explosion of hitherto un-hinted at homophobic rage. Meanwhile, interspersed with the main story is a series of vignettes about a pair of late 1950s' US suburban middle-class couples and their attitudes and observations about sex and sex roles, which stand generally for the proposition that men and women are more similar than different and a lot of standard-issue human attitudes (at least those that can be identified from the vantage of suburban America) don't make much sense and don't correspond with real people's natural feelings. These set-pieces are clearly to be read in the context of Sturgeon's larger thesis, talkily set out in the Ledom sections of the novel, that gender roles and sexual attitudes are chiefly manifestations of the desire for power and superiority.

Opinions differed about this novel. Frederik Pohl agreed with Carnell: "If there has been a better science fiction novel in the past few years—say, since James Blish's *A Case of Conscience*—this reviewer has not seen it" (*If*, January 1961). On the other hand, Alfred Bester said: "This department is so angry with Theodore Sturgeon that we hesitate to review the source of our anger, his latest book, *Venus Plus X*.... The only thing about *Venus Plus X* that shocks and angers us is Mr. Sturgeon's incredible tediousness" (*Fantasy & Science Fiction*, January 1961). P. Schuyler Miller, as usual, fell in between: "it somehow fails to be as good as it should... disappointing because we expect so much more of Theodore Sturgeon" (*Analog*, April 1961). James Blish cited "the dangers of becoming totally bound up in a Thesis. The worst outcome, visible here, is that there is no novel when you are through. As Theodore Cogswell once remarked to me, *Venus Plus X* bears a startling resemblance to one of those common and endless Victorian utopias in which most of the action consists of taking the marvelling visitor to inspect the great Long Island and New Jersey bridge, the gas works, the balloon factory, the giant telegraph center, etc., etc."[7]

My own reaction was similar to Cogswell's. Most of the book is one long info-dump of the type that fortunately went out of style in the 1930s, though I didn't think in terms of Victorian utopias but of a sort of *Atlas Shrugged* for cultural liberals, prompted by certain similarities of plot (the Ledom live in a secluded mountain valley technologically concealed, and there's a John Galtish speech toward the end, though it runs only 10 pages rather than 60). I can't agree with Bester about the novel's "incredible tediousness." It's not long enough to be more than ordinarily tedious, and that only in some parts. But Blish's "there is no novel when you are through" seems to sum things up. The best that can be said of "Venus Plus X" is that

7. William Atheling, Jr. [James Blish], *More Issues at Hand* (Advent, 1970), pp. 74-75.

it is a readable failure containing some incisive commentary about mid-20th Century American culture. The worst is that it is a conspicuous milestone in the failure of what had seemed to be a monumental talent.

Obviously mileage varied, most pertinently Carnell's, and he is due some kudos for what was at the time a pretty daring publishing move. Interestingly, though, despite his assertion that the story is "too good to cut," there are at least some cuts, and the one I identified (I didn't do an extensive comparison) seems to reflect Carnell's judgment of the line he still had to walk. In the book version, a suburban mother is giving her daughter a bath, and the subject of making babies comes up. The scene concludes:

> "Well, darling, it's a little hard maybe for you to understand, but what happens is that a daddy has a very special kind of loving. It's very wonderful and beautiful, and when he loves a mommy like that, very very much, she can have a baby."
>
> While she is talking, Karen has found a flat sliver of soap and is trying to see if it fits. Jeanette reaches down into the bathwater and snatches her hand up and slaps it. "Karen! Don't touch yourself *down there*. It's not nice!"

Carnell omits the second paragraph, which—in terms of Sturgeon's overall argument—completely subverts the point. The fact that Carnell thought he couldn't print that pointed paragraph, but that nobody would blink at the salacities of "Blink," is a sad commentary, but one we've heard a thousand times before in various guises.

Regardless, the readers seem to have liked the novel; all four installments were rated in first place in "The Literary Line-Up." Carnell published only a few readers' comments on it, all in **106**, and carefully balanced. F. Leslie of Yorkshire says "this is just about the most magnificent story I have ever read. It's as if, whereas many of us continue to 'grow' until, say, 40, and some of us until 50 or longer, Sturgeon has managed to grow to be 150, keeping the vitality of 40." Conversely, John Hynam—better known as John Kippax—says "Surely 'Venus Plus X' must be the worst serial you have ever published—even worse than 'Time Out of Joint'—and that was bad enough! For goodness' sake get back to publishing stories, not tracts!"

Kevin Smith of London says "Sturgeon is a remarkable, disquieting writer, and I would like to go into a quiet corner and talk things over with him for a couple of months. He's seen so much others have missed—but, oh, the vast uncharted areas he has ignored!" Mr. Smith does not identify these areas. He does complain of the psychological effect of having to wait for the serialization of such a work ("If you are going to engage your readers spiritually, emotionally and intellectually and then just leave them hanging it is asking for trouble"), but this is a theoretical complaint, since he was able to get the US paperback the same day the first installment went on sale. (Carnell says ominously "that will not happen again.") Mark Irwin of Illinois complains: "I read your magazine to get the British stories, not reprints like that crummy serial 'Venus Plus X,' even though Sturgeon is a good author, this story does no good to your reputation as an excellent s-f magazine." He adds: "I am at present a Physics student at Illinois Institute of Technology, with a full-time job in an electronics lab, and I find that s-f tends to relax me and get my mind off the reams of technological journals and textbooks I have to read." He also claims to read *Punch* and the Manchester *Guardian*.

§

John Brunner's "Put Down This Earth" (**107-108**), later in paperback as *The Dreaming Earth*, is an agreeable if implausible time-passer. In the near future, everything is falling apart under the pressure of population; national governments have given up, leaving the UN to try to hold things together; and on top of it all, there's—Dope! Specifically, "happy dreams," a substance injected into the thigh. It is widely available, five dollars for the first dose and two dollars for more. It is of course addictive; and addicts just disappear after a year or so on the drug. No one has been able to find out where it comes from, or where the users go. We learn this via the protagonist Nicholas Greville, a UN narcotics agent dispatched to a laboratory where happy dreams research is being conducted on monkeys. They disappear too. Then he goes home and his disgruntled wife ("You never let me have any fun," she says, among other complaints) shoots him up with the stuff as he sleeps, giving him a dream all right—of another world, where even the colors are different. The rest is predictable: the other world is real, long-term happy dreams use takes you there, and that's the solution to humanity's problems, a new world to screw up just like the old one. But of course Brunner doesn't say that, and you can bet there was no sequel.

Brunner has the *New Worlds* Profile in **107**, and they are still using his debutante photo from 1955. Unlike Robert Silverberg—see below—Brunner seems not to have minded. Carnell says: "One of the few fulltime British professional writers we have, John Brunner has been producing some interesting plots during the past few years." Brunner says of "Put Down This Earth" that the idea came "From contemplating present-day problems.... I make no secret of the fact that I'm genuinely concerned and worried by the problems I put into my stories. The kind of human apathy which could all too easily get us into the mess I've used as background for 'Put Down This Earth'. The guilt complex which may haunt us because of our unpleasant history of wars and which figures in 'The Analysts'—things of this sort bother me personally and lead me to try and work out solutions in my stories. This is part of what science fiction is for." (Right, solutions like uninhabited parallel worlds—let's get Halliburton on this right away.) "I don't mean to imply that that's the whole function of s-f; merely that it's very important. Call it propaganda if you like. Then consider whether propaganda in favour of common sense and logic in the organization of human affairs is a good thing to have around. I think so."

§

J. G. Ballard's "Storm-Wind" (110-11) is a version of what became his first novel, *The Wind from Nowhere*, likely solicited by Berkley Books in the US as the price of publishing Ballard's first story collections. Ballard's ms.—legendarily written in two weeks—was revised for book publication, and the magazine version is apparently a different revision of the original version, which Ballard had titled "To Reap the Whirlwind." In "Storm-Wind," the wind starts blowing harder and harder for no apparent reason (there is some brief and quickly forgotten hand-waving about the van Allen belts), and various characters (mostly military types and their associates) come together and roam around the surface on armored "crawlers" on various errands while everything falls down or blows away around them.

They all fall into the hands of Kroll, the psychopathic assistant to Hardoon, a megalomaniac builder who has constructed a pyramidal structure intended to survive the wind. Various fistfights, shootouts, and incarcerations ensue. The pyramid falls apart, its foundations undermined by ground-level effects of the wind. The surviving characters catch the last submarine to Iceland, where in a cheery tacked-on epilogue a farm family emerges from its shelter and encounters hope in the form of a cache of canned food and an American military vehicle. En route, there is almost nothing about the consequences of this comprehensive disaster for ordinary people, except for some *en passant* scenes of refugees in the underground.

This novel has never had much respect even from Ballard enthusiasts, and for good reason. It was clearly written only as a career move, and the author's disengagement is apparent. It is almost completely devoid of the wit, flair, and *gravitas* variously displayed in already-published stories like "The Waiting Grounds," "The Voices of Time," and "The Sound-Sweep." It consists chiefly of rather flat accounts of the characters trying to avoid being killed either by the wind or by the clichéd villain Kroll, both of which rapidly become tedious. The writing often descends to cliché as well, as in this scene involving a couple of secondary characters: "Marshall finished his drink, then took her in his arms. Her body was lithe and eager, like a young panther he had once wrestled with, her mouth vivid and devouring." I could only think: "Forget this platitudinous embrace! Tell me about wrestling the panther!"

If one squints and stares, some of Ballard's familiar stylistic quirks are barely visible. For example, in an introductory descriptive section (omitted in the book version), Ballard describes "the diffusing smoke-pall of some distant but enormous conflagration," which is certainly canonical Ballardian usage. It's just not yoked to anything of much interest. Similarly, "an estimated half million deck chairs were swept out to sea" would be a classic piece of Ballardian deadpan irony if he were doing anything other than flat description in the passage as a whole. The protagonist's friend is described as "a small balding man with a round cranium and the intelligent watchful eyes of a first-class bridge-player." (The second phrase, another classic Ballardian note, is omitted in the book version.) There is also the first appearance of one of Ballard's familiar characters, the megalomaniacal strongman who thrives in a newly disordered world. But even from this scavenger-hunt perspective, "Storm-Wind" is uninteresting, a remarkably lifeless text from which it almost seems Ballard has excised anything distinctive or striking. It's tempting to describe it as "not even bad," and it's no surprise that Ballard early on banished it from the flyleaf bibliographies of his subsequent books.

The readers at the time apparently didn't think too much of "Storm-Wind" either. Though the first installment was rated first in its issue (an issue some letter-writers complained was overall lackluster), the second part came in fourth, very unusually for a serial. The only direct comment that Carnell published in "Postmortem" is from John Baxter, who describes it as "the most startling disappointment of the year.... [Ballard is] inventive, ingenious and original, with a writing style that I personally find very exciting. Why then does he have to fall back on the oldest of the old clichés for his first novel?" Carnell himself, who not only published the serial but presumably agented the novel, says in his review of the latter only "Good for a 'disaster' story" (*New Worlds* **117**). James Cawthorn, reviewing the UK paperback edition well into the Moorcock era, is no more enthusiastic: "Filled with his customary vivid imagery, the novel is however badly weakened by some unconvincing melodrama centred upon a megalomaniacal constructor resolved to defy the elements" (*New Worlds* **165**).

Carnell says in his review: "The framework of this story appeared as a two-part serial last year in this magazine ('Storm-Wind') but the new novel is vastly different in almost every respect." Yes, but it's not especially different in any *important* respect. It has the same clichéd and pedestrian quality as the serial. The major plot addition that I noticed is that in the book, the main character, instead of turning back from the airport after his flight is cancelled and immediately taking refuge with friends, goes back to his flat where he encounters the estranged wife he was leaving, and her boyfriend, picks up his suitcases, and *then* goes to his friends' house. This sets up a later scene in which he returns to his flat in the thick of the storm, his wife refuses to leave, and then she essentially commits suicide, blown away to her death. The whole thing seems a pointless detour.

More interestingly, there is material in the magazine version that is omitted from the book. Ballard specialist David Pringle has pointed out that the magazine version starts with a 500-word or so descriptive passage about the beginnings of the storm that does not appear in the book, probably because it was too slow and contemplative for the US audience, too full of distracting British place names. The Icelandic epilogue, in which farmers emerge from their cellar to survey the devastation and to be cheered up by the US military, is also completely absent from the book. There, it's announced that the wind is slowing down, and that's it. Hard SF it isn't.

As noted, the book was sold to Berkley under the title "To Reap the Whirlwind," and there is a text referent for that phrase, a little more than halfway through:

> ...On the whole people had shown less resourcefulness and flexibility, less foresight, than a wild bird or animal. Their basic survival instincts had been so dulled, so overlayed [sic] by mechanisms designed to serve secondary appetites, that they were totally unable to protect themselves. As Symington had implied, they were the victims of completely unfounded assumptions about their natural right to survival.
>
> Now they were paying the price for this, in truth reaping the whirlwind!

The passage appears, slightly revised (and correctly spelled), in the book version.

Ballard has the *New Worlds* Profile in **111**, with not much to say:

> The cataclysmic story is particularly interesting, ...because it shows how even a minor variation in one of the physical constants of the environment can make life totally untenable—a corollary of the biological rule that the more specialised the organism the narrower the margin of safety.
>
> Perhaps because of their climate, English writers seem to have a virtual monopoly of the genre, one or two of the contemporary ones producing almost nothing else. Analyzing the author's hidden motives is one of the quieter pleasures of reading—and writing—science fiction, and from the deluge in the Babylonian zodiac myth of Gilgamesh, from which come Noah and the sign of Aquarius, all the way down to *The War of the Worlds*, the real significance of the cataclysmic

story is obviously to be found elsewhere. "Storm-Wind" is no exception, and anyone wondering why I've chosen to destroy London quite so thoroughly should try living there for ten years. I'm only sorry that I couldn't call it "Gone with the Wind."

§

Kenneth Bulmer's second serial in these issues is "The Golden Age" (**112-113**), under the pseudonym Rupert Clinton, used for this story only, and taken from one of the characters in his mediocre 1959 serial "The Patient Dark." It is a considerable improvement, an unpretentious but tangy pulp novella somewhat in the spirit of *Startling Stories* and its ilk, with a bit of Burroughsian flavor, but off-trail enough to suggest that its real home would have been *Science Fantasy* if it were a little shorter. Carnell says it "will doubtless bring back nostalgic memories to many older readers." Perhaps it might be embraced as an early forerunner of steampunk, which became wildly fashionable half a century later.

It's set in a peculiar world said to have twelve continents but whose inhabitants have names like Larrabee and Henley (not to mention Slater), where steam is king and dirigibles are the chief way of getting around. The Conclave suppresses scientific innovation despite the danger of the encroaching Gurone, orc-like creatures from the neighboring continents. On an archaeological dig, the characters first find a globe that suggests a very different configuration of continents and icecaps, before some of them disappear into a metal-walled tunnel that mysteriously closes. Larrabee heads for home only to discover the hard way that the Gurone are on the march, or the fly, now armed with mysterious weapons that somehow project bits of lead at dangerous velocities.

Larrabee *et al.* manage to find their way back into the mysterious tunnel, along with a hostile member of the Conclave who thinks they should all be condemned for sorcery. They wind up in a world with a golden sky, populated by men who never take their armor off (oh, take a guess). These mysterians show them strange films about this world's history, and Larrabee steals a ray gun of some sort with which he routs the Gurone, converting the Conclave man to a tech fan. Meanwhile, the puzzling tunnel has crumbled into rust and dust. It's never made clear whether this is a time travel story or a parallel world story—it's told from the viewpoint of the relatively unsophisticated characters—which is part of its charm. This is the most enjoyable Bulmer piece I've read; apparently it never made it into book form.

§

The short fiction *New Worlds* published in these two years includes a few of the best, and best-known, stories ever to appear in the magazine. Unfortunately, after those few, things drop off rather sharply. While *New Worlds* is a perfectly readable magazine during this period, there is a dearth of the memorable.

As noted, J. G. Ballard is the most prolific short fiction contributor during these two years, which represent his high point in the UK magazines. His first US sale appeared in January 1962 ("The Insane Ones" in *Amazing*), and thereafter about half of his short fiction output appeared in the US magazines until mid-1964, when his short work started to become more eccentric and largely disappeared from them. The stories in these issues include some of his best and some of his most conventional SF pieces, and a couple which are both.

The least of these is probably "The Gentle Assassin" (113), in the last issue of 1961, as utterly conventional an SF story as Ballard ever published. If it had appeared under, say, John Wyndham's byline I doubt anyone would have questioned it. Elderly Dr. Jamieson, who has invented time travel, comes back to the London of some near future coronation to thwart an assassination attempt that killed his fiancé, but inevitably finds that his own actions caused her death. Quite well rendered, it's just not very interesting, especially by contrast with Ballard's other work. "Chronopolis" **(95)**, on the other hand, is a much jazzier riff on the standard SF story, reminiscent of "Build-Up" ("The Concentration City") in overall approach, but not at all like it in execution. "Build-Up" read like a collection of spare parts while this one is much more consistent in tone and logical in development, done with fine irony and awareness of genre convention—and a good thing too, since it's pretty seriously cracked.

In the future, it posits, there will be no timepieces. As society got overpopulated it also got more and more regimented, necessarily so in order for everyone's needs to be accommodated. You drove to work, ate lunch or shopped when your social classification dictated or there wouldn't be room for everybody. Eventually people rebelled and destroyed all the clocks, and set up the Time Police to make sure nobody made any new ones, and now the young people don't know about it and the old people won't talk about it.

Enter that stock figure of Modern Science Fiction, the young rebel who won't stop asking "why?" Conrad is fascinated from childhood by the remnants of clocks, improvising his own timepieces. One day a man next to him in a movie theatre has a heart attack, and proves to be wearing a watch, which Conrad takes, and it transforms his life. When one of his high school teachers discovers that he is wearing a watch, he's taken on a field trip into "Chronopolis the Time City," which appears to be central London, now almost entirely empty. The teacher explains the secret history to Conrad, hoping to save Conrad from the error of his ways, but Conrad isn't having any: he has seen that one of the clocks is working. He breaks away from the teacher, who tries to run him down and then shoots at him—obviously an undercover operative of the Time Police.

Later he is found by a small gray-haired man with his pockets full of keys: the secret master of Chronopolis, the one who winds the clocks that are still working. Conrad blurts out, "I want to help wind them all up again," and joins him. But his real ambition is to start up the clock in a tower dominating a plaza. Eventually he does, and time returns to the city, however briefly. Conrad is caught and sentenced to prison.

Ballard develops this loony premise with deadpan aplomb and a density of circumstantial detail worthy of Heinlein or Asimov, eschewing florid Ballardisms—though the dead center city of London stands in for his preoccupation with abandoned structures and deserted artificial landscapes. Of course the whole story exemplifies another of his preoccupations, the human experience of time, which he renders with sober wit:

> The water clock had demonstrated that a calibrated time-piece added another dimension to life, organized its energies, gave the countless activities of everyday existence a yardstick of significance. Conrad spent hours in the attic gazing at the small yellow dial, watching its minute hand revolve slowly, its hour hand press on imperceptibly, a compass charting his passage through the future. Without it he felt rudderless, adrift in a grey purposeless limbo of timeless events.

Overall this is one of Ballard's best written and constructed stories to date (maybe ever), even if its contrived premise makes it difficult to take it as more than a *tour de force*. It was the title story of Ballard's first big retrospective collection in 1971, and deservedly so. In his blurb in the magazine, the ever gullible Carnell says of this comic inferno: "Jim Ballard takes our present-day congestion problems to a very logical conclusion."

"Billenium" [sic—spelled correctly hereafter] (**112**) is one of Ballard's best-known stories, anthologized at least 18 times per the Contento online indexes. It appears to be his most-reprinted story, and with good and bad reason. It is probably his best conventional SF story, comfortably within the genre's satirical dystopian tradition, but extremely well executed. People have wondered why it didn't appear in *Galaxy* (probably a couple of years too late—by this time H. L. Gold was entirely out and Frederik Pohl was in as editor). In the grotesquely overcrowded world of the future, everyone lives in a few square meters of space. Two men find that their room has a boarded-over door to a disused and forgotten room, providing them unprecedented vistas of space; but soon enough they've let in a pair of female acquaintances, then their aunt to chaperone (the revolution has started in *New Worlds* but is far from finished), then one of the women's sick mother, then her father, until they are all as crowded as they were to start with, and the newcomers are hinting that the protagonist, who found the room, should move out.

The story is carried (i.e., becomes more than just a farcical sketch) by the weight of careful sensory detail: "All day long, and often into the early hours of the morning, the tramp of feet sounded up and down the stairs outside Ward's cubicle" is the first sentence. After crossing the street, carried ten or twenty yards out of their way by the crowd flow: "There they found the shelter of the shop-fronts, slowly worked their way back to the food-bar, shoulders braced against the countless minor collisions." The requisite short info-dumps are efficient and well-turned:

> The countryside, as such, no longer existed. Every single square foot of ground sprouted a crop of one type or another. The one-time fields and meadows of the world were now, in effect, factory floors, as highly mechanised and closed to the public as any industrial area. Economic and ideological rivalries had long since faded before one over-riding quest—the internal colonisation of the city.

Some of Ballard's preoccupations are visible here, but all in service of the story's main business:

> For an hour they exchanged places, wandering silently around the dusty room, stretching their arms out to feel its unconfined emptiness, grasping at the

sensation of absolute spatial freedom. Although smaller than many of the sub-divided rooms in which they
had lived, this room seemed infinitely larger, its walls
huge cliffs that soared upward to the skylight.

This now-canonical story was rated third in the issue by the
readers.

There are a couple of Ballard's overtly psychological stories
here, in the footsteps of "Manhole 69" (just ignore that metaphor) and the lackluster "Now: Zero." "Zone of Terror" (**92**) is
entertaining but not particularly substantial. Larsen, who works
for an electronics company, has been sent to a company retreat
with a psychiatrist, Bayliss, to recover from overwork. He sees
an apparition of a man in a suit in his garage, and panics. Later,
he sees the same man in his living room and realizes it's himself.
Bayliss tells him it's not an hallucination but "a psycho-retinal
image of remarkable strength and duration" and advises him
to confront himself next time it happens. In fact, next time it
happens he sees not one but two doubles, panics again, and tells
Bayliss to get the gun Larsen had hidden in the letterbox. But
Bayliss himself sees one of the doubles, mistakes it for the real
Larsen (or at least the narrating Larsen), and shoots the *real*
real Larsen—assuming that phrase means anything any longer.
"Now Bayliss too was suffering the same psychotic attack,
seeing two simultaneous images, but in his case not of himself,
but of Larsen, on whom his mind had been focusing for the past
weeks."

Well, this is contrived—much more so than Ballard's
previous bout of overt psychologizing, "Manhole 69," which
offered an actual psychological argument. This hasn't much
more than a gimmick. More interesting than the psychological
McGuffin is the portrayal of Larsen as a man about to jump out
of his skin and of the interaction between Larsen and Bayliss,
whom Larsen resents and fears because he so clearly has his
own agenda and Larsen's welfare is not at the top of it. This is
the first of a long line of shady members of the helping profes-

sions in Ballard's work, robustly represented in the 2003 novel *Millennium People*.

The book version of "Zone of Terror" (in the 1967 collection *The Disaster Area*) was slightly but pervasively revised for book publication, to moderate both the tone and the slightly pretentious vocabulary and verbosity of the original. An example from the *New Worlds* version: "The desert site had been chosen for its hypotensive virtues, its supposed equivalence to psychic zero. Two or three days of leisurely reading, of thoughtfully watching the motionless horizons, and the neuronic grids re-aligned, tension and anxiety thresholds rose to more useful levels, creative and decisional activity heightened." Book: "The desert site had been chosen for its hypotensive virtues, its supposed equivalence to psychic zero. Two or three days of leisurely reading, of watching the motionless horizon, and tension and anxiety thresholds rose to more useful levels."

"The Overloaded Man" (**108**) is another "inner space" epic, which announces itself forthrightly: "Faulkner was slowly going insane." The world is too much with him, and he—a lecturer at the Business School—wants to get away from it all. Unbeknownst to his highly efficient wife, he has quit his job, and spends his days perfecting his newly discovered talent of making things disappear—that is, ceasing to see them in any detail or as anything other than abstract forms stripped of function and meaning. He applies this technique to the houses across the street and the scenery around his back yard, and shortly thereafter to his wife, who returns from work having discovered that he is not really on leave, and begins jawing at him, and then grabs him when he doesn't respond. The abstracted Faulkner responds:

> Her rhythms were sharp and ungainly. To begin with he tried to ignore them, then began to restrain and smooth her, moulding her angular form into a softer and rounder one.

As he worked away, kneading her like a sculptor shaping clay, he noticed a series of crackling noises, over which a persistent scream was just barely audible. When he finished he let her fall to the floor, a softly squeaking lump of spongy rubber.

Then he lies down in the pond in his back yard.

Slowly he felt the putty-like mass of his body dissolving, its temperature grow cooler and less oppressive. Looking out through the surface of the water six inches above his face, he watched the blue disc of the sky, cloudless and undisturbed, expanding to fill his consciousness. At least he had found the perfect background, the only possible field of ideation, an absolute continuum of existence uncontaminated by material excrescences.

Steadily watching it, he waited for the world to dissolve and set him free.

This is an especially interesting early Ballard story for several reasons, not least that it is appearing in *New Worlds* despite the fact that it is a psychiatric fantasy, SF only by a long stretch. One wonders why it wasn't instead in *Science Fantasy*, where Ballard's more eccentric items regularly appeared. Despite its outré premise—or maybe because of it, Ballard realizing that this one had to be well executed to work at all—it seems extremely carefully written and well visualized and developed. To my great surprise, it was voted best in its issue by the readers. It is also interesting because it foreshadows a section of *The Atrocity Exhibition*, the death of Karen Novotny in "You: Coma: Marilyn Monroe":

Murder. Tallis stood behind the door of the lounge, shielded from the sunlight on the balcony, and considered the white cube of the room. At intervals Karen

Novotny moved across it, carrying out a sequence of apparently random acts. Already she was confusing the perspectives of the room, transforming it into a dislocated clock. She noticed Tallis behind the door and walked towards him. Tallis waited for her to leave. Her figure interrupted the junction between the walls in the corner on his right. After a few seconds her presence became an unbearable intrusion into the time geometry of the room.

Epiphany of this death. Undisturbed, the walls of the apartment contained the serene face of the film star, the assuaged time of the dunes.

Departure. When Coma called at the apartment Tallis rose from his chair by Karen Novotny's body. "Are you ready?" she asked. Tallis began to lower the blinds over the windows. "I'll close these—no one may come here for a year." Coma paced around the lounge. "I saw the helicopter this morning—it didn't land." Tallis disconnected the telephone behind the white leather desk. "Perhaps Dr. Nathan has given up." Coma sat down beside Karen Novotny's body. She glanced at Tallis, who pointed to the corner. "She was standing in the angle between the walls."

"Deep End" (**106**) begins to meld the outer and the inner in ways that will become very familiar in Ballard's work, presenting a scenario that is both one of his most unlikely and one of his most characteristic:

The frantic mining of the oceans in the previous century to provide oxygen for the atmospheres of the new planets had made their decline swift and irreversible, and with their death had come climatic and other geophysical changes which ensured the extinction of

Earth itself. As the oxygen extracted electrolytically from sea-water was compressed and shipped away, the hydrogen released was discharged into the atmosphere. Eventually only a narrow layer of denser, oxygen-carrying air was left, little more than a mile in depth, and those people remaining on Earth were forced to retreat into the ocean beds, abandoning the poisoned continental tables.

Here is Ballard's drained swimming pool trope writ globally large. However absurd this account may be, it sets the stage for one of Ballard's classic early landscapes-with-preoccupations:

They always slept during the day. By dawn the last of the townsfolk had gone indoors and the houses would be silent, heat curtains locked across the windows, as the sun rose over the deliquescing salt banks, filling the streets with opaque fire. Most of them were old people and fell asleep quickly in their darkened chalets, but Granger, with his restless mind and his one lung, often lay awake through the afternoons, while the metal outer walls of the cabin creaked and hummed, trying pointlessly to read through the old log books Holliday had salvaged for him from the crashed space platforms.

And:

Mutating kelp, their gene-shifts accelerated by the radio-phosphors, reared up into the air on either side of the road like enormous cacti, turning the dark salt-banks into a white lunar garden. But this evidence of the encroaching wilderness only served to strengthen Holliday's need to stay behind on Earth.

Exactly why the space platforms are crashing isn't explained, though another one comes down during the course of the story. But space travel is not being abandoned; *au contraire*, pretty much the whole population is emigrating to these new colony planets, except for Holliday, who is holding out—and the migration officer is about to make his last pass through the area. Holliday's foil, the above-mentioned Granger, tells Holliday in core Ballardian fashion:

> The seas are our corporate memory.... In draining them we deliberately obliterated our own pasts, to a large extent our own self-identities. That's another reason why you should leave. Without the sea, life is unsupportable. We become nothing more than the ghosts of memories, blind and homeless, flitting through the dry chambers of a gutted skull.

But Holliday's determination is rekindled, or watered, by the discovery in Lake Atlantic, the ten-mile-long remnant of the ocean, of what may be the last fish on Earth—a dogfish, which Granger describes as once "the vermin of the sea." However, a couple of the local louts find the fish and stone it to death, saying to Holliday when he catches them, "Sorry, Holliday.... We didn't know it was your fish." Granger suggests having it stuffed. "Holliday stared at him incredulously, his face contorting. For a moment he said nothing. Then, almost berserk, he shouted: 'Have it stuffed? Are you crazy? Do you think I want to make a dummy of myself, fill my own head with straw?'" Well, subtle it isn't.

"The Voices of Time" (**99**) is hamhandedly foreshadowed by Carnell in **98**'s "Literary Line-Up" as "a complex story built around the fact that Man is sleeping more and more as the pace of presentday life increases." He also discloses that it was initially intended for the 100th issue but was too long. In fact, it's 33 pages long, but still Carnell labels it a short story, while "Chronopolis," at 24 pages, is called a novelette, showing once more either that Carnell couldn't count or didn't care about these categorizations.

This story, along with "The Terminal Beach," seems to be one of the canonical landmarks of early Ballard, the ones all the tour guides take you to. ("The Drowned Giant" is allowed to go abroad on exhibition.) It is widely regarded by aficionados as Ballard's first masterpiece—it's certainly his first wide-screen apocalypse—but it has never quite added up for me, maybe because I approach it too literal-mindedly.

Here's what happens:

Whitby the biologist, who has committed suicide, has carefully cut strange grooves in the floor of a drained swimming pool. Ballard describes these both as "apparently [cut] at random" and as "interlocking to form an elaborate ideogram like a Chinese character," a mandala with four protuberances at its sides. (I'm not sure he can have it both ways.)

Powers the neurosurgeon is able to stay awake for shorter and shorter periods each day; many people are beset by this condition. He says he wants to forget everything. Early in the story he resolves to throw away his alarm clock and scrambles the settings of his wristwatch.

Kaldren, by contrast, doesn't sleep at all as a result of surgery performed by Powers, and stalks Powers obsessively, presenting him with descending 14-digit numbers traced in dust on his windshield, handed to him on index cards, etc. These numbers come in over the radio telescope from the constellation Canes Venatici, and they seem to be a countdown to the end of the universe. Kaldren is also collecting "terminal documents," i.e., "final statements about homo sapiens," such as Freud's complete works, Beethoven's blind quartets (sic; he means deaf, unless it is a clue that we are in an alternative universe), and the transcripts of the Nuremberg trials. This is revealed by his girlfriend, Coma.

Powers finds a frog with lead-lined shell, in the drained swimming pool, no less; many plants and animals are developing their own radiation shields. He puts it in his private zoo along with a chimpanzee, who has a vocabulary of 200 words and has built his own house, and a spider who spins a web of nervous tissue. These developments are said to reflect the existence of the "silent pair" of genes, which Whitby was activating in his irradiation experiments.

Dissatisfied with the way his life is going, Powers naturally goes out to an abandoned artillery range and starts building his own mandala, concentric circles of low concrete wall divided into four quadrants.

We learn that the first astronauts on the moon died, after going on about white gardens and blue people from Orion.

Toward the end of the story, Kaldren soliloquizes:

> "You're not alone, Powers, don't think you are. These are the voices of time, and they're all saying goodbye to you. Think of yourself in a wider context. Every particle in your body, every grain of sand, every galaxy carries the same signature. As you've just said, you know what the time is now, so what does the rest matter? There's no need to go on looking at the clock."

Powers returns to the artillery range and finishes up his mandala, then in his lab kills all the teratogenic creatures with radiation (the chimp has about done himself in anyway), and heads back to the artillery range. On the way he is overcome by waves of time emanating from various geological features and the sky, and dies. Kaldren finds his body, discovers the dead animals in the lab zoo, and shuts himself up in his borrowed house, ignoring the blandishments of Coma et al. "Half-asleep, periodically he leaned up and adjusted the flow of light through the shutter, thinking to himself, as he would do through the coming months of Powers and his strange mandala, and of the seven and their journey to the white gardens of the moon, and the blue people who had come from Orion and spoken in poetry to them of ancient beautiful worlds beneath golden suns in the island galaxies, vanished forever now in the myriad deaths of the cosmos."

This is all very poetic. and many of the elements of the story, maybe all of them, are evocative and memorable. And there's a great deal going on: David Pringle and James Goddard, in their 1976 study *J. G. Ballard: The First Twenty Years*, found the story "a masterpiece of compression, it could well have been a novel." But I find the whole ultimately unsatisfying; the pieces don't add up. Part of the reason, I am sure, is that the supposed unifying scientific rationale seems hokey; it reminds me too much of John Sladek's deadly parody "The Sublimation World" ("For over a hundred years, the sun had been getting dirty"). As a result, the symbolism just doesn't speak to me. That is probably for idiopathic reasons of personality, given the story's widespread appeal both now and at the time it was published. After all, it was Honorably Mentioned by Judith Merril, anthologized by Kingsley Amis and Damon Knight, and even sort of praised by P. Schuyler Miller ("pure nightmare, where things happen seemingly without meaning but with a sense of significance, where symbols may have many meanings or none, and where the universe is crumbling. It suggests that the laws of the universe may be capricious or may go insane" (*Analog,* Sept. 1962)). Now there's a hat trick. Oh, and the readers rated it the best story in its issue.

In general, Ballard was reasonably popular with the readers in these issues. Except for the conclusion of "Storm-Wind," his stories never came in worse than third in the readers' ratings. "The Voices of Time," "Chronopolis," and to my great surprise "The Overloaded Man" were all rated first; "Zone of Terror" second; and "Billennium," "Deep End," and "The Gentle Assassin" third. There's no breath of controversy over his work yet. The only comments on it in "Postmortem" are from Lee Harding (**113**), who says: "Ballard is the finest practitioner I have encountered in your pages. Not one of his stories has failed to satisfy that search for 'wonder' for which my jaded eyes continually search," and John Baxter who, as already noted, described Ballard as "inventive, ingenious and original, with a writing style that I personally find very exciting," while slagging "Storm-Wind" pretty mercilessly.

Ballard makes another appearance in these issues, quoted in Carnell's editorial in **102** on the occasion of watching the Werner von Braun film *I Aim at the Stars*, and suggesting some of his later-appearing preoccupations:

> Rocketry, one of the principal branches of applied science fiction (the other being psychiatry) seems to have appealed to von Braun less for technological reasons than as a means to an end—his obsessive urge into space.
>
> If the film had explored this curious drive it might have been an interesting psychological extravaganza, but instead it concentrates on the politico-moral aspects of his wartime V-2 work, which von Braun himself has never been concerned with. Most of the action takes place at Peenemunde and the pantomime SS men, interminable bunker sequences and approaching Russian guns bring the film dangerously close to becoming the Eva Braun Story.

§

In addition to his mediocre novel, Brian Aldiss has four varied and accomplished short stories in these issues. Aldiss is coming into the height of his powers in his short fiction now, alternately (or simultaneously) comic and grave, gaudy and somber, graceful but not ostentatious. If there are fewer Aldiss stories in these issues than in previous ones, that's because he is now selling regularly to US markets. During this period he published the five "Hothouse" novelettes in *Fantasy & Science Fiction* and another story in *Amazing*, as well as a couple each in Carnell's *Science Fantasy* and *Science Fiction Adventures*, not to mention a couple of US paperback novels, one of which will be serialized later in *New Worlds*.

The best of these four is probably "Moon of Delight" **(104)**

("O Moon of My Delight" in some reprintings), another of Aldiss's sour notes on the Conquest of the Stars, sounding his frequent theme "everywhere you go, there you are." Tandy Two is a Braking Satellite on which is located a Flange, a construction which absorbs the energy of an arriving FTL spaceship, which is then dissipated by the planet's suddenly advancing its axial rotation; day turns into night. The display is spectacular. Murragh Harrison, a footloose poet, is working as an itinerant farmhand while he writes about the planet and the Flange. He's working for the Doughtys, simple-minded farmers with a couple of mercurial children, who are about to return to Earth.

The narrator is a Flange Maintenance Officer who is having it off with the vulgar Mrs. Doughty whenever he can. There's a farm emergency, nobody has any time to pay attention to the children, the younger and more delightful one runs to see the FTL ship spectacle and is electrocuted. (This is reminiscent of "Gesture of Farewell" from a couple of years earlier. Never take your children to an early Aldiss story unless they are well insured.) While all this is going on, Murragh Harrison has his poetic breakthrough about Tandy Two—she's a woman! It sounds ridiculous in synopsis but inexplicably adds up, stupidity played out fatally against a backdrop of spectacular beauty.

There is also some Tuckerization going on, with a Bonfiglioli Geogravitic Layer and the STL Ship *Monteith*. (Charles Monteith was Aldiss's editor at Faber. The first *Best Science Fiction Stories of Brian W. Aldiss* is dedicated to him.)

"Soldiers Running" (**95**)—retitled "How To Be a Soldier" in Aldiss's UK collection *The Airs of Earth* and "Hearts and Engines" in the US *Starswarm*—is in a similar vein, a bitter antiwar piece about a rather simple sergeant whose prospect (or fantasy) of love and a decent life is destroyed by the modern way of war. It manages to be both poignant and as subtle as a mallet over the head.

In a lighter mood—sort of—is the much-anthologized "Old Hundredth," presumably specially written for the anniversary issue **100**. It's another of Aldiss's extravagant far-future visions, this one involving—oh no—the Singularity! Honest. Just look:

> ...And at last, via information theory and great com-
> puters, [man] gained knowledge of all his parts. He
> formed the Laws of Integration, which reveal all be-
> ings as part of a pattern and show them their part in
> the pattern. There is only the pattern, the pattern is all
> the universe, creator and created. For the first time, it
> became possible to duplicate that pattern artificially;
> the transubstantio-spatializers were built.
>
> All mankind left their strange hobbies on Earth and
> Venus and projected themselves in the pattern. Their
> entire personalities were merged with the texture of
> space itself. Through science, they reached immortal-
> ity.
>
> It was a one way passage.
>
> They did not return. Each Involute carried thou-
> sands or even millions of people. There they were,
> not dead, not living. How they exulted or wept in their
> transubstantiation, nobody left could say....

These Involutes are apparently scattered around the landscape, and here's one:

> The Involute was not beautiful. True, its colours
> changed with the changing light, yet the colours were
> fish-cold, for they belonged to another universe.... [an]
> ill-defined lattice, the upper limits of which were lost
> in thickening gloom.

So the animals—generally enhanced, many reconstituted
from extinct species—inherit. Dandi is a megatherium (giant
sloth) who rides around on a baluchitherium (a 25-foot-tall land
mammal) and is on her way home, where she lives in the remains of a human house. But she is confronted by an officious
and dangerous bear who demands the confiscation of her human

artifacts. The ensuing struggle causes her house to collapse and incidentally alienates her mentor, a telepathic dolphin, who cuts her off. Dandi decides it's time to check out, and turns herself into that other common feature of the landscape, a music column, playing—of course—"Old Hundredth," the hymn tune to which the 100th Psalm is sung. This one is a bit forced and contrived to my taste, but charming enough to distract from the skull beneath the skin and account for the story's apparent popularity relative to Aldiss's other work of this period.

Lighter still, in its macabre way, is "Under an English Heaven" (90), another slant on *The War of the Worlds* (the main characters are named Herbert and George respectively), in which aliens land on a farm outside Newbury, and the journalist protagonist determines to take his brother and family to go see it. The English character is satirically displayed, and folks from a nearby scientific installation come and load the spaceship onto a flatbed truck and carry it off. Shortly thereafter they, their installation, and the town are obliterated.

Aldiss appears with a guest editorial, "The Origin of Originality," in 113. Carnell also gives him the *New Worlds* Profile in that issue, portentously reciting his credentials: "...one of the brightest stars in the British science fiction firmament for in five short years Brian Aldiss has undoubtedly become our most prominent author.... Literary Editor of the Oxford *Mail*, he is the logical bridge between the old and new order of science fiction.... He is the present President of the British Science Fiction Association...." After that introduction, Aldiss himself characteristically plays the clown. He says he was going to put together an anthology of favorite excerpts, but instead writes a series of parodies of stories of different vintages all based on the notion of silicon life, ostensibly dedicated to showing that it is treatment and not theme that makes good SF, but mainly an amusing but overlong exercise in pie-throwing. The fact that the magazines in which these non-stories were non-published include *Stupefying Science Sagas* and *Stultifying Stories Quarterly* sums the piece up.

§

After Ballard and Aldiss come a number of familiar and prolific names, but to my taste they are mostly marking time, or slipping backwards. The biggest name in the magazine is surely John Wyndham, with "The Emptiness of Space" (**100**), a final Troon story, and pretty inane, though professionally executed as usual. A Troon descendant (another "Ticker" Troon) finds a derelict spaceship in the asteroids, which proves to contain some folks in spacesuits who have used an obsolete life support/ suspended animation system. One of these is Troon's grandfather, who after being revived becomes obsessed with the idea that his soul has escaped or been lost in resuscitation. At any rate he tells the narrator, who encounters him in a bar, that he is a man without a soul, and the narrator is not the one who could help him. Later another bar patron tells the narrator the whole story, which is pretty hard for a materialist to take very seriously.

Another big name (though more of an honorary *New Worlds* regular than a real one) is William F. Temple, who appears in **100** with "Sitting Duck," a hokey but entertaining story about a man in a space station who watches for bad weather and signs of war, and gets a fatal dose of the latter, but it's stiff-upper-lip all the way. Pursuant to the new liberal dispensation, when the protagonist contemplates the body parts shortly to be shredded by space debris, genitals are prominent on the list.

James White is again one of the mainstays of the magazine, contributing five stories, four of them novelettes and four of them in the Sector General series, but nothing as good as "Tableau" or "Grapeliner" from prior years. "O'Mara's Orphan" (**90**) is an unfortunately busy and turgid concoction, a flashback to the days when O'Mara, later Chief Psychologist, first came to Sector General. He has just been responsible, it appears, for an accident in which two aliens have been killed. Naturally, he is put in charge of their several-ton orphan child, which he must keep in his quarters, pending the official inquiry, in which his fate turns on whether someone who hates him will tell the truth. Why does this individual hate him? O'Mara has been riding him mercilessly, and the reason for *that* is that he has been seriously injured performing some feat of altruism and O'Mara thinks it will be good for him to have someone around him who is not obsequious.

It is thrown into the mix that O'Mara's own frustration is that no one will give him a job commensurate with his responsibility because he's so physically strong that everybody assumes he's good only for manual labor. Meanwhile, he has to rig up a Rube Goldberg device of pulleys and weights in order to comfort the alien child, who needs a lot of petting in the form of hard blows from heavy objects, and has to conceal this arrangement from the station master and the investigator who is interrogating him while he struggles in an artificial gravity several times Earth's. The whole story is a Rube Goldberg device.

"Out-Patient" (**95**) is a bit less busy. Here the patient appears to have a dangerous disorder of the skin, which persists in thickening as the patient's metabolism fails. Conway seemingly refuses to treat this disorder in any sensible way and is being vigorously accused of malpractice, when his behavior and his theory are vindicated: the adult form of the patient emerges from his chrysalis. Of course all of the suspense and a good part of the length of the story is generated quite artificially by the fact that Conway won't tell anyone his theory, since he isn't sure of it. So his behavior appears inexplicable both to his colleagues and to the reader.

White has the *New Worlds* Profile in this issue, and says, "To one with pacifist inclinations—feelings shared on both sides of the typewriter among the s-f fellowship, I think—a doctor character is important in that all sorts of violent, dramatic and emotionally loaded incidents happen around him as a matter of course. So an author who doesn't relish killing off a lot of people or things can inject some legitimate bloodshed into his stories by substituting an accident or natural catastrophe for War."

"Countercharm" (**100**) is shorter than most, consonant with its gimmick, which wouldn't really support a long story. Conway gets introduced to immersion in Educator tapes, which in effect superimpose the mind of an alien practitioner on the tape-recipient's, allowing a doctor of one species to become competent to treat unfamiliar species without having to go through a whole medical education. But it's the whole mind and not just medical training, so Conway finds himself lusting uncontrollably for a crab-like alien assistant, which is a great hindrance to him as he tries to treat another of her kind with her at his side in the operating room.

The solution: Nurse Murchison is assigned to his team. "Nurse Murchison possessed that combination of physiological features which made it impossible for any male Earth-human member of the staff to regard her with anything like Clinical Detachment." Under her influence his preoccupation with Senreth the crab wanes and suddenly his hands are steady again. This gimmick is less inane and offensive than it sounds partly because White is a solemnly well-meaning writer who doesn't play anything for leers and partly because Murchison is a strong character herself and not merely a prop. Carnell's blurb for this story notes that White is the second most prolific author in *New Worlds*'s history (25 stories), outdone only by Francis G. Rayer (26 stories).

"Resident Physician" (**110**) is another formulaic Sector General story: an unfamiliar type of alien shows up very sick under mysterious circumstances. This one seems to have cannibalized the other entity on his spaceship and therefore to be a criminal as well as a patient; Conway finds its condition and response inexplicable. The clever-as-usual denouement is embedded in the title. Letter-writer Robert W. Oswald of London says in **113**: "These 'Sector General' stories are starting to be of a sameness although the unwinding of the plot is exciting to read." Just so.

"The Apprentice" (**99**), the only non-Sector General story by White in these issues, concerns the travails of Nicholson, the personnel manager of a large department store, in dealing with his employee Harnrigg, a centauroid alien who is trying to make it on his own on Earth and whose failure to do so would be a big diplomatic problem. White's dense and sober style is not well suited to situation comedy, and he manages to take 37 pages to tell a story that probably merits half that length, but it's a relaxed and good-natured read.

§

E. C. Tubb contributes seven stories, none of them his best and all of them pretty contrived or overdone or both. "Survival Demands" (**91**) is both, spraying *noir* on all the fire hydrants. ("I studied the smoke of my cigarette. Space is a lonely place, it gives a man time to think.") Humanity has not long ago committed genocide in self-defense, having encountered another species, the Frenzha, which is telepathic and so utterly repelled by the dishonesty of the non-telepathic humans that it's preparing to destroy us. Tolsen, one of the few human telepaths, has winkled out their plot and been driven crazy by telepathically experiencing their deaths when their planet is bombed out of existence. Now we've encountered the Lhassa; will we have to do it again? Not if humanity produces enough telepaths to be their spokespersons to alien races. So they're going to breed Tolsen in his asylum. ("We'll find him a girl, one as near like himself as possible, together they will have children.")

In the same issue is "The Shrine," as by Alan Guthrie, in which Earth has been destroyed and the demoralized remnants of its people roam the galaxy—except that a steady stream of them visit the Shrine, something discovered by accident on an out-of-the-way planet, which bucks them up something fierce: "They came over the low horizon as if they marched to soundless bands beneath the flutter of invisible banners. They came with faces set with purpose and with shoulders stiffened with pride. They had left the ship a defeated rabble—they returned a victorious army." So what's this Shrine? Oh, Tubb isn't telling.

This is followed by "Man of War" (**93**). In an interstellar war, the only hope is having space captains from Earth, because humans have "A refusal to be beaten, a total disregard for anything but doing what had to be done, a ruthless drive which nothing could stop.... It was what had driven them onward and outward." These clichéd sentiments delivered in Tubb's tough-guy style add up to the most fatuous of both worlds.

"Memories Are Important" (**99**) is the best of these stories, a sort of crypto-stealth-New Wave (or New Age) solipsism epic. Researchers have discovered a drug that will permit the selective erasure of memory, and they're testing it out on one of their own. Unfortunately a jet goes by and produces a sonic boom at the crucial moment, leaving the subject with all memories erased and unable to form any new ones. Before long he is walking through walls and teleporting around the streets, because he's forgotten that that's impossible. It is proposed that his power is limitless. Anticlimactically, his colleagues get him back into the hospital and repeat the drug treatment, repairing the damage in some not too well explained fashion.

"Greater Than Infinity" (**100**) is a well turned but ultimately gimmicky story about some space travelers who are snatched and wrecked on an isolated planet, which they discover is inhabited by a very powerful and very bored AI. So, not unlike Scheherazade, they try to figure out how to get it interested in something so it will let them go, and they propose: We believe God made everything, but who made God? Yawn.

"Gigolo" (**104**) is about colonists who are forbidden to return to Earth but are desperate to do so and tell the Earth tourists so at every opportunity. The protagonist has picked up one of them for that purpose; but she turns out to be a big shot and tells him she's going to take him back to Earth regardless, triggering the revelation that things aren't exactly what they seem. This one is badly overwritten and the silliness of the gimmick makes it worse.

"Jackpot" (**107**) is an obvious but succinctly well turned story about space explorers looking for the big score, and finding an artifact that seems at first to absorb energy without limit, with the predictable result by the end of the story.

§

Colin Kapp, the most promising new writer of 1958-59, contributes a number of stories but overall his performance is disappointing. "Enigma" (**91**) is probably his weakest effort yet, strangled in technical detail and suggesting he is beginning to take himself a bit too seriously. There's a war on, but there's so much fallout already that nobody really wants to set off any more nuclear explosions. So the combatants send bombs that don't detonate immediately, but are clearly armed and ready to blow given the proper stimulus, to deny their enemies the use of large swathes of territory which have to be evacuated. The story focuses on the bomb squad who figure out how to defeat the bombs' defenses and booby-trapping with a highly technical solution that begins with blasting soap commercials at it at monstrous decibel levels. There are a few good over-the-top lines ("The naked steel seemed to watch every movement, the surface radiating malice like a cold, metallic sun") but overall it's too sober by half.

That is definitely not the case with Kapp's next offering, "The Exposing Eye" (**99**), which introduces Spike Mickle of Photo Research Services, summoned by Prince Morahn to find out how his intimate domestic scenes with his paramour Lady Lesley are winding up in the tabloids. The solution proves surprisingly mundane, and for that matter so does the whole story, though I suppose the surveillance technology we take for granted nowadays was Extravagant Fiction Today back in 1960. In a blind taste test one would probably guess that this story was from one of the fiction-publishing men's magazines of the time, *Rogue* or one of its kin, rather than an SF magazine. Nonetheless it's highly amusing and well done even if it's ultimately fluff.

"The Glass of Iargo" (**100**) is an overwritten wiseguyish planetary romance: "The *Panamanian Girl*, out of Terra, bound for the Rim, stopped off at Port Suma on Iargo with a cargo of machine tools, Indian hemp, computer memory matrices and a poet." Asked his business by the Company police, the poet says: "Entropy. I represent the random element in human society." In fact, he's there to steal the secret of Iargan glass, the monopoly of which is what the despotic Company is so uptight about. And of course he does, after a brief travelogue of the colorful glassblowing society now ground under the heel of the decadent oppressors.

Kapp's "The Bell of Ethicona" (**101**) is weightier, if lacking the excessive solemnity of "Enigma." In the story it's spelled "EthiConA," the Ethical Control Authority, and Nean is in its clutches after being caught violating the Moral Code by kissing a woman adjacent to a public highway (i.e., visible to the cop who climbed a wall to observe them). It is explained—through Nean's unavailing harangue in his court defense—that after World War III, the world was in a state of moral collapse and strong action was necessary, but it's been 600 years! Lighten up, guys! Nean is carted off to be subjected to the eponymous Bell, which fits over your head and detects your subvocalizations, which (it says here) reflect every word that crosses your mind, and amplifies them and feeds them back.

Says Ophels, the O'Brien figure of this dystopia:

> "It is a sound-mirror of all you ever knew or ever thought, spanning years of experience in an instant, breaking the barrier between the man and the things he has learned to forget. Love, hate, compassion—each emotion has a different signature and the bell can reproduce them all with marvellous fidelity. Only two things can still its tongue: one, that you have learned to face yourself. The second, that you are dead.... Behind the censor there lies a great storehouse of things forgotten, things repressed: the blind, black bogeys of childhood and all the darker, violent shades of things we dare not face. Also the seat of men's ambitions, the

basis of the instincts, and the life-force which drives the living soul. This world we also give to you."

So Nean starts rehashing his past through the miracle of acoustics, and after 18 days of this: "'How do you feel?' asked Ophels. 'Incredibly empty,' said Nean, with quiet resignation." Now, Ophels says, he's entirely rational and it's OK that he still doesn't buy their system. They don't buy their system either, and are trying gradually to break it down by bringing the rebels and freethinkers into responsible positions in the system. Nean falls for it, and then it's revealed that this is another double-cross, and co-opting the rebels is a way to perpetuate the system rather than disassemble it. This one is a nice try, but a bit too stylized and implausible to carry much conviction.

"For the Love of Pete" (**111**) is lighter both in substance and style, featuring an antigravity researcher whose experiments keep crashing and around whom everything breaks or falls apart. First he's fired as a saboteur of the ordinary type, then he's rehired as an unwitting psionic saboteur and therefore a research subject, but then appears to be the victim of a poltergeist who is also the ghost of his vindictive dead girlfriend, but maybe that's just how his own psi talent manifests itself, but.... It's done in an Eric Frank Russellish breezy cod-American-wiseguy style with just a few too many cheap laughs about how much the protagonist drinks.

§

Philip E. High moves in these issues from being an uneven but promising new writer to one who's a bit less uneven but probably not promising much more than what we've seen. "Mumbo Jumbo Man" (**90**) reads like a Campbell reject. An army detachment on an alien planet is about to be wiped out by the alien Seth. As a last desperate measure they turn command over to the agent of the Corps of Magicians, a.k.a. the mumbo-jumbo man, who engineers the aliens' defeat through various ancient arts (any sufficiently aged technology is indistinguishable...). There's not much to it but it's told with High's customary enthusiasm.

"Pursuit Missile" (**95**) is a misfire, a clumsy piece of apparent comedy about the incompetent reinvention of space warfare by an isolated colony planet. In "Routine Exercise" (**103**), a nuclear submarine is suddenly translated back to the Jurassic or Mesozoic (pterodactyls and what sounds like plesiosaurs make cameo appearances), where the crew quickly find themselves in conflict with an alien expedition, popping back to the present when they shoot down the mother ship. Carnell liked this one enough to put it in his anthology *Lambda I*, and it is a very agreeable albeit completely conventional read—it acts out its title. "The Jackson Killer" (**106**) is about an Eliminator, i.e., a man who goes around killing Jacksons, who are rebellious and paranoiac types; but things are not quite what they seem.

"The Martian Hunters" (**112**) is a sequel to High's clever "Project—Stall" (**83**), and is pretty clever itself. One of the Martian artifacts turns out to be a Martian's consciousness which merges with a human investigator, to the consternation of his fellows and the security types, who feel obliged to hunt him/it down. As is common with High, conviction and terseness make a very readable story out of a not very original plot. "Survival Course" (**113**) is less terse but otherwise of the same ilk: on the canonical jungly and rainy Venus, explorers from Earth land, set up camp, and the survivalist among them starts shooting the local fauna—which appear to be literally brainless—with his crossbow. Then the crossbow hobbyist turns up dead with a bolt in his back, and the fauna are suddenly acting a bit menacing. What's going on? The answer is not too surprising but its discovery is well presented. But verve will take you only so far, and, except for "The Martian Hunters," this stuff is all the familiar furniture of SF with not much value added.

John Rackham has become an instant regular at *New Worlds*, but a wildly uneven one. His first *New Worlds* appearance, "The Bright Ones" (**94**), is a farm opera, and not bad. Ben Ford has figured out how to get the dull-blue indigenes of Tau Ceti Whatever (curiously, the planet doesn't seem to be named in the story) to work on his farm. They get to eat cactus that grows profusely as a by-product. He is slaving away to make enough money so that his daughter—back on Earth with his sister, his wife having died in childbirth—will never have to farm, but suddenly daughter and sister show up because sister has taken a job on the planet, much to his dismay.

Meanwhile, the man on the next farm is a biochemist who figures out why a few of the indigenes are bright blue, and brighter generally, and what happened to the ancient civilization (a pretty clever-sounding biochemical explanation). All is revealed when the pig-headed and resentful Ford discovers his daughter is missing and is with the indigenes and goes after her armed and with fists flying. This isn't great literature but at the level of everyday magazine SF it's a well-done story, character- and science-driven simultaneously. Judith Merril gave it an Honorable Mention.

Rackham's next story, "Theory" (98), is lively if risibly dated. Scott is to be captain of an interstellar expedition, and he's been invited to spend the weekend with both his old flame Belle and Parker, the man who beat him out to marry her and who has something to do with the psychological training and selection of the spacefarers. Immediately, Belle begins to act outrageously seductive around Scott, and her husband absents himself most of the time. Scott conducts himself honorably. Then Parker shows up with the woman who was Scott's monitor during his training, heads off to his private workroom, and is obviously disporting himself with her. Scott barges in and demands an explanation.

The answer: he's passed, and the theory is proven. Though he is notoriously hotheaded, he has mostly managed to control himself when exposed to the symbol of the project, a disk with a circular rainbow pattern proceeding from a red outer ring to a violet center, which immunizes the perceiver from the influence of strong emotions. There's an *Analog*-style info-dump about how symbolism has replaced the major tranquilizers in psychiatry. That's how everybody is going to stay calm during a ten-year space voyage. And by the way, the female training monitors are actually the other half of the crew, now that it's been shown it's safe to send them. And Scott has somehow failed to notice that his monitor is actually Belle's younger sister, who had a crush on him way back when and is happy to renew it now. Later, he asks, if all this is true, how was it that half an hour ago, with her, he... er... ah... Turns out the women are all equipped with reverse disks with violet outer rings and red centers—"we girls like a little bit of decontrolled emotion now and then."

"Trial Run" (**101**) is unfortunately drearier, an arid geek epic about an interstellar war against the marauding Arcs (Arcturans). Earth has reverse engineered their space drive, which involves continuous lurches in and out of the "'pseudo' universe," at considerable hazard to one's breakfast. But we're still losing the war. The arrogant "Marsies"—Martian colonists who never let you forget that only high-IQ types were allowed to emigrate there—have developed an idea for sending torpedoes through the pseudo universe, but the lurches make it next to impossible to aim anything. *Now* what to do? The rude Earthmen, who have been recruited to test the torpedo system, come up with the hardware-store solution *all by themselves* and kick some serious Arc butt, forcing the Marsies to eat space-crow and acknowledge their prowess, in this burst of premature Mary Sue-ism. Carnell sums this one up in "The Literary Line-Up": it "deals with the problem of trying to locate a space-suited man lost in sub-space (assuming faster-than-light travel) and involves three kinds of universes." Say what? Maybe Carnell confused this story with a reject from the slush pile.

Rackham has the *New Worlds* Profile in **101**, after having hitherto refused requests for biographical material. "Born 1916 into a family with little wealth and not over ambitious, but great readers, discussers, philosophers." He was surrounded by books and has read a lot since young. He avoids specialization, has "no distinctions, degrees, qualifications of any kind," though he works for the Central Electricity Generating Board and reads and writes in his spare time, or what's left given that he has a wife and three children. His manifesto:

> Have very few convictions, but among them are these: that science fiction is the only fiction being written that has anything worthwhile to say. That it is just about the only field left for exploration on an individual basis. That if it is to last and earn the solid future it merits, it must be aimed at the young. Not the "juvenile" or the "childish," but the keen and tough young minds which can take difficult, challenging concepts, and bite on them. Notice, sometime, the standard of material currently being put out for high-schools on radio and T.V., and you'll have what I mean. Science fiction can reach this level, and be good fun, too.

He is profiled again in **112**, in which he has a guest editorial. Carnell says:

> John Rackham has been in the background of the London s-f scene for many years now. Unobtrusive at Conventions, his presence has been forcibly felt by the pithy discussions he has triggered off when the professionals have been either on the rostrum or in private session. During the past two years his writing ability has increased tremendously, along with his output, and we can expect to see many more fine stories coming from his typewriter in the near future.

It's back to risibility with "Blink" (**106**), dissected in detail above. It's worth noting that this is unusually long for *New Worlds* (59 pages) and highly touted by Carnell: "John Rackham's long novelette this month shows the vast strides he has made since his first short stories appeared in *Science Fantasy* several years ago." "Blink" is followed by "The Trouble with Honey" (**108**), in which the bees on a colony planet are suddenly producing euphoriant honey that suppresses fatigue and depletion-warning centers in the brain. The farmers get out their shootin' irons when the authorities try to suppress this dangerous substance. There's an ecological explanation, and our hero enlists the aid of the saucy lab technician Maria Muldoon (with a couple of stage Irishmen as supporting characters as well) to develop an entomological remedy and swindle the farmers into using it. There's an arch sexual subtext to this one, too.

After all this exasperating junk and near-junk, it is a pleasant surprise to come upon "Goodbye, Dr. Gabriel" (**109**), a humane and thoughtful story about a man who is the victim of a horrible murder attempt but survives as a brain in a box. The heroic Dr. Gabriel keeps him alive, develops senses for him (crude at first but then more refined), ways for him to communicate (ditto), then finally a body, a superhuman one at that. But what's the point? "I'm not a man at all. I'm just a brain, inside a metal and plastic automaton." He resolves to end it all, after taking care of some unfinished business with the man who put him in this position in the first place. Unfortunately the story deteriorates toward the end into overtly Frankensteinian hokum and suggestions of a sequel.

In addition to his fiction, Rackham contributes an article, "The Science Fiction Ethic," to the anniversary issue **100**. Unfortunately, it is rather rambling and tedious, reminiscent of what an ELIZA-like computer program might generate if you fed it a hundred forgettable fanzine articles with similar titles. His point appears to be that SF is no longer fulfilling its function of extrapolating possible futures, and that the people in SF are no different from people now, unlike the good old days when, apparently, SF was about genuinely futuristic people. I must have missed that issue.

Bertram Chandler is back and hugging the shore with a number of unadventurous stories. In **94** he contributes "Lost Thing Found" and also has the *New Worlds* Profile, the latter noting that two years previously he had been complaining about a shortage of ideas, but no more: "stories are now arriving from our favourite Australian author in packets of three or more at a time." Not for long, though, or maybe Carnell was just rejecting them. This is the last appearance of the Chandler byline in *New Worlds*. He has four more under the George Whitley byline in these two years, and that's it for him in this magazine.

"Lost Thing Found" is a slickly written but highly contrived and talky item in which a Survey Service team finds one of the "lost colonies" (descendants of crews lost in space-drive screw-ups), which has been quickly populated because one of the survivors was a genius at genetics. They're also telepathic, and one of them senses that the protagonist is troubled by lost love and offers to recreate her from tiny flakes of skin on articles of clothing she wore, plus any pictures he has, plus his memories. This takes a few weeks. When he meets her, however, he realizes that this is not the real thing and he must go back and patch it up with the original. In this didactic crescendo, what is to become of the woman manufactured to love him is forgotten.

The first of the Whitley stories, "Homing Tantalus" (96), concerns space travelers who come home but land in a different time line, one where their ship blew up and killed them. So not only are they not home, no one can see them and they can't touch a lot of items, like, say, food. Their problem is solved only because one of them manages to find his old girl friend, who is able to perceive him. This one is more incisive than most of the bland and inconsequential fare Chandler has been contributing, though it's odd that it appeared in *New Worlds* rather than *Science Fantasy*. It's also odd that it's followed in **97** by "No Return," *another* story about space travelers ending in a different time line. There's no tangibility problem, but the relativistic time-dilated crew are all put in quarantine with wives resuscitated after 12 years in suspended animation, except that the protagonist (and only he) is greeted by someone not his wife. And he alone remembers, e.g., the Venusberg riots. This one is clever but little else.

"Change of Heart" (**110**), is a typically facile SF/sea story: the dolphins and killer whales have mutated and become intelligent and they've got our number, Wyndham's *Out of the Deeps* writ small. Judith Merril gave it an Honorable Mention. "All Laced Up" (**112**) is one of Chandler's glib, dexterous, and bland tales of domesticity. A couple buys some dodgy-looking iron lace for decorative purposes, a Doctor of Interior Decorating from the future shows up in their living room wanting to do business, and of course the denouement doesn't really disturb the cosmos very much. Carnell liked it enough to put it in *Lambda I* a few years later, as did John Baxter in his first anthology of notable Australian SF (*Pacific Book of Australian Science Fiction*, 1968) and it is indeed a polished artifact.

§

Other *New Worlds* regulars contribute smaller numbers of stories—very small in some cases.

John Brunner, surprisingly, makes only a minor contribution to these issues, both in quantity and interest. (In his defense, he has some good material in *Science Fantasy* and is cranking out Ace Doubles by this time.) His didactic streak emerges in "Badman" (**92**). In a small town, the rumors are starting to fly: "The Badman is coming!" What's so Bad about him? Doesn't say, but everyone is terrified. Young Niles and his buddies try to rid the world of this scourge. When Niles is captured by the Badman, he learns it's all a set-up: they have Badmen so everyone will have somebody to hate and there won't be any more destructive wars. They can't let Niles go, but maybe someday he'll become a Badman himself. It's a smooth performance but still more of an essay than a story, though Judith Merril gave it an Honorable Mention.

"The Fourth Power" (**93**) requires one to suspend disbelief so high the air gets thin. Society is complex enough that we need super-synthesists—not just people who know a lot, but people who can do more with it. Scientists have figured out how neurones (sic—the old British spelling) are connected in three dimensions, but they need more—the fourth power, as Brunner calls it, non-spatial connections within the brain. Hook up a synthesist to the "induction mechanism," which allegedly teaches him how to make such connections, and before long he's taught himself the guitar and picked up music theory, can analyze harmonic structure without interrupting his reading, solves complex math problems at the same time he is memorizing poetry, etc. But wait, he's not really multi-tasking. One task is being finished before another is begun, by the equivalent of psychic time travel, making it all look simultaneous.

It accelerates: "He's asleep, reading a volume of Malinowski, watching TV and listening to a Segovia album, practising one of Segovia's transcriptions of Bach, and writing a short article on—on I forget what." Watching him is "similar to looking at an early three-dimensional film without polaroid glasses on." Shortly thereafter, one of him is in the bedroom while the rest of him are in the lounge. So they ask him which of him was in the bedroom, and he looks unhappy and disappears. Permanently. There is a gibberish explanation. This shaggy savant story is recounted without a shred of humor.[8]

This time Brunner saves the lecture for his *New Worlds* Profile, where—beneath the same downy-cheeked photo that appeared in his first Profile five years previously—he says:

> "The Fourth Power" [...] was first-drafted in a fourth-floor flat in Brussels in October of last year. It was my first story in many months, because my wife and I were touring Europe with a nuclear disarmament exhibition. We covered seven countries in four months.

---

8. Broderick disagrees. These days quantum superposition or the Multiverse might be invoked, or closed timelike loops. In any case, this is a genuine sense-of-wonder story that doesn't quite work mostly because Brunner blinks at the end, but it retains enough gosh-wow to prickle the skin of a responsive reader (and maybe you had to be there at the time).

I think it was probably this circumstance which got me thinking about what I consider the important aspect of this story—the concept of the synthesist. We need something of this sort, and we need it *fast*. We inhabit a shrinking planet. Unless we achieve some method of ironing out the glaring differences in our world, we're likely to be unable to make use of our own major discoveries.

Superficially, of course, world-wide homogenizing is in progress. But that applies to juke-boxes, Italian shoes and General Motor [sic] cars—not to fundamentals. Even in Europe, which is a local district of Earth these days, tremendous discrepancies can be found. The standard of living in Britain, for example, is markedly lower than that of the other countries we visited last year, except France's—and France has been at war for over twenty years non-stop. In Sweden and Denmark, things that the British consider ultra-modern are already thirty years old and slightly out of date. We have our Motorway—but the *Autobahnen*, which enable a fast car to cross Germany in eight or ten hours, date back to the thirties.

And within a day's air travel, you can find medieval feudal societies in the Middle East.

Some technique like synthesis has got to be found, and not just on the economic level—on the security level as well.

Brunner is back in the hundredth issue letting down the side with the meretricious though well turned "Prerogative" (**100**), in which the main character, not the protagonist but the guest of honor at a coroner's inquiry, created life in the laboratory and was struck dead by lightning.

§

Kenneth Bulmer also has three stories in addition to his serials, only one of them particularly notable. "Profession: Spaceman" (**92**) is another of *New Worlds'* human interest stories of the new frontier. A former space ferry pilot has developed a phobia about the loud and dangerous short-term rockets (firecrackers, they're called), but he's a deep space pilot now, so his only problem is the trip from Earth to orbit. There's a disaster in orbit and somebody's got to pilot a firecracker, and of course he steps into the breach. It's readable but overwritten.

Bulmer's "Greenie Gunner" (**101**) is about as dreary as its title. It's another story about the war with the Octos (the other one being "Mission One Hundred" in **63**), conducted in flux-wagons, so called after their space drives. Strickland has failed his exams, so he's going to be a tail gunner rather than a navigator, and his wife Julie has left him for one Bannerman, who didn't flunk and, it transpires, passed his exams and is going to be the navigator on Strickland's first mission, but only after Strickland punches him out. That taken care of, he learns to value Bannerman in the heat of battle, and of course it turns out that Julie was a tramp anyway. Strickland saves Bannerman's life and then while Bannerman is injured and *hors de combat*, fills in and navigates them back to safety, notwithstanding his test scores, which he now realizes were really Julie's fault, since she had just left him at the time. This male bonding/*cherchez la femme* epic concludes: "'You'll make a fluxer,' said the skipper.... *They were a fluxer crew—now.*"

"Hiatus" (**102**), under the Frank Brandon pseudonym, is better. A man wakes up on an apparently long-deserted spaceship, can't quite remember why he's there, wanders around brushing aside the cobwebs and fat brown spiders, entertaining dire surmises. His memory gradually returns and he figures out he's the one designated to thaw the rest of the colonists, who are in suspended animation. It's a bit obvious and overmelodramatic but still effective.

§

Donald Malcolm marks time capably enough in these issues, beginning with "The Pathfinders" (**92**). Shirreff and Grassick project themselves a hundred million years into the future, where they find the author taking on H. G. Wells on behalf of God. Here's the long smooth beach, the endless and featureless sea, the bloated dull red Sun, and the near-omniscient Creature, the last living thing, who is dying and not too pleased about it. But then the two time-travelers show up, primitive but with something "shining deep within them." The Creature extracts telepathically that they consider extinction "not the end, but only the beginning of life! Was this the answer to the elusive longing, to the fear of a bottomless nothingness? Belief, faith, the soul, God?" Apparently so.

The Creature is relieved by this revelation and grants the humans their desires: one of them, a view of the skies from the Equator, and the other, a vision of a shining city of the future (under a smaller Sun and purplish-black sky). Since the city exists, the latter says, his companion needs to go back and put in train the search for a woman time-teleport, and come back with her to this time (of the bloated red sun), and be fruitful and multiply, apparently to help fulfill the prophecy of the city, while time traveler #1 scouts things out further up the line. This thoroughly batty story is lively and economically written, though Malcolm himself didn't seem to think much of it. He says in "Postmortem" in **95**:

> Not all aspects of s-f lend themselves to literary treatment. However, I'd like to see more writers having a shot at such a story. (Obviously, incidental s-f will always be with us). I tried it with "The Pathfinders," (No. 92). I plead guilty to John Brunner's charges. This story is a hybrid. The original piece started as a doodle, an experiment in astronomical description. It became a story—a poor one. Only some remarks you made about the beginning saved these passages for future use. "The Pathfinders," while it succeeded

only in part, was a step towards the literary story. (Incidentally, I do *all* my writing during my 45-minute lunch break.)

"The Winds of Truth" (**94**) is an inconsequential story about Tippy's planet, where everyone tells the truth, and a specialized team of Terrans is there to find out why, their jobs made more difficult by the fact that when they tell the truth about each other they come to blows. "Test Case" (**98**) is a mildly clever and slightly ponderous satire: the Brits land Captain Hamilton on the Moon, much to the annoyance of the United Nations Committee for Space Law, which decrees that there will be no further manned flights to the Moon pending their deliberations (Hamilton will be supplied by unmanned flights). While the lawyers and diplomats argue, Hamilton is mostly forgotten, and nobody knows that he has discovered an alien artifact, gone inside and sat down in the funny-looking chair. "The court was in session."

"The Other Face" (**105**) is prematurely psychedelic, though properly moralistic: men crash-land on a strange planet, drink the water, and—"Minutes later, the tilted lines of the cabin began to writhe, then to melt and flow into each other in the most fantastic designs." Sometime after that, they're dead, found by the crew that otherwise would have rescued them. Apparently they went out into the unbreatheable atmosphere without their helmets. What gives? Lysergic acid diethylamide 25 in the water! But—*They had smiles on their faces.*" And, one of the characters says: "I think they both experienced short, overpowering bouts of mental turbulence that went beyond insanity and during which some deeply personal problem was solved: perhaps *the* personal problem."

Author Malcolm has clearly done his homework in the literature. But, as with "The Pathfinders," there's other literature he's concerned with, too. The story ends with another commercial for God, delivered at the explorers' funeral: "The Captain was a deeply religious man, but not a fanatic or a zealot. Theology was a mandatory course for all men aspiring to his rank. The Academy realised only too well what space could do to a man with power and a belief only in himself." The text: "We commit these, thy servants, to thy care, O Lord, that they may look upon the other face of Heaven, and know peace. Amen."

§

Arthur Sellings has only one story during these two years. "Starting Course" (**102**) is characteristically well written but stunningly inane. The Trendall family has been chosen by lot to receive Eddie, an adolescent android—one of a batch of 50—to complete his education in how to be human. There's an adolescent daughter who becomes captivated by him and wants to share in his destiny of going to a colony planet. The obvious accusations are made, and Eddie reveals that androids don't reproduce (or go through the motions, either, it is implied). So the parents are filled with remorse and suddenly the whole family wants to head for the stars with him, even though they were apathetic schlumpfs before. At the spaceport, Eddie is separated from them and told he isn't going. Why? It's all been a put-up job—the androids are not intended to go into space but to motivate regular folks to go into space. This ridiculously implausible scenario is set out with great sincerity rather than as a Sheckleyesque lampoon.

John Hynam, real name of John Kippax, appears in **100** with "Unfinished Symphony" ("Sympathy" on the contents page), a formulaic but very clever time travel fantasy (the formula being the one about the artist who encounters his future work before he has done it). Carnell's blurb says Hynam "has been devoting most of his time to producing scripts for radio and television plays. His most recent BBC success was 'Someone To Talk To...' with Wilfred Pickles and Jean Anderson in the leading roles." Why he is using his own name and not his accustomed pseudonym is not explained. This is its only appearance in the SF magazines (he did have several stories as Hynam in *London*

Mystery). It's not the only not-very-interesting name trick here. The story's narrator is Julian Frey, a pseudonym Hynam used for a couple of stories in *Science Fantasy* in 1958 and 1958.

He reverts to the Kippax name in "Nelson Expects" **(110)**, which features a mid-fortyish, but very fit, repressed and milquetoasty fellow who has been spacewrecked on a comfortable planet with four pulchritudinous stewardesses (sic) and a 14-year-old boy for company, his domineering and strait-laced wife having been killed in the crash. The entire story is about his getting over it and getting ready to move in on the women, who are becoming impatient. Carnell says of this arch period piece: "Outside of science fiction one of our favourite Magazines (sic) is America's *Playboy*, noted for its brilliant fiction and satire—which strongly influenced the purchase of John Kippax's 'Nelson Expects,' a story that could well have been published in that magazine." Indeed. Carnell is probably one of the three or four people in the world who *did* read *Playboy* for the written matter. This story is Kippax's last appearance in the Carnell *New Worlds*, and his last in *Science Fantasy* and *Science Fiction Adventures* appeared within a few months of this one. He made one more appearance in the Moorcock *New Worlds* in 1966 and that was it for his SF magazine career, though he did have a couple of stories in *New Writings in SF* shortly before his death in 1974.

Several of the familiar names are present but winding down, mercifully in some cases. Lan Wright's "The Jarnos Affair" **(93)** is the last in the seemingly interminable Johnny Dawson series, possibly the most contrived yet. To deal with an aggressive and telepathic race, Dawson and confederates fake the history of Earth's military deeds and cause themselves to believe their own fabrications by means of hypnotic "impulsion," so the Jarnosians pull in their horns. The usual satire directed against innocuous targets is present (describing Dawson's boss: "Hendrix's bloodshot eyes popped in disbelieving rage and the ragged stump of a mashed cigar dangled precariously from the lower lip of his open mouth.")

After this suffocating formula piece, "Star Light, Star Bright" (**104**) is considerably less irritating, almost refreshing in fact, a sort of updated *Planet Stories* pastiche: "'From Telverlorn Skarn had come to Kantor's World some twelve years before, there to live while her alien beauty faded, and her cat's eyes became a permanent mirror for the haunted longing in her heart.'" But she's dead by suicide, and the reporter protagonist snoops around and pumps her old acquaintance Carlin.

> "For a man of your position you are astonishingly ignorant. No, we were not lovers." Carlin swallowed another mouthful from his glass, grimacing slightly as the harsh fluid caught at his throat. "How do you love a hermaphrodite? There is no sex, no life as you and I know it—there is only beauty, a cold awesome beauty that is totally alien. Skarn's race was parthenogenetic. To call her 'she' is merely to recognize her beauty, not her sex."

So why's she dead? She ran away with Carlin to see the rest of the universe, and her sun went nova, and only now is the light from the nova reaching her present abode so the death of her home planet is undeniable.

"The End of the Line" (**111**) is in the same rhetorical and atmospheric vein: "Now I am the last of my world—there is no other like me, no one to whom I can turn for companionship, and no place where I can stay, no world that I can call my own. Earth is as alien to me now as my world would have been to you, Florian, and the only thing I have left is the flight through all eternity—with death as my salvation." This is the Barbarian, more formally known as Peter Yorgen, last of the Longship pilots, superannuated by centuries of relativistic time dilation. The story goes on in the same vein for some time, and culminates with Yorgen being escorted back to his ship to pick up his stuff. Instead of hijacking his spaceship and heading out—the correct conclusion if this really were *Planet Stories*—he grabs his (small) bag and exits, weeping. This is close to the end of the line for Wright as well: it's his next to last piece of short fiction in the SF magazines, followed only by a serial in *New Worlds* and a novella in *Science Fiction Adventures* in 1963.

Dan Morgan's last story for Carnell (he published one in Moorcock's time, and then moved on to paperback novels for a while) is "Stopover Earth" (**102**). A spaceman has two hours to find his long-time pen pal, marry her, and get back on the ship with her, but she's nowhere to be found and her household robot is unhelpful. Morgan has had the sense to keep this hyper-contrived "Fondly Fahrenheit" variation very short and therefore sharp.

Peter Hawkins' desultory career ends in these issues. "The Edge of Oblivion" (**102**) is aptly titled, since it is his next to last story in *New Worlds* and in the field. Unfortunately it's a bit of a muddle, as was frequently the case with Hawkins. As the magazine's overall level of writing and thinking has improved over the years, some of the long-standing contributors such as Hawkins have been left behind. This one posits that Venus used to have a moon, but it disintegrated and all the pieces fell to the surface (already a plausibility problem there). In these deposits are found "marbles," which if properly irradiated will glow indefinitely (another plausibility problem), and which are sought out by the company that employs the protagonist. The marbles come in black and blue, but he's found a red one.

It turns out the red ones are in some mysterious way hemmed in by invisible walls of force, so when they try to fly one to base in an aircraft it rips a hole through the back window because it can't go any further. What to do about all this is left completely inconclusive, except that the ne'er-do-well protagonist is ready to take charge of figuring it out. Here's an indication of the persistent amateurishness of Hawkins' writing: the protagonist is looking at the marble, studying the notes of the man who found another one, and thinking hard: "Pieces of a jigsaw puzzle began to pop into place like rabbits into holes at the sound of dog." Not only does he gild a metaphor with a simile, but a ridiculous and distracting one to boot.

"Black Knowledge" (**113**), Hawkins' finale, is equally dire. The characters land on a planet that proves to be the library of destructive techniques compiled by the Cresparians, one of the extinct principals in a long-ago interstellar war—or, as Hawkins calls it several times, a University of Death (a phrase that J. G. Ballard appropriated or reinvented some years later for what became a piece of *The Atrocity Exhibition*). One of the four gets vivisected in an obscurely described way, another commits suicide, and one of the remaining two decides he's going to blow the place up and does, only to be upbraided by his remaining companion that somewhere there's a duplicate library and some other species is going to use it against humans. All this is conveyed in a style that ranges from the infelicitous to the grossly incompetent: "A stellar explorer, like Somers caught in a Cresparian trap elsewhere on the planet was an impossible situation because if another spaceship had arrived anywhere near the world all the alarms aboard would have been ringing as if tolled by a convention of lunatic bellringers." "Now all the evil knowledge was in Man's hands and fortunately he had no adversary against whom to use it, except himself and it was by no means certain he wouldn't do that." Hawkins managed one quite good story in *Science Fantasy* a few years earlier—"The Daymakers" (**23**)—but never reached that level again.

Alan Barclay's "The Scapegoat" (**105**) is another of his explorations of military characters and milieus, mildly satirical—like dilute Eric Frank Russell. Here's an alien incursion into the solar system, and brash young ambitious Captain Slesdyke is assigned to assist canny old General Turnock, who figures out how to manipulate the contentious forces of dozens of countries into an effective fighting force and to win the war in spite of them all. It's a bucket of clichés, but Barclay has become a very smooth writer and it goes down painlessly.

"Haircrack" follows in the next issue, a genial puzzle story about a robbery from a computerized banking system, but it's all a set-up. Barclay has designed the system to have an unnecessary flaw which the robber has exploited and eventually reveals. Still, it plays out very pleasantly. Judith Merril gave *both* these stories Honorable Mentions.

Unfortunately all this facility, developed over a decade, will now go to waste. These two are Barclay's last stories in the SF magazines. The score: 25 stories, including one under Barclay's real name, George B. Tait. Two articles; one early story in *Astounding*, two in *Authentic*, the rest in the Nova magazines. Two stories reprinted in the short-lived US magazine *Saturn* in the late 1950s; two appearances in Carnell anthologies in the 1950s.

§

The dinosaurs, too, are headed for extinction. E. R. James is nowhere to be found. Francis G. Rayer has only two stories in these issues, though Carnell notes in passing in a blurb in **100** that he has overall been *New Worlds*'s most prolific author. "Static Trouble" (**91**) is another of his high-science epics, this time on a hot, dry planet covered with dust, which hovers in the air in layers because of the static electricity generated by the heat, dryness, and friction. But when something comes along that is grounded, like a human being or a spaceship or a building, the charged particles "sped like dust towards a rubbed ebonite rod, and clung." (That is, the dust sped like dust. Remarkable!) So the Earth explorers are about to crack and mutiny is in the air, but then the protagonist sees through the dust clouds...a native. Off they go on a quest and find a native city, with clear sky and no dust. How can this be? Insulation! Probably silica glass, so the city is at the same potential as the dust rather than grounded. "Men could do the same." This one is actually better done than Rayer's usual. In fact, Judith Merril gave it an Honorable Mention, perhaps out of surprise.

"Spring Fair Moduli" (**103**) is more wistful and wispy, suitably for a writer who is inexorably being left behind by the rising standards of sophistication and competence in this magazine and the genre. Joe, an apparently very humanoid alien with golden-brown skin, goes on a carnival ride with his girlfriend Judy, who disappears from his arms. Of course he is accused of doing away with her, and when he returns to the fair to look for her again, he is pursued by a wannabe lynch mob—at which point he has the sort of epiphany that only a left-behind SF writer could recite with a straight face:

> A new, intense awareness had grown in Joe's mind. While crouched under the canvas he had thought of Kirchoff's Law. There was an equation, a balancing. Each circuit loop was an unknown, but you guessed current flow. When the simultaneous equations were worked, you merely got a negative sign if you were wrong. And here, at the fair, there seemed to be an over-fullness of action and of motion—an equation that did not balance.

So he jumps back on the ride a few steps ahead of his persecutors. "Astonished faces stared up at the roundabout. Beyond it sang and roared the other machines, vast, human-laden wheels in endless, repetitive pattern. Momentarily the fair was an integrated whole, an oscillation and orbiting of power. Mass balanced mass, motion balanced motion, each integrated with the other." Joe disappears too, and finds himself in a wooded Arcadia where Judy is waiting for him and tells him the folks here are kind and friendly. This story's gimmick, and title, are a bit overtly repetitive of an earlier story, "The Jakandi Moduli" (**42**), in which the bustle of spaceships landing and taking off results in some of them taking particularly convoluted courses and disappearing.

§

Several new voices are heard in these issues—new to *New Worlds*, at least—in addition to the omnipresent chatter of John

Rackham. Unfortunately, most of them didn't last long, and none of them made it to the front ranks. One of the relatively more lasting was David Rome (Boutland), who managed 20 stories in the SF magazines, mostly before 1965, and a few stragglers in original anthologies, before moving to a more lucrative career in TV and movies. His stories here are competent but not much more. "Time of Arrival" (**105**), his first story in the SF magazines, is a short and bitter piece about a kid who is dying to get into space and the old wannabeagain spacer who betrays him—effective if you buy the premise, I suppose. Judith Merril apparently did, giving the story an Honorable Mention.

"Trinity" (**108**) is a piece of unpretentious pulp. We're at war against the alien Lipp, who are trying to infiltrate the Area. (You get to it, once you've landed, by going through the Gap to get out of the Field). The protagonist has come to investigate the fact that two Area workers disappeared for a day but have no memory of anything but being at work as usual. Of course a game is afoot, and the day is ultimately saved by the beautiful Geshtian who proves to work for the Security Force rather than being mere decoration. It's readable enough but is almost irritating for its lack of ambition, rearranging standard SF pieces on the board.

Rome/Boutland has the *New Worlds* Profile in this issue. He's 22, family emigrated from UK to Australia, started writing as a child, worked in a newspaper starting about age 15 as messenger boy, clipper, filing clerk, then a printing-trade apprentice. "Three years of technical school, plus intense dislike of routine, drove pen to paper once again." He started being published in Australia in 1958, published stories and articles under various names in 1959 and 1960, then went freelance. He says some of this material was SF ("mostly near-future shorts"), but it's not listed in Miller/Contento—not surprisingly, since there weren't many genre publications in Australia at the time. He began to specialize in SF after returning to England, works 9 to 4 six days a week. "Still have a sneaking affection for the BEM, and like to use him in a mild way, now and then.... Always fascinated by the psi powers...."—both of which are on display in "Trinity." He lives in the Pennine foothills with his wife.

"The Fortress of True" (**110**) is also vigorously pulpy, but shorter. The protagonist is an Earthman resident on Manat, with whom Earth is about to be at war. The Manatians know he's an agent; but he figures out a way to deliver his payload and destroy the Manatian munitions factory. "Protected Species" (**113**) is a slightly pious story of two spacemen who settle down on a planet to do some (sort of) agriculture, find the indigenes are interfering with their business, and react to them in very different ways.

Lee Harding's first *New Worlds* story "Conviction" (**111**)— slightly preceded by a couple in *Science Fantasy*—is much ado about very little. A slightly nutty specimen is convinced that nuclear war is imminent and blows the family savings on a bomb shelter. The war arrives, or so it seems, and we discover the guy is even nuttier than suspected. "Echo" (**112**) is more substantial. Explorers on Mars see a mysterious cloud appear; it expands, gets denser and warmer, finally breathable. They see a crowd of walking Martians, and there's a city in the distance. What's going on? Obviously a temporal disturbance, explained when the city vaporizes in what sounds like a nuclear explosion (but the characters still have their photographs). This is an agreeable middle-of-the-road SF story well enough written to maintain interest despite the familiarity of its subject and modus operandi. After these, Harding had a few more stories and lasted a few more years than David Rome.

The freshest of the new-to-*New Worlds* writers (although also the oldest, at 45 in 1960) is Wynne N. Whiteford, who contributes three stories. The least of them is "Bill of Sale" (**92**), a well-done if inconsequential story about a trading post on an alien planet, the protagonist's scheme to take one of the very humanoid alien women to Earth, and how the tables are turned. "Moment of Decision" (**96**) is equally efficient and capable and has a little more to it. A man graduates as a computer specialist, has no plans, and decides to head for Eltanin VI, where the entire economy is run by a computer, the Solmak of Milos. He's sure he'll find programming work. But everybody discourages him, on Earth and on Eltanin. There, he finds that the original Ninety-Eight colonists seem to be a class apart from the more recent emigrants, and he is told there is no work for him. Of course he sneaks into the Solmak installation and finds it hasn't been used in decades, and the elite are passing their decisions off as the computer's. He is released only after, apparently, persuading the Eltanians that he won't blow the whistle because their system works and that's all that matters. Back on Earth, he decides that's right and keeps his mouth shut.

Whiteford (1915-2002), a little-sung Australian pioneer with an erratic career arc, has the *New Worlds* Profile in this issue. Born in Melbourne, he had a few stories and articles published in his teens, couldn't sell "literary" stories, switched to engineering and operated a display business (whatever that is) for a few years. He resumed writing after he got married in 1950, publishing suspense and SF short stories for Australian magazines, and was Technical Editor of an Australian motoring magazine, "specialising in road-testing of cars and covering motor-racing events." He started writing novelette-length SF while living in Washington, D.C., moved to New York in 1957 writing sports-car articles and SF for US magazines, then came to London. Now he's about to return to Australia.

This account is fleshed out by the Miller/Contento index, which lists stories in *Australian Journal* and the *Australian Science Fiction Monthly* in 1956 and 1957, but the *Science Fiction Encyclopedia* says he was publishing SF as early as 1934 in something called *Adam and Eve*. He had half a dozen stories in US magazines in 1958-59, five in the Nova magazines in 1959-60, and then nothing more until 1978, when he had five stories over the next six years in the dire Australian magazine *Void*. He published half a dozen mostly drab novels from 1980 to 1990.[9]

---

9. See Russell Blackford, "Taking Wynne Whiteford Seriously," in Broderick, ed. *Chained to the Alien* (Borgo Press, 2009, 125-43).

"The Doorway" (**98**) is the best of Whiteford's stories in these issues, economically told and crisply written, a pleasure to read compared to much of its company, which remains variously arch, stuffy, or just a bit dull at the basic word-and-sentence level. It begins:

> "I've had the stuff analyzed," said Conway as they sat down in the living-room of his flat. His eyes had a haunted look.
> Smith's mouth twitched nervously to one side. "Was it blood?"
> Conway lit a cigarette before he answered, belatedly holding the packet out.
> "It was blood," he said. "Green blood."

The green blood is from the veins of the attractive woman next door to Smith in his rooming house, and he begins a campaign of surveillance and illegal entry that suggests a less perverse and more prosaic version of Sturgeon's "The Other Celia." The woman has a cabinet inside a cabinet in her room, and Smith follows her into it and finds himself in Washington, D.C. rather than London. The obviously alien woman and her companions find him out and it looks like he's come to a bad end. Carnell's blurb says, "We hope that now Wynne Whiteford has returned to Australia he will not forsake writing science fiction, as his latest story (written two days before he sailed) indicates that he is capable of producing a wide range of plots." In fact, this was Whiteford's last appearance in the SF magazines until 1978.

Robert J. Tilley is described by Carnell as a new author in the blurb to "The Wingys and the Zuzzers" (**96**), but he had five stories in *Nebula* and *Authentic* and one in *Fantasy and Science Fiction* before this one, his *New Worlds* debut. He published another nine, mostly in *Fantasy & Science Fiction*, before hanging it up in 1986. This one is arch and insubstantial if competently written. A spaceship of the alien firgs is attacked by the evil four-limbs (obviously us). and there are only two survivors, one of them a princess, but they have the last laugh. When their captors leave them alone for a while, they mate and by the time the Earthfolk return, their fast-growing progeny are ready to clean the Earthmen's clocks. This is all scandalous, since the male firg is a commoner, but their resourcefulness is recognized and a new dynasty is born. The wingys and zuzzers of the title are the firg equivalent of the birds and the bees.

"Reason" (**101**) is sharply written and effective, though its logic is skimpy in retrospect. The protagonist, a retired doctor, sitting on a park bench, encounters a man who is distraught over the chalos. These are, apparently, intangible intelligences that have appeared from across the universe in people's heads, suppressing their hostile and aggressive impulses and allowing them to live rationally and peacefully. But what if they are not going to stay? What if they are going to withdraw suddenly and leave humans. whose self-control has atrophied under this benign stewardship, alone with their savage selves? The man panics, runs, and is run over by (or runs into) a car and is killed. There's a long epilogue in which the elderly doctor wonders if the man was right, and he's glad he won't be around to find out.

W. T. Webb's "The Red Dominoes" (**99**) is an acerbic, rather Padgettesque morality tale about a really rotten and small-minded man who finds an alien device which, when its domino-like keys are pressed, confers visions of other worlds and alien creatures, and sometimes mental contact with them—including the shapeshifting one that is looking for the lost device. This is the first *New Worlds* appearance by Webb (b. 1918) (of two—he had another in 1965, under Moorcock), but he had previously placed several in *Nebula* and one in *Science Fantasy*, and will have several more in *Science Fantasy* and *Science Fiction Adventures*, then a scattering in UK fantasy/horror magazines from the late 1970s to late 1980s before he's done.

John Ashcroft, who contributes "This Wonderful Birthday" (**106**), is also new to *New Worlds*, but he had a couple of stories in *Science Fantasy* in 1954, the first accepted (he says in the

New Worlds Profile in this issue) when he was 16. He had a few more in *Nebula* and *Authentic* through 1957, then disappeared for several years during RAF service, and now he's back looking grown-up and reasonably dapper in his photo. He says that for him "the gulf between the juvenile comics and adult s-f was bridged by the late John Russell Fearn; as 'Vargo Statten' he introduced me to most major s-f concepts (and we need a successor to continue this recruiting activity)." This of course has been a recurrent theme of Carnell's.

He concludes: "Apart from reading, sketching, tape recording, enjoying New Orleans Jazz and Afro-American folk music, I hope to go on producing occasional stories keeping on the narrow path between the blaster and the soapbox. If I can enjoy myself, entertain people and be paid for it into the bargain, I'll be quite happy." And he produced a couple of stories in 1961 in *Science Fiction Adventures*, and one more story and an editorial in *New Worlds*, and that was it for his SF career. "This Wonderful Birthday" is a talky and sentimental, but reasonably pleasant and competently written, account of the ceremonial opening of a new world for colonization—Earth, which has had to be returned to habitability after a destructive war which left only the Mars colony alive.

Richard Graham appears in **96** with his first story, the heavy-handed "The Realists," in which little Jimmy shocks his parents by saying he wants to be a tech. It's not to be countenanced, they're not our kind. Then they watch the fantasy show on TV in which alien invaders are trouncing Earth's defenders. Of course, it's not fantasy at all, and little Jimmy survives only because his parents put him down the air raid chute to make the alarm stop before going back to bed themselves. "The Spirit Is Willing" (**102**) is a little subtler but not much: Earth is the imperial exploiter, and a member of the garrison goes down to have a drink in town, drinks a lot of the native liquor, meets some of the cute aliens and plays a gambling game with them, then he sort of passes out. When he wakes up, he heads back to the base clearly reprogrammed and intent on sabotage (but so crudely that he is easily stopped). This Little Known Writer[10] had five stories, all in the Nova magazines, between 1960 and 1963, and no more in the SF magazines.

Mike Davies' "The Singing Grasses" (104) is a nice try that doesn't quite gel. An Earth woman is serving as a biologist on a spaceship of the colony planet Moltar. War is declared, she's an enemy alien, and is to be "interned" by being left on a deserted planet. The Lieutenant who has been romancing her starts to desert to stay with her but can't do it and comes back. The Captain, who has been silently captivated by her, resigns his commission and takes advantage of the rule that says a former captain can't serve in a lesser rank on the same ship. It's lyrically written without getting too bathetic. This is followed in 109 by "The Ship of Heaven," a variation on the same theme. A military ship has landed on what proves to be a paradise planet, inhabited by colonists whose ancestors destroyed their ship and the rest of their technology after landing. The crew is getting restless, an attempted mutiny is fostered by the seductive natives and put down by the captain after they learn war is declared. It's hardly original but it is unusually well developed and visualized. These are the only two SF magazine credits for Mike Davies; Carnell says nothing about him.

D.S. Stewart's "Five" (104) is a quite clever alien contact story. Six explorers land on a planet where the inhabitants are organized in groups of five. One of their number goes missing, and the natives allow that they've helped the humans out by getting rid of the superfluous one; the answer to his disappearance also reveals the aliens' heretofore mysterious means of reproduction. This is the only appearance in the SF magazines of the D.S. Stewart byline, but the story is identified as the first by a new Australian author, and here in 108 is "Junior Partner"

---

10. This recurrent phrase reflects the view of members of the listserv on which this material was first aired that Attention Must Be Paid to the obscure and forgotten producers of decades-old magazine fiction, a preoccupation in which I enthusiastically joined.

by D. *D.* Stewart, another one-credit byline, whom Carnell describes as "a 'down under' writer [who] joins the select but growing band of Australians who are bringing a freshness of approach to science fiction, at least as we see it through western eyes." Same writer, victimized by Carnell's proofreading? Most likely.

This one features a rich loner solicited by the Ministry of Employment in a rather regimented future to become a Messenger, i.e. an exploratory space pilot, who will be absent from Earth for centuries on their missions. He snaps it up, puts his money in trust, and by the time the story is finished many hundreds of years later he owns the world, women have become dominant in society, he has grown two inches, and it is shortly revealed that he is a near-immortal alien finally reaching pubescence and beginning to get interested in girls as he anticipates reaching his natural height of twenty feet. Well, yes, hard to deny it's a fresh approach. Judith Merril gave it an Honorable Mention.

David Porter's "The Third Word" (**92**) is a cleverly turned trifle in which Broughton, apparently a businessman, receives a visitor who tells him he is an extraterrestrial and he can prove it by uttering the words that will bring back his memories (the first one of which is "mescalinability"—as noted, the Sixties are here). And he does, except that things prove not to be what they seem to seem. Porter's "Still Time" (**97**) is in a similarly facile vein, with the protagonist solving a mysterious bank robbery in a world dominated by psi talents (hundreds of them). Under *New Worlds*'s new and frisky dispensation, there's a pause for an interlude with the cashier from position four, "the number one scenic attraction of the Egerton branch." These two stories are Porter's only credits in the SF magazines.

George Langelaan (misspelled "Langalaan" throughout the magazine) makes his first SF magazine appearance with "Cold Blood" (**111**). The other was in *Fantasy & Science Fiction* in 1961, but he is presumably best known to Anglophone SF as author of "The Fly," published in *Playboy* in 1957 and reprinted in Judith Merril's annual anthology before the film appeared. Carnell says that Langelaan is French and the story is translated, though there's no translation credit. Merril says that although "The Fly" is his first US publication, "American audiences have seen his work, if not his name... for some thirty years—during which time the *English* (born in Paris) journalist has worked for the Paris staff of AP, UP, INS, and the *New York Times*."

Clarification can be found with some digging, which reveals Langelaan to be the author of *Masks of War: From Dunkirk to D-Day—The Masquerades of a British Intelligence Agent* (Doubleday 1959), one bookseller's entry for which says: "The author, a bilingual British Intelligence agent, as fluent in French as in English, underwent extensive plastic surgery to change his features, and after the retreat from Dunkirk was parachuted into France as a 'Frenchman.' Thus began a series of extraordinary adventures that continued throughout the remainder of World War II. George Langelaan tells of his arrest by the Vichy government and of his subsequent escape over the Pyrenees into Spain with the aid of the 'Woman in Red.' His capture of a German spy in a crowded London movie theater was but one of many adventures that befell him back in England."[11] He published a number of other titles; most of them are either in French, German, or Spanish.

But I digress, chiefly because this is more interesting than the actual story, in which a mental patient who has killed an elderly woman by stuffing her into a refrigerator is revealed by a not very reliable narrator to have been her husband, who was frozen some decades earlier in an Arctic expedition and then revived by a mad, or at least slightly cracked, scientist, or facsimile thereof. It's amusing enough but a bit ponderous and retro to be appearing in an SF magazine later than, say, 1939.

---

11. Variations of this text can be found in listings for the book at www. addall.com, probably taken from the book jacket copy, though it appears that someone bought the copy associated with the complete text as quoted, after I had transcribed it. Such are the vicissitudes of low-resolution Internet research.

But Judith Merril gave it an Honorable Mention.

Kathleen James' "Mantrap" (**107**) is a sharply written but slightly meandering story about the efforts of the imperial-istic Earth-dominated Galactic Union to locate and annex some colonized star systems that are clearly documented, but somehow can't be found when searched for. Their inhabitants slip out on trading missions and other forays, but if captured, reveal nothing and promptly die. So the Earthmen figure out how to decant one of their personalities into a duplicate body already occupied by one of their agents' personalities as well, and send this composite spy to find the systems and figure out what is going wrong, with unpredicted results. This Kathleen James had three stories in the SF magazines—this, another in *New Worlds* in 1962, and one in *Fantasy & Science Fiction* in 1966—but is revealed by Miller/Contento to be the pseudonym of one Joyce Carstairs Hutchinson (b. 1935), who also wrote as Wilhelmina Baird, whose only magazine credit is an excerpt in *Amazing* in 1993 from her novel *Crashcourse*.

Bill Spencer (b. 1925) was a friend of J. G. Ballard's from Cambridge who worked in advertising, invented gadgets on the side (like a quick-release safety-belt buckle), and eventually disappeared into academia. En route, he did some avant-garde sculpture, and may have played some part in inspiring Ballard's story "Venus Smiles." He had half a dozen stories in *New Worlds* from 1960 through 1963, then a couple more as William Spencer in the last issues, four stories in scattered volumes of Carnell's *New Writings in SF* anthologies from 1966 to 1971, and, decades later, a handful in *Interzone* from 1993 to 1997. His account of Carnell, whom he visited in his office, gives a rather different slant than Michael Moorcock's:

> He had a gentle and considerate manner. He wasn't a very big chap; he was rather slight in physical stat-ure and he had an unassuming manner. If he'd stood next to you in a bus queue you wouldn't really have noticed him. His voice was quiet, but it was nicely

modulated. It often seemed to me that when he was talking to writers he spoke to them in this reassuring tone as you might speak to a nervous horse, a wild horse that might at at any moment kick up and gallop off into the distance…. [H]is manner was almost as if he was close to and quietly conversing with a rather dangerous maniac who might suddenly burst out into some unpredictable behavior.[12]

Spencer's first story, "The Watchtower" (**97**), deserves special notice, being the runner-up in salacious risibility to Rackham's "Blink." It is an incompetent but entertaining alien contact story, in which one member of the crew of a station that watches for fluctuations in radioactivity on an alien planet is taken sick and goes to the hospital, leaving behind his wife Ilsa and the third crew member, Jon Mitland. As soon as hubby is out of the way, Ilsa begins behaving seductively towards Mitland. He starts taking long walks into the jungle outside, where he finds a disused SETI station wrapped in plastic. Naturally, he opens it and cranks everything up and starts listening in, despite having looked at the old logs which showed nothing over a period of many years. Curious, Ilsa follows him, points out the futility of his activities, and then starts pulling the levers arbitrarily, pointing the receiver in a random direction. And of course:

> Finally he caught her, and held her tight in his arms.
> He was flushed and very angry. "You little…" he started to say.
> "Look," said Ilsa. "Look, you great dumb oaf."
> She pointed to the central display, which had swung over unmistakably. The trace quivered, alive with meaning, in the "significance" zone. Coloured lights

---

12. "The Sonic Sculptor: William Spencer Interviewed by David Pringle." *Interzone* 194 (January 1994), p. 43. The biographical details in the text are also taken from this interview.

were winking. Cathode tubes glowed and rippled with strange meaningful waveforms.

"So much for your methodical methods!" said Ilsa scornfully, wrinkling her nose at him and putting out her little pink tongue.

Suddenly, they are getting results, a modulated signal that carries a diminishing arithmetical series, i.e., 4, 3, 2, 1, and it's back to business. Ilsa's tongue is not seen again, though there are a couple more flirtatious outbreaks that don't go anywhere.

The signal proves to be coming from "a nebula—and an extra-galactic one at that." And now the signal is truncated: 3, 2, 1, and then 2, 1, and then... reminiscent of the descending series in Ballard's "The Voices of Time," reduced for clearance. When zero hour arrives, there's suddenly a red-blue glow in the radio telescope, and when Jon climbs up to look—"Ee... it's all over you!" says Ilsa. "Seems harmless," says Jon, but warns her not to touch him. (Convenient under the circumstances, and more science fictional than a headache.) Ilsa asks if he isn't going to try to get rid of it—"Have a bath—*anything.*" There's a brief change of viewpoint in which it is made clear that Jon is now inhabited by an alien intelligence, and a concluding scene in which it is suggested that this has happened before—indeed, "Man became man by the addition of an alien intelligence" 30 million years ago. Then it's announced that Ilsa's husband is coming back. The End, everything hanging.

Spencer's "Button-Pusher" (**105**) is not quite so over the top, or maybe it's just over a different top. It's a *Galaxy*-gone-to-seed or early Laumer-style dystopia, in which the protagonist goes to a job every day and pushes buttons according to an arbitrary scheme, earning credits with which to pay for a Sleeping Cubicle and Happy Pills and every now and then a Travel Shop. He dives behind his desk with a screwdriver and establishes that his buttons aren't connected to anything, so they take him away, lock him up for a while, and then make him a Supervisor with various special privileges, and the duty to push different buttons. It's not badly done of its type, but the attitude is laid on thickly enough to become annoying rather than amusing.

§

A few American writers appear in these issues, mostly with original stories rather than reprints. Carnell says in his editorial in **103**, after noting that three of five short stories are by Americans: "With the American science fiction market now reduced to about seven regular magazines, most of the leading writers have moved into other literary fields but I find that more and more material is being submitted to the Nova magazines from newer American authors who would like to have stories in print but can find no favour in their own country."

The most prolific American is (of course) Robert Silverberg, with two reprints and an original story. "Ozymandias" **(94)**, from (appropriately) the last issue of *Infinity* (November 1958), where it appeared under the Ivar Jorgenson pseudonym, is one of his sharper early stories. A military space mission finds a planet that initially seems abandoned, but proves to contain a library of advanced military technology, which of course they take back to Earth with them, because that's their job. Fade to black, or to lone and level, as Percy Shelley's eponymous poem puts it.

The other and lesser reprint is "Company Store" **(109)**, reprinted from Frederik Pohl's Ballantine anthology *Star SF* 5. A man signs a contract to colonize a far planet, in return for which he gets all the necessities of life free but has to pay a premium for anything else, quickly finding himself in disastrous debt. The problem is solved through the kind of facile manipulation of words all too familiar from the inconsequential magazine SF of the '50s. Judith Merril liked it enough to give it an Honorable Mention.

The non-reprint, "The Man Who Came Back" **(103)**, is an extremely well assembled and written, if repellent, story about the first man who buys his way back from the stellar colonies, all for the love of the woman who left him 25 years ago and caused him to depart. She's manipulative and grasping but ultimately does his bidding, because one of the aliens on his colony planet taught him how to control other people. The US *Fantastic Universe* folded before it could be published; ultimately it found US publication in *Galaxy* (December 1974).

Silverberg has the *New Worlds* Profile in this issue, complete with the same near-pre-pubescent photo that appeared in his previous profile four years previously, as the text acknowledges: "Since the picture above was taken he has grown a trim van Dyke beard and looks the part of D'Artagnan. He and his wife Barbara paid another visit to Europe last summer, spending a few days in London visiting the science fiction writers before returning to New York. Trans-Atlantic tripping is becoming a commonplace vacation these days." More substantively: since he was voted most promising new writer in the Hugo awards, "he has been forced to graduate to other fields of writing for the bulk of his income, where markets are wider and higher paying," and he's more successful and making three times as much money. "Despite this—and Bob states that it is easier writing general fiction than it is science fiction—he still likes to turn his hand to the occasional s-f story and this month we publish one of those rare stories from him."

Silverberg again has the *New Worlds* Profile in **109**, for reparations: after the last one, "we had a horrified letter from him pointing out that the photograph we had used was years old—taken at a time when he was still an amateur writer. To assuage his ego he sent us a new photograph, proving that time certainly marches on." This photo depicts the above mentioned and now familiar beard. The text notes that he is no longer writing SF regularly and that he and wife are house-hunting outside New York, looking for lebensraum and library space.

Richard Wilson's well written but ultimately bland "The Best Possible World" (**98**) is his fifth story in *New Worlds* and his first not reprinted from a US magazine (the US SF market having drastically contracted with the demise of more than half a dozen magazines between 1958 and 1960). Father and young son are alone on a well-stocked space station after a war that destroys civilization, leaving them stranded. The father's project is to splice together fake radio news programs comprising humanity's greatest hits which he plays for his son weekly, pretending they are current. When the kid starts reading the World Almanac, father knows he can't keep the fakery up, so he comes clean. About that time he turns on the real incoming radio and discovers that there are people alive on a Moon base trying to contact them and rescue them. The kid says, when he's told that it may take a while to get rescued, "I don't mind. It'll give us a chance to get to know each other." So the catastrophe suddenly becomes cozy, at large and small levels, and a bit claustrophobic for my taste. (But not for Judith Merril's—she gave it an Honorable Mention.)

Wilson has the *New Worlds* Profile in this issue, which says (aside from the familiar and obvious) that a film of his novel *The Girls from Planet 5* "goes into production at the end of this year (retitled 'Take Me To Your Leader'). Despite the satirical new title (after all, the book was a satire) the film is to be a serious production in colour and may well influence Hollywood to break away from the 'horror-cum-fantasy' rut the script writers have ploughed during recent years." Apparently it never appeared. Further: "Night editor on a New York wire service, he hears most of the astronautical news almost as soon as it happens and his stories have a ring of truth about them." More like the ring of conventional sentiment, I'd say. But Carnell obviously thought otherwise. He says in the book review column of **102**, where he reviews Wilson's novel *30-Day Wonder* (to my taste, a typically insipid Wilson production): "Let me admit that I am a Wilson fan (as much as I am an admirer of Heinlein, Sturgeon, Bradbury and Asimov)."

Theodore L. Thomas's "The Moon v. Nansen" (**103**)—his only story in the UK magazines except for a few BRE (British reprint editions of US magazines) appearances—features a legal dispute on the Moon. A *chlorella* tube on farmer Nansen's spread blows, and various people sue him with the backing of the sinister Lunar Enterprises, Inc., looking to put him out of business. The intrepid firm of Centerton, Westgate and Hogan gets to the bottom of things and saves Nansen's bacon, or oxygen. There's not a lot of plausibility to it, and it's never clear exactly why the bad guys want Nansen out of the way, but it's amusing enough, and Thomas—a practicing attorney himself—manages more verisimilitude in portraying law practice than most SF writers, who seldom get the tune even when they get the words.

Robert Hoskins' "A World for Me" (**103**) starts as a mildly Sheckleyesque piece about the problems of socializing a sentient robot for domestic service and then unfortunately veers off into the pathos of the robot's search for its place in the universe. "Morpheus" (**107**) is a nice try—first astronaut finds that the physical stresses of space flight trigger a psychiatric breakdown by recalling his brutal childhood traumas—but Hoskins is too pulpy a writer to bring it off effectively.[13]

Larry Maddock appears in **95** with "Creatures, Incorporated," an amusing farce about a down-and-outer who encounters a telepathic shape-shifting alien named Webley who mostly masquerades as a cat. Together they rent an airport kiosk and set up a service for visiting aliens, finding them lodgings suited to their body chemistry, etc., with the alien hiding inside a fake machine, like Maelzel's chessplayer, for greater credibility. Judith Merril gave it an Honorable Mention. Maddock is back in **97** with another innocuously good-humored Webley story, "Alien for Hire," in which a giant birdlike alien appears looking for a job. They get him one as a ride on Coney Island.

"When In Doubt" (**101**) features an Aldebaranian priest

---

13. It's perhaps interesting that such recurrent SF tales of psychiatric consequences of space flight were to a surprising extent borne out a decade or more later among the Apollo astronauts. Most notably, the second man to step on the Moon, Buzz Aldrin, was plagued by alcoholism and depression (see http://www.psychologytoday.com/articles/200105/buzz-aldrin-down-earth, visited 9/6/11). Other instances are reported in Andrew Smith's *Moondust: In Search of the Men Who Fell to Earth* (Fourth Estate, 2005).

looking for a job and sand-boring Venusian slugs that Creatures Inc. has set to work digging tunnels for a construction project. When a seventh joins them, they seize the occasion to down tools and engage in an orgy ("You're familiar with the 'daisy-chain' idea among humans?"), since the opportunity doesn't come that often, given their extremely complicated reproductive setup. The blurb for "When in Doubt" says "Unfortunately, this will probably be the last of the Webley stories.... We have lost touch with the author." This seems odd, and likely a euphemism for "the author doesn't want to write any more, especially at what we pay." Actually the author is one Jack Jardine of California, and these Webley stories are Jardine's only contribution to the SF magazines or anything close except for a 1954 *Imagination* story, one in *The Man from U.N.C.L.E.* in 1967, and an article about Skylab in *Vertex* in 1973, the last under his own name. Jardine also published the "Man from T.E.R.R.A." series of paperback novels in the late 1960s under the Maddock name and, with his wife Julie, a couple of other paperback SF novels under the name Howard L. Cory.

§

And now to the dregs. There are as usual a few stories by people who have no other credits at all in the SF magazines, and for the most part that's a relief. An exception here is Derek Lane's "The Destiny Show" (**91**), an amusing *Galaxy*-type satire about a TV show, *This Will Be Your Life*, made with the assistance of a precognitive time viewer, and the unplanned demise of a coarse Hollywood producer who takes the show over to liven it up with the future life of a sociopathic gangster. One can regret the lack of any more stories by Derek Lane, but not so the rest of these one-shot authors.

Phillip Heath's "Delete the Variable" (**107**) is a harmless item about a computer that predicts the future, develops consciousness, and of course foresees its deviser's attempt to pull the plug on it. The plot and development are pretty old-fashioned but it's smoothly enough written. D. E. Ellis, identified by Carnell as a new writer, has "Stress" (**110**), in which a space crew in suspended animation tanks find that they are awake, and discover their inner psi talents. It's clumsily written and poorly thought through (at the end, one of the crew is sure that their children will also have these talents; Lamarck, take another bow).

In M. Lucas's "The Ark" (**105**), some guys are looking for the remains of Noah's Ark, and find it, and it's a spaceship. And that's the story—a throwback to the John Russell Fearn stories in the Pendulum issues of *New Worlds*, except competently written. Harold Parsons contributes "The Funnel" (**97**), in which a spot of anomalously low gravity appears next to the desk of the low-level bureaucrat protagonist, and starts to grow, with disastrous consequences. This one is a completely archaic story, and one suspects the writer was reading too much Wells, or maybe too little. Finally, we hit bottom with Lance Horne's "Nuclear Justice" (**96**), a lame spy vs. spy joke about nuclear research and golf. Astonishingly to me, both these last two items, the worst of the two years to my taste, got Honorable Mentions from Merril.

§

So what's for the Permanent Collection here? Four Ballard classics ("The Voices of Time," "The Overloaded Man," "Chronopolis," and "Billennium") and a couple of near misses ("Deep End" and "Zone of Terror"), a couple of near-great Aldiss stories ("Moon of Delight" and "Soldiers Running") and a couple more just a tick behind ("Old Hundredth" and "Under an English Heaven"). And then... hard to say. Rackham's "Goodbye, Dr. Gabriel" and Whiteford's "The Doorway" are about the most memorable remaining items. While I've complimented a number of stories in passing as sharp, brisk, clever, or what have you (like Tilley's "Reason" or Hynam's "Unfinished Symphony"), I really can't imagine ever wanting to reread them or anything else in these issues, including the serials, with the possible exception of Bulmer's pleasantly odd "The Golden Age."

§

And now to the non-fiction in 1960 and 1961, aside from the Kenneth Johns and Sam Moskowitz articles mentioned above, and the editorial about Sturgeon's "Venus Plus X," discussed in connection with that story.

Carnell's editorials continue as before, albeit somewhat longer, consisting mostly of commentary on the SF field in general as well as the affairs of *New Worlds*. Most noticeable difference from past years: he's realized that dialogue is more interesting than monologue, and he engages the readers and writers a bit. (Though in **98**'s editorial "Life Line," he explains that he can't get all the letters into "Postmortem" timely so they won't all get published, and anyway some of them misconstrue his editorials or other letters and printing them would just eat up more space.)

Carnell's editorial in **90**, "Plot Nots," summarizes Donald Westlake's article in the September 1959 *Writer's Digest* listing hackneyed plots to be avoided in SF:

1. The characters prove to be Adam and Eve.
2. The solar system is an atom in a larger universe.
3. Young Johnnie is lonely because he's different—he can lift things with his mind.
4. John Smith stumbles into town talking of Martians who are taking over people's bodies. Turns out everybody in town is a Martian.
5. Beautiful stowaway on spaceship: "Eight men and a woman, there'll be trouble."
6. Alien Frank Buck type comes to get pairs of animals, takes hero and heroine for the zoo.
7. Time tourists told "don't bring anything back."

8. "He's growing younger!"
9. Time traveler kills grandfather.
10. Police are telepaths.
11. Fate of galaxy depends on struggle between one man and one alien.

Dan Morgan, who sent Carnell the *Writers' Digest*, adds two more:

12. Hero gets the idea that everybody else on the spaceship is acting like a robot. He's a robot.
13. Superweapon developed, disaster forecast, it's Atlantis.

To this Carnell appends his own "Nots": "...we do not use stories that are located in the past, contain bug-eyed monsters, mad scientists, flying saucers, or are based upon presentday power-blocks [sic], atomic wars or post-atomic war civilisations." But, he allows, any cliché can be revived.

The editorial in the next issue is mostly turned over to a long and well-thought-out response from Dr. Arthur Weir of Westonbirt Village, Glos., responding to "Plot Nots":

> First: my own Plot-Nots, for which I draw examples indifferently from *New Worlds, Science Fantasy* and your chief rival *Astounding* BRE:
>
> (1) Stories of people enmeshed in an incredibly complex and/or corrupt society, which they can neither understand nor control, e.g., Wilson's "It's Cold Outside," Aldiss's "The Towers of San Ampa," Poul Anderson's "The Long Way Home," or van Vogt's "Weapon Shop" stories, while Asimov's "The Currents of Space" was barely saved from this by superb writing.
>
> (2) Stories in which humankind beat the aliens by stupidity or luck, when they in no way deserve to do so, e.g., Damon Knight's "Idiot Stick," Eric Frank

Russell's "Wasp," (and many shorts of his such as "Plus X," "Nuisance Value" or "Basic Right"), while even Murray Leinster has fallen into this gulf with "Short History of World War III" and to some extent with "Pirates of Ersatz."

(3) Computers capable of thinking qualitatively (as opposed to quantitatively or faster) ahead of their creators, e.g., Harrison's "I See You" or Stanley Mullen's "Guppy."

"Your own Plot-Nots," he continues, "strike me as ill-chosen, since if adhered to they would have debarred a number of your more conspicuous successes, and other very noted examples of s-f of recent years; for example:

B.E.M.s:—This would bar out all James White's "Sector General" stories, as also the highly successful "Jacko" series of Alan Barclay.

Presentday Power Blocks:—This should have debarred John Wyndham's "Idiot's Delight"; in any case to overlook or to refuse to admit the existence of presentday power blocks is a very dangerous kind of wishful thinking.

Atomic Wars and Post-Atomic Civilizations:— This would have ruled out E. C. Tubb's "Tomorrow," (one of the most striking stories *Science Fantasy* ever printed) and also the last two of Wyndham's "Troon" stories; it would also disqualify such masterpieces as John Wyndham's "The Chrysalids," or James Blish's "A Case of Conscience," either of which, I fancy, you would have been thankful to serialize, had you had the chance!

Mad Scientists:—This would have debarred another success: Colin Kapp's "Life Plan."

Flying Saucers:—And here, for once, we are in agreement, since, like guided missiles as observed by the U.S. engineer in 1946, "there ain't none!"

But Weir suggests that "Plot Nots" should actually be an Editorial Not, and offers a friendly amendment to the whole discussion: "Surely it would be better to put your advice to your contributors (or would-be contributors) in this form: Nothing is forbidden, and anything will go if done well, but all the commoner plot situations have been done so often that they can only be accepted if done supremely well—which is not likely with a newcomer to the highly-specialized craft of science fiction writing." (Harry Harrison responds similarly in "Postmortem" in **93** and gives this advice to wannabes: "Every idea you can think of has been done before. If you want to re-do it well enough to sell, go away and read some more SF. At least 50 novels, 100 anthologies, and 200 magazines. Examine all new ideas in the light of past stories.")

Weir concludes: "Luckily, you neglect your own precepts at least as often as you fulfill them; e.g., the story that I would describe as the best you have yet published, James White's 'Tableau,' is doubly damned by the standards of Editorial No. 90, since it introduces a B.E.M. and also is exactly situation No. 11 in the U.S. writer's list:—J.S. and the alien stood facing one another, both unarmed. Which, of course, also applies word for word to Alan Barclay's 'The Real McCoy' and 'The Thing in Common.'"

In **92**, the editorial is titled "Soul Searching," because that's what's going on in the SF community, says Carnell. He notes Earl Kemp's "Who Killed Science Fiction?" questionnaire (which begins "1. Do you feel that *magazine* science fiction is dead?"),[14] and says "Postmortem" is open for airing of the issues, which are pertinent to the UK as well as the US. He adds:

---

14. The resulting publication, which won a Hugo Award, has been reprinted with supplementary material. See Earl Kemp (ed.), *Who Killed Science Fiction?* (Merry Blacksmith Press, 2011).

"With Import restrictions lifted we shall soon see original U.S. editions of magazines and pocketbooks on sale in Great Britain and this added competition will certainly have some effect on our own market, small though the percentage of s-f titles will be." Carnell goes on to note a fanzine, *Quantum*, published by John M. Baxter of Bowral, New South Wales, who wants more scientific accuracy in SF. Baxter thinks that "Men like Bradbury, Sturgeon, Sheckley and Matheson have abandoned s-f for the more lucrative fantasy field, in which they excel, leaving pure science to those authors who have mastered it."[15]

In **93**, Carnell has "Soul Searching Continued" and expresses surprise at the reader reaction to "Soul Searching." Though opinions differ about what's wrong with SF and what to do about it, everyone seems to agree that there's a problem. He notes "the repeated requests for *New Worlds* to radically experiment with stories that are 'different.' This I am quite willing to do if any of the authors submit such stories, providing the literary standard is maintained." He observes that good SF is now harder to find than five years previously, but says in part that's because SF is no longer published as such, and much of it is "streamlined for the general novel market and are far more everyday in theme than the great novels of a decade back—*which were written originally for the magazine market as serials*. The day of the mighty opus as defined by Kuttner, Smith, van Vogt and others is temporarily over."

Carnell surmises that many older readers consider SF to be in the doldrums because of the absence of "the great names of the recent past." And he pronounces these famous last words: "It may well be that with s-f more difficult to find, the magazine markets will again assume their former eminence...." All

---

15. Bowral was then a small isolated town of 5,000, where by a bizarre coincidence the 16-year-old Broderick, from distant Melbourne, was installed in a junior seminary, but permitted by Father Superior to purchase one sf magazine a month, *New Worlds*. He contacted 21-year-old Baxter, who kindly allowed him to borrow endless amounts of new and old SF, and was thereby branded forever as a science fiction devotee and future writer.

this said, the only substantial response to "Soul Searching" that Carnell actually prints in this issue is John Brunner's. Brunner asks

> What is it that in science itself captures the imagination of the public? The breakthrough, rather than the skilful, craftsmanlike application of existing principles.... Science fiction writers of today tend rather too often to prefer engineering to invention.... Too many writers in our field today—and too many readers, into the bargain—seem to have acquired a snob sophistication which demotes excitement and promotes flip cleverness.... Let's have some sheer size!... Let's stand back from man the individual and take another look at Man the race. Let's calculate with absolutes again—s-f was for a long time the only field in which absolutes were being considered at all, and in many ways remains so.

He submits that he tried to do this in his long novella "Earth Is But a Star" in *Science Fantasy*. (Before the decade was out, he'd have done it fairly definitively in the Hugo-winning *Stand on Zanzibar* (1968).)

In **96**, Carnell presents the "Final Summary"—of "Soul Searching," that is, consisting of his own answers to the "Who Killed SF?" questionnaire. Is magazine SF dead? No, just in a transitional period resulting from "the vast strides astronautics has made during the past few years." He can't comment on who or what is responsible in the US, but agrees with John Campbell that "the mess Hollywood movies have made of labeling weird and horror films as science fiction" is significantly to blame. The explosion of paperbacks is diverting new readers from the magazines. Carnell also notes the collapse of distribution in the US. "However, *any* commodity that works on 25%-50% wastage to effect a profit cannot be operating at maximum efficiency. To be allowed to operate in the land of Time and Motion study seems fantastic to me!" What can we do? Beats him. Look to the original paperback for salvation? No, except for the novel—outside the US, the anthology and short story collection "is practically dead." (Within four years, he would abandon *New Worlds* and the other Nova magazines, and move on to a quarterly anthology of original short fiction, *New Writings in SF.*) He adds that magazines in general appear to be in a period of consolidation in the face of declining readership and advertising revenues, and that perhaps SF "has only been taking part in the present phase of redistributed leisure time" to movies and paperbacks.

Carnell devotes a couple of editorials to complaining about not getting any respect, though of course he doesn't put it that way. In **94**, "Credit Lines," he genteelly vents his spleen in an unusually long (three pages) editorial. First he notes that half of the books in Damon Knight's top ten for 1959 are by British writers, two of them—Aldiss's *Vanguard from Alpha* ("Equator") and Wyndham's *The Outward Urge*—originating in *New Worlds*. Also one of Knight's two favorite story collections of the year is Aldiss's *No Time Like Tomorrow* (half from *New Worlds* and *Science Fantasy*), and P. Schuyler Miller in *Astounding* is praising John Brunner's *The 100th Millennium* ("Earth Is But a Star" from *Science Fantasy*). But the magazines get no credit whatsoever for this.

"Apparently" this has something to do with American and British copyright law (Carnell doesn't say what; one would think that he would actually find out).

> As far as we are concerned, this lack of credits is a particularly vicious circle. Naturally, in publishing as in any other business, we all thrive on publicity, and credit lines could well introduce new readers from the ranks of the book buyers. It also seems to me that without *New Worlds* and *Science Fantasy* as natural outlets for the original publication of short stories and

some novel-length material many a hard cover collection or novel would never be born.

About halfway down the third page we learn what he is really exercised about: the US reprint edition of *New Worlds*, discussed above, which completely obscures its origins. "In fact, there is even a different editor's name on the contents page!" Carnell continues:

> There are, obviously, a number of logical reasons for this decision to present the magazine as a new American one rather than the reprint of a British one and we commend the American publisher for presenting it this way.... as far as we are concerned, we would rather have sales than prestige.
>
> Therefore this editorial is not intended to be a complaining one against imaginary circumstantial injustices—I am merely telling you these facts *because it is very obvious that no one else will!*

Carnell rehashes the US reprint edition fiasco and the obscuring of the magazine's origins in **99**, "Missing Links," previously discussed, and announces that the UK magazine is now going to be distributed in North America, surprising some readers who will see the jump from No. 5 of the defunct US reprint to No. 99 of the real thing.

In **103** he takes another angle on Anglo-American relations in "Changing Patterns," noting the presence of four American authors in the issue. The magazine has published "a wealth" of "outstanding" material from North Americans, seeking it out themselves although for a long time the British market "did not offer any tempting financial returns for Americans wishing to sell their material to Great Britain." But now markets have dried up in the States, most leading writers have moved into other fields, but he's also getting more and more submissions from Americans who can't get published at home. He continues:

These changing patterns of literary submission remind me of a statement I made at last year's British Conference at Easter—that the success of *New Worlds* has largely been based on stories rejected by American editors. Stories, that is, by British writers, most of whom have the logical desire to earn the higher rates paid across the Atlantic. Many such stories have been exceptionally good but not found favour with American editors—some editors there do not favour British material at all unless it conforms to American writing standards (Eric Frank Russell is the successful example of this) while other editors have ploughed a furrow so deep they can no longer see over the sides and *all* stories must conform to one pattern or another. Also, as Alfred Bester pointed out in a Guest Editorial in *Science Fantasy* some time ago, the cultures between the two countries being considerably different tend to make the literary styles correspondingly so. Especially in science fiction.

So a good story by British standards would not necessarily be good by American. For which *New Worlds* and myself have been extremely thankful over the years. This particularly applies to such radical writers as J. T. McIntosh and Brian W. Aldiss, who seldom conform to the known requirements of the American market. In fact, for a long time I have had an arrangement with both of them—and a number of leading British authors—that they only submit material to myself *after* rejection in America. Even this policy is not adhered to too rigidly, however, for many of our top British authors write material specially for this magazine which later sees publication in America. Quite a number of our novelettes have later been rewritten into book-length novels—Arthur Clarke's "Guardian Angel" in 1950 later became the beginning of the now-famous *Childhood's End*.

There's a certain irony in the foregoing observations, since just a few months previously Carnell had published what proved to be J. T. McIntosh's last story in the UK magazines. The rest of his considerable short fiction production appeared in the US. Brian Aldiss too was beginning to appear more frequently in the US magazines at the expense of the UK ones.

Carnell continues:

> Most of Arthur's early stories were originally published in this magazine but I must confess that I missed out on one novelette—the original MS which later became his novel *Earthlight*—and he seldom omits to quote me (jokingly) as the only editor who ever rejected a Clarke story. At that time (1952) I considered that a Moon colonisation story was out of date! Reader reaction show that even today colonisation stories of the Solar System are still in the front rank of popularity with most readers.

Carnell grossly exaggerates. As noted in Chapter 1 of our companion volume *Building New Worlds*, Clarke published only four stories in *New Worlds* (one of those a reprint) through the mid-50s, a small fraction of Clarke's prolific production of short fiction.

In **104**, "Old Hundred," Carnell combines his editorial with "The Literary Line-Up" and says *nobody* rated the stories in anniversary issue **100**, despite there being more correspondence than ever; every story was praised by somebody, Rackham and Russell were praised, Alfred Bester said it's the best balanced issue he's seen in years, Jack Williamson bemoans that he doesn't have time to write SF. Carnell also revisits one of his pet peeves, stating about the brief return of interior illustrations in **100**: "The other big surprise was... lack of reaction from that most vociferous section of the community known as science fiction fandom—the same section that, in the main, has been requesting the return of art work in *New Worlds* ever since we dropped it some years ago." He says it was easier to cancel the idea out than persevere. "My final summary, therefore, is that you couldn't care one way or the other and as it is easier, editorially, not to have art work in the magazine, I see no reason to belabour the fact." He does, however, allow Harry Douthwait (correct spelling Douthwaite) of Manchester to belabor it in **108**: "the majority of fans would like to see the return of interior illustrations, but from past experience it seems as though it would be a waste of time writing to you about this subject."

Several editorials are devoted to the shifting situation of SF publishing in the UK. In **107**, "Complex Situation," Carnell notes that US paperback books are starting to be imported. UK paperback publishers have hitherto focused on the best US titles by the most prominent authors, crowding out British authors except for Clarke, Wyndham, Christopher "and to some extent Maine and McIntosh." Now UK publishers are wondering what to do. Also some US paperback publishers are now adding a contractual clause giving them the right to distribute throughout the English-speaking world. "The fact of the matter is, the last barrel has been well scraped and by early 1962 I predict that there will be very few British-published s-f titles on the market." UK trade journals list 70 forthcoming fiction titles, none SF; last year there were 160, none SF. He concludes: "While not competing directly with the paperback book trade we ourselves are directly affected by the fact that we shall probably never have the opportunity of publishing another American book as a serial." This is an odd thing to say—the majority of US books serialized in *New Worlds* were hardcovers—and in any case it was not quite true even of paperbacks. Brian Aldiss's *Minor Operation*, published by Ballantine, was serialized the following year, though it was the only such instance during the rest of Carnell's reign.

Carnell continues in this vein in **109**, "Interesting News," noting the advent of the new Gollancz SF line—the now-famous yellow-jacketed books that dominated UK SF for years. "This country has long been in need of a publisher with sufficient courage to make a determined effort to sell s-f under a well-known imprint *and make a success of it*." He mentions the checkered history of UK hardcover SF publishing: "the disastrous 1952-54 period when everyone tried to get on the bandwagon and published titles indiscriminately," with no one on the staffs who knew anything about SF, which also saw a "spate of the most appalling rubbish" in paperback. The period ended in a "blaze of adverse publicity" for the genre. Then publishers tried to drop the term SF (Michael Joseph and Faber & Faber), but they couldn't find enough writers of the "Wyndham calibre" to keep it going.

More recently a lot of SF "has appeared disguised as general fiction," most of it by unskilled writers who don't know SF. So it's not surprising that Gollancz expects to be publishing much American material—though an American publisher said good luck, there aren't 12 good titles a year, so Gollancz will have to publish some story collections. Carnell notes in closing that in the diminished US magazine field there is reduced opportunity of making a serial sale, and authors are more and more writing for book publication and there are lots of paperback originals. So now it's the editorial staffs of hardcover and paperback houses that are shaping policy re SF novels, not magazine editors.

Carnell expands on this last thought in **110**, "Comparisons Old and New." He's been saying that the shape of the SF novel is changing from causes outside the magazine field, indeed outside the "regular SF field." He decides to compare two examples, Philip José Farmer's *The Lovers*, newly issued by Ballantine, and Arthur C. Clarke's just-issued *A Fall of Moondust*. Concerning *The Lovers*: "Nine years have mellowed the original critics' opinions and it will be interesting to see whether any of the current reviewers will have the courage to bluntly state what a bad novel this is. Basically, it is the *idea* behind the story that is classic in its conception—and this and the metabolic explanations which form the *science* fiction part (the crux of the story) take up only a few thousand words. The rest of the story is typical of the racy style required magazine presentation [sic].

where every word must count and where cliff-hanging climaxes come monotonously every few thousand words or so.

The overall impression, as Farmer endeavours to build his pseudo-culture of the future, is one of a vast breathless welter of words in which brief glimpses of his intended meaning flash past one's mental eye like telegraph poles viewed from a speeding train. Unfortunately, this is the overall impression I get from almost all the novels which are written first for magazine presentation. There is no time for the normal development of background details—one is plunged willy nilly into the mainstream of the plot and expected to immediately comprehend what is happening. By and large, this is the *basic* fault of all magazine science fiction.

How different to the mechanics of a novel written specifically as such, with its slower tempo in which the author settles his readers into the framework of his story and gradually unfolds the plot step by step.

He notes that Clarke's *A Fall of Moondust* is to be serialized in the London *Evening Standard* before publication—"(in itself an unprecedented event for this particular newspaper). How different the sales approach for an s-f novel written as such with top paying mass markets immediately wide open!" Carnell compares this to *The Death of Grass* and *The Day of the Triffids,* serialized in the *Saturday Evening Post* (sic; actually the latter was in *Colliers*). "Such prestige sales immediately open the gates of the film industry without any undue effort on the part of agent or author." (There was no film of *A Fall of Moondust,* though a version of *The Death of Grass,* apparently with bikers, appeared in 1970.)

Admitted that every author cannot spare his valuable time to such a project. With the *immediate* cash return for magazine publication often of vital importance in making a living, only secondary consideration can be given to book-length presentation. So no-one can really blame the authors for continuing in the pattern already laid down. It does seem to me, however, that magazine editors in general will have to re-evaluate their requirements in the light of the drift towards book presentation *first*. Then perhaps that elusive "sense of wonder" will return to the magazine field.

I am quite willing to accept the fact myself.

Several of Carnell's editorials are more narrowly directed at events in the SF scene. The **97** editorial, "Big Book of 1959," is devoted exclusively to *Starship Troopers*, which Carnell thinks won't be published in the UK, since only four of Heinlein's 25 novels have been in UK hardcover and only one in paperback. He praises it highly. And someone is paying attention: in "Post-mortem" in **103**, there is a letter from Arthur George Smith of Norwalk, Ohio, who declares that much of the philosophy expressed in the book is actually Heinlein's personal philosophy.

> Both this country and England are infested with a plague of minus-brained "do-goods" who have forgotten that the prime object of laws is to protect the law-abiding, not the law-breakers. Also that the young of the human race are merely the young of the fiercest of all animals, who have to be civilized.

For anyone who has forgotten, *Starship Troopers* is dedicated "To 'Sarge' Arthur George Smith—Soldier, Citizen, Scientist—and to all sergeants anywhere who have labored to make men out of boys. R.A.H."

On the other hand, F. Leslie of Yorkshire says of *Starship Troopers* in **106**: "I don't think I have *ever* read such monumental claptrap and drivel (sheer and unadulterated) from a previously assumed highly intelligent man."

103's editorial also contains a half-page "Important Notice to British Readers" stating that people are complaining they can't get the magazines, but Nova has not made any changes in distribution. "This error is due to the distributors of the American magazines *Galaxy* and *If* ceasing to supply the wholesale trade. Please notify your retailer of this fact if necessary." Also: "The title of this magazine is not being changed." That's *Astounding=>Analog*.

In **105**, "So This Is Hell?" Carnell takes on Amis's *New Maps of Hell*, starting with two paragraphs about the publicity it has garnered ("we are all the richer for it"). Carnell thinks highly of the book, but emphasizes that it's about American and not British SF, adding: "I have long emphasized the fact that British s-f broke away from the American mainstream immediately after the last war and the gulf is still widening." The "no respect" theme emerges again; Carnell notes that the book does not mention post-war British SF at all, though there was apparently a special Foreword in the UK edition[16] that mentioned *New Worlds* and *Science Fantasy*. He complains that Amis appeared on the BBC and mentioned only the US magazines, though he thinks the BBC would have deleted any mention of his magazines anyway under its no-commercialism policy.

I understand from authors and publishers alike that a mention on radio or TV here is worth a thousand sold copies the next day. With my usual single-mindedness of purpose, I cannot think of a more deserving case for free publicity (apart from *New Maps of Hell* itself) than this magazine which has pioneered along for fifteen years without very much official recognition (it really *is* surprising how those copyright acknowledgments elude us despite the vast amount of material republished from our pages). Certainly we recently hit the feature page of the Sunday *Times*, opposite a large

16. The first one, at least. The Foreword in the UK Four Square paperback (1963) makes no such mention.

portrait of Princess Elizabeth, in a down-beat article headed "What Happened to Science Fiction?"

In **108**, "Science Fiction in Russia," Carnell reviews the Foreign Languages Publishing House anthology *The Heart of the Serpent*, with the title novella by Ivan Yefremov, which he says he was tempted to try to acquire as a two-part serial, "but there were long passages of very 'heavy going' which detracted from the smooth flow of the narrative by our standards"; all of the stories display a scientific meticulousness which reminds him of American SF of the early '30s. Indeed, Carnell reports, one of the authors is a physicist at the USSR Academy of Sciences, another is a recent graduate of the Azerbaijan Medical Institute, and one of the Strugatsky brothers is an astronomer. Carnell expresses his ambition to publish a Russian s-f story, and says "I already have an eye on the possibility of a Polish also." As far as I can tell he never published either.

A couple of editorials recount SF-related socializing. In **95**, "Easter Parade," he reports on the Easter Convention, noting that while 20,000 Aldermaston marchers were approaching London and TAFF representative Don Ford was taking pictures in Hyde Park, the BSFA (British Science Fiction Association) elected Brian Aldiss over Kenneth Bulmer as its new president. Carnell recites other highlights of the Easter Convention (like replacing the hotel on 48 hours' notice), and mentions that 70 people (he still insists on calling them "delegates") attended.

More bizarrely, in **102**, "The Stars and von Braun," he recounts an outing of *New Worlds* regulars, at the invitation of the Columbia Pictures publicity department, to the film about Werner von Braun, titled *I Aim at the Stars*, to which someone with a gift for getting to the point appended "—and hit London."

Carnell notes the relatively unfavorable publicity the film received in Germany and Scotland (wonder why) and says its London premiere "didn't add any lustre either." Columbia Pictures "must have thought they had a tiger by the tail. Or a rocket by the touch paper end." Their PR department had approached Carnell "with the idea of inviting all the leading science fiction writers to the London premier, but one can only assume that when they saw the list and failed to find such names as H. G. Wells, Jules Verne and Olaf Stapledon, they had second thoughts and sent us press tickets for an afternoon show instead." The party included SF writers John Wyndham, Arthur Sellings, William F. Temple, and Lan Wright, cover artist Brian Lewis, book reviewer Leslie Flood, and J. G. Ballard. Not surprisingly, the film was not too popular with this audience of Londoners and neighbors.

"The film had apparently started when we sat down and we were regaled [sic] with one of those typical science fiction time travel themes—von Braun dying sometime in the future by falling from a roof. Ten minutes later we realised we had been watching the end of a drama called 'Portrait in Black.' It was the best ten minutes of the afternoon."

Carnell quotes Temple at length on the moral incoherence of the film, mentioning in passing von Braun "aiming at the stars and hitting almost everything else," and then moves on to Lan Wright's praise for its technical aspects and his suggestion that the filmmakers were trying to "whitewash von Braun." Ballard's more colorful reactions were discussed earlier in this chapter.

§

A number of guest editorials are featured in these issues, the first in the anniversary issue **100**, in which Carnell has no editorial but is the subject of the *New Worlds* Profile, looking (of course) dapper in his photo. The profile is nothing more than the well-known facts. The editorial is by Eric Frank Russell, "A Trench and Two Holes." It is stupefyingly inconsequential, but don't say you weren't warned: "I have been told to write an editorial about it [the number 100], or else. Being in one of my sterile periods, when I revert to the status of a low-grade moron, I find the task impossible. To me, 100 looks like a trench and two holes or a thin man followed by a couple of fat ones. The best I can offer is a hodge-podge of ruminations as weighty or as weightless as the belly-rumblings of a meditative cow. So sorry." Well, he wasn't kidding about the sterile period. It had been a year since he had published a story in the SF magazines, he published one more four and a half years later, and a last very weak novel around the same time, and appeared once more with a presumably very old story (a collaboration with Leslie Johnson) in one of Phil Harbottle's productions, and that was it. In retrospect, this was Russell's *de facto* farewell to the field.

Kingsley Amis rears his head again in **106** in David Kyle's guest editorial, which reports Amis's appearance at the Eastercon with a talk titled "Anti-Science, Anti-Fiction" in which he "proceeded to demolish some of the favourite conventions (mumbo-jumbo some would call them) of the s-f fans. Time travel, interstellar space travel, psionics, extra-sensory perception, and the universal translation machine all came under fire as being not merely fantasy but philosophic nonsense and fundamentally trivial.

"After the first breathtaking shock of Mr. Amis' unsympathetic assertions, the reaction of fan and author alike was swift, hot and intense. As Editor Carnell later remarked, 'he had virtually slashed the plot bases of modern science fiction in half and delegates took exception to this.'" E. C. Tubb "used ridicule to emphasize what he believed was the extremist positions which Amis had taken...." Kyle disagrees with Amis's emphasis on satire and literary standards: "*ideas* must always come *first*."

The guest editorial comes into its own toward the end of this period—or maybe Carnell was just running out of gas. After the weighty essays on the whence and whither of SF publishing in **107**, **109**, and **110**, he does not appear in the editorial slot again until **116** (March 1962), and after that not until **140** and **141**, the last two Nova issues of the magazine in early 1964—though he does have several articles on film festivals and a TV show, and one called "Survey Report of 1962" which under prior practice would have been an editorial. In the Tymn/Ashley compendium on SF magazines, Mike Ashley cites Carnell's diminished editorial presence in connection with the general decline of the magazine and of Carnell's apparent interest in it, and the inference is probably right.

In any case, in **111** he announces the guest editorials as a series to be written by "prominent SF authors" who will have a "completely free hand" to opine about SF. The first, "Where Now?" is by Arthur Sellings. Sellings, a bookseller by day, claims to see matters from "where it counts—the cash counter." SF has a terrible image problem, people assume that any bad SF story must represent the genre, this problem has to be solved in the magazines, and it's time for a revolution: "a return to roots.... [A] story should be intelligible—*in itself*—without reference to any other. The explanations may not be necessary to the hardened fan, but they can be made without offending him.... Science fiction has become too glib. That sense of wonder is the prime thing which s-f can offer to the newcomer." He then cites George R. Stewart's *Earth Abides* as an example, without noting that its author came completely from outside the world of SF. Or maybe that is his point.

John Rackham, in "On a New Level" (**112**), says the conflict between those against and for "messages" in SF (citing Kingsley Amis for the latter) is a phony one because you can't write any decent story without some sort of message. "There must be an ethic, a set of social values, in any story, if it is to make sense to the reader." It is only when the writer questions conventional viewpoints that "the reader begins to feel uncomfortable, and to suspect that he is being encouraged to think." Rackham thinks SF writers should take the daring approach that science should govern our affairs because it works.

Frankly, both these essays seem a bit tiresome and *pro forma* to me. Perhaps having a similar reaction, Brian Aldiss takes a different tack in "The Origin of Originality" (**113**), discussed above in connection with Aldiss's own fiction: parodied SF stories claimed to be from *Stupefying Science Sagas* and *Stultifying Stories Quarterly*. Refreshingly, once more he can't resist subverting the exercise he's engaged in.

§

The book reviews, which once appeared nearly every month, appear in about two-thirds of these issues—a considerable increase from four issues in 1958-59. The reason for the increase is chiefly that *New Worlds* has decided to acknowledge the realities of SF publishing, which is that there are few British SF hardcovers any more but paperback publishing is growing, and American paperbacks are becoming more readily available. Leslie Flood ceases to be the only or even the predominant reviewer; he continues to do the British hardcovers and some British paperbacks, but Carnell now regularly reviews British and US paperbacks and on at least one occasion US hardcovers. Flood continues to make an art form of praise, describing Aldiss's *The Canopy of Time* (**92**) as "A coruscation of a book this, product of a fertile imagination and an able literary style." Similarly: "Congratulations to Messrs. Faber and Faber for maintaining, almost alone, a high standard of hard-cover science fiction publishing in this country and for their progressive presentation of one of the foremost writers in the genre today—James Blish" (**94**, praising Blish's collection *Galactic Cluster*).

Like Carnell, Flood goes ga-ga for Clarke's *A Fall of Moondust* (**112**): "Mr. Clarke has come up with a cracking science fiction novel, thoroughly 'British' in approach and treatment, beautifully and authentically descriptive, uncannily plausible and well-characterized." He even gives an uncharacteristic good notice to Charles Eric Maine ("I have never rated his previous works very high... and this is probably one reason why his hardcover publisher no longer sends review copies"). Absurdly, in **99** he compares Maine's *The Tide Went Out* to *Earth Abides*. But he is not uncritical. Of Harold Livingston's *The Climacticon*: "Given patience and a good ploughshare you should be able to get through this acre of verbosity." More ruefully, he mitigates his disappointment with *Trouble With Lichen*: "Being an ardent Wyndham enthusiast, I am comforted by an idle thought—W. Shakespeare fretted with 'Much Ado About Nothing' when his mind must have been occupied with 'Hamlet.'" If only his analogy had been correct. (Both quoted from **99**.)

Even Blish gets the boot, at least in part, for *A Clash of Cymbals* (**92**): "An epic of cosmic scope which gets bogged down frequently in sesquipedalian scientific mumbo-jumbo (sorry, technical jargon) and, apart from Amalfi, cardboard characterisation, enlivened only by some interesting theological aspects of his theory and the truly dramatic climax."

As always, Flood acknowledges a few books I've never heard of, such as (in **94**) Digit's "strangely interesting novel by Desmond Leslie, *The Amazing Mr. Lutterworth*, which is an idealistic yearning for world salvation by almost metaphysical visitation, divulged after an absorbing first-person narrative by a man whose identity and purpose are unknown." (The Honorable Leslie was the Theosophically-inclined co-writer, with US "Professor" George Adamski, of the infamous *Flying Saucers Have Landed*.) Flood's feelings are considerably mixed about the dystopian/apocalyptic *And So Ends the World* by Richard Pape (**110**), "One of the strangest books to come my way," which proposes that salvation is through... salvation.

Carnell's reviews are generally more pedestrian, though he occasionally has something interesting to say, or a particularly dissonant clinker to drop (e.g., in **113** he describes James H. Schmitz's "Grandpa" as a story about "weird vegetables"). In **104** he recaps 1960's novels: "Only five titles stand out in my mind as verdant oases in a vast desert of ground down corn— *30-Day Wonder* by Richard Wilson...; *Death World* by Harry Harrison...; *Venus Plus X* by Theodore Sturgeon...; *Drunkard's Walk* [by Frederik Pohl]; and, my vote for the outstanding novel of the year—or the past five years—Walter M. Miller's *A Canticle for Leibowitz*...." A few were better than average, e.g. *Trouble with Lichen*, but most were well below standard; "but my nomination for Rubbish Novel of the year with black crepe trimmings goes to Poul Anderson's *The High Crusade* (Doubleday). Publisher and editors concerned should hang their heads in shame at foisting this one off as modern science fiction. I am the more irritated because this one came out of the Street and Smith *Astounding* S-F stable, who also published *Death World*, and one doesn't expect stinkers from this source or from Anderson." (I thought it was pretty nifty myself, back when I was 11.)[17]

Generally Carnell seems not to think too much of Anderson, of whose first collection *Strangers From Earth* (**110**) he says: "Regrettably, I disagree with American reviewers on the greatness of Poul's writings, for, so far, I do not think he has fulfilled the great promise he showed when I first met him some years ago. Somewhere along the line he has become side-tracked in his plot ideas or the presentation of them." Admittedly that was one of Anderson's weaker books, containing none of the pre-1961 stories for which he is best remembered.

Carnell thinks Frederik Pohl's *Drunkard's Walk* (**104**) is "a deeply thought-provoking future-society novel"; "an excellent example of the wordsmith's art—a fine, understandable, futuristic setting, good dialogue and characterization, and an intense plot"—not an opinion shared by many. (In *Analog*, May 1961, P. Schuyler Miller described reading it as like being "gummed by a toothless minnow.") He has much praise for Sarban's *The Doll Maker* and "Mathiesen's" *A Stir of Echoes* (he means Matheson), and in **107** he praises Constantine Fitzgibbon's dreary *When the Kissing Had To Stop* as "'required reading' to the pacifist-minded, the Ban-the-Bomb mooters, the 'Yankee-go-home' factions, and anyone else who doesn't realize that the velvet glove covers a mailed fist."

Carnell slags Fred Hoyle's *Ossian's Ride* in **107** (and does worse in the editorial, calling it "probably one of the dullest pieces of fiction in the genre in recent years"). Fredric Brown's *The Mind Thing* "falls far short of the high level of story writing

17. Broderick still thinks *The High Crusade* is damned nifty, and he's much older than 11.

Mr. Brown was producing two or three years ago." Carnell says that several writers have admitted an "awesome 'drying-up' period" to him recently: John Wyndham, Eric Frank Russell, Theodore Sturgeon, and "many others."

There is one film review in these issues, in **100**, by Arthur Sellings, expressing his mild disappointment at George Pal's *The Time Machine*: "The film does not *compel*." But you should see it anyway, he advises.

§

The letter column "Postmortem" appears in half the issues. Many of the more interesting comments have already been discussed. The contents include a number of manifestos about SF, some from the magazine's writers, of varying degrees of interest.

Robert J. Tilley has a long letter in **95**, describing himself as a "comparative newcomer to the genre"—at 31, he's been at it for a mere 4-5 years. He thinks SF is a bad name. "S-f has been at the pigeon-holding [sic] stage for some time now, and the gradual introduction of an awesome number of taboos has led it down the inevitable path to self-strangulation." Readers don't want experiment but get bored with the result. He still can't think of a good name. "Down, I say, with science fiction before it's too late, block up the pigeon-holes or put pigeons in them, exorcise the taboos and for the sake of the literature that we love, can't we all at least consider making a fresh start."

Donald Malcolm, also in **95**, says writers pay too little attention to precision of language and says reading poetry has helped him with his writing: "Good language automatically elevates a story.... On the question of literary work, such stories must have *depth* and *breadth* of theme. John Brunner's term, huge concepts, sums it up, and I agree that we need to take stock of Man the race. Too much science fiction is incidental, even trivial—most of my own efforts included."

John Ashcroft goes on at length in **108** after reading "a small mountain of back issues," catching up after being out of the country for several years. They confirm his impression that "simplicity is the keynote of good design" as applied to SF. He's foursquare for the sense of wonder. "While it's dangerous to generalise, I'd say British s-f satisfies me more than American s-f in this matter of conveying the wonder of things and people instead of the excitement of fast plotting or narrative."

Lee Harding suggests in **111** that letterhacking is the salvation of SF, and says Carnell should put a letter column in *Science Fiction Adventures*. Two issues later he tries to put his views into practice, writing: "What a lifeless, trivial thing magazine s-f has become!" *Cherchez les* professional writers, those who "invaded the field during the fifties and brought with them the formula of the pulp/detective/mystery/adventure magazines that until then had provided them with the greater part of their livelihood." If SF is saved it will be by the amateurs, and he doesn't see this happening in the US; but it is happening in Carnell's magazines. "Ballard is the finest practitioner I have encountered in your pages. Not one of his stories has failed to satisfy that search for 'wonder' for which my jaded eyes continually search." He also cites John Ashcroft, and Aldiss, though the latter's best work is published in "dollar land." He complains that "Rackman" "has brought to the field the familiar 'British' (ugh!) Method of detective story writing...." In the US it's been left to *Amazing* and *Fantastic* "to try and inject some new life into the corpse of s-f. The houses of Gold and Campbell seem to be immune to change, and it is in those two magazines that the signs of decay are most pronounced."

Carnell responds: "It is not our usual policy to 'knock' at contemporary magazines and editors—its [sic] a big world and we all have to live in it—but of late your criticism about the American scene has been echoed by scores of readers." He invites champions among North American readers to respond.

There is some comment on the art in the magazine, chiefly from Harry Douthwaite of Manchester, who is quoted above berating Carnell for persisting in the omission of interior illustration. He says Carnell's attitude to readers is approaching that of John W. Campbell. "At the present moment, the paintings of Brian Lewis, though well executed, fail dismally in their task of stimulating the reader's imagination. The general effect obtained from your magazines, now, seems to be that you are trying to conceal the fact that they are science fiction; ordinary drab covers, no interior art, plain interior layout." "So shall we come down to earth now, Mr. Carnell, by saying (with all due respect) that you should finish your rather unsuccessful experiments and return *New Worlds* to its traditional Science Fiction format: full size cover, proper illustrations, good, exciting *science* fiction."[18]

Mr. Douthwaite is back in **113**, expressing gratitude for the return of Gerard Quinn, who he says inspired his own attempts to become a commercial artist. Kevin Smith, no address, agrees in **108** with part of Douthwaite's program: "Confirmed finally a growing conviction through the Lewis series that a good cover artist deserves—in fact *needs*—a full cover and should not have to share it with a contents listing. Several covers which, as full-size pictures, would have been impressive, came out as claustrophobic and fussy on a three-quarter page."

Answering a letter in **106**, Carnell discloses his story length classifications: short stories are 3,000 to 10,000 words; novelettes up to 20,000. Short novels up to 35,000; novels, 3-parts, 54,000, 4-parts 70,000. He doesn't say how often he actually pays attention to them; on the evidence, it's pretty scattershot.

For the "be careful what you ask for" file, David E. Reid of London in **108** endorses the proposal to "revitalise science fiction with a more adventurous policy.... Not long ago the British cinema and theatre were in the same position that s-f finds itself today but they have swept out of the doldrums with a 'new wave' of stimulating, realistic and controversial plays and

---

18. Mr. Douthwaite, like more than one young devotee of traditional SF, seems to have had a change of artistic view in later years. See his brief memoir at http://www.jacktrevorstory.co.uk/harry_douthwaite.htm (visited 9/16/11).

films which have also been, in most cases, immensely profitable.... And why not get Kingsley Amis to write a story set in a Socialist future?" (He would get that wish two decades later, in *Russian Hide and Seek,* by which time Amis was not as friendly to socialists as he'd formerly been.)

Finally, but far from least, in **95**, Mrs. J. Curzon of Marlborough, Wilts., apparently a reptile hobbyist, criticizes James White's "Trouble with Emily" on the ground that one could not possibly get a dinosaur to play, and scoffs at radiation theories of reptile extinction: it was the cold, stupid, she says. In **100**, Laurence Sandfield takes vigorous issue with Mrs. Curzon's reasoning, essentially accusing her of lacking a sense of herpetological wonder.

§

Advertising remains sparse during these years. There are at least a few small ads in all issues but **113**. Other than that, the only regular non-house advertiser is the UK SF Book Club, which has a full page in nearly half the issues. (The Jazz Book Club puts in an appearance in **93**: "Do you believe in parallel worlds?") G. Ken Chapman of Fantasy Booksellers and Leslie Flood of the Fantasy Book Centre have congratulatory ads in issue **100**. Publishers' advertising remains rare. Digit paperbacks take the inside back cover of **96**; Pergamon Press has a full page for Tsiolkovsky's *Beyond the Planet Earth* in **98**; Blackie has a half page in **100** for the first *Out of This World* anthology. Then there is half a page in **104** for *Realization* by Geoffrey A. Dudley, B.A., from Psychology Publishing Co. Ltd.: "It's almost uncanny what this book can do for you! Test its amazing powers *Absolutely Free.* A strange book! A book that seems to cast a spell over every person who turns its pages! ...Self-consciousness changes to confidence, timidity gives way to courage. Humility retreats before self-reliance." Etc. There's a fair number of ringers: Charles Atlas in **93**; the Rosicrucians in **93, 101, 113**; the International Correspondence Schools on the back cover of **99** through **102**. And there's the occasional half-page for the BSFA or squib for a UK convention.

§

Meanwhile, something new had stirred in Carnell's Nova kingdom of *New Worlds* and *Science Fantasy*: a magazine intended, perhaps, as a gateway drug to those two, aimed at younger readers who craved excitement rather than whimsy, cerebration or pomposity. It will "bridge the gap," Carnell hopes, and for the next chapter we'll leave *New Worlds* and its slow slide toward a new wave, and concentrate on this brash newcomer. It ran from March, 1958, through until May, 1963, and perished just 11 months before Carnell's and Nova's *New Worlds* closed up shop and was reopened by Michael Moorcock in May/June, 1964. In chapter 3, we'll return to the mixed blessing of those final years before the fabled New Wave slammed across the landscape of science fiction, bringing with it anger, incomprehension and vituperation, or delight and rejoicing, depending on whether you were drowned or raised high by its strange tides.

2: PARALLEL WORLDS: NOVA'S *SCIENCE FICTION ADVENTURES* (1958-63)

The UK edition of *Science Fiction Adventures* began with the March 1958 issue. At first it was a reprint edition of the American magazine, companion to *Infinity*, published by Royal Publications and edited by Larry T. Shaw. The US magazine had started in December 1956 and ran 12 issues, at first bi-monthly and then, says Mike Ashley in Tymn/Ashley, six-weekly from August 1957 to June 1958. The British edition ran 114 pages exclusive of covers, cost 2/-, and was initially bi-monthly. As with *Science Fantasy*, the date did not appear on the cover or in any other prominent place. It was buried at the lower right of the contents page ("3/58" et seq.).

The UK magazine ran for five issues entirely as reprints from the US edition. The colophon in these issues says the American edition is edited by Larry T. Shaw and the British by Carnell. But there was no issue-by-issue correspondence between the two versions; each UK issue included stories from at least two of the US issues. The US edition had featured "short novels" (novelettes and novellas), with a limited number of short stories, and so did the UK edition. The UK covers bear the slogans "3 Action Packed Adventure Novels" or "3 Complete Action Novels." Most of the stories have illustrations (one, at least), mostly by Emsh, which, unlike the covers (see below), appear to be taken directly from the US magazine.

The UK magazine initially had a minimum of editorial personality, at least on the inside. The only feature in the first five issues is a monthly editorial, very short; four of the five were by Larry Shaw. The exception is Carnell's editorial in **3**, in which he thanks the readers for their "enthusiastic support," says the policy is to publish two or three short novels each issue, gives story ratings from the first issue, and reports the death of C. M. Kornbluth, who had a story in the first issue. To the extent Carnell had an editorial manifesto, it appeared in *New Worlds*, in **68**'s editorial, "Bridging the Gap."

Carnell announced there that "the formula for all the stories will be action-adventure against a science fiction background, written by most of the leading American writers in the field," reprinted from the American magazine. Shaw, he says, is "one of the liveliest of live-wire editors to enter the publishing field in recent years"—indeed, he has found the missing sense of wonder. The UK *Science Fiction Adventures* will provide an "introductory medium," because SF in the long established magazines is often "incomprehensible to casual readers.... As a final testimonial, let me say that with over thirty years science fiction reading behind me, and despite many years professional experience, the stories in *Science Fiction Adventures* are once again giving me the same thrills I encountered a quarter of a century ago." It's tempting to say "All too true," but that would be unfair and lacking in nuance.

Aside from the editorials and the fiction, the only contents in the early reprint issues are the familiar house ads for the other Nova magazines and the Nova novels, a page for the SF Book Club in **3**, an inside front cover ad for *Planned Families* ("Please send me, under PLAIN COVER...") in **4**, and a couple of ads for Blue Centaur books in Sydney. The US edition had book reviews, a fan column, and a letter column. There's none of that in the British reprint edition.

On the outside, however, the UK *Science Fiction Adventures* had plenty of personality, though you have to dig to find it. There is clearly a deep ambivalence about the cheesy American sensationalism with which the US edition presented itself. The cover of **1** illustrates Kornbluth's "The Slave." First look at the corresponding cover from the US edition (September 1957),[19] then go to the UK version.[20]

The US version by Emsh features an anguished buxom woman in torn bright orange garb in the foreground, hideous one-eyed alien—seemingly supervising her torture—behind. The UK cover, credited "by Rubios from an original by Emsh," tones things down considerably, moving the woman back and dressing her in a less alarming color, and adding in the foreground a concerned and intrepid male head and shoulders, which looks like he wandered in from the Crime shelves. The one-eyed alien is mostly obscured by the male and is almost indistinguishable. Some other rather abstract picture elements are introduced as well. The result is to soft-pedal the Weird Menace sadism angle a bit and also to create a picture that is to my taste more balanced and interesting and much less blatant and crude than the Emsh original, notwithstanding that the cover blares "3 COMPLETE ACTION NOVELS."

There's an even more startling transformation in the cover of **2**. This time, look at the UK version first.[21] This one, credited "by Rubios from an original by Schoenherr," is considerably cruder than the previous issue's cover, with a rather badly rendered buxom and scantily clad woman wielding a stylized ray gun and striking an equally stylized pose, reminiscent of

---

19. The US *SF Adventures* covers are not at www.sfcovers.net, but are at http://www.philsp.com/mags/science_fiction_adventures.html#y1956. They can also be found at the French language site http://www. collectorshowcase.fr/sf_adventures_page_1.htm and on the following page, preceded by an earlier US magazine of the same title and followed by the UK magazine. The US cover discussed in the text is at http://www. collectorshowcase.fr/IMAGES2/sfa2_5709.jpg (sites visited 9/10/11).

20. The UK *SF Adventures* covers can be found at http://www.sfcovers. net/mainnav.htm and at http://www.philsp.com/mags/science_fiction_ adventures.html#uk (sites visited 9/10/11).

21. http://www.collectorshowcase.fr/IMAGES2/sfad_5805.jpg.

Hannes Bok's work, of warding off something that is unseen and seems to be out of the picture, against a backdrop of futuristic buildings and flying machines. Now go to the US original (the January 1958 issue).[22] There, the same woman striking the same pose is actually grappling with and seemingly about to get eaten by as stereotypical a Bug-Eyed Monster as we have seen since the demise of Erle Bergey. For the UK version, this major picture element has simply been excised, replaced by a sedate background that doesn't appear in the original at all.

On issue **3,** Carnell gives himself a break and uses an original by Brian Lewis, an abstract or surreal, as you prefer, Richard Powers-influenced scene, gaudily but tastefully colored like the covers Lewis was beginning to do for *New Worlds*. It supposedly illustrates Calvin M. Knox's "Earth Shall Live Again!"—not a cover story in the US edition—and has no discernible relationship to any of the US covers. Similarly, on **4** there is an innocuous spaceship scene by the *New Worlds* about-to-disappear regular Bradshaw, illustrating nothing and not derived from any of the US covers.

But on issue **5** they're back wrestling with an American cover. On both versions, there's another woman, foregrounded in tight bodice (these US-derived covers were largely boob-driven one way or another), but again, take a look first at the UK cover, which is actually credited to Emsh, though I can't find his signature and can't tell for sure if the cover is really his or a very good imitation.[23]

The woman is striking an anguished pose against a backdrop of smoking wreckage suggesting a bombing run just finished, with a small male figure in the background standing on a low hill; it's hard to tell if he's posing triumphantly or desperately. But now look at the US version (the June 1957 issue).[24] The small backgrounded figure is clearly triumphant, and why

---

22. http://www.collectorshowcase.fr/IMAGES2/sfa2_5801.jpg.

23. http://www.collectorshowcase.fr/IMAGES2/sfad_5811.jpg.

24. http://www.collectorshowcase.fr/IMAGES2/sfa2_5706.jpg.

not: he's standing on a large heap of corpses, which have been completely excised for the UK magazine.

§

I haven't read all of the fiction in these early issues all the way through, since I'm interested in the development of the British magazines and not in the incidental detritus of a fairly lackluster segment of US SF publishing. However, I at least started all of the "novels" that were new to me; I had also read some of this material long ago, mostly in the form of Ace Doubles. Jerry Sohl's "One Against Herculum" (2) was an utterly routine stand-up-guy-against-a-rotten-system opus, and looking at the first few pages, I don't have a shred of interest in rereading it. Robert Silverberg's "Chalice of Death" series, under the Calvin M. Knox pseudonym, comprising "Chalice of Death" (1), "Earth Shall Live Again!" (3), and "Vengeance of the Space Armadas" (5), is probably adequately described by the story titles; as *Lest We Forget Thee, Earth*, I found it pretty uninteresting in 1959 and it hasn't improved since.

Silverberg had at least one story in nearly every issue of the US *Science Fiction Adventures* under one name or another. In the UK 5, he has another proto-Ace Double, "This World Must Die," as by Ivar Jorgenson. It's more smoothly written than a lot of the other material here, but illustrates the fundamentally hackneyed and meretricious level of much of this magazine. The protagonist Gardner is the leader of a team whose job it is to destroy the planet Lurion. Why? Because the computers show that if it isn't destroyed, it will launch a devastating attack against Earth 67 years later (margin of error eight months). This proposition obviously raises a lot of questions, but they're not asked. Gardner does meet an attractive woman, an anthropologist studying the rather distasteful culture of Lurion (knife fights to the death are a common nightclub amusement there), and he has some qualms about killing her, if not the millions of other people on the planet. These qualms are resolved when one of the team members betrays the mission, and suddenly Gardner needs a fifth for genocide, so he spills the beans to his woman friend, who seems to have fallen fruitlessly in love with him for no discernible reason. She'll do it!—so of course she gets to leave with the boys. En route there are such innovative plot maneuvers as a newly arrived team member's showing up at Gardner's hotel room with a briefcase, telling him it's necessary for Gardner to describe the plan briefly before they can talk about the next steps, which Gardner does. Of course this man is a turncoat and has a tape recorder in his briefcase, as revealed after a fistfight in which Gardner knocks him out. Later, the stirring end of the story, view from space:

> "It ought to happen just... about... *now*," Gardner said.
> As he spoke the black dot that was Lurion suddenly—*crumbled*!
> The job was done.

The expanded Ace version was called *The Planet Killers.* Critic Rich Horton notes that it is changed in what one hopes would be the obvious ways—instead of recruiting the anthropologist to the detonation crew, Gardner has a crisis of conscience: if the computer chose a traitor as part of the crew, how can its predictions be so perfect? So he and the anthropologist flee and ultimately head out to a colony world, and years later are offered a job to go help a reform movement on Lurion. Despite this, Horton describes the book in his on-line review as a "paint-by-numbers book" and "Silverberg at close to his worst."[25]

The same phrases might apply to "Secret of the Green Invaders" by Robert Randall (Silverberg and Randall Garrett) in 2, a labored satire about the revolt of (some) Earth people against alien domination and the inability of Earth people in

---

25. http://www.sff.net/people/richard.horton/aced75.htm (visited 9/10/11).

general to govern and be governed. It reads like a Campbell reject, dollop of Russell and dollop of Anvil and dilute heavily. (In fairness, I should mention that at least one of Silverberg's US *Science Fiction Adventures* novellas was pretty good— "Valley Beyond Time." which Carnell had reprinted in *Science Fantasy* **27** the previous year—and there are a number of others I've never read.)

A couple of the stories in these issues are more familiar. C. M. Kornbluth's "The Slave" (**1**) is a piece of violent yard goods about humans kidnapped to be psionic galley slaves on an alien spacecraft. It displays Kornbluth's professionalism while wasting his talent. Algis Budrys's "Yesterday's Man" (**1**) is considerably better, a post-nuclear quasi-character/leadership study that was later incorporated into *Some Will Not Die*, even though it was completely unrelated to the other stories that had been fixed up into *False Night*, the earlier version of that book. This was done at the insistence of Regency editor Harlan Ellison, according to Budrys in *Non-Literary Influences on Science Fiction* (Chris Drumm, 1983). Budrys continued: "Other scholars may be intrigued to know that 'Yesterday's Man' was written not for money but for title to editor Larry Shaw's 1954 Aero Willys four-door sedan with a missing front chassis member."

There are a couple of other stories by reasonably well-known names. Harry Harrison's "The World Otalmi Made" (**4**) is readable albeit ridiculous, about a member of a futuristic Mafia-type organization who is summoned to another planet to deal with the menace of Otalmi, who is grabbing power by making people like him through psychosurgery. It's implausible and bloody but at least slickly enough written to keep one going. James Blish and one Phil Barnhart ("his poetry and astronomical articles have appeared in a wide variety of magazines") contribute "Two Worlds in Peril" (**2**), in which the protagonist has crash-landed on Venus and finds himself underwater between contending factions of mer-people. He's been sent to Venus because Earth is beset by the Gas, which is venting up through subterranean cracks and killing everything; but it turns out Venus has the

Gas too. That's as far as I cared to pursue matters.

There are several stories by even longer-term veterans than Blish. One, Edmond Hamilton's "The Starcombers" (5), is a bleak and overdone, albeit readable, novelette about a seedy crew of interstellar scavengers (the most agreeable of whom, the protagonist, is merely a drunk) who happen upon a near-dead world where survivors of a humanoid civilization hang on in ruined buildings in a huge crevasse that has retained an atmosphere and is also inhabited by a variety of gigantic and nasty carnivores, in a sort of kitchen-table version of William Hope Hodgson's *The Night Land*. The humans and the indigenes undertake to trade food for ancient technology, each looking for a way to cheat and exploit the other, culminating perfunctorily in inconclusive bloodshed.

The other veterans' stories are by has-beens or never-wases. I managed about 10 pages of John Victor Peterson's "Mission to Oblivion" (4) before expiring of boredom, but I couldn't tell you reliably what it's about (then or now). Peterson had a long but sparse history with Carnell's magazines—he had a story called "Empyrean Rendezvous" in *New Worlds*, the fanzine predecessor, in March 1939, and his photograph appeared in **65**, showing him picking up a Hugo at the 1957 London world SF convention for *Science Fiction Times*. The blurb for this story may have as much biographical information about Peterson as ever seen: "John Victor Peterson works for the Civil Aviation Administration, as Chief of the Property Management Branch at New York International Airport. When he writes of future developments in radar, instrument landing systems, and similar devices, it is with the authority of long experience in this field. Though his fiction has been appearing for almost 20 years, he is strictly a 'spare-time' writer—unfortunately for his many fans." Peterson published seven stories from 1938 to 1942, in *Astounding, Thrilling Wonder, Comet* and *Uncanny Tales*. He returned in 1954 and had another 11, mostly in *Fantastic Universe* and *Infinity*, before hanging it up in 1959; none was ever anthologized.

Henry Hasse (1913-77) contributes "Clansmen of Fear" (4), involving a peculiar post-nuclear-war set-up (the protagonist's tribe has to stay *near* the bombed-out ruins because they need the radiation) and some aliens who seemed to be about to make an emergency landing on Earth at the point where I gave up. The high point of Hasse's career, which began in *Wonder Stories* in 1933, was probably the inclusion of his 1936 story "He Who Shrank," one of the universe-within-an-atom stories that were popular back then, in the notable anthology *Adventures in Time and Space* edited by Raymond J. Healy and J. Francis McComas (1946). He managed to place another 50 or so stories either in the pulps or in lower-end digests through about 1961, when he sold three stories to Cele Goldsmith's *Amazing* and *Fantastic*, and was then not heard of until a couple more stories in *Whispers* in the early 1970s.

So that was the reprint *Science Fiction Adventures*. The rug was yanked from under it rather summarily.

The US edition folded with the June 1958 issue. The UK edition could have remained a reprint magazine for some time, since there were 12 American issues to draw on, but it did not. The reprints continued through the fifth issue (November 1958), and then Carnell announced that *Science Fiction Adventures* would continue as a British magazine. Its circulation, he said in the editorial in **6**, had been increasing "by leaps and bounds," and the readers "have been letting us know in no uncertain terms that a first-class action-adventure magazine in the science fiction field was long overdue. At least in our part of the world." So they sought out material from "British, Commonwealth, and American writers," and Carnell says that what they've got is probably better than the material in the reprint issues. (Some of the "new" material—four stories in the seven 1959 issues—had, in fact, been previously published in *other* American magazines, but none in the US *Science Fiction Adventures*.)

§

During its first year, 1959, the new UK *Science Fiction Adventures* looks a lot like the other Nova magazines, with the contents listed on a vertical strip on the left of the cover (this began with issue **5**, around the time *New Worlds* made the same change), and the title on a strip at the top. The price remains at 2/-, the date stays buried at the bottom of the contents page, and the page count remains the same, but re-numbered. With **12**, the front cover is no longer treated as if numbered, so the table of contents is now page 1 and the last page of text is numbered 112 rather than 114.

As with the reprint issues, blurbs appear both after the story names on the table of contents and at the beginning of the stories. The Table of Contents blurbs resemble what you'd see on the cover of an Ace book of the time, e.g.: "Powerful and opposing forces were out to stop Edison North representing Earth at the Galactic Federation Council on Xaron. Throughout the journey death stared over his shoulder." The story blurbs are more sedate: "Australian writer Wynne Whiteford is still living in London and the popularity of his two former stories, 'Shadow of the Sword' (No. 6) and 'Distant Drum' (No. 9) prompted us to request another galactic adventure from him. You won't be disappointed in this one either." Both are for Whiteford's story in **12**.

The interior illustrations continue, though they are now two years gone from *New Worlds*; all are by Brian Lewis, one each for most stories, and the quality is variable. There's a slogan at the bottom of each cover—"Action-Adventure Science Fiction," "All New Science Fiction Stories," etc. Most of the covers are by Lewis (five of them), with one each by Bradshaw (**6**), a pleasant spaceship take-off scene, and Hutchings (**10**), rather cartoony.[26] The Lewis covers are in his literal-minded, wax-people vein and are mostly pretty simple-minded as well, consistently with

26. See these covers at http://www.sfcovers.net/mainnav.htm, at http://www.philsp.com/mags/science_fiction_adventures.html#uk, and at http://www.collectorshowcase.fr/sf_adventures_page_2.htm and the following page.

the magazine's declared mission. The worst are **9**, in which it appears that Humphrey Bogart is punching somebody out with a buxom woman looking on, and **7**, soldier with cartoon face and futuristic-looking rifle. The most interesting of the lot is **11**, with a couple of men on horseback looking down from a ridge at a spaceship, while a couple more men with peace signs on their helmets skulk in the bushes. Peace signs?

There's still a minimum of editorial matter. "The Editor's Space" appears in **6** and **7**, with the latter promising a letter column if readers will just separate their comments on *Science Fiction Adventures* from those on the other Nova magazines. "The Reader's Space" appears in **9**. Neither feature appears again in the remaining issues through **12**. There are scientific articles in **9**, **11**, and **12**, the latter two by Kenneth Johns, the former ("Cave Painting") by one George Chailey, who also had a short story in *Science Fiction Adventures* **6** and is otherwise unknown to the SF magazines.

For some unexplained reason, 1959 has seven issues. *Science Fiction Adventures* first departs from its bimonthly schedule by missing the September issue (no doubt accounted for in part by the printing strike that caused *New Worlds* to miss an issue in the fall), but then there are issues dated October, November, and December before the magazine reverts to bimonthly after a February and a May 1960 issue, and stays that way for the rest of its life.

The fiction policy continues to favor longer and fewer stories. The lead stories often run more than 50 pages, whereas *New Worlds* lead stories seldom go much over 40 and are often shorter. Only one issue has as many as four stories. The policy is made explicit in the ad, "In the Next Issue," on the inside front cover of **12**, which advertises James White's "Deadly Litter": "Too long to publish in *New Worlds*—but outstanding in any magazine." There are only half a dozen short stories in the seven issues; one of them, Chailey's "Death of a Telepath" in **6**, is labeled "Bonus Short Story." Almost all of the non-reprint stories are by established contributors to *New Worlds* and *Science Fantasy*:

Bulmer, Sellings, White, Clifford C. Reed, Tubb, Presslie, Lan Wright in these issues. Eventually, Aldiss, Ballard, Brunner and Moorcock put in appearances. And of course the indispensable E. R. James and Francis G. Rayer had cameos.

The first post-reprint issue (6) in fact begins with a reprint, the short novel "Shadow of the Sword" by Wynne Whiteford, which had appeared in the October 1958 *Fantastic Universe*.

"Shadow of the Sword" is a thoroughly naive story that is frankly refreshing after a lot of the preceding US material, much of which (Silverberg, Harrison, Hamilton) seems virtually decadent by comparison. Scott is dispatched from Earth to Triton on an urgent mission to take possession of some alien artifacts before the enemy Eastern Alliance gets hold of them. He's accompanied by Brenda (it's her and her brother's ship), who is prepared to serve as co-pilot, and a good thing—they need to accelerate hard and she grew up in Jovian gravity, two and a half times Earth's. As a result she's short and stronger than Scott, but she's lost an arm to a pressure suit malfunction and the prosthetic isn't good for much. So they set off, Scott deals with her predictable attempt to take control and head for home, then some EVA is called for. She's ready, but he does it, despite the risk of leaving her alone inside. "It wasn't a job for a woman." She reminds him how strong she is. "'You're still a woman.' She began to say something, then stopped. Her eyes looked bright and a trifle moist." They get to Triton, the artifacts include a super-fast antigravity spaceship which could win the war for whoever gets possession of it, but Scott has a different idea. After they outwit an Eastern Alliance crew by clever manipulation of the ship's gravity fields, they head off to Earth to make cameo appearances in the skies over both belligerents' cities in hopes of bringing humanity together, "Unite and Conquer"-style. Clearly an item by now, they zip back to Triton to find that in the interim the aliens have returned and packed up their other artifacts as well as the remaining humans and their spaceships. Sequel obviously on the way.

Recall that Carnell said (*New Worlds* 68) that his intent in

Science Fiction Adventures was to provide an "introductory medium" for new readers, because SF in the established magazines is often "incomprehensible to casual readers." This plain tale of appealing characters strikes me as a much more attractive introduction to the genre than the weary and wearying pieces in the reprint issues by Silverberg, with their stylized palace intrigue (the "Chalice" stories) or flip genocide ("This World Must Die"), Harrison, with his hyper-capable protagonist effortlessly running up the body count, or Hamilton, laying on the cynicism with a trowel.[27]

The sequel, "Distant Drum" (**9**) is equally pleasant if a bit more cluttered. Scott and Brenda head for Earth in the alien spaceship, but the aliens are on their tail. Off to Jupiter they go, thinking the aliens can't handle the gravity, but they're wrong. There ensues a reasonably well done cat-and-mouse game between the alien spaceship and the domed Earth colony, during which Scott performs improbably well in the high gravity, and the colonists' superior knowledge of the planet culminates in the humans defeating the aliens and their robots. Scott and Brenda enter their ship. Suddenly it takes off for parts unknown, fetching up at the aliens' home planet a very long way away (relativistic effects are not mentioned), and there are the missing human archaeologists to explain that the aliens' civilization is decadent, only the robots know what's going on, and there's a lot of rebuilding to do. The couple find a nice alien bungalow, already renovated, and are about to set up housekeeping, planning periodic forays to Earth to keep everybody scared and united (as I said, relativistic effects do not feature).

Whiteford's short novel "Who Rides the Tiger" (**12**) is just as readable but more humdrum. Edison North, a prominent anti-Isolationist, has been selected by the Isolationist government of Earth to send off as its representative to the Galactic Council.

---

27. If indeed the circulation was going up by "leaps and bounds," as Carnell said in **6**, that might discredit all my criticisms of the appropriateness of much of this fiction for Carnell's avowed purpose——or maybe he was reaching a different audience from the one he intended.

Why? Obviously to kill him en route and make sure the aliens get blamed, an agenda played out and thwarted through a series of stock maneuvers (e.g. he's pursued, he realizes the pursuit is ahead of him as well as behind, he jumps up a fire escape into somebody's window). At the end the schemes are revealed, the Isolationists will lose the next election. Earth will join the glorious Federation, with its flag depicting a human with torch leaping up to the stars. Some bald, earless telepaths put in cameo appearances, but otherwise it could be happening in Dubuque.

§

Kenneth Bulmer, the magazine's most prolific contributor, had some 13 long stories in *Science Fiction Adventures* under his own name and the Nelson Sherwood and H. Philip Stratford pseudonyms, as well as several collaborative "Kenneth Johns" articles. In these seven 1959 issues he has three "short novels," a novelette, and a couple of articles. The first, "Galactic Galapagos" (**6**) as by Nelson Sherwood, is a lackluster "short novel" (29 pages) about a colony planet with several large islands, one of which is overrun with bugs and with predatory eagles that steal people's children. The islands are described as not dissimilar to the Galapagos Islands as observed by Darwin, a comparison that goes nowhere because the solution to the mystery is that the planet's previous occupants killed off a couple of ecological niches on that island, so the answer is not to exterminate the pests but to restore the missing species. This short story's worth of idea is stretched out to purposeless length.

The rest are a bit better. "The Sun Creator" (**7**), as by Sherwood, would have seemed at home in *Planet Stories*: Larry Shackleton, star polo player and the son of the mastermind of Galactic Re-Planning, has just scored the winning goal that will put Earth in the finals against Eridanus when he is informed that his father has died, he's in charge, and the powers that be need him right away. Mabel, a device made by his company which turns planets into stars, has been accidentally diverted from its destination and lost on the politically turbulent planet Greensleeves; would he mind accompanying them to go find it? He would mind, but soon enough agrees to take on the evil Baron responsible, only to learn that Mabel is hidden in the Baron's castle, has been activated, and will blow in four hours. "Then he was blazing a meteoric path across the stars, pulverizing space and reaching out and across into the storm and fighting its last dying anger as he settled down onto Greensleeves." Alone, of course, for no visible reason. A little later: "On this planet, quite near him, was a machine which was set to turn this planet into a sun in—in just about an hour's time!" But of course it doesn't. This is a competent turn on bog-standard pulpery.

More or less the same is true of "Don't Cross a Telekine" (8), as by Stratford, in which a telekinetic and slightly telepathic guy, hoping to make some money shooting craps with suckers who don't know of his talent, is recruited by two sets of people for what turns out to be the same mission, rescuing a piece of film from a booby-trapped safe in a derelict spaceship in the asteroids. One employer is a malevolent politician who wants Venus to secede from the rest of the solar system, the other a benign politician who wants everybody to stay together, who has a good-looking daughter. (This is pretty close to the same plot, if not the same ultimate revelation, as Jay Williams' "Seed of Violence" in the same issue.) It's not hard to guess where the protagonist's loyalties wind up.

"The Halting Hand" (12), allegedly a novelette but two pages longer than "Galactic Galapagos," is pleasant fluff about humanoid aliens assigned to keep Earth's space program from succeeding; but one of them, Vinter, meets a girl (sic). More precisely, Tessa is "a slip of a girl filled with ideas of inter-planetary travel and exploration for the sheer doing of it, for the wonder, the freedom, the outward urge of a vital race," etc. She's also a "technologist working on large scale rocket guid-ance systems," and besides that, a dead ringer for the woman whom Vinter was forbidden to marry by the Central Registry. By the end, she's asking him why he's doing what he's doing.

Answer: because it's an assignment! Yeah, but why *this* assignment? Pressed by Tessa, he presses Central Control, and finally learns that they would really like to *help* backward races into space, but they can't right now, because they have to defeat the marauding Terentii and they really can't spare any mentors for the next 50 years. So Vinter asks Tessa to marry him, and says if things don't work out on his home world, he'll come back to Earth with her. She goes for it: "I'll follow you—into space—where I belong."

§

The Whiteford and some of the Bulmer stories seem to me to quite well fill Carnell's declared SF 101 agenda—straightforward SF for an audience that is mostly young. The best story in these issues, however, is decidedly trickier. James White is wrestling again with the evils of warfare in "Occupation: Warrior" (7). In the far future, the Guardians keep the peace around an otherwise libertarian galaxy, except that some folks just have to fight wars. So the Guardians arrange them, under tightly controlled circumstances. Special planets are designated for warfare, only the most cowardly are selected as soldiers, and the Guardians have a repertoire of maneuvers to discourage and demoralize the combatants so as to wind things up as quickly and with as little damage as possible. The protagonist Dermod, who is not cowardly at all, fakes his way into a war determined that Earth will win this one, and applies his considerable military talents to doing so, causing much more carnage among the enemy than anyone bargained for, and arresting the Guardian observer when he tries to blow the whistle.

This sounds like the basis for a compact lampoon in the Robert Sheckley manner, but in White's earnest hands it is long, somber, and a bit ponderous, though quite readable and ultimately admirable. Consistently with White's previous work, in which nobody is irredeemably bad but just misguided, Dermod ultimately lacks the courage of his insanity. After delivering to the captive Guardian a rant about how they are stifling human freedom (though he can't cite anything humans are not free to do except fight wars), the consequences of what he is doing start to sink in, and he becomes a remorseful convert—the Guardian predicts he will join them. The war is also exposed as totally stupid, based on a misunderstanding. If all this sounds a trifle familiar, it's because the idea of canned warfare administered by a universal peacekeeping agency was set out prominently two years previously in White's famous "Sector General" (*New Worlds*, **57**), where the Guardians were called the Monitors.

So why isn't this a Sector General story? Apparently it was, initially titled "Classification: Warrior." David Langford describes it as "a story whose Sector General links were removed by an editor who thought it too grim for the series."[28] This seems odd to me; a future in which warfare is as carefully controlled as in this story seems like a thoroughly optimistic vision. But then Carnell often displayed a genius for missing the point. One might also ask why this one didn't run in *New Worlds*, since it's considerably subtler and denser than the usual *SF Adventures* fare. The story's signposts are not clear at all: Dermod is the viewpoint character, the early parts of the story show him doing his job without any apparent question on the author's part, and the author's point emerges only gradually along with Dermod's change of heart. The story is also written in White's capable but densely expository style. The answer is apparently its length (as Carnell said about the later "Deadly Litter"): it runs 54 pages, and stories of such length were generally relegated to *SF Adventures* or *Science Fantasy*.

Jay Williams' "Seed of Violence" (**8**), from the November 1958 *Fantastic Universe*, is a well-meaning if slightly pedestrian novelette about an archaeologist who falls into the middle of a political scheme to scapegoat the gentle and primitive Martians, label them as animals, deprive them of their legal protections, and exploit Mars unhindered. After a few sedately rendered

---

28. http://www.sectorgeneral.com/articleslangford.html (visited 11/1/11).

chases and shootouts with the sadistic villains, right prevails, the archaeologist's work proves crucial to understanding who the Martians really are, and he's about to get next to the beautiful and hypercompetent secret agent. It's benignly readable.

Williams (1914-78) was one of those writers, rare in his time, who wrote unabashed genre SF in the course of a wider literary career, and actually knew what he was doing. He published ten stories and an article in the SF magazines from 1956 to 1962, all but this one in *Fantasy & Science Fiction* or *Astounding*, and a couple more in anthologies. Otherwise, from 1943 to his death in 1978, he published some 75 books, including historical novels, the best known being *The Witches*. A bit over half of them were juveniles, including, collaboratively, the Danny Dunn series—*Danny Dunn and the Antigravity Paint*, etc. Of course he's forgotten as an SF writer, never having published an SF novel and having given up on the magazines after a double handful of stories.

§

Clifford C. Reed's "Halfway House" (**8**), a short story on the cover but a 24-page novelette on the Table of Contents, is consistent with the Intro to SF agenda, probably too consistent. It's an irritatingly *pro forma* item in which the protagonist Hart is dispatched to Valeria, an unprepossessing planet used as a way station between Earth and the more salubrious Sirius 2, and also as a penal colony. But something funny is going on. Hart discovers there's more economic activity (like farming) going on than realized, and there are outlaws who have escaped penal discipline and have their own outposts just over the mountains. When he gets to the outlaws' lair, he learns that they've discovered ore valuable enough to win them their freedom (he says). But the woman who took him there is exposed as a double agent, and there's a shootout because they insist on handing her over to be paralyzed and eaten by the giant spiders that infest the planet. The government cavalry arrive and rescue everybody, and Hart gets the girl seconded to go back to Earth with him. So what are the cons going to get for finding the ore? The question is forgotten. And those giant spiders—what did they live on before they had humans to stalk? There's not a word about the ecology of the planet. And the square-cube law? Fuggedaboutit.

This is followed by Reed's short novel "Children of the Stars" (**9**), which starts out in an equally formulaic way, with a combination of political prisoners and criminals being transported interplanetarily, amid the usual sort of scenery-chewing:

> A warder on this level pushed Marth roughly. "On to the end," he snapped. "Into that last cage." He slapped the club he carried against the rails. "Unless you want to feel this," he hinted.... "Four rats in each cage," the guard announced. "Get in!"

But the prisoners take over the ship and head out for parts unknown, finding an inhabitable planet without inordinate difficulty, crash-landing, setting up shop and almost immediately dividing into factions.

The sequel, "Forgotten Knowledge" (**11**), takes place 80 years later, by which time everybody speaks in a sort of faux-archaic baby-talk, and there's a different set of factions and rigid social stratification, with a poorly developed conflict between those who want to go back into space (how? Reed doesn't say; but it's the province of the folks who "wear white cloth" in the Science House) and those who want to head over the horizon, and the whole thing was so boring I gave up on it. One notable characteristic of these stories, like "Halfway House," is an almost complete lack of attention to the fact that they're supposedly set on an alien planet. There are beasts to be rounded up and herded, crops to be grown, but there's no more detail or discussion than that about this world and its life. These stories could as well have been set in Australia, or Kansas. So much for "action-adventure against a science fiction background." For Reed, at least, it's at best a painted scrim.

There's another story in this series the following year, and the three of them were fixed up into a deeply obscure book called *Martian Enterprise* (Digit, 1962—named for the hijacked prison ship), which is subtitled or blurbed *The Battle of Inter-Planetary Supremacy*. Reed published one more short story in *Science Fiction Adventures*, a few more in *New Worlds* and *Science Fantasy* in 1964-65, and was then gone, not before time, from the SF magazines.

§

E. C. Tubb's short novel "Galactic Destiny" (**10**) is a half-hearted experiment, a stylized space opera-cum-morality play told in short scenes of nearly uniform length. In Tubb's slightly twee far future, starships are operated by the Folk, who all seem to have three-letter names (Jak, Ric, etc.) and who talk the Talk, which apparently carries oceans of meaning in a few words. The passengers are called the People, who just talk. On this particular voyage, the three No-space engines blow and leave everybody stranded in space. The captain cobbles together one replacement out of the debris, but the mass of the ship will have to be cut down drastically, and after all the luggage and fittings have been thrown out, some of the people will have to go too. So there is a series of homicides, all of which seem to be intended to suggest who and what is valuable or not, but the whole thing seemed so contrived as not to be worth even trying to follow the argument, if that's what it is.

Silverberg is back, as Calvin M. Knox, with "The Silent Invaders" (**10**), from *Infinity*, October 1958, a 37-page novelette which was later expanded into an Ace Double with a number of subsequent editions including a Dobson hardcover. One of the Silverberg sites reports: "There is an amusing introduction to the 1977 Ace edition (and the Hamlyn as well) in which Silverberg tells of his surprise when he saw this book on a newsstand in

1973 and couldn't remember having written it."[29] This may be understandable. The short version could have been written in his sleep. It's reminiscent of "This World Must Die" from the all-reprint issues: morally preferable (the killing is smaller-scale and there's a slightly better reason for it), but equally perfunctory. Major Abner Harris is really Aar Khiilom of Dharruu, heavily reconstituted and come to infiltrate Earth to help tilt it Dharruu's way in the titanic conflict with the Medlins. Shortly after arrival, he is informed by the leader of his group of ten Dharruuvians that the Medlins are here, a hundred of them, including the woman in his hotel whom he has been about to seduce (or vice versa).

His alien spy instruction manual says developing a sexual relationship with a native is a good way to firm up his cover, and he's eager to try this human sex business anyway. Instead, he's instructed to kill her. When she gets the drop on him, the Medlins introduce him to some particularly robust Earthfolks who they claim are the new master race that everyone should serve and foster. Will he kill the other Dharruuvians to help out the cause? Of course, he lies, and gets back to his fellows, who outfit him to go back to the Medlins, claim mission accomplished, and then kill them. So he tries, and has them all unconscious and ready for the coup de grace, except that the superhuman woman is pregnant and her fetus, even more superhuman than she, takes control of his mind and muscles. Now he's a real convert, so he goes back to the Dharruuvians, claims the Medlins are dead, and then kills his own group. Now he's a fake Earthman for life. That's all there is to this arid game of spy vs. spy ping-pong. Apparently the book version added length but not much more. Rich Horton says of the Ace Double version: "All in all, a silly story, very minor Silverberg, a bit too rapidly resolved—nothing special at all."[30]

Silverberg's short story "Venus Trap" (12), from *Future* 30

29. http://www.majipoor.com/work.php?id=1024 (visited 9/10/11).

30. http://www.sff.net/people/richard.horton/aced43.htm (visited 9/10/11).

(1956), is probably the most enjoyable of his stories in these 1959 issues. The sinister Venusians are engaged in genetic engineering (and that's what Silverberg called it in 1956—not the first. Jack Williamson was a few years earlier, but a good early pickup). A geeky Earth spy has smuggled out of the Venusians' Earth laboratories a two-headed pigeon with knifelike claws. Meanwhile, the diplomat protagonist's brother-in-law has developed a method of growing gigantic vegetables, so the protagonist hotfoots it to Venus and applies the treatment to the local equivalent of a Venus flytrap. When he displays the menacing ten-foot result to a Venusian diplomat (homage to Ballard's "Prima Belladonna"? No, looks like the Silverberg story appeared at the same time or earlier), the Venusians are scared witless and readily agree to abandon their activities with Earth life if Earth will just destroy the giant flytrap and all its seeds. Of course, there are no seeds—this is an acquired characteristic and not inherited or heritable. Thus Silverberg repudiates Lamarck!—unlike some of Carnell's other contributors. This story's lightweight tone matches its substance, unlike his longer and more portentous—and emptier—ones in these issues.

§

A couple of *New Worlds*' more incisive regulars contribute decidedly un-incisive and badly padded items. Arthur Sellings' "The Tycoons" (6) is a sharp and amusing short story that is unfortunately stretched out to novelette length (29 pages). A buttoned-down tax inspector pays a call on a firm that moves a lot of money but doesn't have any personnel expenses. Of course they are aliens bent on world domination through a device that, when completed, will make all humans devoted slaves. To protect themselves from exposure, they tell him they make novelties, give him a personal loyalty treatment and recruit him as their PR man and chief salesman—at which he is so diligent and successful that they can't get their mind control device finished for filling orders for novelties, and are thwarted.

Robert Presslie's long novelette "The Savage One" (11) opens bracingly by presenting Kramer, an utterly hostile and amoral character about to be executed for murder:

> He was conceived in abandon, born in the gutter and raised in an alley. Yet he climbed out of his environment, stood on it and built a kingdom of crime and corruption which he ruled like a tyrant. He lived without fear and died with a defiant curse on his lips. In the death cell he laughed at the padre. In the lethal chamber he spat in the face of the executioner.

But his personality is hijacked by alien Mirfakians looking for entities to be re-embodied to fight their endless wars. He objects vehemently to no avail but ultimately (30 pages worth of ultimately) learns how to fight back from a race of intelligent, telepathic, and telekinetic sandworms, with their assistance psionically destroys the Mirfakians, and this time welcomes death. The momentum of the beginning is dissipated by the story's length and contrivance.

There is only one completely new author in these issues, George Chailey. "Death of a Telepath" (6) is a short and mildly clever detective story—how do you kill a telepath in a spaceship without leaving any clues? Carnell says nothing about him in his blurbs either for this or Chailey's article "Cave Painting" in 8. If he's a pseudonym, Miller and Contento don't know about it.

The rest of the shorter stories are by Carnell regulars, except for N(orma) K. Hemming, who had one story each in *New Worlds* and *Nebula* as well as some earlier Australian publications. "Call Them Earthmen" (10) is her last published story. She died the following year, at 33. It's a creaky item that might have made an impression in *Wonder Stories*. An alien invasion is on the way, and humans have just found the Citadel, a relic from just before the last alien invasion, which destroyed human civilization because it was fought with weapons that attacked the brain. The invaders were killed, humanity lost all its memories. Inside the Citadel, they find what must be a member of the last invading race—except it is revealed that he's actually a human. The humans were destroyed, and the invaders lost their memories and now think *they* are the survivors of humanity. To cut to the chase, of course the human succumbs to argument ("Your race died, Bendal—but I can promise you that we will make the name of Earth ring far through all the stars"), relents from his hatred, and decides to admit these pseudo-humans to the rest of the Citadel, which contains weapons or something that will help them fight off the new generation of invaders, who aren't like us (either us) at all.

E. R. James "Refrigerator Ship" (**11**) is a characteristically clumsy but uncharacteristically melodramatic item in which a spaceship full of frozen colonists arrives at its destination just in time for the colony planet's star to go nova, blinding the captain. So they've got nowhere to go but back to Earth, 400 frozen people without nutrients for a return trip, and barely enough food for three people. They wake up the colonist who used to be a captain, and his girl friend, which makes five; one of the crew kills another, then the blinded captain pulls the switch to dump the colonists and the crewman who has gone to wake them up, leaving three. Then he says to the new captain "There's you, and your girl... and you will comfort each other during the long years to come... so that there may well be three to reach Earth," and shoots himself. "And all around the ship, the stars drew out into red lines which faded into the gathering flux of lightspeed and beyond."

Lan Wright's "The Easy Way" (**12**) is another of his facile and cartoony stories, a perfectly capable example of the kind of colonialist Hamburger Helper that filled the mid-ranges of American magazines during the 1950s. Dallow is having a hard time getting the primitive and ferocious Sharonians to provide enough of the native weed Kiprit to meet the Terrans' needs. His boss, the unprepossessing Don Jaime, shows up with his aide, a large, mute Japanese named Tanashi. So they head out to roust the Sharonians, who continue to have their own agenda, and it ain't pickin' cotton, er, Kiprit. Don Jaime insults the headman, who challenges him to a duel; Don J. then says (through Dallow) that he's such a puny specimen it would be less insulting for Tanashi to fight the headman. Tanashi trounces the headman (Wright makes a point of his using Karate rather than Judo), takes over, and will shortly contrive to be defeated by Dallow, who'll remain headman as long as he wants because only the headman can challenge. Obviously Dallow won't—he'll just take the insults. So the Sharonians will pick all the Kiprit Earth wants. Why will this possibly work? "As is the case with all primitive tribes, they will defend to the death certain taboos and traditions—especially those on which their tribal life has been based for so long." Ah yes, those Lesser Breeds, incapable of seeing when they are being outrageously exploited.

§

Science Fiction Adventures keeps to the same course in its third and fourth years as in its first post-US-reprint issues in 1959: 112 pages exclusive of covers (except for **21**, which has 116 pages, but no explanation for the difference), digest size. There are a couple of changes: the price goes from 2/- to 2/6 at the beginning of 1961 with **18**, and the interior illustrations disappear after **15**. The schedule remains bi-monthly, with one glitch, as noted above: **13** is dated February 1960, but **14** is May, and the magazine continues bi-monthly from there. So there are only 11 issues in the two years.

As before, there is relatively little editorial matter, and a smaller number of stories per issue, although longer ones, than in *New Worlds*. Two of these issues have only two stories and only one, **18**, has as many as five items (one of them a short article). There are two articles in these issues, one by Kenneth Johns, of the same general length and approach of his (their) *New Worlds* articles, and the other by Alan Barclay extolling the virtues of "The Bow" (**17**) ("unquestionably the most fascinating weapon invented by man"). The tables of contents continue to contain blurbs for the longer stories, different from the ones on the stories' title pages. The former are more in the way of advertisements, though not very captivating ones ("The peace treaty between Takkat, Shurilala and Earth was to be a lasting one, but behind the scenes the Takkatians had other plans"). while those on the title pages tend to tout the authors' backgrounds ("Kenneth Bulmer has written a number of exciting short stories round the hypothetical three-system war....")

Visually the magazine starts out and continues through **18** with the familiar *New Worlds* format, white bands at top and left side for title and story titles respectively. With **19** the bands are gone and the cover picture expands correspondingly, with the magazine title in a box. Some of the covers are indicated as illustrating one of the stories, and some are not. The covers are almost all by Brian Lewis, still in his literal-minded mode, but the resulting damage is lessened by the fact that he plays to his strengths and minimizes the human figures in most of them, in favor of machinery, planets, jungle, etc., with relatively pleasing and colorful results. Compare, say, the covers of **18**, **22**, and **23**, quite attractive to my taste, with the tediously waxen and cartoony human figures on **13**. There are also a couple of Jarr covers, both of them well done extraterrestrial scenes (**15** and **17**). In general, the covers do a pretty good job at the magazine's avowed purpose of presenting the stuff of SF simply, for an audience that is not too familiar with it.

I wish I could say the same about the fiction contents. The problem with the material is both its quality and its relationship to the magazine's ostensible purpose. A lot of the stories in these issues simply aren't very good even in the terms stated in the magazine's prospectus. They may be action-adventure stories but they are not particularly well plotted or written, in some cases just boring. More importantly, one would think that an introductory medium for new SF readers needs to do more than present action and adventure. It should presumably also present the other and to my mind more important attractions of SF: ingenious ideas well worked out, strange and interesting settings, some vision of the unrealized possibilities of human existence. Otherwise the readers would do just as well—or much better—to go back to the likes of Eric Ambler and Louis L'Amour, or their more elementary colleagues. The stories from the Carnell magazines that leap to mind in response to Carnell's statement of policy are some of John Brunner's novellas from *Science Fantasy*, especially "Echo in the Skull" and "Earth Is But a Star." There's nothing on that level here.

Take, for example, Clifford C. Reed's "The Road Back" (**13**). The story is the third and last of his Sumedin series, in which political and non-political prisoners who hijacked their prison ship have split into factions, and here's their war. It is reasonably readable, assuming you can tolerate the stilted dialect:

> "This business here, in this place, is fighter business, and here *I* speak."... "Not after his speak," he denied. "I calculate the Council will wish to hear this man.... Calculating so," he said, "I touch him. He becomes my charge. I touch him for the Council."... "He has been speaked that whether good or bad comes to him in Newtoun will come from his own self. His own speak will prove him."

As in the earlier stories, the background is poorly sketched. There is absolutely nothing about any differences between Sumedin and Earth; for the author's purposes, the planet is just a place where the action occurs. The history and events are poorly rationalized: the colonists landed with one spaceship and its contents, and the spaceship has been blown up, and it seems only a few generations have passed. Nonetheless, one faction specializes in building trucks, and the other has just invented what appears to be a laser rifle (though the word isn't used, the first laser not having been built until 1960), and a sort of acoustic gun capable of making cliffs collapse at a distance. They are also determined to get back into space, and at the end of the story they shoot off the chief bad guy in their first experimental spaceship. Not bloody likely, I'd say, and not a story that would have encouraged me to read more SF as a kid had I not already become fixated.

The same is true, though to a lesser degree and for different reasons, of the other long story in issue **13**, James White's "Deadly Litter." It's another of his hard-working and well-meaning pieces, and became the title story of his first non-Sector General collection, from Ballantine in 1964. In the future, throwing things out of one's spaceship has become a grave offense because bread crusts and potato skins have ways of becoming fatal missiles to other ships. People have careers tracking down miscreants and investigating just when, where, and what was tossed, so its path can be tracked and people can be warned. The protagonist has arrested such a culprit and they are off into space trying to reconstruct what happened when he and others lightened ship near Jupiter to save their lives after an accident. There's a mystery about who's who that really isn't very mysterious by the time it's unraveled after 40 pages. There is an admirable if labored ingenuity here that is largely missing from the Clifford Reed story. Despite his faults White remains as likeable a writer as the Nova magazines could boast. Nonetheless, this story is painfully slow.

§

The dominant contributor in these issues is Kenneth Bulmer, with seven stories in these 11 issues, five of them lead "short novels" and the others novelettes. His work demonstrates both the weaknesses and the limited strengths of the material in this magazine. His long (83 pages) "Of Earth Foretold" (**14**) postulates an Earth characterized by "the acceptance of one great universal religion of light and grace, power and perfect understanding." Exactly what this religion teaches and why everybody believes in it isn't explained, but that's the way it is, though there are varying degrees of enthusiasm for it on Earth, and "relifan" (religious fanatic) is a derogatory term for some. In order to keep the universe peaceful, Earth sends out spaceships full of Prophets of Earth, one per planet, androids wired to preach this unspecified gospel and convert any alien races that might otherwise be tempted to believe... otherwise. But some alien Evil Ones—that's what the characters call them—turn up, and must be stopped.

Meanwhile, a space crew is out to rescue Abd al-Malik ibn-Zobeir, who has accidentally gone out the airlock with one of the Prophets and is marooned on the relevant planet. They get attacked and shipwrecked themselves by the Evil Ones, find the local indigenes, and then the Evil Ones—who, it turns out, call *themselves* the Evil Ones!—show up again with a mind-controlling transmission that converts everyone to *their* religion, something about the promise of the four caves. Rescuers from Earth appear, are gobsmacked that the space crew is spouting the Evil One nonsense, and then... the lost Prophet of Earth, the one that Abd al-Malik etc. rode down on, shows up radiating *his* transmission, and the crew is converted back. Actually it's Abd al-Malik himself—the Prophet got smashed but the "mental radiation equipment" was intact, so Abd has impersonated a mass-produced android messiah. Right and Terra triumph! And one of the re-converts can figure out from the "four caves" propaganda (which refers to star formations) where the Evil Ones come from, so our men can go there and whack them.

One might hope that this is all satirical, but apparently not. One might also suspect that the explanation for why everybody accepts one religion on Earth is another mind-controlling transmission, but there's nothing in the story to support that, and it seems inconsistent with the variety of degrees of devoutness on Earth. Apparently mind control is for the lesser races, while Earth humans retain free will; they just all happen to exercise it in the same direction. Excuse me if I am not persuaded, or sympathetic, and if there's a shred of irony in here it has eluded me. There's a certain amount of mechanical ingenuity but nothing much interesting is done with it, and there's really no reason to root for one side or the other except that the other side is wearing a big sign that says Evil. Bulmer also, as is often the case, overdoes the pulp pizzazz, e.g. (describing the Prophets):

> Made by the cunning hands and brains of men they yet possessed the chilling power of striking awe into those charged with their care and protection and delivery. The knowledge that these godlike beings were composed of steel and plastic, of synthetic flesh and bones and blood, with memory-sponge brains and nuclear battery hearts, did not dispel that cloying aura of unease and dread.

This story became an Ace Double half under the title *The Earth Gods Are Coming*.

Bulmer's slightly longer and considerably more tedious "Earth's Long Shadow" (**17**) is a dreary piece of yard goods. The galaxy is a stew of squabbling cliques; everybody is steeped in cartoon nationalism; Earth is believed to be mythical, but at the same time it is also believed to be within the unexplained Blight, an area of space no one can enter because of the consequences of past wars.

A traveling salesman who seems to be a spy comes to Gamma-Horakah ostensibly on business, but he really wants to get to Alpha-Horakah, the system's capital, to see what aggression is being brewed. Along the way it's hinted that he's from Earth. Then it's confirmed that he's from Earth. Then it's revealed that he's really the super-duper emperor of Earth, or was before he quit to engage in two-bit espionage jobs in the middle of nowhere. Meanwhile he's doing the usual action hero number, outfighting, outshooting, and outthinking a series of set-up adversaries, and eventually gets to the Horakah citadel, where he's about to be killed, except that the cavalry in the form of half a million ships from Earth arbitrarily shows up and rescues him.

He takes the obligatory alluring girl with him. She's named

Allura. He's operating under the pseudonym John Carter, and encounters somebody else—apparently another Earth agent—using the equally Burroughsian name Carson Napier. Why? No apparent reason. What's done with it? Nothing. In addition to the clichéd action, there's no real sense of place—it could be happening anywhere or nowhere—and certainly nothing to evoke any semblance of the fabled Sense of Wonder to which this magazine was supposedly dedicated. The whole thing is made of cardboard. It's also remarkably badly written, probably out of haste to be done. A sample: "The line waiting was growing restive. One or two children were playing with increasing violence. And it seemed as though the customsman had flexed his status flaunting mental muscles enough."

This became half of an Ace Double as *No Man's World*, and though I didn't read that one, this story reminds me why I largely gave up on the Ace Doubles at about the time this was published.

Bulmer's novelette "The Dedicated Ones" (**15**) is a leaden satire that reads like an *Astounding* knock-off. On Lancion III, there is a lot of work to be done because the native society is full of injustice and exploitation, and the Dedicated Ones—galactic do-gooders—have come to set it right. But it is eventually revealed that it's all a put-up job. The natives are trying to accommodate human racial guilt over their bloody past, so they've faked up some sweatshops and nasty-looking factories to give the humans something to reform. But matters get out of hand, with one of the Dedicated going bonkers and undertaking to bomb the nearest native city out of existence, saved only by Colonel Ramsden, who literally gallops back to the human camp to intervene. Ramsden, it was previously explained, got pretty racked up a while back, and the natives sewed his top half onto the lower portions of a horse, so he goes about his duties in centauroid fashion. Unfortunately the story, with its ridiculous premise developed in utter solemnity, is as much of a chimera as Ramsden.

Bulmer's "The Aztec Plan" (**18**) is a rambling and generally snoreworthy novelette about intelligence agents who learn that Earth's enemies are scheming against Earth notwithstanding the just-concluded armistice in their war. They have to get a message back to Earth; but the bad guys know they are trying to carry a message. How to get through? The ultimate answer is a pretty uninteresting Mr. Wizard job involving directional magnetic fields, and the route there is a pretty conventional spy plot involving such greatest hits as eavesdropping from the ventilation ducts.

Matters look up a bit for Bulmer in the later issues. "Design Dilemma" (19), under the Nelson Sherwood pseudonym, is a romance of defense contracting. Honest. Despite the subject matter, it's considerably more simple-minded even than most of Bulmer's other stories, and frankly refreshing as a result. Despard is Director of Design of General Spaceship Associates, and he's under pressure to do the technically impossible—the available engines won't carry the mass that the politicians want carried. The only way to get the battleship contract is to skimp on armor, compromising the safety of Our Boys in Space and the principles of General Spaceship Associates. But it's also the only way to protect the futures of his daughter Minx and all his employees, including his devoted, prematurely white-haired secretary Miss Lincoln.

Of course when he caves, his daughter is shocked and Miss Lincoln and his closest associate quit. But the day is saved when the crackpot inventor whom Despard has brushed off, but Miss Lincoln has been championing, proves to have the goods: an improved Transmat that will work ship to ship, so the battleships will no longer have to carry tons and tons of lead shot ammunition—they can resupply in flight. That's right, in the future space battles will be fought with volleys of lead shot—cubical lead shot, if you please. Anyway, problem solved, contract signed, Earth secure, domestic harmony restored, and Miss Lincoln married to the inventor rather than continuing towards her rendezvous with spinsterhood. So ultimately it's a story about maintaining one's integrity, and much preferable to the earlier stories, which are not about much but shuffling card-board markers labeled good guys and bad guys.

Bulmer's "Wind of Liberty" (20) is another long novella (72 pages), this one portraying the struggle of humanity every-where against tyranny—sort of. In fact it goes through the motions of canvassing Big Ideas by throwing a couple of carica-tures against each other in the course of a clichéd plot—sort of a cartoon supercollider. On the other hand, it is more carefully assembled and finished than some of Bulmer's other work here, so it is more amusing and less irritating to read.

Vickery, who we are told a couple of dozen times has a wolf-like face, is a rebel against the Friendly Combine. When the story opens he has intruded upon the fat City Warden Armstrong for some tiresome dialogue ("In the galaxy there is a wind of liberty blowing!" "All this is very fine and fancy free.... But we have proved that our system is more efficient—" "Efficient! Is that all, then, that your puny mind can conceive?"). But he slips up and is captured, only to be spirited away in a daring rescue in an underground tunneling machine by the beautiful Tania Sevlon, daughter of another revolutionary leader, who makes reference to "that arch-brute Armstrong" while "her long pale hands hovered over the butts of twin machine cannon" as they flee. By the way, just what are they rebelling against? Vickery ruminates:

> Monopoly, Financial Trust, sheer money-grubbing trickery.... What businessman's cankered twaddle it all was.
>
> The members of the civilization spawned among the stars by mankind were no better than slaves—they were slaves, in everything but name.... He regarded himself as the devouring flame that cleansed the galaxy of the parasitical businessmen's monopolies brought world after world out of the shadows into the light of Freedom, Equality and Liberty.

This is the gospel according to Pillengarb's *Treatise on a Free Economy*, the Bible of Vickery's cause.

Meanwhile, some light-years away, the swells of the Friendly Combine are elucidating their own principles, from the mouth of Cluster Executive Gerald Wain, but derived it seems from the social philosophy of Snively Whiplash, Ph.D.:

> "The proper study for Man is Man.... But not in this day and age and not, most certainly not, for any man or woman of the public. And not for any member of the F.C. below the rank of System Executive.
>
> "To allow the ordinary run of humanity too much knowledge of self, destroyed too many empires for us to allow it here. Men work and play, are born, marry and die. What else do they need to know? Any soul-searching must be done for them by their priests—of whatever religion they choose—who are themselves rudely skilled in applied psychology. The galaxy was saved much toil and bloodshed and agony of mind when the art of psychology was lifted from the hands of ordinary men and reserved for System Executives and above."

Exactly what if anything people would like to do that they are not permitted to under this regime is not quite spelled out—is retail discounting forbidden? There's some stuff about the subjugation of individual planets—is this a revolution for protective tariffs? Anyway, the swells decide to go after Vickery with their secret weapon, the beautiful Elaine Caitlin (Ms. Sevlon of the long pale hands and machine cannon is not mentioned again). There ensues a cliff-hanger plot, almost literally. At one point Vickery and Elaine, having stowed away on a spaceship escaping the revolutionaries, are clinging by their fingers in a ventilation duct (always the ventilation ducts!) in which a powerful fan is threatening to suck them in and chop them up, and is stopped only by a strategically thrown shoe. During all these diversions, by the way, Vickery is carrying in his plastic suitcase a wrapped package which contains a tactical nuclear weapon.

Later, they slip out of the ductwork into the cabin of one of the swells, where Vickery finds and takes several books, which on examination reveal the secret workings of the F.C. system—as disclosed above, psychology!—which has been kept secret from the masses. Even the double agent Elaine becomes infuriated to learn how she has been manipulated: "They'd used it on her, turned her into a secret service operative when all she'd really wanted was a good cybernetics job, a husband, home, and family." Vickery recounts the ancient secrets: "It all started with a character called Freud, or Jung, or Adler, the old records are confused.... But this modern stuff is vitriolic. A System Executive can just talk to you for half an hour and you agree to everything he says!" Unfortunately no technical details are provided.

But in addition to these revelations, there is a copy of Pillengarb's revolutionary Bible, annotated in the margins by a System Executive, e.g.: "Freedom as an ideal is above reproach but the F.C. denies the sort of freedom that is prevalent today and leads only to a freedom to be inefficient, a freedom to wage war, a liberty to murder when the whim takes one, a freedom of thought that thinks only of self and self-aggrandizement and devil take everyone else." Reading these annotations, Vickery becomes half de-converted from Pillengard; whether this is an ironic confirmation of the "talk to you for half an hour" notion, or just a device to move the plot, is not clear (but I'm betting on the latter).

Elaine, who has been torn between heart and conscience, as Bulmer might have put it, finally blows the whistle on Vickery, and they are brought before the men in charge in the usual sort of plot-driven confrontation. As they are nominally being tried for subversive activities (Elaine having been deemed unreliable at this point), the *real* head cheese shows up and reveals that the F.C. has just been attacked by the menacing alien Mongs, and Vickery needs to go convince the Freedom Fighters that it's time for everybody to put aside their squabbles and fight the real bad guys. "'We'll win,' Elaine said. 'We'll win—because we'll be a team.'"

This story, remarkably, seems not to have made it to Ace Doublehood—I can't find an American edition at all, the *Science Fiction Encyclopedia* gives no alternative title, and its only reprinting seems to be as the title story of a Digit paperback collection.

Bulmer's "Trial" (23) may be his most engaging story in these issues, clumsy as it is. Harrington of the space navy or whatever is on leave, inherits his uncle's toy company, and is immediately dispatched to Terpsichore, which is covered in aggressive jungle growth. This appears to comprise a single plant that has spread over the whole planet and in which there is a complex ecology of predators and prey, including small sentient beings who never go down to ground level. Sound familiar? This is the November 1961 *Science Fiction Adventures*, and the first of Aldiss's "Hothouse" stories had appeared in the February 1961 *Fantasy & Science Fiction*. But little matter. The story moves on quickly, as Harrington rescues a couple of Terpsichorean kids and is, apparently, rewarded with a gift of Zana, vegetable creatures which, when trained and installed in toys, animate them. (This is so poorly explained that it's hard to tell if it's bad writing or if the story was edited with a hatchet.)

An evil industrialist starts pressuring Harrington to sell Zana in bulk so he can train them to run his factories (he can't just buy the already manufactured dolls—"The factory indoctrination wouldn't take," and soon enough they would be acting like animated toys again). If Harrington doesn't comply, he will be driven out of business. So he sells the man some Zana and then turns himself in to be prosecuted for enslaving intelligent aliens, risking the prospect of life on a "penal asteroid" and confusing the hell out of his defense lawyer, since he acts as if he wants to be convicted. (This plot device is apparently borrowed from Vercors' *You Shall Know Them* (1952), a.k.a. *Borderline*, barbarically retitled *The Murder of the Missing Link* for US paperback publication.)

The bulk of the story consists of Harrington's trial, and Bulmer displays the usual lack of understanding of how these things actually work (though I've seen a lot worse). The jury finds (a) the Zana are intelligent, but (b) he didn't enslave them. Unfortunately the interesting question of how one defines and recognizes intelligence gets superficial shrift—the trial witnesses just opine without discussion—and we never see enough of the actual behavior and characteristics of the Zana to care much about them or their status, unlike other stories on this general theme, like H. Beam Piper's *Little Fuzzy* and Heinlein's "Jerry Was a Man."

§

Lan Wright has a couple of lead short novels, done more slickly than most of Bulmer's. "The First Return" (**15**) is a modest thriller, much more readable than his leaden *New Worlds* serials, just don't think too much as you're reading. Dr. Kello is asked by Security Section Leader Garvey to do an autopsy, but then gets a message it's called off. Later, he meets the doctor who supposedly did it in his stead, but who knows nothing about it. Then he is struck from the rolls of autopsists. Naturally, he becomes an amateur detective, finds out that the dead man (whom he saw) is from the returned first interstellar expedition, supposedly quarantined safely on the far side of the moon. They've been taken over by alien symbionts, except for the ones who got out in a lifeboat, and the possessed ones have convinced the authorities that it's the escapees who are possessed and must be hunted down. Having learned this, of course, Kello doesn't do anything so rational as *tell* the authorities himself. He continues his gumshoeing, almost gets killed for knowing too much, etc. Apparently it never occurs to the authorities to put him under surveillance and tap his phone, so they would find out faster what was going on. Incidentally, the story takes place in Nairobi, but there is not a single African-sounding name on display (though some of the space crew have Asian names), and the only reference to African ethnicity is that one of the characters has a "uniformed coloured maid." So much for the literature of tomorrow.

Wright's "Should Tyrone Fail" (22) is a more overtly James Bondish novelette set on a fecund and vicious jungle world ("primeval horror," of course) with a single large domed city ("The facade of ease and elegance and luxury was a hard veneer for the rich, cut-throat world of trade and profit that was the reason for the Jewel City's being."). Tyrone is there because a spaceship has crashed somewhere in the jungle, and it's full of Rimrock:

> Rimrock—the fabulous mineral born in the heart of some exploding star aeons before and now spread like an asteroid belt around a vast, endless section of the Galactic Rim. Rimrock—ten times as hard as diamond, the ultimate in cutting capacity, the base for bearings in the engines of the new fleets of stellar ships, the priceless ornamentation of a few thousand pampered women, the rock that cost the life of a man for every pound that was mined—the new lodestone that lured men to a fortune—and to death.

All the movers and operators converge to find this bonanza, and Tyrone's going to be in the middle of it. ("Behind his laughing eyes Tyrone's mind was icy. There was about this stumpy, pudgy man with his bald head and sleepy eyes an aura of danger that could almost be smelt by a man with the right sort of intuition, and Tyrone was never one to ignore his own hunches.") Tyrone can play the game with the best of them. ("Tyrone sat quiet and studied the fat man through hooded eyes. He was smart all right—just as smart as Tyrone wanted him to be, and the grim elation he felt at Sedaka's summary could have no place in his facial expression.") It hurtles on in this vein—those quotes are all from the first eight pages of a 48-page story—to the predictable bloody contretemps in the jungle (the aforementioned "primeval horror" where somebody gets eaten every 20 paces or so). Something even graver than advertised is going on, and at the end the beautiful blonde conspirator proves to be an intelligence agent just like Tyrone and they're going to get to know each other on the trip back to Earth. It's perfectly slick and basically empty. Wright can crank these out in his sleep by now, and probably does. But he certainly makes a smoother job than Bulmer of "action-adventure against a science fiction background," in Carnell's phrase.

The same cannot be said for Wright's story "Transmat" (17), in which a lazy and corrupt bureaucrat in charge of a receiving station for goods teleported from Earth to a colony planet is beset with equipment failures, as incoming shipments are crushed or slimed with such unexpected items as heavy steel bars and decomposed rabbits, which also wreck the receiving units. This one is described by Carnell as an attempt at "sustained humor." It's sustained all right, far longer than its gimmick warrants, and the ultimate explanation is both predictable and as uninteresting as the protagonist's caricatured temper tantrums.

§

Robert Silverberg's novelette "The Wages of Death" (20), reprinted from *If* (August 1958)—the only reprint (or Silverberg story) in these issues, or during the rest of the magazine's life—is a smooth and professional job, not surprisingly. It is a capable story about some Loyalists—adherents to Earth—who are fleeing an edict that they must swear allegiance to the new independent government of their colony planet on pain of death. A bunch of effete intellectuals, they hire a real man's man to smuggle them across a couple of thousand miles of country to a rendezvous with their rescue craft. The protagonist learns not to be so effete en route, first killing their escort who is planning to collect their fare and then sell them to the Truthmen (the cops), and then deciding he's not really a Loyalist and is going to take the oath and work for the kind of planet he wants. There's a certain strawman quality to the story's argument, but it's considerably less cartoony than many of the other contents of the magazine.

Francis G. Rayer's novelette "Adjustment Period" (**16**) is another in his Mens Magna series, about the world-dominating supercomputer that talks like a bad movie: "'Your classification of me is incorrect,' the Mens Magna stated. 'My motivation is not derived from clockwork, and my primary function is not that of addition. Furthermore—'" Here we are dealing with Mens Magna in Space, with an instantaneous hookup to the mainframe on Earth. On a far planet, Earthfolks are trying to figure out why the otherwise benign natives are always stealing from them and then fervently denying that they have done it, and being highly offended at the accusation, and passing lie detector tests about it. There's another, less numerous, fiercer, and seldom seen alien race too, and an obvious explanation for the mystery. Rayer ignores the obvious explanation for a less obvious but more contrived one.

"Contact Pattern" (**19**) is another Mens Magna story, and one of Rayer's better-executed ones, though the premise is arguably fatuous: irresistible force versus immovable object. Somebody has invented an absolutely immovable force field (furious hand-waving in background), Mens Magna is having it installed over a colony planet's capital city because mysterious aliens keep buzzing it in their spacecraft. The protagonist, who is governor or director or whatever, gets the force field installed in a spaceship to facilitate the getaway of his plucky assistant who's got the goods on the crooked businessman who is extorting the colony government for millions. But the force field goes on over the city because of a fake alien alert, the shielded spaceship hits it and disappears, with assistant and evidence. Even Mens Magna is baffled. After several more melodramatic turns, the protagonist takes off in the *second* force-fielded ship, triggers the city force field, and finds himself several years in the future, coming down to land, with the first disappeared ship in sight too. What happened to the crooked businessman and his claim? Things look prosperous from the air, so everything must have come out all right. It's ridiculous on examination, but more carefully written than most of Rayer's stories and otherwise relatively clanger-free. Granted, that's praise only by comparison to a rather low standard, and I can't imagine these stories offering much encouragement to new readers.

§

So is there anything less generic and more distinctive among the longer fiction here? Yes, though that's not always such great news. Brian Aldiss's "A Touch of Neanderthal" (16) is one of his peculiarly sour stories, a sort of half-lampoon, cartoony without being funny. Anderson is dispatched to a planet from which no one returns, and discovers people looking and acting odd and menacing. For no reason anyone explains, on this planet people revert to their prehistoric ancestries, becoming either Neanderthals or Cro-Magnons. There is talk of the great division in human nature between Neanderthal magical thinking and Cro-Magnon devotion to cause and effect. Anderson takes refuge with a couple who, also for some unexplained reason, have not reverted and who also hate each other. The connection between these facts, if any, is not apparent. Aldiss is at pains to say how homely the woman is. At the end, Anderson and woman are going to escape to Earth in his spaceship, but they get into an argument, she runs back to her husband, and he reverts to Neanderthal. One is left wondering what the point is, other than a nose-thumbing *non serviam* to the prevailing To The Stars SF ideology—always worth a go, but Aldiss has done it so many times so much better that this one doesn't add much, and it seems particularly out of place in this magazine.

Aldiss himself seems to have been at best ambivalent about this story. In his collection *Intangibles, Inc.* (Faber, 1969), it is drastically "rewritten" (as the acknowledgments page puts it). In fact, most of the revisions to the story proper are just ordinary second-thought polishing, with a few trendy late-'60s intrusions (cigarettes have become "mescahales"; on Earth, at peace in the magazine version, the book has it that "the Have-Not Nations are fighting a conventional war against Common Europe. But our latest counter-attack against South America seems to be going well, if you can believe the telecasts."), and a few that are just incomprehensible. For example, the protagonist announces himself in the magazine as having come from Trotsky's Planet. In the book it's Lenin's Planet. Parse that, from the author of "Basis for Negotiation" and *Life in the West*!

However, Aldiss has now encysted the original story in a frame in which the robots who dominate the world after Nuclear Week and keep the surviving humans in a zoo are pursuing Anderson, who is the author of the story "A Touch of Neanderthal," because they don't understand what a story is and are trying to figure it out. In the course of the resulting bizarre conversation, Anderson says "The story was a lot of nonsense because I injected this Crow-Neanderthal theory, which is a bit of free-wheeling young man tripe." Now, he distinguishes between the limbic system and the neo-cortex, and says the former is the root of all our troubles. The automata vanish into the invospectra ("an entire new stratum of reactive quanta"), leaving the humans to flee the zoo if they wish and Anderson and wife to raise pigs. It's all a bit self-indulgent and patience-trying.

John Ashcroft's novelette "The Lonely Path" (**18**), by contrast, is a pleasantly naive story about space explorers who find a strange artifact on Mars, a high tower that also extends a long way under the ground and appears to be very old. The characters figure out how to get inside this artifact of the ancient Martians. Sanderson is snatched back into the very distant past where he encounters a robot called Guide, who explains that Mars is about to be comprehensively wrecked by a stray planet passing through the solar system, so the Martians have packed up and are ready to leave in their space fleet—to where, they don't know, but they're sure they'll find a place. But, it says, they're lonely, and want to know what happens after they're gone, so they've built this tower with time-travel installed and also with space-viewers that allow them (and their human guest) to see what's going on around the solar system. Sanderson permits them to record the entire contents of his mind. In return they will send him back to his present, in long temporal leaps so he can reconnoiter as he ascends. Also, Guide—not really a robot, but a Martian acting through one—finally shows himself. He's basically a rat, which triggers an ancient childhood phobia of the protagonist, but he gets over it quickly enough:

> Then the creature ran along his arm, clawing delicately at the fabric of his clothing to keep a grip, and sat on his shoulder and rubbed its side against his cheek like a contented cat. Sanderson thrilled to an almost physical sense of brotherhood, while his brain cleansed itself to [sic] poison that had clogged it for thirty years. He felt suddenly healthier.

When the last spaceship arrives, Guide scampers into it just before catastrophe strikes and Sanderson embarks for his home century. Channeling my inner 13-year-old, I'd say this story comes as close as anything in these issues to the magazine's supposed premise of entry-level SF comprising relatively simple adventure stories that evoke the lost sense of wonder. Ashcroft's name, by the way, is rendered as "Ashton" on the cover and table of contents, but correctly on the title page of the story itself. There was a *New Worlds* contributor named John Ashton, but his profile in *New Worlds* **78** (December 1958) makes clear that he is a different person from Ashcroft—though Carnell seems to have hopelessly confused them when the Ashton byline appeared again in *New Worlds* a couple of years later, as noted in Volume One.

Ashcroft's "No Longer Alone" (**21**) is, as the title suggests, a sequel to "The Lonely Path," though a distant one. Centuries hence, humans are spreading through the galaxy, mindful of the lessons learned from the Martians by way of the tower, and they intervene on a world where a couple of races (one green, one blue) are about to go to war over diminishing resources. Their planet is getting hotter, there's not enough water, and the humans are prepared to solve all their problems through such means as bringing in excess water from uninhabited planets if they'll accept the help and learn to live in harmony. This one is overly preachy and therefore a bit wearing, but still more palatable to my taste than some of the cardboard-valued epics of Kenneth Bulmer.

William F. Temple's "A Trek to Na-Abiza" (21) also delivers on the magazine's premises, a bit less naively than Ashcroft, and is one of the more enjoyable items in these issues, the sort of oddball item that usually tended to show up in *Science Fantasy*. Sherret is a crew member of a spaceship that has landed on Amara, which follows a complex orbit among three stars of different colors. Sherret is tossed off his ship for not following Goffism (in which everybody gets a chance to run things for a while) rather than Reparism (very hierarchical). He says he's neither, but to no avail, so he has to leave and hike a considerable distance to the *other* Earth ship on the planet. This sets the stage for a series of good-natured and bizarre picaresque adventures, Jack Vance Lite in spirit, which fulfill an unintelligibly cryptic warning given him by one of the alien species, and which I'm not going to recount in detail because somebody might actually want to read this story someday, unlike most of the other contents of these issues. This is the first of Temple's stories in the UK SF magazines that I have actually liked. It was Ace Doubled as *The Three Suns of Amara*, and P. Schuyler Miller (*Analog*, September 1962) aptly said: "Praise be that English writers haven't forgotten science fiction can be fun." (Of course he also said "Monsters, landscapes, people—all are utterly strange and totally believable at the time we encounter them." Well....)

John Kippax's novelette "Stark Refuge" (23) also fits the declared *Science Fiction Adventures* model pretty well: a spaceship struck by a meteor must land for repairs, but the only nearby stop is a closed planet. Its government relents and lets them land under strict conditions of isolation, which of course one of them breaches. The cover-up unravels. The planet is closed because its colonial masters, needing enough population to colonize, have manufactured androids who can't reproduce but aren't in on the secret until one of the crew sneaks away and tells some of the locals about his family. As one of the colonial administrators remorsefully confesses: "Think of the contradiction here. Beautiful, warm, eager, intelligent beings, who were denied one of the basic sources of human dignity, and happiness—the supreme joy of bringing forth their own children." Further: "It is against the will of nature." "Now, the news is everywhere. The people of Draneth know that they are not human. They have the terrible shock of finding that they are scientist's creatures. It is the end. The end." So they're going to shut the place down. And do what with the sterile androids? Doesn't say—one would think they would leave them in place. But: "There is no life, or progress here, now." God invoked, fade to black. However implausible the whole scenario is, it's well written and developed and free of the pulpy excesses of most of Bulmer's stories.

"The Game" (**22**) by David Rome—Australian David Boutland—is a bit excessive but doesn't suffer too much from it. It's an overblown melodrama featuring a sort of homicidal psionic dodgeball, in which Players telekinetically manipulate huge iron balls and try to kill the Scarlets, so named because that's what they wear in the arena. If the Scarlets manage to survive a few bouts, they supposedly retire reasonably well off on the remote worlds where most of them are from. Molineux is about to marry the daughter of a Game mogul, despite his revulsion against the Game. But he learns too much: the Scarlets really don't get paid off to live in ease, they are incarcerated in secret catacombs under the arena, as is Molineux when he stumbles on the secret, after apparently being betrayed by his fiancé. It all comes good in the end and he even gets his girlfriend back. This story actually works pretty well; enough happens, fast enough, to balance the mood of dystopian revulsion.[31]

§

The remaining shorter fiction is mostly so-so. The biggest name is Brian Aldiss, whose second story in these issues is the deservedly never-reprinted short story "Original Sinner" (15). It's a piece of hackwork, but high quality hackwork: a space-faring soldier gets overnight leave on Mars, looks up his old married flame and discovers her husband has died and she's free, but they only have the day and night and he'll never be back. Then leave is cut short and he's ordered back to his ship, resisting; but at least he's lived and fought back against his fate, however briefly. The pleasures of love are contrasted with those of drink and comics.

E. C. Tubb has several stories in these issues. His short story "Grit" (14) is one of his clawing-the-noir-walls jobs: a little intellectual nebbish is shanghaied onto the Long Drag, a ten-year spaceflight (from where to where, and why, is ostentatiously not explained), where the food is rotten and the crew is abused and the captain is a sadist. The nebbish gets scapegoated for some quasi-mutinous activity and "junkered," thrown out the airlock with five hours' air and shot full of some drug so "he ain't wholly a man no more." The bosun, who is the first-person ungrammatical narrator, recounts all this degradation and at the end has decided to stand up for once, and he's off to murder the captain and the officers. It's probably well done given its premises, but those are so over the top it's like an exercise in self-parody (in fact, maybe it is).

"Umbrella in the Sky" (18) is one of Tubb's occasional pieces of sociologizing, this one about industrial relations. The Sun is going to explode because of a swarm of contraterrene (anti-

---

31. Half a century later, of course, the mood of dystopian revulsion has become a major selling point to young adult readers of, say, Suzanne Collins' *The Hunger Games* trilogy.

matter) meteors heading for it. Earth's only hope is to build a large shield in space—the umbrella of the title, nowadays known as a soletta—but the construction is falling behind. Why? The protagonist is dispatched to find out. Well, the workers are making book on who will be the next to die and naturally this makes everyone work to rule and slow down. Of course there's an attempt on his life en route to uncovering this, otherwise the story would have been even more boring than it is.

The best of the lot is "Iron Head" (**16**), probably because it is overtly satirical. A cowpuncher for the Apex Delicacy Co. loses his job and can't get another because he's one of the few who can't learn telepathy. He signs up with the Guard, mercenaries that Earth hires out to keep its balance of payments in acceptable bounds. He quickly rises in the ranks to become emperor of the galaxy, married to a beautiful extraterrestrial queen he has conquered. His secret? If no one can read his mind, but the people around him can read the enemies' minds, that's quite a battlefield advantage. Tubb sends up all the clichés of mediocre space opera and keeps it short enough not to become wearing.

Several other Carnell regulars appear. John Kippax's short story "Last Barrier" (**16**) is about Kanov, a member of the Steel Legion engaged in colonial warfare, who is manning an outpost in the company of his dead brother. A mysterious figure who claims to be a general, and has the proper ID, shows up, and they engage in portentous conversation. The general is a veteran of campaigns including Gallipoli, Austerlitz, and Bunker Hill, none of which Kanov has heard of. The whole rationale for Kanov's existence and the Legion comes unraveled and Kanov dies begging for "resolution tablets" (for the general was a plant, of course). This is actually a more effective antiwar screed than it sounds in synopsis.

A. Bertram Chandler's "By Implication" (**23**), his only appearance in *Science Fiction Adventures*, is a didactic number in which a spaceship is hijacked by Martian rebels and the evil government is ready to destroy it complete with innocent crew and passengers. The fortune cookie please: You're a pirate if the government says you're a pirate. This one might go over well in Somalia if there were anywhere to publish it. Clifford C. Reed's "Ivory and Apes" (14), his last in the magazine, is an unpleasant item in which an alien freight operator is hauling some animal specimens to the home planet, with their alien captor and another passenger who proves to be a sort of animal rights type who believes that specimens should be put out of their misery, and schemes to accomplish that end. Of course the telegraphed revelation is that the animals are human beings. The Biblical title is a phrase from II Chronicles 9. 21: "Every three years once came the ships of Tarshish bringing gold and silver, *ivory and apes*, and peacocks."

There are several American authors here, though not to much effect. Robert Hoskins' "Weapon Master" (18) is a trivial item about a traveling salesman who shows up on a planet whose inhabitants are much exercised about their neighbors, and offers to trade them high-powered weapons for the small arms that they presently possess. As he's blasting off, they discover that the weapons are all duds; a pacifist, he's off to run the same scam on the neighbors. Jim Harmon's short story "Messenger Boy" (15) is the 5,271,009th variation on the arrogant and belligerent aliens who are outsmarted by the peace-loving ingenious Earthmen, built around a pretty unlikely gimmick; but that's no surprise, the likely gimmicks having all been used up long since. This is the kind of thing the US magazines were full of, except that by this point the US magazines have mostly died out and there's no room for mediocre specimens of hackneyed plots. Gordon R. Dickson's "The Amateurs" (19) is a pleasant item about four people who survive a poisoning incident on a spaceship; everybody else dies and they don't know how to run the ship; but they figure it out collectively by combining their various lower-level talents.

And then there's what must be a ringer: Tevis Cogswell, with his short story "Machine Record" (19), a farce about a mad scientist who has invented a machine with which he can destroy the world. He hires a political affairs researcher to help him achieve world domination; but nobody much is interested, so he eventually gives up. It's not really very funny, and the most interesting thing about it is the author's name. It's hard to avoid thinking that it must be a collaboration between Walter Tevis, who had several stories in the SF magazines from 1957 to 1961, and Theodore Cogswell, who was fairly prolific through the 1950s and into the very early '60s, and had a story in *Science Fantasy* the following year. Miller/Contento doesn't support this theory, but you know the one about absence of evidence and evidence of absence. The Internet SF Data Base says Tevis Cogswell is a pseudonym of Theodore R. Cogswell,[32] based on what is not stated.

And so to the (deservedly) Little Known Writers. Dale Hart's "Conquest by Proxy" (**19**) is an archaically silly item about colonists who accidentally find the last Martians, who just want to be left alone, but one of them is willing to advise the Earthfolk telepathically on how to deal with the problems of the Martian environment. This byline also appeared in *Fantasy Book* in 1949 and *Haunted* in 1964. Noel Baddow Pope has no other credits in the SF magazines than "The Thin Red Line" in **23**, and his middle name about sums it up: BADDOW! is *le mot juste*, as would be BARROOM! and THWACK! and other comic-book expletives, for this incompetently written alien combat epic in which the Terran combat team prevails over the savage Vhazas by painting themselves red, thus taking advantage of the limits of the Vhazas' visual system. Don't let anyone tell you SF is not a literature of ideas.

§

As previously noted, there is very little editorial matter in this magazine. In the entire two years, "The Editor's Space" appears just once, in **20**, in which Carnell professes to be horrified to find that the last editorial was over two years previously.

---

32. http://www.isfdb.org/cgi-bin/ea.cgi?94201 (visited 11/2/11).

He says: "Make-up of a magazine specializing mainly in long complete stories seldom leaves the odd page to fill." (That seems odd—one would think a few long items would be harder to fit in a fixed page count than more numerous items of varied lengths. Well, I've never edited a magazine, especially with 50-year-old technology.) He says the long stories are very popular, which gives him an opportunity to publish things too long for *New Worlds* as single stories and too short for two-part serials. He admonishes: "If you want to give the magazine a boost recommend it to a friend, *but don't let him borrow your copy!*" But this is followed by an unusually generous offer: send your friend's name to Carnell and they'll send a free sample. Carnell also touts some of the upcoming stories, which points up something unusual: this magazine has no "coming next issue" feature after issue **15** (until then, it appears on the inside front cover).

Advertising is essentially the same mix as in *New Worlds*. In addition to the house ads, the SF Book Club is the major advertiser, with full-page ads in **14, 16, 19, 20, 21,** and **23** (the inside front cover). Charles Atlas takes a page in **14,** the Rosicrucians do the same in **14** and **18,** and the International Correspondence School takes a page or the back cover in **17** and **18.** The BSFA takes half a page in **15, 16,** and **23,** and half the inside front cover in **19, 20, 21** and **22** (and there's an Eastercon notice in **13**). The magazine *Film User* takes half a page in **19** through **23,** usually on the inside front cover with BSFA. Odd items include Digit paperbacks on the inside back cover of **16,** the Pergamon edition of Tsiolkovsky's *Beyond the Planet Earth* (**17**), and the Psychology Publishing Company's prematurely New Age *Realization* (**19**).

"The Readers' Space" appears only twice in two years. In **13,** Julian Reid of Victoria, B.C., suggests an idea exchange, whereby readers who can't write would send their ideas in to the editor, who would farm them out to writers who can't think. Well, I caricature, but you get the idea. Carnell thinks it's a capital suggestion and the idea-wallah should get half a guinea for a gimmick and up to two guineas for plots, if and when used. He also notes the possibility of plagiarism allegations and says "the reader will have to trust the editor." Derek Blyth says Carnell's magazines "have the American market beaten wholesale."

In **16**, Derek Oldfield of Peterborough pooh-poohs Reid's notion of idea franchising, saying that gimmicks don't necessarily make plots, and the trend in SF is to use the SF background as a vehicle for stronger character development and less development of *science* fiction. About the field generally he says:

> What is disheartening is the growing trend of stories inferring [sic] that Man is the centre of the universe—the kind we turn to science fiction to avoid. Witchcraft (with the inference that it has some form of scientific basis), financial juggling and politics, sex and sadism in spaceships indistinguishable from tramp steamers at sea.... There seems to have been practically no attempt to follow up the path of true science fiction in recent years.

About this magazine, he says:

> Basically, I think you are on the right lines with *Science Fiction Adventures* although some of the recent stories have been singularly empty of any sustained plotting; on the other hand they have somehow begun to bridge the gap between the presentday clever-clever type of story and that left vacant in 1940 when World War II turned our values upside down. The pre-war stories provided that much-vaunted "sense of wonder" which disappeared after 1946 and I estimate the possibilities of *Science Fiction Adventures* sparking a similar sense of wonderment in newer and younger readers very high.

Carnell reports that Reid's idea trade suggestion "produced no replies or suggestions at all."

Also in **16**, Carl Frohmayer of Brooklyn is pleased to see the magazine and surprised it is now printed in England. He says the stories seem to be more mature than the old US *Science Fiction Adventures*. D. H. Lewis of Toronto is pleased to see *Science Fiction Adventures* and *Science Fantasy*, and are you the same people who used to publish *New Worlds*? Indeed we are, says Carnell; "a prolonged shipping strike here in 1956 successfully killed the Canadian edition of that magazine."

§

Science Fiction Adventures **24** through **32**, January 1962 through May 1963, continues its bimonthly schedule, 2/6 price, and 112-page size to the end, which is...right here. In **32** there is a "Special Notice" which says: "We regret to inform readers that this is the last issue of *Science Fiction Adventures* we shall be publishing, at least for the time being. Well-liked though the magazine is in certain circles, sales no longer warrant keeping it on our lists. Subscribers are offered a choice of either *New Worlds Science Fiction* or *Science Fantasy* to fill out their existing subscriptions. Write to us immediately with your instructions." Carnell assures readers that the latter two magazines are unaffected.

Too bad. After the longueurs of 1960-61, during which the magazine published very little worthwhile, this final year and a half represents a startling improvement. The enhancement is visual as well as verbal. 1962 begins with an eye-catching Brian Lewis rendition of a shiny modern building rising from water, with jungle fronds in the foreground, obviously illustrating the novella version of Ballard's "The Drowned World"—even though title and author do not appear on the cover. Perhaps Carnell thought the *Science Fiction Adventures* readership would not likely be attracted by the Ballard name? Probably not—most likely he just thought it was a nice picture that would go well unsullied by type, and he's correct. This cover has little to do with Ballard's vision of drowned London, but it's quite striking in its own right.

Lewis has three more covers, one in his uninteresting wax-people mode (25), of which more below, and two colorful abstracts celebrating but not really illustrating John Brunner's "Society of Time" series. After Lewis there are a couple of Lewis imitations by one Singleton (29 and 30), not on the level of Lewis's best but colorful and interestingly cryptic, and then the brief return of Gerard Quinn on 31 and 32, the former a painting that looks like a graphic depiction of multiple personality disorder, and the latter a more perfunctory but well enough done two-color drawing of a space scene. [33] (By this time all the Nova magazines have given up on painted covers, possibly to save money, possibly not.[34])

The fiction and the covers are basically what there is in these issues. There are no more editorials, letter columns, or articles. The advertising, as before, mirrors what's in *New Worlds* and *Science Fantasy*.

§

Leading off the first issue of 1962, "The Drowned World" is, in the context of the preceding issues, a reading experience comparable to rummaging through a pile of old newspapers and grabbing a live electric wire. Maybe that's the wrong metaphor for a story that so conspicuously foregrounds ennui, at least

33. See these covers at http://www.sfcovers.net/mainnav.htm, at http://www.philsp.com/mags/science_fiction_adventures.html#uk, and at http://www.collectorshowcase.fr/sf_adventures_page_2.htm and the following page.

34. Carnell disclaimed such a motive in connection with *New Worlds*, stating his belief that a more sedate cover would attract more readers. http://www.gostak.co.uk/skyrack/skyrack45.htm (visited 10/19/11). However, he also said a few lines later, "Cover illustrations already on hand for *New Worlds* have been switched to *Science Fiction Adventures*, where I do not contemplate a change of face." Nonetheless the change of face occurred.

early on—and in a magazine with **ADVENTURES** in the title! How oxymoronic is that? But Ballard's crisp and vivid writing, whatever else it may do, signals a refreshing level of professionalism as well as literacy compared to most of the contents of previous issues.

"The Drowned World" is also thoroughly over the top. Early in the story, here's the protagonist Kerans looking at a picture: "On another wall one of Max Ernst's self-devouring phantasmagoric jungles screamed silently to itself, like the sump of some insane unconscious." And a couple of pages later, his dream:

> As the great sun drummed nearer, almost filling the sky itself, the dense vegetation along the limestone cliffs was flung back abruptly, to reveal the black and stone-grey heads of enormous Triassic lizards. Strutting forward to the edge of the cliffs, they began to roar together at the sun, the noise gradually separating until it became indistinguishable from the volcanic pounding of the solar flares.

One can only wonder what readers accustomed to the likes of Lan Wright and Francis G. Rayer made of this (and in the absence of a letter column we'll never know). Ballard rather quickly thereafter reveals his theme, through the learned Dr. Bodkin:

> "The innate releasing mechanisms laid down in your cytoplasm millions of years ago have been awakened, the expanding sun and the rising temperature are driving you back down the spinal levels into the drowned seas submerged beneath the lowest layers of your unconscious. This is the lumbar transfer, total biopsychic recall. We really remember those swamps and lagoons."

Of course this would be quite familiar and comforting in substance to the Wright and Rayer fans, since it's just a more educated version of one of the lamer gimmicks of the genre—"racial memory." But it certainly sounds classier, if no more plausible, in the hands of a writer with an imagination and a style.

What happens in "The Drowned World," as most SF readers probably remember, is that global warming is in train and sea levels have risen, worse than any imaginings of Al Gore. Humans have retreated to the polar caps except for a few eccentric stragglers. Kerans, overtaken by the above-described dreams and the psychological resonances of the altered climate, eventually abandons his research expedition and heads south—"a second Adam searching for the lost paradises of the reborn Sun." But earlier, midway through, the charismatic scavenger Strangland—one of the larger-than-life hoodlums and mountebanks that figure in so many of Ballard's works—arrives, with his party of black retainers and herd of semi-tamed alligators, for a spell of looting and psychodrama. The major plot differences between the novella and the book version are a subplot in the book concerning one Hardman, another member of the research expedition not present in the novella, who is overcome by the dreams and Sun obsession and heads south before Kerans; a diving expedition into a sunken London planetarium in which Kerans nearly commits suicide by asphyxiation; and an episode in which Kerans is brutalized and left to die by Strangland and his crew.

But aside from this modest addition of incident, the book version is expanded pervasively throughout (looking to be a bit more than twice as long as the novella), sometimes just by the elaboration of detail, usually telling and amusing, and sometimes more substantively. For example, the above-quoted passage about "innate releasing mechanisms" in the novella is the first real intimation of the story's argument; in the book version, that passage is preceded two chapters earlier by a nearly three-page lecture by Dr. Bodkin about time-codes and spinal levels. In this more developed presentation, Kerans is much more aware of what is happening to him, much more of an agent when he, too, heads south. In general, the argument, the characters, the language, and the imagery are much better developed in the longer version. My first thought was that Ballard would have written the novel first (having already had one published) and then stripped down a shorter version for magazine publication, but having reread the novel, I am persuaded that Ballard expert David Pringle is correct: the novel was a later expansion and refinement of the magazine story. Unlike the novella, it reads like the work of a writer who now knows where he is going and takes the time to get everything right. This is not to disparage the novella version excessively, since it is surely the best, as well as the most out-of-place, piece of fiction this magazine published. But it remains a sketch for the novel.

§

The next issue (**25**) begins reasonably well with "Spoil of Yesterday," the first of John Brunner's Society of Time stories, set in a world in which the Spanish Armada prevailed and Spain dominates Europe, and the major North American power seems to be the Mohawk Nation. Time travel is accepted though allowed only to a tiny elite, while space travel is inconceivable. "Spoil of Yesterday" is the weakest of the stories, involving a mask brought without authorization from historic Mexico to Brunner's alternate present, where Don Miguel of the Society finds it in the boudoir of a dimwitted society lady, and is assigned to crack the case so it can be returned and the timeline preserved. It is murkily revealed that time-meddling generates alternate worlds, or maybe they are there anyway. En route Brunner invokes such pulpy crutches as drugs, antidotes, and hypnotism, and the characters are cardboard.

"The Word Not Written" (**26**) is considerably better. At a royal celebration of the Armada's victory, someone has the bright idea of bringing over some Amazons from one of the parallel worlds, and they naturally burn down the palace and kill the King. Don Miguel and the learned Father Ramon contrive to forestall these events, sending Don Miguel into the past and persuading the earlier Father Ramon to take his word for it that he will need to remove the responsible idiot from the celebration early, thereby creating a closed time loop. There is much meditation on how he keeps his memories of what have become non-events.

In "The Fullness of Time" (**27**), Don Miguel is on sabbatical in California when someone finds an anachronistic drill bit in a site that's been buried for centuries—clear proof that someone is stealing resources. But in fact something deeper is afoot, an attack on the historical foundation of the time-traveling society.

These stories were quickly collected into a fix-up Ace Double, *Times Without Number* (1962), which I found quite enthralling during my Golden Age of 13. It was later revised, Brunner's frequent practice. I find the stories less satisfying now because I have mostly lost patience with time travel stories even when they are well done—but they are still very readable and ingenious (especially the third), and among Brunner's best of the period.

§

The other major item of interest in these issues is Michael Moorcock's first long piece of SF (as opposed to fantasy, for he's well into the Elric stories by now), "The Sundered Worlds" (**29**), which is followed by its sequel or second half "The Blood Red Game" in **32**, the last issue. These novellas were later combined for book publication as *The Sundered Worlds*. This is a sort of cozy space opera in which the characters go careering about a universe—nay, multiverse—that seems about the size and navigational difficulty of a shopping mall parking lot during off hours. It gives every indication of having been written in a big hurry, without revision, probably most of it between 2:00 and 5:00 in the morning. Of course Moorcock even then, at age 22, was a glib and competent writer so the results are not as disastrous as could be expected, though there are moments that bear a certain resonance of the Rev. Lionel Fanthorpe:

> Renark and his companions watched the screens as the shoals of craft from Migaa entered the Shifter's area of space. After half-an-hour, when the ships were fairly close, the Thron ships came slashing upwards from their planet like sharks. There was an insane anger in their ferocity which, to Renark, was inexplicable. From other directions, a large, motley force of Entropium warships helped the Migaa craft dispose of the outnumbered Thron vessels.

Other passages bear a certain resemblance to E. E. Smith, or at least my 40-years-old memories of him:

> So a squadron of ships, each armed with the device, reached the Thron home-system of Yito and directed their beams on to the planets. At first they succeeded only in shifting the planets through their own space and time, altering the position of the planets around the suns, resulting in the equidistant position they now occupied. The Thron retaliated and the Shaarn hurled the Thron warships effectively, into another space-time continuum. Returning their attention to the system, they blasted it with warp rays time after time and, quite suddenly, it was gone—vanished from the Shaarn's space-time into another.

A mysterious solar system, the Shifter, pops in and out of our continuum every now and then, and people hang out on the nearest planet Migaa hoping it will show up—or, in Moorcockian rhetoric, "So the outlawed and the damned, the searching and the hunted came to Migaa when there was nowhere else to go—and they waited." Renark has an advantage, being a Guide Senser, which means he has some combination of Cosmic

Consciousness and GPS and sort of knows where everything is around the universe. When the Shifter shows up, Renark and his companions head for it, are attacked by one indigenous fleet and rescued by another, and wind up in the city of Entropium, a sort of Interzone of washed-up and on-the-lam characters.

Renark has been informed by refugees from yet another continuum that ours is doomed, and he's looking for the answer. He is directed to one Mary the Maze, who has been driven insane by her experiences exploring the "ragged planet," which apparently is partly in and partly out of this continuum and also is the site of the Abyss. So he heads out:

> ...Renark steered the ship through the malevolent currents of the unnatural area of space and howled his challenge to it. And the three words: "*I am human!*" became his war-cry as he used all his skill to control the metal vessel which plunged on the random spatial and temporal currents and forced its way through blazing horror towards the angry planet of Thron.

He and his companions are attacked by the Thron and befriended by the Shaarn, who we are told are "the golden children of the galaxy—the searchers, the wanderers, the enquirers. They were the magnificent bringers of gifts, bestowers of wisdom, dealers of justice." The Shaarn in turn direct Renark to the Ekiversh, glutinous metazoans who pass along some history lessons about the Dance of the Stars and the Dance of the Galaxies and urge him on to the lattice planet, giving him a "conservator" to protect him from the travails of Chaos. ("Once again they thanked the metazoa and then were plunging upwards, cutting a pathway of Law through the tumbling insanity of interstellar space.") At the lattice planet, Renark and friends find the Abyss of Reality and of course jump into it, are told that they are expected, and are ushered into the presence of the Originators, who note that they are late ("your rate of development was not what we had hoped"). The Originators explain that they have set things up so humanity can evacuate their universe for another one, and send Renark and company home to organize it, explaining in passing humanity's ultimate purpose: "To exist." (Thanks, guys.) But Renark stays behind and witnesses the end of our continuum (from where? "the void," of course).

"The Blood Red Game" picks up during the evacuation, led by Renark's pal "Asquiol of Pompeii, captain of destiny, destroyer of boundaries, becalmed in detachment...." (This is Pompeii the planet and not the buried Italian city.) However, the universe they are entering proves to be occupied, and the occupants are not pleased by the sudden appearance of the entire human species. But they're willing to be good sports about it—they offer to play the Game, winner take all, the Game being a sort of tech-assisted mind-wrestling. It's obvious what happens—lots of cliff-hangers, and the good guys beat the natives—so I won't recount the plot, except to note that Mary the Maze shows up again, lucid and married to a new central character.

These stories, with their extravagant rhetoric and plotting, are as sharp a departure in their way from the buttoned-down run of the *Science Fiction Adventures* mill as is "The Drowned World" (and, of course, as were the Elric stories from the run of *Science Fantasy*). As with "The Drowned World," it would be interesting to know how they were received at the time, but there's no letter column (and no issues to have one in anyway, after "The Blood Red Game"), and the book version was delayed by several years, by which time it had ceased to be so unusual. The only review of it in the SF magazines, quite brief, is by Langdon Jones in the Moorcock *New Worlds* (**149**), who says: "The main attraction of this story is the ideas with which it is packed.... Unfortunately the ideas tend to get slightly in the way of the story."

§

These Moorcock stories could of course be justly dismissed as a farrago of overblown clichés, but that would miss the point.

Moorcock's clichés are mongered with a color, vigor and enthusiasm largely absent from the more routine performances of the magazine's regulars, like Kenneth Bulmer. In fact, part of the appeal of these late issues is that Bulmer's work is much less dominant than formerly, comprising only two sequential novellas under the Nelson Sherwood pseudonym. The first is "Scarlet Denial" in 26, and brightness falls starting with the front cover, Brian Lewis at his worst, which portrays a cartoony-looking guy in a uniform smirking at another uniformed character who seems to have been given a hotfoot.

Which is exactly what's going on: the protagonist Carson, an orphan working as a spaceship-breaker, is pranking a member of the Galactic Guard. At about the same time, the local GG commander is assassinated. Carson's girlfriend is picked up, accused, and interrogated and tortured to death by Statque, the Bureau of Status Quo Enforcement—the bad cops. Carson goes berserk looking for the perpetrator, and runs through a door into what seems to be a chlorine atmosphere, is saved by a sort of giant Venus flytrap but is in imminent danger of digestion. His central nervous system is invaded by an ancient symbiotic intelligence that has been riding in a dragonfly analog also caught in the flytrap, and which quickly identifies itself as Sandoz, saving Carson and itself by switching his metabolism to anaerobic so he doesn't have to breathe the chlorine. It levitates them both to the spaceship that carried Sandoz to this planet, with his now deceased prior hosts, some centuries ago.

Can we say kitchen sink? This is the plumbing outfitters' showroom. It is disclosed that Sandoz is hunting his girlfriend (no details on gender arrangements among the symbionts, but "she" is the pronoun usage), from whom he has been separated for centuries. Carson, inevitably, is revealed as a very special person: the long-lost child of the former head of the Galactic Guard and one Helen Ross ("the loveliest creature that ever walked God's Galaxy")—"The union of the two, with scientific help, would produce an infant who would combine everything that was best and desirable in a Guards officer." Statque disapprove of this threat to their supremacy. In the midst of a ridiculously protracted shootout between the Galactic Guard and Statque, Carson and Sandoz levitate to catch the spaceship on which Sandoz's girlfriend is about to depart. In the meantime, Sandoz has developed a mildly petulant and supercilious personality. Having him as a symbiont sounds a bit like being infected with R2D2.

The next installment, "Scarlet Dawn" (28), is in similar vein. In the course of the hugger-mugger, Carson bumps into a woman who looks exactly like his deceased girlfriend, with whom he falls immediately in love, and who turns out to be the daughter of the *current* Galactic Guard chief and to have been bred to marry Carson and found a super-race of GG offspring. She not only likes the idea *a priori*, but also has been dispatched to vamp him out of harm's way. Events are manipulated so in the course of disposing of the Statque bad guys, Sandoz's girlfriend switches from the cat in which she has taken refuge to Carson's designated mate, setting up an interspecies *ménage à quatre* that will meld the personal and the political. Or as Carson telepathically pronounces to his mates at the end: "I think between us [sic] we're going to sort the Galaxy out."

En route to this resolution, Sandoz, through his physiological manipulations, first saves Carson from exposure to vacuum when he is tossed out the airlock, and then from a thermonuclear explosion during the final confrontation with the Statque and the man who tortured Carson's previous girlfriend to death. Which reminds me: in the second part, Bulmer introduces in passing a telepathic interrogation device. So why did Statque torture Carson's girlfriend to death while interrogating her, rather than using the device? Just for fun, I suppose. Maybe that's the point.

There is a certain ingenuity to this relentless bombardment of cliffhangers and other out-of-the-grab-bag plot devices, rendered in familiar breathless pulp style, like a ransom note taped together from clippings, and on some level these stories exemplify *Science Fiction Adventures*'s mission. But it's a pretty boring exercise—unlike Moorcock's stories, it's just not crazy enough—and I can't imagine that even in the early 1960s anyone took it as much more than a way of killing time. Rich Horton more or less concurs in his review of the Ace Double version, *The Million Year Hunt*, describing the first part as "a fairly minor effort" and the second as "by-the-numbers" and "not really as interesting." And he can't figure out the "Scarlet" titles any more than I can.[35]

§

Once past these conspicuous pieces, there is a readable B list of novellas and novelettes. Two stories in the same issue as "The Drowned World" are near-paradigms of the magazine's mission statement: entry-level presentation of the standard matter of SF. David Rome's novelette "Bliss" (**24**) is the generation starship fallen into decadence plot, with the denizens of the upperdeck lording it over the lowerdeck Plebs. The young upperdeck protagonist who can't stop asking questions ("'What are stars?' I persisted") and his Pleb girlfriend sit in the disused transmitters and are precipitated to another part of the Ship (pretty big ship, this one) where the people know what is going on. A rebellion is brewing to overthrow the Presidium and gain control of the Power Room and maybe try to land. First they must get through the Ruins, which are populated by a couple of varieties of nasty mutants (not Mutants, fortunately). These stock moves are made tolerable and even enjoyable by fast pacing and by Rome's brooding style, which becomes energetic and not just oppressive when there is enough happening fast enough.

The plot of Lee Harding's "Pressure" (**24**) is equally familiar in broad outline: in the future, everybody takes vitamin supplements by order of the government, but our protagonist—another one who can't stop asking questions—has stopped taking them to see what will happen, and begins to realize how crowded,

---

35.   http://www.sff.net/people/richard.horton/aced57.htm   (visited September 5, 2011).

regimented and oppressive his society is, what meaningless makework people's jobs are, etc. And of course the denouement and revelation: he decompensates, winds up in a mental hospital, and then the folks in charge show him what's really going on and tell him "We need every rebel we can get." Not unlike Rome, the author's habitual overwriting becomes a feature rather than a bug when the action is moving fast enough, e.g.: "He ran and ran, faster than the whirring plastic strips themselves, weaving his way through a barrage of noise, wading through the molten symphony of discord when the going got heavy. Sound had never assaulted him with such force. His mind was a raw, gaping wound reeling under the impact of the snarling, snapping noise the City had unleashed upon him." Etc. There is similar appeal, too, in Philip E. High's "Blind as a Bat" (**25**), a bracing space war story saved from intolerable geekishness by fast pace and High's no-wasted-word style.

John Rackham's long novelette "The Rainmakers" (**30**) is an agreeable piece of retro space opera, what Kyril Bonfiglioli would later call a "solid-fuel job." Mars needs water, and the characters are Martian colonists bringing home big chunks of a huge ice asteroid by brute rocket force—except this crew gets cleverly entombed in a 90-foot-diameter chunk by a nut case who is jealous of one of the crewmen and his fiancée. But the joke's on him, because the fiancée is on the ship, having switched places with one of the crew to be with her intended. Frantic struggle to escape the ice ensues, involving science that most fourth graders could probably follow, and character interplay ditto. This would have sat perfectly well in *Startling Stories* of 1952—and that's close to the definition of success for this magazine.

Equally agreeable is Richard Graham's "Breakdown" (**31**), which connects several familiar dots, proceeding from "The Machine Stops" through "Nightfall" through..."The Last Question," I guess, with another purposeful or accidental stop near the beginning: "Without any fuss, the readings were going down." In the future, machines run everything. While there are Maintenance men, their duties seem mostly ceremonial and they don't really understand what's going on. One day it all stops. Panic and irrational aggression ensue. But one of the Maintenance men doesn't give in, finds the emergency flashlights and rations, and journeys into the deep tunnels, where he discovers that the computer in charge of everything has achieved consciousness and doesn't see any point in continuing its useless rituals. So he finds the input device and persuades the computer by Cartesian and Socratic means that humanity exists, then bribes it to turn the lights et al. back on with the prospect of a continuing flow of information.

§

Things go downhill in various directions among the remaining longer stories. John Brunner's "Jack Fell Down" (**31**) is a clever nice try that somehow misses fire, probably because it tries to cram too much instruction into novelette length. Starting as a murder mystery—who caused a member of an interstellar negotiating team to fall a couple of thousand feet into the ocean on Earth?—it turns into a sociological one—why is one colony planet resisting the construction nearby of a "builderworld," a sort of technological cornucopia that will bring Earth-style prosperity? After a few *pro forma* plot twists the protagonist figures it out and explains it to everyone. This is an exercise in *Analog*-style didacticism and very likely was rejected by that magazine.

W. T. Webb's novelette "Earthmen, Farewell" (**28**) starts out reasonably promisingly. The colony planet Ecti exports the fabulously valuable shed pelts of the indigenous and maybe sort of intelligent "goldies," but someone has killed a dozen of the goldies for no apparent reason. Detective Inspector Knox from Earth, who would really rather retire, is on the case, finding the colony divided between the respectable types who are working to bring Free Enlightened Democracy (for the humans, that is), and the low-lifes and no-goods who live in Shedtown and are the obvious suspects. This adequately-begun police procedural is aborted by an attempted onslaught by the Shedtowners and the appearance of the legendary giant goldie, who announces that he or it is the "emanation of their group-mind" of the goldies, and their ancient and mysterious artifact is really the spaceship they rode in on, and they've had it with humans and are heading out. Oh, and the dead goldies killed themselves when the well-intentioned Security Officer rounded them up to start an experiment in goldieculture. Inspector Knox, who has taken up with the local biologist and goldie-admirer (Astra, no less), submits his report and declares his intent to settle in and help make Ecti a place the goldies would like to come back to. This piety may be admirable in principle but doesn't do much for the story.

Alan Burns contributes the genially ridiculous "Placebo" (**30**), a novelette which begins with the protagonist, who we are told is a "watcher," banging up his aircar on the moor and taking refuge with Meg, who is a witch and prone to saying things like "Some folk prefer me to the doctor. The simple folk believe what I say, and I think better of my brews and drenches than packets of pills from the World Health Authority." He explains that he was drawn to this district by something strange, but that he has lost his weapon. Going into town, he learns it will take a while for his car to get fixed, and decides to look for a job, getting one at a chemical factory opening up in an abandoned distillery. He also finds a room, and shortly sees that the land-lady's young daughter has contracted Cher, an extraterrestrial disease (stop snickering). Turns out the chemical factory is run by aliens spreading this disease so they can offer a cure which will make humans vulnerable to mind control. The watcher knows, they know he knows, but they let him continue in his new job and sabotage their efforts. Meanwhile, he has enlisted Meg as a confederate to save the child from Cher: "'Get professional,' she told me. 'I can follow.'" So he explains:

> "Life force emanates from the prefrontal lobes of
> the brain in certain cells which are not detectable by

present-day apparatus.... Cher is caused by the dormant cells being awakened by a resonator unit. Only a small charge, given out as a beam, is needed.... The rogue life force has to be polarised long enough for the cells that give it out to die, just as the brain cells normally die if air or blood is cut off to them. One of us must believe that Jeannie will live, that is our polarising unit, the other must believe that she will die, and that will complete the cancelling."

Fortunately they don't have to click their heels. There's plenty more, but hardly worth bothering with. The aliens are vanquished and the watcher (who is revealed about halfway through not really to be the watcher, but the vehicle for the watcher, which is a disembodied intelligence that comes and goes) discovers that Meg is perfectly suited to be his new weapon, serving as a sort of psionic amplifier. Happily ever after, etc.

Burns has another story earlier in these issues. "Deviant" (25) is a benign piece of social work. In the future, there will be psi-talented mutants called devs, who will have to work for Deviant Control so everybody else will feel safe. A group of devs rescues an adolescent girl from being raped in an alley and takes her on as an assistant to their "de-junglising" survey of a planet slated for colonisation. Of course she turns out to be a dev too, with a talent for making friends with all the deadly fauna; with her help they find the intelligent life that will save the jungle, and lessons are learned by all.

A couple of the other novelettes are repellent in ways that transcend their literary qualities or lack thereof. Joseph Green contributes one of the mellower apologies for genocide in "The Fourth Generation" (30), in which a crash-landed group of interstellar colonists yearning for rescue is beset by the Uglies, who have faces like wolves but enough intelligence to make some artifacts. The two main characters are following a pack of Uglies who have snatched the girl they both covet, referred to only as the Redhead; a fate worse than death is suggested. They rescue her, but on their return no one pays any attention because the lost colonists have been found, and rescue is in the offing. This is not what our heroes have in mind: "We had barely touched the surface of what this planet had to offer. With a little help from Earth in the matter of weapons and power equipment, we could expand out over the face of this bountiful world, wiping out the Uglies and claiming it for humanity." (Hey, why not wipe them out, they really are ugly, they don't deserve a planet, or life.)

Lan Wright closes the show with "A Task for Calvi" (**32**), the final story in the final issue, one of his well-machined but formulaic thrillers, and once more his crypto-fascist tendencies come to the fore. Mr. Calvi of the Stellar Bureau is on a distant planet on a mission to meet somebody, is subject to a mysterious telepathic attack that disables his telepathic implant, the somebody he's to meet doesn't show, various people are killed, somebody tries to kill Calvi, Calvi follows and is followed, threats and warnings are issued, the local law enforcement honcho is suspicious, and here's what all these standard-issue moves boil down to: another member of the Stellar Bureau is about to sell them all out by disclosing the secret of interfering with the Bureau's communication (like the telepathic attack that Calvi experienced). It seems that only the Bureau can communicate across interstellar distances and hence is the secret master of everything, and this betrayal has to be stopped, by violent means if necessary. In fact, preferably so, it seems. As Calvi has already explained: "'The law,' sneered Calvi. 'The law is hamstrung by its own inefficiency. Langert, space is too big and planets too insular for the law to operate with any speed or efficiency. You know that—every Law man admits it, yet nothing has been done. The Bureau is the one thing that keeps the planets of Mankind stable—'" And again, talking to the local lawman about a particular bad guy: "If you get to him first he will be arrested, tried, recommended for psychological treatment. There will be legal battles because he is not a citizen of Norval. There will be postponements, delays, appeals—all the sordid paraphernalia of your kind of law and order, and then, in a year or two, he will be free."

§

There are a couple of at least noticeable debuts in these issues. Steve Hall's first story in the SF magazines is "Einstein's Universe" (25), a contrived but painlessly readable time travel piece about a sort of mad scientist who thinks he has found the end of the world, not too far off, but the explanation is more prosaic. It doesn't help that the protagonist, the mad scientist's friend, is an SF writer who name-checks van Vogt's Nexialists.

Hall's "Takeover Bid" (27) is much more ambitious, almost ludicrously clumsy, but nonetheless readable and modestly clever. It starts with a portentous prologue from the dawn of time that recounts the formation of Duomatter, molecules comprising both matter and antimatter, and the arrival of a few atoms of it on the primordial Earth, where in the fullness of time they wind up in the sample Tony uses to demonstrate an induction furnace at a trade fair. It explodes, and Tony awakes to find that he is inhabited by a telepathic symbiont, the Multiman. This entity has either replaced or invaded his white cells, and is capable of spurring him to great physical feats, or paralyzing him so he can't take risks that would endanger the Multiman. (Whether the symbiont *is* the Duomatter or was merely created or transmitted in some fashion *by* the Duomatter explosion is not explained.)

Pat, the good-looking assistant who was standing next to him at the trade fair, got a dose too, and the Multiman and its Multi-other half decide that these human characters should marry so the Multis can reproduce. Pat has doubts, but these are resolved after Tony defeats the Multiman's instinct of self-preservation and, now as the Integrated Man, rescues her from an about-to-burn wrecked car, demonstrating his retention of free will. Interestingly (or not), the Multiman uses a virtually identical plot device as Bulmer's "Scarlet" novellas. These ran in the issue before and the issue after, so one obviously did not influence the other. I suspect both were at least partly inspired by Hal Clement's *Needle*, a 1949 invaded-by-symbiont novel which was published in the UK by Gollancz the year before these stories were published.

Hall next appears in **29** with another novelette, "The Third Law," published under the pseudonym Russ Markham for no apparent reason. This one is an inept Asimov rip-off in which the Third Law is tweaked but the first two Laws of Robotics are more or less as Asimov prescribed them. Here, the robot has killed somebody. How could that be under the Laws? The contrived explanation is revealed through that favorite lazy writers' plot device, a trial—in this case the trial of the robot for murder. There is plenty else wrong with this story, though as with "Takeover Bid" its faults seem to be the sins of enthusiastic amateurism rather than of cynicism or haste.

Hall sold 20 stories to Carnell, and none to anybody else, from 1962 through 1964, and then vanished from the field, in which he is unanthologized.

Of greater world-historical significance, I am sure, is John Baxter's first published story. "Vendetta's End" (**29**)—the first of eight stories and a novel in Carnell's magazines and their successors—is immediately distinguishable from the rest of the contents of *Science Fiction Adventures*: it's denser and more pretentious. The paragraphs are visibly longer, and the beginning is positively bulging with set-up:

> The Houses of Parliament in New London was one of those curiously incongruous buildings inevitable in a city which has been rebuilt sometime during its history. Some enterprising architect had visualised a new Acropolis, cool and aloof, with the city sweeping up to it as if in worship. The final effect, however, reminded one of a dowager duchess knee deep in dirty water.

Baxter introduces his character Jaime Hilton: "His face set deeper into its characteristic hardness. There was great power and a little brutality in the manner of this tall spare man—one realised without being reminded that his would be a feared enmity." Yes, yes, we surrender! You can write better than Kenneth Bulmer! Now get to the point!

Once one gets past the ostentatious scene-setting, it's a pretty stock story. In the future, everything is dominated by vicious family cartels and in particular the rivalry between the Hiltons and the Waldens, which manifests itself in a duel every year. Jaime is on his way to the dueling grounds, where he shortly discovers that his opponent is "a young and beautiful girl." She came because nobody else from the family would. So of course (after he has knocked her unconscious and she's revived), he unveils his plan to end this futile bloodshed, and she is charmed. As they leave the dueling park, where the families are assembled at the gate to greet the surviving champion, he lags behind, then cuts off her head in view of her relatives, and easily kills the Walden patriarch when he attacks in a rage, leaving Hilton as unchallenged Master of the Universe or whatever. Fade to black and a quote from Machiavelli, with Hilton's wingman reaching for his tape recorder: "He had history to write."

So here we have another point on the line between "The Cold Equations" and "A Boy and His Dog," in which tough-minded auctorial sophistication is demonstrated by ostentatiously killing women characters. Baxter gives the impression of a writer on a mission, ready to show the old dogs how it ought to be done, and in fact he had just published a nearly eight-page manifesto in *New Worlds* **122** in Carnell's series of guest editorials. Of course if you actually read the eight pages, it's quickly clear that what he has written has not much to do with what he advocates: "We can see in science a new kind of beauty."

> We should trim our plots of the outdated thinking that motivates them. Stop worrying whether our stories "mean" anything: the beauty of art is "meaning" enough. Stop worrying if the characters "stand up and

cast a shadow"—stop worrying about character development at all if you like....

§

The best of the shorter stories is probably Harry Harrison's "War with the Robots" (27), not a reprint, unlike some of his other contributions to Carnell's magazines. This one is early-Philip K. Dick-ish in theme if not in tone: soldiers and their robots are fighting a grim and apocalyptic war underground against the other side and *their* robots. The foe's robots are about to make our characters' base uninhabitable with various ingenious remote attacks. Trapped, the soldiers have no alternative but to follow a disused tunnel towards the surface, where they find some people trying to farm as the robot-guided missiles sail overhead, and an envoy of the Enemy looking for someone to surrender to—but it doesn't matter, because at this point nobody can stop their robots from fighting, or even communicate with them.

Barrington J. Bayley continues his stealth SF career with two stories under his pseudonym P. F. Woods, again for no discernible reason except possibly to shake off the taint (if any) of his prior work in *Authentic* and in *Vargo Statten* and its heirs. He did not use his own name in the Carnell magazines, reclaiming it only after Moorcock became editor of *New Worlds*.

Bayley is a refreshingly odd writer even for SF, and these stories are no exception. "Fishing Trip" (26) is about a couple of men (one of them a physicist who can't get a job since he punched out a Director of Sub-Nuclear Research, the other an ordinary nebbish) who are engaged in particle monitoring or something beyond the orbit of Neptune, and mainly drinking and wisecracking a lot. They encounter a large object, match velocities, find it has no mass (how? they read the massometer, of course) and doesn't conduct sound. The ex-physicist tries to drill a hole in it and his drill bit comes out the other side, fifty yards away. Then his drill and body start to distort and to be drawn towards the drill hole. Conclusion? There's no space in there, but space is now flowing into the hole. It's like a ship floating on space, and now it's leaking. So they get drunk and have a fistfight and the ex-physicist heads off to go into the place with no space, but before he can get into it, it sinks—"That is, she took on greater, more meaningful proportions, became more majestic.... Slowly, the true nature of the vessel heeled over into the sidereal universe as currents of space swirled in and around her." And there's the drowned crew and the noble passengers, about 30 feet tall.

This is followed by "The Radius Riders" (27), a geekily and clearly intentionally retro story—maybe intended as a Jules Verne pastiche—about "the subterrene vessel *Interstice*." "We were jubilant. We had no suspicion, as we approached the West Coast, that a grave misfortune was soon to befall us, provoking us into reckless folly, and causing us to be caught helpless in the grip of the mighty terrestrial planet." They discover they can't surface as planned—there's a field that would disrupt their polarisors! So they go deep, heading for the center of the earth, hoping to come out on the other side, only to discover (after some pitched battles with "intra-Earth intelligence" in their own matter-penetrating vessels) that they don't seem to be getting anywhere. Captain Joule (!) figures it out—geological relativity! "Matter is a distortion of space. As matter becomes more concentrated... so the space it occupied becomes more concentrated.... Within the Earth, space itself is compressed in proportion to density. What from the surface looks like an inch, might really be a thousand miles. The Earth's radius is the same at all levels—we shrink as we enter denser matter, so it always looks the same. There's always the same distance to go." When the vessel finally emerges, after centuries or millennia, there are 11 light-years on the odometer.

Several more of the short stories are of at least some interest. Michael Moorcock's "Going Home" (25) precedes the two novellas discussed above, and in fact seems to be his first published SF story (as opposed to fantasy) save for his pseudonymous collaboration in *New Worlds* with Barrington Bayley ("Peace on Earth" as by Michael Barrington (**89**)). An Earth colony sends a ship back to Earth to find out why their ancestors were sent so far away; nobody wants to tell them. They finally wring out the answer, that their ancestors were the last incurably neurotic or otherwise disturbed people on Earth, and since then Earth has been free of craziness; but it's also sunk in mediocrity, so they're all glad to be heading back to their colony. It's entirely too long for its didactic point, and is told in an unconvincing and stilted faux-*Planet Stories* style completely inappropriate for its content, but even then, and when making misguided choices, Moorcock was a more competent writer than many of his competitors in these magazines.

Equally pastiche in style is Sydney J. Bounds' "Out There" (**28**), which features a man whose obsession is to hook up a radio telescope to a television receiver, and winds up summoning Something slimy and frightening, which fortunately dies and starts decomposing immediately, but the protagonist remembers that men are building rockets... "—and all the while, something waited, out there." The retro feel of this piece is reinforced by the fact that the character's name is Ayrton, suggesting it's a purposeful, not accidental, homage to John Russell Fearn via his pseudonym Thornton Ayre.

Mark Streeter's "The High Edge" (**29**) is more contemporary in approach, though now it is a sort of museum piece of Cold War qualms. The captain of a nuclear-armed submarine has been dispatched to the deeps with a safe full of sealed orders, to be opened daily, which say: "Manoeuvres—none, drills—none, maintenance—as needed." To make a long and overwritten story short, Cap'n goes nuts from boredom and anxiety and eventually shoots off all his nuclear missiles, which prove to be dummies, and the whole enterprise is revealed as a psychiatric test. This is Streeter's only credit in the SF magazines, though Miller/Contento notes "They Who Must Hide," a short story in something called *International Storyteller Omnibus* 3 (1964), which is the only SF issue of this series and contains 19 short stories by writers unfamiliar in the SF genre.

Claude and Rhoda Nunes' "Inherit the Earth" (31) is a rather meandering but agreeable short story on a familiar theme: a man buys some unusually animated, seemingly sentient, dolls for his child, they develop personalities, but have to be left behind when the family emigrates to the stars to avoid the coming war. Soldiers take over the house, get along fine with the dolls and are actually a bit humanized by them. When they move on, it's revealed that the dolls are variant humans genetically engineered to be radiation-resistant... hence the title.

§

And finally to the dregs. David Rome, author of the much better "Bliss" discussed above, delivers a clinker in "Confidence Trick" (27), which musters all his overbearing stylistic and attitudinal resources in service of a very silly story. In the spacefaring future, distressed spacecraft are rescued by tele-kinesis—to wit, the Telekinetic Recovery Corps—but an arrogant, lip-curling R-ship skipper gets there first, only to find he can't do the job with his machinery. A fistfight ensues, a Corps guy arrives and sorts him out telekinetically. Unfortunately the spaceship is still stuck in the mud, seemingly forgotten.

Colin Denbigh's "Walk to a Star" (30) is a prehistoric epic, in which the characters say things like "Long ago was my first walk. That time the Star looked into my belly and sent a spirit. It was Dan, who was eaten by the fish-with-teeth. He was a good boy. He had nice brown hair." Prehistoric then turns out to be posthistoric in the entirely predictable end of the piece. Finally, Peter Vaughan's fatuous "Foolproof" (31) is a gimmick on a familiar theme: spaceship won't go when you push the button, why? The computer's developed its own agenda, of course.

§

So what, in the end, did *Science Fiction Adventures* add

up to? Mike Ashley says in Tymn/Ashley that it "contained a greater percentage of more enjoyable and memorable stories than any other British magazine." We beg leave to differ, albeit with qualifications. *SFA* was at best a mixed bag, in terms both of its explicit agenda and in the simpler terms of the quality of the material it published. Carnell set out, he said, to publish an entry-level magazine, by implication directed at younger readers: an "introductory medium" in which "the formula for all the stories will be action-adventure against a science fiction background" (*New Worlds* **68**).

Certainly a number of stories filled this bill nicely, notably some or all of those by Lee Harding, David Rome, John Ashcroft, Wynne Whiteford, John Rackham, and Richard Graham. But much of the "action-adventure" material was entirely too formulaic, often drearily and carelessly written, indifferent to setting, and laden with clichés, sometimes wearyingly cynical, displaying little either of the ingenuity or the idealism that could be expected to draw intelligent younger readers to SF. Much of the reprinted US material in the early issues, and much of the prodigious production of Kenneth Bulmer and the *oeuvre* of the less prolific Clifford C. Reed, fits at least part of this description.

Of the stories that escape this indictment, a number were a poor fit to the magazine's mission statement for other reasons, meritorious or interesting though they may have been. White's tricky "Occupation: Warrior," Tubb's stylized "Galactic Destiny" and lampoonish "Ironhead," Aldiss's peculiar "A Touch of Neanderthal," and most especially Ballard's "The Drowned World" fall into this category. Possibly the most successful in fulfilling *SFA's* mission in a manner agreeable to the broader SF audience as well were Temple's "A Trek to Na-Abiza" and Brunner's Society of Time stories. The latter, under their fix-up title *Times Without Number*, along with the novel-length expansion of "The Drowned World," have proved the most lasting works to originate in *Science Fiction Adventures*.

3: *NEW WORLDS*: MARKING TIME (1962)

New Worlds enters 1962 looking good, with Gerard Quinn's striking black and white rendition on the cover of **114** (January) of Sector General hanging in space.[36] It is followed over the next several months by three of Brian Lewis's best-composed and most colorfully surreal covers and a pleasantly sketchy one by Enrique, with the only clinker being an ill-conceived effort on **116** by Quinn to portray someone with a head full of recorded alien personalities.[37]

In midyear, however, the bottom drops out of the front as it were, and painted covers are abandoned entirely in favor of black and white photos against a colored background—photos that are poorly reproduced and mostly not very interesting in the first place (drab, shrunken author photos; a publicity still of Boris Karloff hosting an SF TV show; and a shot of Arthur C. Clarke receiving an award). Note particularly the covers of **121**, with murky postage-stamp-sized author photos and short dull story blurbs ("Alien on Earth. Alien Psychology. Future Earth."), and **122** (similar but murkier and duller). Some grudging kudos are due to the cover of **125**, picturing Colin Kapp, with pipe and pompadour, in front of some gigantic industrial installation (oil

---

36. See these covers at http://www.sfcovers.net/mainnav.htm or http://www.philsp.com/mags/newworlds.html.

37. Broderick disagrees, finding this image highly effective—not great art, but good cover. Not as appealing as Lewis's **115**, **117** and **119** covers, admittedly.

refinery?), and Francis G. Rayer, about to plug something into a truly alarming array of now-antique electronic gadgetry.

I had assumed that the reason for this change was to cut costs, in the absence of any comment or explanation by Carnell. However, there is some background on this subject in the fanzine *Skyrack*.[38] First, concerning the Enrique cover, from *Skyrack* 44: "Harry Douthwaite reports on *New Worlds*: The recent cover on *New Worlds* **118** (by Enrique) was bought from an agency which handles a number of Spanish artists and on the day after publication Carnell received three phone calls, five letters and two personal callers, all praising the cover. Ted says that he will be buying others and has on hand two completely revolutionary lay-outs. It will be interesting to see the final outcome of this experimentation."

But in the next *Skyrack*:

E. J. CARNELL, editor of the Nova chain, noticed that in the last issue Harry Douthwaite inferred that Ted is experimenting with new art cover layouts and so Ted writes: "I'm not. One of the experimental covers was the July one with the Karloff TV photograph. This will be followed from time to time by other photographs, either from films, TV or pictorial articles, when possible. The second cover layout is on the August issue and once again dispenses with cover art. I know that there will be howls from some quarters but I have a strong line of reasoning behind this radical change, primarily that over the years a vast number of ordinary s-f readers (other than regular magazine readers) will not pick up an s-f mag because of the cover picture. To date, about 100,000 people have bought *Penguin S.F. 1*, edited by Brian Aldiss and I feel that many of those people will be tempted to purchase *New Worlds* from the bookstands if they see a sedate non-pictorial cover.

---

38. Available at http://www.gostak.co.uk/skyrack/ (visited 9/10/11).

We shall see. Cover illustrations already on hand for *New Worlds* have been switched to *Science Fiction Adventures*, where I do not contemplate a change of face. This means that at least two Gerard Quinn paintings will appear on that magazine. I have also found another new artist named Singleton so Spanish artist Enrique is not likely to have anything coming up for a long time, if at all."

And, indeed, he did not—the **118** cover is apparently his only appearance on an SF magazine.

I can't help thinking that Carnell missed the point a bit in contrasting *New Worlds*' sales with those of *Penguin SF 1*. But whatever the reason, *New Worlds* goes instantly (with the vivid exception of Lewis's cover on **119**) from a rather spiffy magazine to a shabby-looking one. Had the photos been in color and better reproduced, they might have worked better—though they still would not have been very interesting. The covers are the only visible sign of decline—the page count stays the same (128 exclusive of covers), as do the schedule (monthly) and the price (2/6). But the covers make a big difference, and one suspects they contributed to the magazine's ultimate failure notwithstanding Carnell's professed rationale.

The other thing that fades during 1962 is Carnell's editorial presence. The era of guest editorials, begun late the previous year, continues, and Carnell has only one editorial the whole year, though he does contribute some very brief book reviews, plus praiseful reviews of *The Day the Earth Caught Fire* (**114**) ("One scene here alone is worth the price of admission as the beatniks go berserk in Chelsea"), *The Pit and the Pendulum* (**115**), and the ABC series *Out of This World* (**120**).

This last is four pages long and more of a puff piece than a review, since Carnell doesn't seem to have viewed any of the episodes at the time of writing. This is consistent with the boosterish preoccupation he has periodically shown with film or TV SF (except when it's really awful, in which case he takes it quite personally). In addition to the cover still and Carnell's article, the back cover and inside back cover of **120** are given over to stills and PR shots from the series, and show host Karloff gets the *New Worlds* Profile in **121**, extending over *both* front and back inside covers. The most interesting points to be found there are that Karloff loathes the word "horror" and prefers "macabre," and thinks SF is a "natural development from the macabre stories of a generation ago." He and the producer add that the greatest difficulty in doing SF for TV has been "learning the vocabulary of science fiction writers," with terms being seen differently by script writers, directors and actors, requiring development of a common understanding before shooting started.

There is also a bottom-of-the-page squib in **124**, seemingly editorial matter and not paid advertising:

NEW BBC SERIAL:

Provisionally planned to start on November 8th is the first of a four-part, 45-minute serial entitled *The Monsters*, based on the possibility of prehistoric monsters still surviving at the bottom of the Great Lakes. Produced by George Foa, directed by Mervyn Pinfield, and written by Evelyn Fraser and Vincent Tilsley, the story centres round Professor Cato (played by Robert Harris), a former Chemical Biological Warfare expert, who, disillusioned by modern methods of destruction, becomes a violent nuclear disarmer. Once over that hump, the plot should thicken rapidly.

"Hump" indeed. Violent nuclear disarmers? Like those old ladies who sneaked into a missile base and banged on the missiles with hammers? Early in 1963, Carnell expressed his disappointment with this one, describing 1962 as "a dismal and cheerless year on the BBC TV front" in part because of this "third-rate 4-part serial" (**127**, "Survey Report of 1962").

Despite these quaint sidetracks, overall, the magazine has less personality than before, and more of a sense that it's running on autopilot. The guest editorials may have been designed to liven things up. Carnell makes plenty of room in "Postmortem" for comment and argument about them, and maybe these discussions seemed more interesting at the time. But from the vantage point of half a century later, they mostly don't add much. There is little that is more tedious than yesteryear's polemics, with a few exceptions like Ballard's editorial, discussed below.

§

Once more, Carnell has a lineup of serials by his homegrown veterans, and once more they add up to less than one would like. 1962 leads off with James White's three-part serial "Field Hospital" (114-116), the latest in his Sector General series. I've previously noted, and quoted at least one letter-writer as saying, that these stories are starting to get a bit formulaic. Now here's John Baxter in "Postmortem" in 114: "White has just exhausted the possibilities of his 'Sector General' idea, and it's about time he dropped it and started writing things like 'Tableau' and 'Dogfight' again. There is, after all, only a small number of variations in the hospital situation, and these descriptions of unusual cases and even more unusual treatments are becoming tedious."

White has either gotten the hint or figured it out for himself. This first novel-length Sector General story has more space opera than alien surgery to it. It was also clearly written and plotted with three-part serialization firmly in mind. In Part One, Conway is dispatched with a Federation medical expedition to the recently discovered Etla, a planet whose population is afflicted with debilitating and mysterious diseases, for which it receives assistance every decade or so from a distant Empire whose representative on Etla won't meet with the expedition. Soon enough they get chased off the planet, and the utterly corrupt situation, in which the Empire has been keeping Etla sick and using the results as a pretext to raise money for other purposes, becomes clear. The Empire doesn't know where the Federation is, but they can get the location of Sector General, so soon enough in Part Two the attack comes—a non-nuclear attack, since the Empire needs a trophy for propaganda use with its brainwashed population, and also because otherwise the story would be over pretty quickly.

So Part Two is largely a disaster/space war epic, at the end of which the hospital's translation capacity is destroyed. In Part Three, Conway tries to deal with the translation problem by taking tapes (i.e., assuming personalities as well as languages) of a number of different alien species, which ultimately drives him temporarily nuts. Meanwhile, the hospital is filling up with war casualties from both sides, which raises the temperature of the military types running the war, but also results in ordinary folks from both sides talking to each other. Empire casualties realize from the fact that they are well treated (and particularly from the selfless example of Conway) that their government has been lying to them about the Federation ogres. So a citizen's posse partly led by Conway mutinies against the military types, who come around quickly enough, and peace is made, per White's predilections.

There are a couple of other things going on here, neither of them new but both of them better developed than previously. One is the character of Conway, which seems intended as a counterargument to the usual monolithically heroic protagonist of SF. He is filled with ambivalence and self-doubt, and a lot of selfish motivations that he suppresses but feels guilty about anyway. But his actions are heroic enough, and that's how he is perceived by others, though he doesn't quite get it himself. The other thing is his romance with the pulchritudinous but chilly Nurse Murchison, which becomes considerably less cartoony here as Conway tries to figure out how to get past her aloof surface (the answer seems to be to behave selflessly—stay tuned).

"Field Hospital" is ultimately a pretty routine performance, if more well-meaning than most, but it is certainly a much better-made novel than White's previous *New Worlds* serial, "Tourist Planet" a.k.a. *The Secret Visitors*, about which the best that can be said is he really didn't know what he was doing. This one also represents a sharp break in White's writing career, a drastic shift from short fiction to novels. He had been producing four to six pieces of short fiction a year—mostly novellas and novelettes—for the UK magazines for a number of years. But after "Resident Physician" in late 1961, he drastically curtailed his short fiction production. A few stories appeared in *Fantasy & Science Fiction* in 1963, but there was no more White short fiction in the Carnell magazines.

For that matter, there was no more White short fiction in any SF magazine for more than a decade, though he did produce several Sector General novelettes for Carnell's *New Writings in SF*—presumably a higher-paying market than *New Worlds*—a few years later. (These were collected as *Major Operation*.) White's next several appearances in the SF magazines were serialized novels, all of which achieved book publication as well, starting with "Open Prison" in 1964 in the last three issues of the Carnell *New Worlds*. And of course he published other novels that had no serialization, such as *The Watch Below*.

"Field Hospital" was fixed up with "Resident Physician" in the Ballantine volume *Star Surgeon* in 1963. Its only review, apart from a very brief and admittedly biased note by Carnell in *New Worlds*, was P. Schuyler Miller's in *Analog* September 1963, which is mainly just descriptive but concludes: "With these stories, the English author has a tiger by the tail—and it's purring."

§

The biggest noise among 1962's serials is Brian Aldiss's "Minor Operation" (**119-121**), reprinted and abridged from its Ballantine paperback publication as *The Primal Urge*. This is another big step in the Romans-becoming-Italians line, and no doubt it had an impact in its time, for pushing the envelope if nothing else. Not so much, decades later. A big part of the problem is the sheer unlikeliness of the premise: the British government decrees that everyone will be required to have implanted on their foreheads a metal disk—a Norman Light—that will turn pink when one is sexually aroused. It would take an awfully broad farce to distract the reader from the gimmick's utter implausibility, and Aldiss doesn't manage that—what he delivers is a fairly low-key and mild satire of English foibles, couched in a not very interesting thriller plot that he becomes entirely too absorbed in by the end.

Jimmy, who works at the International Book Association, is secretly enamored of his brother's girlfriend, which ceases to be a secret when he gets his Norman Light installed. Meanwhile he has an evening's fling with one Rachel, who rebuffs him when he becomes obsessed and tells him "You didn't give me a thing," a line which echoes through his self-esteem for the rest of the story. Reactionary opposition to the Lights develops and there is a genteel failed *putsch*, with Jimmy and company held hostage in a country manor. Rachel has proven to be closely connected with the company that makes the Norman Lights and is helped to defect to the Soviet Union by the end, where it is hoped that she will complete her next project, a disk that will reveal whether a speaker is telling the truth. Jimmy is on his way out of his brother's house and in with his brother's girl-friend, and the Norman Lights are triumphing.

So what? Insofar as there is any answer, it is in a sort of throwaway paragraph towards the end, which shifts to omni-scient voice to refer to "the future as we are now living it, when ER's are as universal as foreheads; for under the intense scru-tiny which Emotional Output has enjoyed since ER's came in, sexual activity has slumped to an unprecedented minimum, and birth rates everywhere have dropped to a small percentage of their previous levels. One happy result of this decline is that the world famine so frequently and zestfully predicted throughout the forties and fifties of this century has been, like Utopia, indefinitely postponed." Earlier on, there's a description of an anti-Light demonstration by actors and actresses in which an orator declares "we are cut off from our past by the Emotion Register. To act in any play written before this year is to falsify it and ridicule ourselves."

Well, those might have been interesting ideas to develop, with an interesting if difficult society to portray, but Aldiss doesn't. There is a scene at the end at the Societal Therapy Clinic, where those who won't accept ER's are drugged with a peyote derivative (!) and shown perverted (sic) pornographic movies to condition them for the new age and help with their neuroses, but nothing much is done with this either—it's interrupted by dead-ender gunfire and then everybody goes and has a drink.

The novel is all readable enough, and Aldiss has his usual quota of showy lines ("If hell is a city much like London, it follows that purgatory may resemble an address in Mayfair." A character named Croolter B. Kind—an "unfrocked Canadian alienist with advanced ideas and a slight stammer," co-proprietor of the Societal Therapy Clinic—is a sort of dilute version of William S. Burroughs' Dr. Benway. The last line has the main characters emerging "into the London air, evening-calm, gasoline-sweet.") But there's not a lot of there there, to my taste at least.

Leslie Flood reviews the Ballantine paperback in **117**, calling it "a gem of a new novel... an hilarious extravaganza, a political satire, good s-f a la Wyndham, and a first-rate novel rolled into one, and—to misplace a metaphor—it looks sex squarely in the face." Oh, and "an extremely witty and entertaining story." I guess you had to be then. Or, maybe, there: P. Schuyler Miller, trying to be respectful in the May 1962 *Analog*, says "we get a fondly humorous dissection of British society, British character, British traditions. Only a reader who knows England well will get most of this second-level satire."

As noted, the serial version is abridged from the US paperback. The versions have the same number of chapters, but the book version's chapters have titles, and are divided into Part 1 and Part 2. These features are eliminated from the serial. I looked fairly carefully at the last two chapters of each, and it seems that the book text is reduced by 15% or so for the magazine. But there is nothing omitted in the serial that much changes the substance or emphasis of the book version, unlike some of the revisions we have seen from Aldiss (see notes on "Basis for Negotiation," below, or "Oh, Ishrael," discussed in Volume One, or "A Touch of Neanderthal" in Chapter Two, above).

Instead, they seem mostly to be routine space-saving edits by Carnell, with a bias towards removal of lines and phrases that are especially arch, risqué, or self-indulgent. For example, here the bracketed material has been removed: "Now a curious effect, [like the aftermath of making love,] began to steal over Jimmy[: an effect compounded of lethargy and lightness]." And a few pages later: "No. 8 was now undone and half carried through the [salacious pink *pointillist*] gloom to a guarded exit." The Author's Note, which takes up over a page at the beginning of the book, is reduced to a single sentence in the magazine, and a good job too.

The last word should probably be Aldiss's. He doesn't mention this novel in *Trillion Year Spree*, *The Twinkling of an Eye*, or "The Glass Forest," but I finally found in *Bury My Heart at W. H. Smith's: A Writing Life* (Hodder & Stoughton, 1990), end of chapter 8, a reference to those "trivial novels, *The Primal Urge* and *The Male Response*." Just so.

§

John Brunner's "Crack of Doom" (**122-123**) was published under the pseudonym Keith Woodcott for no apparent reason except maybe that it isn't very good. It is a turgid and perfunctory potboiler set in a future starfaring society in which the Starfolk (so named because they eschew planetary surfaces and live in their ships) dominate colony planets because they make the colonies' economic success possible through trade and aid, and ask only for a levy of breeders to keep their population up (outer space makes you sterile). A population of mutant "psions" lives a marginal existence on the colony worlds, or at least on the world where the action takes place. Humanity is puzzled by the ruins and artifacts of the Old Race, who have disappeared aeons previously. Now the psions are being driven crazy by a sort of psionic shout suggesting that the end of the universe is near.

Brunner sets things in motion with a pogrom against psions, a secret agent from Earth, and other stock devices, and ties them up with a not-surprising revelation linking the psionic shout and the Old Race. Carnell's blurb says (once you figure out how to read the misprinted lines): "A reader once stated that the right type of psi story had never been written for British science fiction. We contend that Keith Woodcott's two-part serial is just right internationally and introduces a slan-like atmosphere into what has become a highly controversial theme." The "slan-like atmosphere" presumably means the pogrom. As to the story's Brit-friendliness, it went straight to Ace Doublehood (as *The Psionic Menace*, no less) and seems never to have had a UK edition of any sort.

In fairness, my jaundiced opinion is not universal, or at least not as intensely so. P. Schuyler Miller said (in *Analog*, November 1963) of the Ace Double rendition, which was accompanied by Samuel Delany's *Captives of the Flame*, that "an English author handles a similarly way-out adventure yarn smoothly. It's fun, but you won't remember it as you will Delany's.... As Harry Golden would say, 'Enjoy, enjoy!' And if you can, believe a little." I can't, or can't be bothered. Meanwhile, I would suggest to Carnell, if I had a time-telephone, that he need look no further than, oh, across the Atlantic for the definitive British psi story of its time, Arthur Sellings' *Telepath*, which was about then being published in the US by Ballantine. Gollancz issued it the following year as *The Silent Speakers*.

§

The most enjoyable of this year's serials, oddly, is John

Rackham's "The Dawson Diaries" (**117-18**), a sequel to "Good-bye, Dr. Gabriel" (**109**). Johnny Dawson (no relation to the Lan Wright character of the same name!), the brain in a box to whom Dr. Gabriel has provided an artificial body and a wireless hookup to the brain (which remains in a closet), is back, having been rescued from his philosophically motivated suicide attempt. Dr. Gabriel has obtained the surviving brain of Frances, a young woman paralyzed all her life and then catastrophically injured in a fire, and proposes to do the same for her. Dr. Gabriel's company boots them out because people are talking, and they must cooperate with Mr. Klein, their mysterious, aged, and wheelchair-bound benefactor.

Klein's brilliant but sociopathic nephew Mike also gets in on the act, offering improvements to the tech, and switching Frances and Johnny back and forth in Johnny's body. Dr. Gabriel covertly jimmies the rig so they both wind up together in Johnny's body, able to converse. Meanwhile, what about a body for Frances, who has never really had one worthy of the name? Johnny takes her shopping, showing her unclad store mannequins and assuring her against her diffident protests that real women look like that, and it's what she should aspire to. Dr. Gabriel advises:

> "She has never had a body before, remember, Johnny. You must not expect her to feel that its *looks* are important. But, Frances, you listen to me, too. If a body is going to 'feel' good to you—smooth, neat and active, graceful—then it will look good, too. These things go together, always. Johnny, take her to see some nudist films, eh?"

When Frances is decanted or switched into her own newly constructed body, she says it feels different, as if there was something missing, and her sculptor speaks up, holding a brown paper bag:

"This is what you need," she said, severely. "What with two silly old men, and one clever-but-stupid mechanical copy—it's no wonder you hadn't realized. My dear, you're stark naked! That's what's wrong." And, you know, we hadn't thought of it! Trust a woman to remember that kind of detail.

But all is not well. Mr. Klein dies, and leaves everything to Johnny and Frances, causing Mike to storm off in a villainous huff, with premonitions sown all around that they haven't seen the end of him. The fateful denouement occurs at a carnival, where Frances suddenly seems possessed at the top of the Ferris wheel, leaps off, climbs down with her ravishingly superhuman body and runs amok through the grounds, bending the bars of the lion cage to go in and kick the lions around (having by this time lost most of her clothing), and clearly trying to lead Johnny to his death, or at least the death of his body. Of course she's been taken over by Mike, who has improvised his own remote control arrangement and is seeking revenge, and Dr. Gabriel's efforts to shut Frances down wind up killing him, so everyone except Mike (and the late Mr. Klein) are on track to live happily ever after, and Johnny is thinking he and Frances should get married, a notion whose implications are not pursued at all.

This is an odd combination of sophistication and naiveté, almost Gernsbackian or maybe even Tom Swiftish, with a great deal of reasonably intelligent talk (for 1962, anyway) about the problems of arranging a workable brain hookup to a remote body, though not much about actually making a body that would be human in appearance but serviceable, much less superhuman as Johnny's and Francis's are. And of course the characters are all two-dimensional and in primary colors, and Johnny's narrative voice is impossibly innocent. The more risqué aspects of the story, hinted at above, are played obliviously rather than Thorne Smithishly—a bit surprising coming from the author of the previous year's bizarrely salacious "Blink." At one point it is suggested that Frances doesn't really know the difference between men and women, even though she's spent considerable time traveling around in Johnny's body learning to operate it. How things change. How hard it would have been for anyone to take this seriously after 1962. The ceremony of innocence has since taken a pie in the face. But it makes a diverting and novel experience for the time-spelunker rummaging the back files and trying to take things on their own terms.

Not surprisingly, this novella and its predecessor seem never to have appeared in book form.

§

The short fiction, unfortunately, mostly marks time, though at a reasonable level of competence. There is little by the most impressive contributors of recent years: James White is gone, Aldiss and Ballard have only two stories each (and, for each, one of them is inconsequential), Colin Kapp has only one (albeit a striking one), as does Brunner. There are some new and prolific contributors but they mostly don't break any new ground.

Colin Kapp's "Lambda I" (**125**, and "Lambda One" on the cover) is his first piece of short fiction in a little over a year, and he clearly took some time with it. Carnell selected it as the title story of the first *New Worlds* anthology since the mid-'50s (*Lambda I and Other Stories*, Berkley, 1964 and Penguin, 1965), and with good reason. It is a flamboyantly melodramatic geek epic, full of memorable FX and bouncy rubber science, recalling the breakneck audacity of Kapp's first stories in 1958-59.

In the future, people travel by means of Tau technology, which makes matter resonate so it can pass through other matter, meaning you can travel through the Earth rather than around it or on top of it. Of course if something goes wrong you could materialize inside and take out half a continent. In these pre-Ralph Nader days, Kapp says Tau transportation has put planes and trains, if not automobiles, out of business despite the lurking presence of poorly understood risks and the suppressed legends of weird disasters. Porter, whose wife has recently left him, is an official at Tau Corporation. His old friend Brevis, now a prominent psychologist, drops in to visit him just in time for him to get called in for an emergency: the incoming Tau ship *Mu Elektron* won't pop into the right mode, so everybody's stuck in Tau space. And Brevis has just disclosed that Porter's wife wants to return to him and is bearing his child, but it turns out she's on the Tau ship.

The *Mu Elektron* is dispatched to a distant location, so it will only take out part of the Atlantic rather than part of England when it blows. The specter of chaos looms when the passengers figure out they're doomed. Porter and Brevis realize that they must break out the very first Tau ship, *Lambda I*, from its museum home and go after the errant ship, like sending a handcar to a stranded locomotive (though Kapp says it's like a lifeboat). So they're off into Tau space and Kapp pulls out all the rhetorical stops:

> Then, with a wrench, they were gone. Miraculously, the grid of cold, black iron seemed to fade and run as though painted in water colours on a window flooded with water, and a crushing insubstantiality broke over their heads like the surf of some dry, inhuman sea. They were bathed in nausea, and the black wave as it rose and fell tripped every sensory nerve cell in their bodies with twisting spite. Then, after what seemed like an eternity, they were through, and a new scene coalesced like droplets of rosewater condensing on the brain. Involuntarily Porter clutched at a stanchion and swayed, sick with dizziness and dismay. Brevis merely went a deathly white and stared ahead, his thoughts unknown.
>
> The *Lambda I* appeared to be suspended in an illimitable space, a space tinged in some unfathomable way with a monochromatic pinkness which tainted every surface and made nonsense of visual perception.

Below them was nothing, no end or limit or foreseeable confine; neither was there anything above them or on any side....

Of course this is all illusion : "There must be some interaction between Tau-matter and the fabric of the brain itself," a theme which is pursued effectively and enthusiastically to the end of the story, working in Porter's unborn child as a crucial plot element. The story is sufficiently dense with plot that Kapp's sharp (quasi)visualization and near-over-the-top language enhance rather than overwhelm it. Also the reader is less likely to stop and ask questions like—"Wait a minute. They go and drag an antique prototype out of a museum and it *works* right out of the exhibit case?" Hokum it may be, but it's really first-rate hokum. Judith Merril gave it an Honorable Mention, admittedly less of a distinction than it used to be.

Brian Aldiss, as noted, has two stories here. "Basis for Negotiation" (**114**) is a Cold War artifact and also an experiment on his part. China has declared war on the US, the Soviet Union has joined it, and Britain has declared neutrality. Sir Simon Challington, an academic and former politician of reactionary bent (he still resents the US failure to back Britain over the Suez Canal), regards Britain's posture as utterly dishonorable and disastrous and heads for London, overthrow of the government on his mind. He is accompanied by a left-winger whose heart turns out to be in the right place but whose head is a bit unreliable, and who is also homosexual. They manage to reach high levels of the government. The general in charge of U.S. forces in Britain shows up, irate that the British military is skirmishing with them and trying to kick them out of the country; gunplay ensues.

Then the U.S. President comes on TV and announces that the nuclear bombardment of both coasts has been ineffectual because America now has the Shield, a force field that will stop nuclear explosions, and the bad guys better meet us in London to negotiate a peace within 48 hours, and by the way it's good that the U.K. was neutral because otherwise it (not having the Shield) would have been annihilated. At the end, Sir Simon tells one of the government ministers that he is coming back into politics, and the likes of the minister and the Prime Minister are weak. The minister tells him not to kick a man when he is down, referring to the PM, who will resign.

The story is quite uncharacteristic for Aldiss, dead serious, told in a forceful and plain style, short sentences and short words and no metaphors or reflections or other gaudy and decadent distractions, just the way its man-of-action protagonist would think and speak. It seems to be Aldiss's bid to establish himself as a chronicler, at least from a distance, of the character and characters of the British establishment. It works pretty well, at least to one who's never been near the British establishment, up to a point: that point being the *deus ex machina* of the American force field, which lets the air out of the story rather decisively. The story also—especially combined with "Minor Operation"—gives the strong impression of a writer who is becoming discontented with the strictures of SF and is starting to look around for the exits.

Aldiss says in the Introduction to his collection *The Airs of Earth* (Faber & Faber, 1963) that this story "caused much discontent" at *New Worlds*. "I was accused of holding certain attitudes to certain political parties, and to certain sexual propensities, even of taking the name of C.N.D. in vain; one reader, bolder than the rest, suggested I had written in my cups. Not all these charges do I deny, though I hope a perceptive reader will find the story fights its real battle on other battlefields.... I should say that 'Basis' is somewhat revised. For that I must thank John Baxter, an Australian reader whose criticisms have been very useful."[39]

The discontent at *New Worlds* appears to have been localized, since the story was voted the most popular in its issue.

39. These suggestions were not those published in "Postmortem," but made privately during a vigorous correspondence (Baxter, personal communication to Broderick).

ahead of James White's serial. The "in his cups" remark is by John Rackham, whose letter is printed in "Postmortem" in **116**, and who says the story "was a bust, and explains, all by itself, why Brian prefers mythopoetical purple. This, an attempt to write ordinary s-f, in plain English, is a pastiche of pseudo-politics, with cardboard characters striking attitudes and mouthing clichés. The plot-line itself offers one of the oldest gags in the business, the 'gadget out of the hat' especially invented to rescue the author from an impossible situation of his own devising. I'll leave it to those better qualified than myself to scrag the pitiful politics." He further complains about "careless mistakes" such as misspelling Aldermaston twice (surely the work of Carnell) and a technical error about one-way glass.

Two issues later, in "Postmortem" under the rubric "On Aldiss and That Story...," two more comments appear. John Baxter says, "As far as I know, no writer, British or otherwise, has ever been courageous enough to tackle a theme as controversial as this, nor has an editor been brave enough to publish it.... It shows people as they really are, and not as we would like them or imagine them to be." But he too trashes the rug-pulling revelation, and also the portrayal of the secondary character as homosexual: "By assuming that the public is unsympathetic to homosexuals, Aldiss may find himself in deeper waters than he expected. That sort of conviction by association is no longer in fashion." Now that's news, in 1962.

Lee Harding says, "Superb! But—s-f? No matter. Aldiss managed to cram more sheer brilliance into his forty scintillating pages than the last dozen issues of the magazine!... The writing was superlative!... But whereas it was consciously s-f, Aldiss's tale almost shocked with its realism—until the 'force field' gimmick was dragged in at the finale and made me realise that I *was* reading an s-f story after all." (So the two Australians praise the realism of this story of the inner workings of Britain, while the Brit talks about "pseudo-politics" and cardboard characters. Hmmm.)

The revisions in *The Airs of Earth* version of the story are actually pretty minor, a phrase or a word here and there, until the end, where Simon Challington's exchange with the government minister is much longer and more poisonous than in the magazine version: Sir Simon accuses him and the PM not just of weakness but of moral weakness, and says the minister should resign with the PM. The minister accuses him of "holier-than-thou cant" and vows to stick around: "Now more than ever the country needs experienced leaders." So the bottom line of the *New Worlds* version is that weakness is routed; of the book version, that the snakes won't change their spots.

This story, by the way, appeared in the first (1965) version of Faber & Faber's *The Best Science Fiction Stories of Brian W. Aldiss*, but was removed from the second (1971) version in favor of newer material. It also appeared in *Lambda I and Other Stories*, the 1964 US anthology of *New Worlds* stories, with this comment in Carnell's foreword: he says it "was rejected by all the American s-f magazines (on the basis of theme only) yet, despite its Munich-type political theme, produced a veritable snowstorm of correspondence when published in England, with commendations even from British readers!" So naturally it was left out of the 1965 UK edition of that anthology.

Aldiss's only other short fiction in *New Worlds* this year is "Conversation Piece" (**115**), a lame and silly satire, too forced and farcical for extended description, about an overcrowded future in which only those men who keep their ratings high will be allowed to get married (only the docile are allowed to reproduce), and "proxis"—civil-servant concubines, it appears—test their fitness for marriage by provoking them. This one appears never to have been reprinted, and just as well.

§

J. G. Ballard's presence, dominating in 1960 and 1961, is much diminished in 1962, but not for lack of production. Ballard has hit the American market. He published ten pieces of magazine fiction in that year, but six of them are in *Amazing*

Stories, Fantastic, and *Fantasy & Science Fiction:* "The Insane Ones," "The Garden of Time," "The Thousand Dreams of Stellavista," "Thirteen to Centaurus," "Passport to Eternity," and "The Singing Statues." Of the others, the novella version of "The Drowned World" appeared (as discussed last chapter) in *Science Fiction Adventures* and "The Watch-Towers" in *Science Fantasy,* leaving only "The Cage of Sand" and "The Man on the 99th Floor" in *New Worlds.* Presumably, these are the stories he could not sell in the U.S., and it's easy to see why, though the reasons are quite different for the two stories.

What Ballard is lacking in fictional presence he makes up in manifesto. His guest editorial "Which Way to Inner Space?" appears in **118** (May 1962), and by comparison to some of the other tedious screeds in this series, it is quite bracing if a little irritating as well. It is easy to quote but hard to summarize (and hard to stop quoting), but I'll try to restrain myself. Ballard thinks that most of the present ills of SF derive from its preoccupation with space travel. The bulk of "space fiction" is "invariably juvenile" and imposes narrow imaginative limits, transcended only by writers as good as Ray Bradbury. SF won't be able to survive on this diet. Already most readers can tell that most of it is based on "the most minor variations on [familiar] themes, rather than on any fresh imaginative leaps"— it's becoming academic, its virtuosity a "sure sign of decline."

So it's time for SF to turn its back on space, interstellar travel, extraterrestrial life forms, galactic wars, and the disastrous influence of H. G. Wells. It's time to "jettison its present narrative forms and plots. Most of these are far too explicit to express any subtle interplay of character and theme. Devices such as time travel and telepathy, for example, save the writer the trouble of describing the inter-relationships of time and space indirectly." And now we're at the famous pronouncement: "The only truly alien planet is Earth"—one of the irritating lines, a piece of hyperbole that outruns Ballard's otherwise interesting argument. But here's his program:

More precisely, I'd like to see s-f becoming abstract and "cool," inventing completely fresh situations and contexts that illustrate its theme obliquely. Instead of treating time like a sort of glorified scenic railway, I'd like to see it used for what it is, one of the perspectives of the personality, and the elaboration of concepts such as the time zone, deep time and archaeopsychic time. I'd like to see more psycho-literary ideas, more meta-biological and meta-chemical concepts, private time-systems, synthetic psychologies and space-times, more of the remote, sombre half-worlds one glimpses in the paintings of schizophrenics, all in all a complete speculative poetry and fantasy of science.

And here's where *you* come in: SF sets higher standards than any other literary genre, "and from now on, I think, most of the hard work will fall, not on the writer and editor, but on the readers. The onus is on them to accept a more oblique narrative style, understated themes, private symbols and vocabularies. The first true s-f story, and one I intend to write myself if no one else will, is about a man with amnesia lying on a beach and looking at a rusty bicycle wheel, trying to work out the absolute essence of the relationship between them. If this sounds off-beat and abstract, so much the better, for science fiction could use a big dose of the experimental; and if it sounds boring, well at least it will be a new kind of boredom."

A few years later, Ballard actually delivered on this promise or threat, more or less. The last (paragraph? section? chapter?) of "The Assassination Weapon," which became an (episode?) in *The Atrocity Exhibition*, reads:

THE TERMINAL ZONE. He lay on sand with the rusty bicycle wheel. Now and then he would cover some of the spokes with sand, neutralizing the radial geometry. The rim interested him. Hidden behind a dune, the hut no longer seemed a part of his world.

The sky remained constant, the warm air touching the shreds of test papers sticking up from the sand. He continued to examine the wheel. Nothing happened.

Ballard has the *New Worlds* Profile in this issue, with piercing gaze out of lean face. It is mentioned that he has just been on the BBC's Home Service with Amis, Aldiss, Bulmer, Brunner, and Wyndham, preaching the gospel of "Inner Space."

So how do Ballard's stories, in the two issues immediately after his guest editorial, stack up in his own terms? In one case, not very well. "The Man on the 99th Floor" (**120**) is one of Ballard's weakest stories, in a league with "Track 12." A man has a fixation about getting to the 100th floor of buildings, but when he tries he can't get past the 99th. When a psychiatrist tries to help him, the nefarious scheme is revealed. "Oblique narrative style, understated themes, private symbols and vocabularies"? Nah, it's a crime thriller with a post-hypnotic suggestion gimmick—"far too explicit to express any subtle interplay of character and theme" is more like it.

"The Cage of Sand" (**119**) is another kettle of fish, Ballard's most overt tilt yet at the verities of SF, his first anti-*ad astra* piece—though I'm not sure it connects with any of the pronouncements or catchphrases in his editorial other than "psycho-literary ideas." In the future, Florida has become a desert and has largely been abandoned because of plant viruses brought back from Mars in Martian sand, which spaceships have used as ballast [sic!] to avoid lightening the Earth and causing it to orbit closer to the Sun. (This backstory with its grotesquely nonsensical rationale is revealed only two-thirds of the way through.) The space age appears to be over, though Ballard is not explicit on the point.

A small band of neurotics lives, and hides from the authorities, in the half-buried hotels of Cocoa Beach, near Cape Canaveral, pursuing their obsessions with the seven dead astronauts orbiting Earth in their capsules. Bridgman was an architect, whose company lost the contract for design of a Martian settlement, and who realized his own inadequacy for the task—hardly cause to become an extralegal recluse in a contaminated zone, one would think. The other characters have more powerful stories—the woman's dead husband is in orbit, and the other male character is a former astronaut who panicked on the launch pad. At the end of the story, one of the vehicles falls out of orbit and explodes over Cocoa Beach. The characters are caught by the wardens who want to take them away and detoxify them. But Bridgman is permitted a triumph of sorts:

> ...A flange of hot metal from Merril's capsule burned his wrist bonding him to the spirit of the dead astronaut. Scattered around him on the Martian sand, in a sense Merril had reached Mars after all.
>
> "Damn it!" he cried exultantly to himself as the wardens' lassos stung his neck and shoulders. "We made it!"

This passage is interesting as an ironic inversion of SF's Conquest of Other Worlds motif: instead of voyaging far and conquering what we find, we've brought back the other world and it's conquered us. But still, this failure of a space conqueror can sink his hands into Martian soil (never mind that it's a form of waste) and claim victory, on terms that are meaningful to him if no one else.

It's also interesting to compare the above-quoted end of "The Cage of Sand" to the end of another famous SF story, Theodore Sturgeon's "The Man Who Lost the Sea" (1959), in which the space conqueror is dying of anoxia after reaching Mars and suffering a banal accident:

"'God,' he cries, dying on Mars, 'God, we made it!'"

Surely Ballard was consciously throwing that line back into the face of standard SF. As David Pringle has pointed out, Ballard is almost certain to have seen the Sturgeon story, since after its publication in the October 1959 *Fantasy and Science Fiction*, it was reprinted in Judith Merril's fifth annual *Year's*

Best SF—along with Ballard's own "The Sound-Sweep." Note that the capsule that falls out of orbit at the end of "The Cage of Sand" is that of astronaut Merril.

In any case, standard SF seems not to have noticed or cared about this act of *lese majeste*. "The Cage of Sand" was voted the best story in its issue by the *New Worlds* readership.

§

John Brunner has only one short story in 1962, "Stimulus" (**116**), which begins with the definition of "stimulus" from *Webster's New Collegiate Dictionary*, and continues in that authoritative vein as Lee, an agent from Main Base, is dispatched to the outback of its unnamed colony planet, where he finds a hostile bunch of colonists—hostile because he has the power to toss them off the planet. He's there to investigate the death of a colonist family at the claws of the predators ("spitcats," though they look nothing like cats) that Achmed, one of the colonists, has been breeding, hoping to make them dominant in the local ecology, to the supposed benefit of the colonists. Actually he was pushing them towards intelligence by selecting away from production of the enzyme that metabolizes the analog of urea to the analog of allantoin, thereby stimulating their nervous systems, and speaking of analogs, doesn't it sound like *Analog* is exactly where Brunner aimed this story? (He was starting to sell to Campbell with some regularity about this time.)

It's turgid, not to mention sternly righteous and didactic, as Lee tells the colonists that they have to pack up and leave their planet, since allowing another species to develop intelligence will be a stimulus for *us*, and of course they all want to be rational about this, don't they? Reviewing Brunner's collection *No Future in It* (**125**), Leslie Flood listed this story along with several others in a sentence that begins "He is very effective with straight *science* fiction" and concludes with "are as good as, and similar to, Clarke's work, which is high praise indeed." If only.

Brunner has the guest editorial in **114**, "Our Present Requirements," in which he complains about getting rejection slips saying his stories don't meet them, mostly from the American market, "from which I make my living when I do." Brunner is light on chapter and verse, but says generally that nobody wants to deal with non-clichéd clinical psychology ("What about the real nature of madness in a future setting? What about new psychological disturbances? What about new—if you like—perversions of basic instincts?") What about the way attitudes to love and marriage can change? If he wants to write Lesbian pornography, he could sell it. He couldn't sell SF about a future or an alien society "in which this problem was a central one." Nor could he sell a political novel that was "a serious treatment in fictional form of trends already visible here and alarming to people with their eyes on the future.... The world is now in a mess because we know more about what makes atoms tick than about what makes people tick." Have to do better, he says, "Yet in s-f we're missing out on a whole area of this kind of progress. It's labelled with a rejection slip."

In **116**'s "Postmortem," one Rod McLaughlin rubbishes this piece, saying that if Brunner wants to write about Lesbians he should do it already and if the stories are any good they will sell—look at what Sturgeon has already published ("and the fact that I think his fantasies are often diseased and unhealthy is neither here nor there. They are well written stories and they have sold.") Brunner also gets the *New Worlds* Profile in this issue, with the same juvescent photo *New Worlds* has been running since 1955. The profile contains no comment by Brunner, just praise from Carnell, who thinks his best story is "Earth Is But a Star."

§

After Ballard, Aldiss, and Brunner, the biggest name in these issues is probably Harry Harrison. His "The Streets of Ashkalon" (**122**) (rendered Ashkelon most other places, such as newspaper stories about missiles from Gaza), his semi-celebrated piece of religious iconoclasm, is more interesting as event than otherwise. In the story, told from the viewpoint of an atheistic trader, the well-meaning Father Mark arrives on Wesker's World to bring the Gospel to the simple and literal-minded inhabitants, who have no concept of supernatural entities or life after death, and also no concept that what somebody tells them might not be true. So they cotton to the idea of miracles and eternal life, decide they need a miracle right away, and crucify Father Mark—who of course does not rise from the dead. The story concludes (in the rain):

> "Then we will not be saved? We will not become pure?"
>
> "You were pure," Gath said, in a voice somewhere between a sob and a laugh. "That's the horrible ugly dirty part of it. You were pure. Now you are..."
>
> "Murderers," Itin said, and the water ran down from his lowered head and streamed away into the darkness.

Carnell's trepidation is evident in his blurb: "To our knowledge there has [sic] only been three good religious science fiction short stories ever published (and two of them are by Ray Bradbury). It is a subject not readily acceptable to the genre and requires a delicate touch to avoid the pitfalls of conflicting theological beliefs. We are convinced that Harry Harrison's story is the fourth good one—but, naturally, controversial." Presumably Carnell's three good stories are Bradbury's "The Man" and "In This Sign," and either Clarke's "The Star" or his "The Nine Billion Names of God." But this is an odd claim to make in light of the number of other well-remembered SF stories about religion published before 1962: Anthony Boucher's "Balaam" and "The Quest for St. Aquin," Katherine MacLean's "Unhuman Sacrifice," Walter M. Miller, Jr.'s "Canticle" stories and the resulting novel, Eric Frank Russell's "Hobbyist," Lester del Rey's "For I Am a Jealous People," James Blish's "A Case of Conscience," Henry Kuttner's "A Cross of Centuries," and no doubt others. Well, maybe Carnell didn't like any of those.

There's a backstory here, which of course Carnell does not mention. Harrison says in his essay "The Beginning of the Affair" in Aldiss and Harrison's *Hell's Cartographers* (Harper & Row, 1975):

> I wrote this for a Judy Merril anthology of "dangerous" ideas that was never published due to the publisher going broke. The story came back and went out, and returned rather quickly from all the American markets. It was too hot to handle since it had an atheist in it. This is the truth. Even my good friend, Ted Carnell, would not take it for the more liberal British *New Worlds*. I asked Brian if he had any idea what could be done with it. He had some critical remarks about the priest's characterization, which I agreed with, but said as well that he would like to use it in an anthology he was doing for Penguin. (And I must add that Carnell, once he knew the story would be anthologized, felt it would be all right to use it in his magazine. This might indicate that his spine needed stiffening, but if so it indicates as well that the American editors had no spines at all.) The story has a happy ending in that it was eventually anthologized three times in the United States and translated into Swedish, Italian, Russian, Hungarian—and twice into French.

As to the story itself, it is perfectly workmanlike and not the least bit subtle, as usual for Harrison.

Harrison has the guest editorial in **120**, "What Is Wrong with British Science Fiction," which is surprisingly insubstantial. The answer, in the first sentence, is "the regrettable fact that it suffers from the disapproval of the Establishment." His evidence: he was engaged by a newspaper to write SF reviews, but they never got sent any review copies by publishers, who seemed not to want to have it known that they were publishing SF. He admits Gollancz as an exception. He says things will get better, citing *New Maps of Hell* and the potentially subversive effect of G.D. Doherty's school text *Aspects of Science Fiction*. Harrison also has the *New Worlds* Profile in this issue, even more wispy than usual. It consists of eight small snapshots with captions such as "I'm ALWAYS glad to meet a fan who likes my stuff, particularly one as young and feminine as you."

§

Many of the lower-profile regulars are present, generally at or near their accustomed level of achievement. Kenneth Bulmer's novelette "Flame in the Flux Field" (**116**) is at the low end of his, another piece of yard goods in his series about the war, conducted in fluxwagons, against the alien Octos, whom no one has actually seen. This one features a Professor of Anti-Octo Technology Daisy Yolande Hillary a.k.a. Damn You Hillary, and an obnoxious rookie bombardier who shapes up all right after all, and there's a new model of fluxwagon to test, and it's all too tedious to relate.

The stalwart Francis G. Rayer and E. R. James both reappear for their next-to-last hurrahs in **119**, James after a three-year absence from the SF magazines. Rayer is closer to the top of his range, such as it is. His stories here are all relatively concise, which is a good move for him—the shorter, the less trouble he can get into, and tightly wound plots are proving to be his forte insofar as he has one. These stories are all readable if not particularly memorable.

In "Sacrifice" (**119**), a dangerous mental parasite—a mindorm, Rayer calls it—is looking for a more sophisticated host, and here comes a woman artist to rent an isolated cottage. The locals who take her there act kind of funny. Could they know something she doesn't? Sure enough, the mindorm riding in its wolf host comes after her—but aha! She's a robot simulacrum controlled from a spaceship! So the mindorm can't get in and dies. This denouement would seem cleverer were it not recycled from Rayer's earlier story "Consolidation Area" (**46**, April 1956), which also featured a mental parasite fatally deceived into trying to take over a robot.

In "Sixth Veil" (**120**), a man working on a construction project is sent underground by supervisor McGregor for one last inspection. While he's down there, they start pouring the quick-setting concrete, entombing him. There won't be time to break through to him before he runs out of air. But McGregor appears to him in a vision, tells him it isn't a dream, and invites him "Come—*come*—" And we find ourselves in an elaboration of the jaunting backstory of *The Stars My Destination*.

In "Variant" (**121**), Rayer is back to recycling his own plots, specifically that of his early story "Of Those Who Came" (*New Worlds* **18**, November 1952). An alien cop is tracking down some aliens who have gone bad on an unsuspecting Earth. The twist is that these "variants" are aliens who decide they like the luxury of Earth's easy living, compared to their own hard world, and the cop succumbs himself after killing both his quarry. Judith Merril gave it an Honorable Mention, maybe for old times' sake. "Capsid" (**125**) features a desolate planet full of intelligent, telepathic, and predatory amorphous organisms that snatch any spaceship that lands and drag it underground into their burrows, more out of curiosity than hunger; they eat minerals they find in the ground around them, and a good thing too, since there's apparently nothing else on the planet to eat. Rayer comes up with a clever rescue scenario that is almost enough to keep one from wondering how these things evolved—and evolved intelligence—in the first place. A capsid, by the way, is the shell of protein around a virus core; I'm not sure what the point is of using that word here. Were the humans—or maybe their metal spacecraft—almost fated to become the aliens' protective surround?

James' "Six-Fingered Jacks" (**119**) is a geek space opera. Earth prospectors, about to land on a small moon, discover a 50-mile-wide alien ship closing on them. After much hand-wringing and acting out, one of them shuts himself up in the engine room and seems to be hand-rolling nuclear explosives, when they establish a video connection. The aliens have six fingers per hand, and start flashing signs at the humans—hey! It's the base 12! And the signs add up to 92! Uranium! It's a bit murky, but I think James is saying that they are warning the humans they are about to land on a moon virtually made out of it (which of course will make them rich). "The Thousand Deep" (**121**), I cautiously guess, is meant as a comedy. It's the overcrowded Earth again, the "thousand deep" refers to underground city levels, and there's a thriving interstellar colonization movement that uses press gangs to kidnap qualified crews. The protagonist has just graduated with the highest marks at the University and is ready to marry his girlfriend and ship out, but she sends him a Dear John letter indicating excessive influence by her relatives. He goes after her, but a squad from his ship is on his doorstep to escort him there, and when he gets away from them there's another gang after him, and he goes careering up, down, and across the levels, with his girlfriend trying to steer him to the press gang of the ship belonging to her uncle.

Incidentally, the fanzine *Skyrack* provides a window into Mr. James' involvement with the SF community.[40] At the British national SF convention,

> long standing Nova writer E. R. James surveyed the sf scene, defining sf as having a basis of scientific fact explained logically. He claimed that Yoga thought of the concepts of science fiction long before sf did so. James amazed his audience by removing his jacket and standing on his head Yoga fashion. He spoke of the claims of Yoga and the manner in which *Analog* was using stories based on the off-beat sciences, and mentioned how to work even slight scientific concepts into stories. He wound up by reviewing his own sf

40. *Skyrack* 42, April, 1962: http://www.gostak.co.uk/skyrack/ (visited 9/10/11).

history and the trends of sf during the last ten years. One major theme, he said, is that of overcrowding and survival. As one gets older one writes better, said James. One has a better insight into human nature and this is all important to writing.

Well, maybe.

Donald Malcolm, another former regular whose appearances have dropped off, is back after 15 months' absence with "Yorick" (120), and as usual he's brought his big dumb friend God with him. Yorick is a planet with some funny-looking continents, hence the name, and strange astrophysics. There's a larger star, about four solar masses, in a very eccentric orbit around a smaller star (about one solar mass)—stop right there! Wouldn't it be the other way around? Guess not; after all, Malcolm belongs to the British Interplanetary Society and three astronomical societies. In any case, Yorick is orbiting around one or the other of them, and the theory is that when conjunction arrives (any day now), the planet will either swap primaries or do a figure eight around them. One would think there might be some more apocalyptic consequences—climatic, vulcanological, etc.—but nothing is said about them.

However, the air is full of charged particles, everybody's in a bad mood, and the indigenous humanoids won't let the humans into their villages. This mildly mysterious set-up quickly becomes more mysterious, though not necessarily more interesting, and the indigenes (the vast majority of whom have proven to be in suspended animation) all wind up marching to a big crater for a ritual to commemorate the passage of the big star and the end of the solar wind ("The planet was free.") That fast? Seems unlikely. But never mind. How did they manage suspended animation? A symbiosis between the local trees and flowers. And here's the money shot: "'Funny,' he said, turning the petal over in the sunlight, 'how man has long sought a kind of immortality and God, in His infinite wisdom, has enshrined it in a flower.'" This story appears to be the first in Malcolm's

Matthew Brady series, since that's the character's name.

Robert Presslie, too, is back and much heralded after a three-year absence. Unfortunately he begins his renascence with the unimpressive "One Foot in the Door" (121), a contrived and silly story about a traveling salesman/secret agent outwitting the aliens who are accustomed to prevailing through psi in all their business arrangements. It's as sterile as it is glib, and a comedown from Presslie's past fare, some of which was quite good, and on other occasions was at least fetchingly crazed.

But things are back to abnormal with "Remould" (123), a novelette that begins with about 30,000 people getting ready to cross the Bosporus, some of them on rafts, the rest swimming and pulling the rafts. Seven thousand of them proceed to die in an unexpected storm. It seems that aliens have set off nuclear bombs around the planet 100 miles above the surface, causing everyone to become sterile from latitude 20 North to 60 North—but if you get out of the Sterility Belt, your puissance is restored. So the population of the Northern Hemisphere is on the move, in tribes led by those few men who have escaped sterility in some unexplained fashion.

Much macho leadership is on display from big man Henneker. His remaining thousands continue their trek over the mountains to Iraq, and through the now-all-too-familiar landscape, from Mosul down to Baghdad, and then an advance party heads down to Basra on a hand-operated railroad bogie, hangs a left into Persia, and finds... the aliens, who explain it was all an accident and they're trying to rectify it by temporarily reversing Earth's magnetic field, and in a week or so everybody can go home. Oh, and they'll help set things up again. The protagonist announces: "But before you start helping us to remake the world I think we should have a conference. There's a whole heap of things in the world we probably won't want restored. When the time comes, let's make it a better place." Now *there* would be the more interesting story. But no, there doesn't seem to be a sequel.

Presslie is back in the next issue with the pure lunatic quill, "Lucky Dog" (124), which if it were adapted as a B movie would have to be called *Psychedelic Werewolf versus the Bonsai Space Invaders*. Kirk the failed astronaut is participating in experiments with a Ditran derivative called Propytran, and it's starting to release the beast in him, almost literally. He says his sense of smell is getting much sharper, and then while having dinner with the woman he loves, he takes her hands in his and breaks both of her thumbs. Meanwhile, something weird is going on in orbit: one of the abandoned satellites is starting to emit strange signals, and then starts up with the recordings of the astronaut who died in it.

But Kirk is on the scent—metaphorically, this time. Propytran has sharpened senses nobody else even has, and he's listening in on the aliens who have invaded the satellite, and who of course are up to no good. There are about 10,000 aliens on their small spaceship, and that's only the waking ones—there are several million more deep-frozen pre-fertilized ova. It seems the aliens were having a population crisis:

> ...Their biologists came up with the answer. They found a way of limiting the growth of their progeny, something like the Japanese can grow trees in miniature. The idea was to move these tiny people to a new world—being so small they could get many more into each ship—and being so small, they computed that their stay on their new world would be practically indefinite since no matter how fast they continued to breed, their food and space requirements would perhaps never exceed their chosen planet's potential.

But it didn't work out that way.

> In two generations the new Menkarians [the first dwarfed colonists] were twelve inches tall, weighed around the same number of ounces. The fourth generation Menkarians were as tall as their original ancestors

and it became apparent that sooner or later they would be back where they started as regards over-population.

What had started out as a purely internal project, entirely peaceful in purpose, had to be transmuted to one of deliberate aggression. Using the same technique of miniaturization, the Menkarians embarked on a cold-blooded policy of spreading their own population over as many habitable planets as they found, regardless of the priority of any existing inhabitants.

Their biologists worked on the flaw in their original plan and developed a miniature Menkarian who could assume full five-feet tall proportions, not in a few generations, not even in one, but in himself. Their technique was to land on a planet, ingest the hormone which had been developed to accelerate growth and before the planet's true inhabitants knew what was happening they had been taken over.

And for lagniappe they bring with them fertilized ova, which can be brought to maturity in a matter of months.

After this revelation, Kirk is set to be dispatched upstairs to go after the invaders, full of Propytran so he can eavesdrop on their thoughts and foil their evasive maneuvers. And there we leave him, and his love, who will be waiting and whose thumbs seem to be healing well. Judith Merril was sufficiently charmed to give this one an Honorable Mention—but did the same with "One Foot in the Door."

Philip E. High, who once seemed like a breath of fresh air but now resembles a boring party guest who just won't go home, has four stories. "The Psi Squad" (114) is a typically fast-moving story that ultimately goes nowhere. A police officer is suspected of having psi talents, is sent on a mission, gets in trouble, he's being tested in earnest. His "psi" talent is actually reading the chemical traces of moods and emotions (he sure reads a lot from them, though), and other psi talents have similarly materialistic explanations. Carnell's blurb says: "We do not publish many psi stories—it is a plot motive which has been so overdone in recent years that readers have become heartily sick of the word psi itself. However, try this one for a change." A change it is, but not a very interesting one. Judith Merril gave it an Honorable Mention, devaluing that currency a bit more.

"Probability Factor" (115) is also breezy but formulaic. A high-powered, top secret computer is being delivered by truck, a fog comes up and suddenly the truck crew is in the future, where Earth has become home to giant golden crocodiles. They are shortly back in the present but without the computer, and their story is obvious nonsense to the hard-headed investigator, until the report comes in of a giant golden crocodile attacking traffic on the A20. "Dictator Bait" (118) is less breezy and more smug and turgid, starting with memos to the Divisional Officer, Interstellar Intelligence, Sector 6, and from him to Operator 2/8, suggesting there's a shape-shifting alien about on the planet Rause cleverly fostering cultural deterioration. So the omni-competent Operator hies himself there, sets himself up as body-guard to one of the local strongmen, works his way to the top by being smarter and tougher than everybody else, and is restoring some order in his fascistic way, so the shape-shifting alien is compelled to attack him and be defeated. It's a stale breath of Campbellian didacticism.

"The Method" (124) is worse, with several mismatched ideas strung together in a spavined plot which opens with Marsin, the military hero, illicitly channeling a twentieth century soldier. The revelation is that everybody back then was a generalist who could field-strip his weapon *and* engage in hand-to-hand combat, unlike these decadent days where everybody has a tiny piece of things and nobody has the whole. Then we get filled in on the background. The alien Levanoon dominate the other sentient races, staging small set-piece wars as a means of dispute resolution, dividing and conquering everybody. Marsin figures this out, takes his squad into a city where Earthfolks are disliked and generally attacked in barroom brawls. This time they kick ass in a barroom, then head to an embassy and kick more ass and persuade some of the aliens to support them in an attack on the Mickeys, who are the Levanoon's tools on this world. They shoot the place up with their loud replica twentieth century weapons; and here's the moral! "Perhaps this is the first time in history that subtlety has been defeated by—brute force." The story is as disjointed as this account of it.

High has one of the guest editorials, "Why Explain S-F?" (117), which takes about six facile pages to say nothing very interesting, consistently with its title. Reader H. Higgins endorses it in "Postmortem": "the only way to retain [the] sense of wonder is for authors to let their imaginations run loose with a vengeance"—"but please, no 'sick' stories." P. Hickey says "I thought that no lover of s-f would again use the odious comparisons which were produced again in Philip E. High's guest editorial"—i.e., comparing it to "Westerns," "Romances," and "Detectives" rather than "Literature." SF provides "food for thought"! The sooner everybody accepts that SF is a serious art form, "the sooner we will see regular reviews by responsible critics in every newspaper." (Be careful what you ask for.)

High also has the *New Worlds* Profile in the issue with his editorial, and is revealed to have had the stereotypical writer's history—he's been a commercial traveller, insurance agent, bus driver, reporter, salesman, "and many other things." It does not disclose his work habits, for which we must depend on Phil Harbottle's interview and profile: "ninety per cent of his writing took place in the works canteen of the bus company for whom High was employed as a driver! High wrote his stories in longhand during his spare time. He always carried a notebook in his pocket (a hangover from his earlier days as a reporter) and wrote during his stand-by periods, typing it out when he got home."[41]

David Rome—whose SF career is only a year old, but who had four stories in 1961, regular enough for me—is back with three

---

41. "Phil High—Literary Craftsman," interview and profile by Philip Harbottle. http://www.infinityplus.co.uk/nonfiction/intpeh.htm (visited 9/10/11).

more, all burdened to some degree by an excessively portentous style. In "Moonbeam" (122), the author's atmospherics get the best of him. Bianchi was to be transmitted to Alpha Centauri ("Think of a shout"). But he doesn't seem to have gotten there. He's here, instead. But he's really just a reflection. He also seems to be an Artificial Person (another character refers to him insultingly as "Newt"), so he of course races to the scene of his manufacture on some ill-defined errand, then goes back to the Moonbeam project center and destroys the apparatus with a gun he has wrested from a guard, and finds himself on a planet of Alpha Centauri, with the gun still in hand, and shoots a man he finds in a tent, and the story ends in a burst of italics suggesting that nothing has really happened at all. The point is lost in the noise.

"Jogi" (123) is another strident one: pet animal escapes from spaceship, everybody thinks it's cute, and they try to feed it milk, while it starves for hostile emotions to batten on. "Meaning" (125) works better because the story is loud enough to be heard over the accompaniment. A space crew is marooned in Mars orbit, maintained in a VR fantasy world by the ship's computer, but what's fantasy and what's real, and is there really anybody else alive on this thing? It's a trope revisited at length in Philip K. Dick's 1970 novel *A Maze of Death*, and in the recent TV drama series *Life on Mars*, in both the 2006-07 UK and 2008-09 US versions, not to mention a 2009 Spanish recension. This time the stylistic oppression is worth it. Merril bestowed an Honorable Mention on it.

Lee Harding is not yet a regular, since his first two *New Worlds* stories appeared in late 1961, but he's also appeared in *Science Fantasy* and *Science Fiction Adventures*. However, in 1962 he has four stories in *New Worlds* and comes into sharper focus. "Late" (115) is a pleasant short transcendence opera. Everywhere you go in space, the Race has already been and left, so where could they be? A space expedition dedicated to finding out comes upon a gold-shrouded planet (hard to focus on for some reason) and lands a couple of men. One of them hikes over towards a strange-looking artifact, runs into an invisible wall, and being unable to get through it, shoots it. The wall defends itself and he's dead, except that the Race who are lurking behind it resurrect him and repair him, after taking him briefly into their collective consciousness. This is first *and* last contact, because they are heading out where we can't follow them, using their planet as vehicle. But it's not a total loss for the protagonist: "And although they had taken him like a fish left gasping on the short of an unknown lake, and cast him back into the human sea and forbidden him the knowledge of the universe, he could not find it within him to hate them, for they had cast him back a better fish."

In "Dragonfly" (**117**) the fish seems to be a keeper, though the metaphor has obviously changed. Carnell's blurb starts: "We do not often have a story dealing with the first astronaut to attempt a sub-space journey to the nearer star system...." Well, who does? Often, I mean. Ramsay the star pilot is off on his experimental journey to Alpha Centauri, five days each way, when the Shadows—amorphous shapes—appear diaphanously on the second day, get more and more substantial, and on the fifth day one of them enters him. He feels "alien fingers kneading the stuff of his mind." Then it and all the other Shadows seem to leave. He lands on a barren planet of Alpha C and there's a man waiting for him, "a ridiculous figure in brown shirt, slacks and *desert boots*." (Emphasis in original. What's the big deal? It's a desert!)

Ramsay goes out with a gun. The man explains that he's been waiting for Ramsay, and that it's unnecessary to shoot him because "We just wish to —— with you." He says —— is hard to explain. Ramsay shoots him ineffectually, runs back to his ship, takes off, and arrives back at the Solar System in an extreme state, still inhabited by the Shadow, and shortly dies—"forced to discard the crippling husk of his own body and his own reality before he could ever hope to understand all that the Shadows had to offer." He, now it, considers telling the bereaved wife and colleagues what's happening but quickly loses the desire. "It would never go back, no more than a dragonfly could return to the naiad beneath the water and extol the virtues of its wondrous new life."

Harding ups the transcendence ante in "Terminal" (**118**), in which (again) space explorers make it to a planet of Alpha Centauri, which proves quite Earth-like except for the rudimentary life. Even so, they feel like they are being... watched. After an interval of collective heebie-jeebies, Lassiter heads for the mountains, and Harding wrestles manfully with that which cannot be described: "Oddly enough, he didn't feel like a man sailing blithely into the jaws of danger. He should have felt, perhaps, like a mesmerized bird awaiting the cobra's lethal blow but the human part of his mind was too clearly orientated to lose itself in a miasma of fear. Instead, he felt more like a man about to experience something profound." And soon after: "Quite suddenly, everything seemed *doubtful*." Well, I guess that's sort of profound, maybe.

"Birthright" (**119**) is less grandiose than the others, but more burdened by Harding's irritatingly overblown style. Earth is visited by an extraterrestrial but clearly human couple. Kinnear, head of Earth's space program—called "Operation Deep Freeze" because its modus operandi is to shoot off ships full of humans in suspended animation in hopes that maybe someday one of them will land somewhere habitable—is visiting the extraterrestrial guy. ("No octopi-inspired monster this, but a noble being who carried his very existence like a proud heritage, who seemed to know pride in every inch of his superbly muscled, grey-tinged body and who regarded him with eyes devoid of deceit and possessed only of an open curiosity.")

Kinnear's goal is to pry loose the secret of faster-than-light travel. In the course of conversation, the alien Arl suggests that Operation Deep Freeze is cruel and pointless, and if it wasn't for Earth's great music he and spouse would have moved on rather quickly—and, by the way, there's no FTL drive. "A creeping, tortuous paralysis seemed to suddenly move over Roul's body as the first inkling of implication behind the alien's words crept up upon him." The aliens have such long lifespans that they don't need FTL (I guess they are not easily bored either). "Roul still stared with mounting horror as the alien's last words struck a death knell to his dreams, to everybody's dreams, and brought the door of the universe closed against their scrabbling fingers.... His right hand curled into an angry fist that was raised briefly, against the uncaring sky." Annoyingly, Judith Merril gave this, rather than one of the better Harding stories, an Honorable Mention.

Harding has the *New Worlds* Profile in **116** (an issue in which he does not have a story): 25 years old in 1962, he'd discovered SF through Buck Rogers and other comics, was involved in fandom, pursued a career in photography (covering film-making, including *On the Beach*), is married to a "beautiful Dutch girl" and plans to go to Europe "with an eye upon either a professional writing career or motion pictures"[42]: favorite SF writers are Sturgeon, Blish, Clarke, Leiber, Aldiss and Ballard.

§

Of the new, new contributors, the most impressive is Steve Hall, though more for quantity than quality. Under his own name and his pseudonym Russell Markham, he published 13 stories during the year in the Nova magazines, and he didn't even get started until the March *Science Fiction Adventures*. Seven of the 13 are in *New Worlds*. Hall might be described as an instant hack, a reasonably facile writer, but often an amateurish one. For example, one of his stories, "Pandora's Box" (**122**) contains the following third paragraph: "Greg mentally reviewed the sequence of events which had led to him being appointed as the Chief Construction Engineer of the United Nations' base on Earth's natural satellite."

---

42. He didn't get to Europe for another 42 years, and despite some significant Australian awards, including the 1980 Children's Book of the Year Award and the A. Bertram Chandler Award, had abandoned SF and fantasy by 1983.

Overall, though, the story is modestly clever. People are on the moon, matter transmission has been invented, a box with flashing lights mysteriously appears in the general area of human activity. Opened, it contains an 18-inch egg-shaped object with a button on it. What to do? Don't push the button, obviously. But maybe there's a timer and it's already started ticking; maybe moving it again will set it off. So they matter-transmit the box to Alpha Centauri, which four years later disappears from the sky. "One month later, a United Earth government was an accomplished fact."

"Think of a Number" **(118)** is another boring iteration of the one about the superior aliens who menace humanity but are sent packing by some variety of human ingenuity, in this case stage magic disguised as psi.

"Visual Aid" **(119)** is a clever idea incompetently rendered. A bunch of kids is on a school tour of a spaceship, somebody pushes the wrong button and they are off into space with no food or return fuel. But here's a planet, so they land, and nobody notices because it's Earth right after the end of World War II and everybody in Europe is a bit preoccupied. Well, that's an interesting plot setup—how human-like alien children could survive and fit into a human society in chaos—but Hall proceeds to throw it away and flash forward some unspecified number of years, where a psychiatrist has just hired a new receptionist, who is smart and good-looking, and he asks her to help him out at a dinner party, where she displays psi talents. Lo, and ho hum—two of the refugees have found each other.

"Paradox Lost" **(120)**, a title used no fewer than seven times in the SF magazines, is the old "time machine, kill your grandfather" gimmick, but this one is from the grandfather's viewpoint. He persuades his grandson (who says his mother has already been conceived so he's not afraid) to send him to the future rather than shooting him; but then somebody else shows up ready to shoot the grandson for interfering with his timeline, and quickly there's an infinite regress (progress?). This one is more clever and compact than its predecessors.

The same is true of "Just in Time" (**124**), of which Carnell says: "In six short months Steve Hall has made quite an impression in the British science fiction field and as his experience grows so does the stature of his writing technique." Several rich and sociopathic types are sitting around trying to come up with an idea for their next criminal exploit when a misdirected time machine appears in their living room. They get the time traveller drunk and use his machine to perpetrate an ingenious art theft, then send the traveller on his way. But then the time police appear in the living room in *their* time machine, acting out a Scotland Yard routine about the protagonists' activities, wipe out the events and their memories and give the perps a particularly poetic if unexplained comeuppance. This is of course all outrageously contrived, but Hall has learned to move things along quickly and economically so it goes down smoothly.

The first Russ Markham story appears in **124**, "Who Went Where?", a competently formulaic space exploration story. The team of astronauts—two married couples—arrives on a planet where all the artifacts of civilization have been abandoned Mary Celeste-style, and solve the problem stated in the title from available clues. Per Miller/Contento, it is the first of the Galactic Union Survey series. "Mood Indigo" (**125**), also as by Markham, is Hall's try at a technical puzzle. The characters are testing a force field, which has been erected around an island with them on it, and which proves to shift the wavelength of light (hence the title). Not much is done with that idea (if anything could be); but when they turn the field off, it stays on, because the energy from the ocean waves lapping against it is enough to keep it going. They're trapped. What to do? Hook up the generator to the field again, turn it on, then turn the power off, and it will drain the stored energy from the field. Does this have any relation to reality? Hard to say with an imaginary invention. And I don't know if it is accident or design that the main character's name is Don Channing, same as the protagonist of George O. Smith's pioneering geek epic *Venus Equilateral*.

These stories are all readable enough despite their occasional infelicities. What's irritating is their lack of ambition. Hall seems only to want to learn the game as played, and play more of it. There's nothing distinctive or edgy about any of them.

A solider if not scintillating performance comes from Joseph Green, an American writer who worked for NASA. Green makes his debut in **115** with "The Engineer" (his first published story) and quickly follows it with four more stories during the year (plus one in *If*). "The Engineer" is a didactic tale of psychotherapeutic virtual reality. The protagonist is a henpecked and rat-raced fellow who has had a nervous breakdown in a competitive and regimented near future. In his induced fantasy he is stranded on a planet with simple natives, takes up with one of their beautiful women, and turns off his distress signal. Soon he's bored with the agricultural life, his paramour's sexual appetite outruns his, and he comes down with appendicitis before being retrieved from this fantasy, having learned his lesson— but he knows his reconciliation to his own world won't last. It's capably enough written but quite talky, the sort of thing you'd expect to see in *Analog* except for the no-way-out ending and the talk of sexual appetites.

The next four are all part of the series that was fixed up in 1965 for Ballantine and Gollancz as *The Loafers of Refuge*, which I read at the time and remember finding benign but not compelling. The scene: humans have colonized and homesteaded Refuge, which is inhabited by the indigenous and very humanoid but hirsute Loafers, so called because they don't seem to work much, and live in harmony with nature by such expedients as telepathically controlling the animals. In "Initiation Rites" (**117**), Carey, the first human child born on the planet, announces that he is going through the Loafer initiation so he too can control animals. The usual conflict between bigotry and tolerance is played out in the usual way, and Carey shows everybody by using his new abilities to keep his disabled uncle from being trampled by a giant *grogroc*, the beast that killed his father.

"The Colonist" (**121**) opens on Earth, where Sam Harper

walks out on his wife and son and the idle and constricted life on a completely urbanized planet (he lives in one of the high-rises that cover the South Island of New Zealand). He volunteers for the colonization draft, finds a suitable woman to marry on the ship out (courtship takes about a minute and a half), and gets set up to farm and sell his produce to Earth—except some alien trees are strangling his peanuts with their roots, and the Loafers take great exception to chopping the trees down. Strife is avoided (except for one hothead whom the Loafers handle with ease) when Carey and the Loafer Timmy talk to the Loafer elders, figure out that these *breshwahr* trees are intelligent and that the peanuts have something that they really want—borax from the colonists' fertilizer, plentiful and cheap as dirt. Problem solved through tolerance and understanding and fertilizer delivery, Honorable Mention conferred by Judith Merril.

"Life Force" (**124**) is a detour, much more incisive and less benign, with no visible connection to the Loafers and their planet, though it appears in *The Loafers of Refuge*. On the planet Barren, a young poet making a living as a biologist attends the Pageant with the head of the Earth legation, and gets a running commentary. A thousand years ago, a ship full of Earth colonists crash-landed, tried to survive, encountered the primitive and humanoid Hued Ones. The humans first reduced them to sexual slavery and then began eating them when other agricultural and gustatory expedients failed, after a ceremonial declaration that they are animals. The Pageant concludes by slaughtering another dozen of them. The legation head explains: "To stop it is to acknowledge that it has been wrong all along, to admit that the Hued Ones are not animals." So he puts it to the poet: do you want to stay here and try to stop all this by developing some meat agriculture, so Barren can enter the community of civilized worlds? Here's a terrifying turn on the "problem solved through tolerance and understanding" theme—monstrous evil to be coaxed out of existence by providing a more palatable (as it were) alternative, the skull beneath the smiley face—or vice versa, I guess. One wonders if Green appreciated the utter grimness of what he was writing. Probably not.

"Transmitter Problem" (125) is cheerier, returning to the Loafers' world. The big problem with matter transmission is that it kills living animals, but Doreen—sister of the above mentioned Carey—has learned from Phazz, her pet *breshwahr* tree, now uplifted by the colonists' borax fertilizer, how to keep her mind right and survive the transmission. But the man in charge won't let her try it out, and nobody will support her. That all changes when news comes through of an anarchistic rebellion on Earth: "The world's leading psychologists had been called in on the problem, and had issued a statement within twenty-four hours. They blamed the breakdown of authority on a mass psychosis which had been building up for years, and of which they had repeatedly warned authorities." The gross crowding and regimentation of Earth have reached a breaking point. So Doreen and her brother, and Loafer friend Timmy, force the transmitter operator to send her (and the tree, in its pot) to Earth. She uses her Loafer mind control skills to get the man on the other end to send her back, and here's the solution to Earth's problems: "'We could take a million people a year here, for the next thousand years,' said Carey in a slow, thoughtful voice." Oh dear.

Bill Spencer is not quite new and not quite regular, having had one story each in 1960 and 1961. "Little Horror" (114) is a proto-nanotechnology story, about a man who programs tiny machinery to make ever smaller replications of itself and then generate near-microscopic consumer goods like transistor radios, which make him rich. But something else is going on in his micro-factory—first some gray fuzz in a corner, then what looks like a developing insectile form, then a wasp-like creature that stings him nearly to death—suggesting that if you build something small enough, unknown malevolent forces that can't influence anything bigger will use it to come after you, Lovecraft meets *Popular Mechanics* or maybe quantum physics. This one is modestly well done, unlike Spencer's earlier ones, which were floridly ridiculous.

He splits the difference in "The Analyser" (**118**), which, like "Minor Operation," might have been closer to the cutting edge in 1962, but is yesterday's news now. In a utopian future, Lisa is smitten with Don, and the last step before they get married is to check in with the Analyser, which of course tells her that they are incompatible and fixes her up with the wonderful and considerate Harry. It takes a week or so for her to get bored with Harry, so she goes back to Don, who promises fights but also "fire, light, exaltation, sudden joy, swift happiness."

Barrington J. Bayley, as P. F. Woods, makes his first solo appearance in *New Worlds* (following a 1959 pseudonymous collaboration with Moorcock) with "Double Time" (**120**), a peculiar parallel-worlds story about a professor whose wife has been killed by one of his experiments and who snatches a counterpart from a world close enough to ours that she doesn't know the difference. Understanding his crime, he ceases to be jealous. This is all framed in a discussion of transverse particles, which pass energy perpendicular to the direction of time. Bayley's stories tend to read as if he hasn't seen any SF later than Gernsback, and this is no exception.

Alan Burns' "Pixy Planet" (**117**), his only *New Worlds* appearance (he had another half dozen in *Authentic, Science Fantasy* and *Science Fiction Adventures*), is a pleasantly Vanceian short story with a rambling plot and a strange and remote human society lightly sketched. The Federation has been militarily defeated by the Thrag (The Holy Rebellion Against Government). 20-year-old anthropologist Dela leaves the isolated Federation garrison on Foresdel to marry Tass, a native wind-seller. The simple Foresdelians, with the aid of the indigenous Pixies, prove to be more sophisticated and powerful than anyone had expected, and repel the Thrag with ease. They also eliminate the Federation base, about which they had been having doubts anyway, while saving its people. Judith Merril gave this one an Honorable Mention.

B(rian) N. Ball's "The Pioneer" (**115**), the first of his handful of stories in the SF magazines—he had one more in *New*

Worlds—is a fairly tedious Cold War period piece, a not-quite-thriller about a space launch. The man in charge defected from Eastern Europe somewhere, except he didn't really—he secretly helps kill real defectors. He wouldn't mind killing the astronaut, who he thinks is dallying with his wife; poetic vigilante justice is administered.

Richard Graham's "Schizophrenic" (**123**), last of his four stories in *New Worlds*, is an SF sitcom and quite an accomplished one. Protagonist Raymond is walking down the street minding his business when the world twists and jerks and a couple of men snatch him into the future, because he's just the right size and shape to be swapped temporarily for Crowther, a future-dweller who wants a week's Twentieth Century vacation. So Crowther pops back into our time with Raymond's clothes and the contents of his pockets and a great deal of attitude, goes to Raymond's house, interacts with Raymond's wife who thinks he's Raymond gone nuts, goes to his job, goes shopping (though the idea of paying for things takes a while to sink in), enthusiastically accepts the wife's suggestion that he see a psychiatrist, winds up in the toils of the law and then is rescued by his contemporaries, with Raymond returned to face the music. It's done at the right length with the right tone (slightly Pythonesque) and would make a good half-hour TV show in the right hands.

Kathleen James (pseudonym of Joyce Carstairs Hutchinson, who also, we recall, wrote as Wilhelmina Baird), makes her second and final appearance in *New Worlds* with "The Seventh Man" (**117**), a capable and amusing space opera/mystery involving smuggled drugs, a stowaway who turns up dead, missing cargo and stores, a peculiar smell, and a captain who unaccountably heads the ship into the Sun. The denouement is strictly used furniture, but then so was most SF by this time, and it is well enough turned. Too bad she didn't write more.

§

And now to the dregs, or the crumbs at the bottom of the

box. H. L. Draper, whose other credits in Miller/Contento include five stories in *London Mystery* 1962-68, but none in the SF magazines, contributes "The Bundenberg Touch" (**115**), a smoothly written but tediously contrived spaceship-in-distress comedy involving an aquatic creature named Agnes grown in a tank by the ship's hydroponicist. H. B. Caston's "A Question of Drive" (**123**), his only credit in the SF magazines, is a pulpishly competent run-of-the-mill piece about a man trying to spy out and steal the Sirians' near-instantaneous space drive, with an out-of-the-hat techy surprise about what's going on. Archie Potts' "The Warriors" (**124**), the first of his two contributions to the SF magazines, is an almost Gernsbackian if reasonably well written story about an old guy who has figured out how to train ants with electric currents to act out war games. He comes to a bad end, but then so do his ants, and the whole thing is thoroughly passé.

Robert Ray's "The Craving for Blackness" (**122**) is an incoherent and incompetent story the gist of which seems to be that the characters spend most of it in an elaborate Chinese-box virtual reality scenario to escape from the fact that only women can go into space ("They bend where we break."). Astonishingly to me, the readers put it in second place. This is one of four stories in the SF magazines from 1950 to 1967 under the Robert Ray byline. It is said in Miller/Contento to be a pseudonym for one Al Bernstein, who published nothing under his name but seven stories as Donald Bern during the early 1940s in *Amazing* and *Fantastic Adventures* (e.g., "Mystery of the Amazing Battery") plus one more as Albert Bernsen in *FA* in 1950.

In Morris Nagel's "Serpent in Paradise" (**122**), the intrepid space explorers are lured by the survivor of an earlier shipwreck into a sort of pocket Shangri-La with addictive hallucinogenic flowers; once you're hooked, you can't leave because lack of the flowers will kill you and they don't travel well, and now they are dying out so everybody's going to die. It's pretty archaic-seeming, though unaccountably Judith Merril gave it an Honorable Mention. This is the only appearance of Nagel's byline, a pseudonym for Australian Stephen Cook, who had one story in *Science Fantasy* this same year. He took his own life shockingly young, at 25.

Paul Corey's "Operation Survival" (**125**) is a stupid and offensive story in which the residents of the Willegar School for the Mentally Retarded—"feebs," as they are described repeatedly—are commandeered by some stereotypical military types for a tryout at launching nuclear weapons in the event of an attack that knocks out the more conventional responders. The "feebs'" performance is analogized to monkeys on typewriters composing a book. Paul Corey's only other genre credit is a vignette in *The Diversifier* 15 years later.

§

As noted, Carnell has only one editorial during the year, and it's pretty dry.

"1961... in Retrospect" (**116**) proposes that 1959 and 1960 were lean years in world SF, and that if anything 1961 was even more dismal, yet it may be called the Year of the Renaissance. Magazines were stable and contents were improved if not sensational; paperbacks were booming but there was a sharp decline in quality. Paperback originals were up in the US but still resisted in the UK. Carnell notes that there is now limited importing of US paperbacks, which stops British publishers from buying British rights, leaving them little to publish. The myth of the endless backlog of good material is over.

Meanwhile, US firms are trying to buy into UK publishers—they want access to the whole British Empire. UK writers can make more money selling in the US, where they can get an extra payment for British rights—as much as, or more than, British publishers normally offer. Hardcover SF "has just about reached rock bottom again" in both US and UK. Carnell likes Aldiss's *The Primal Urge*, Anderson's *Three Hearts and Three Lions*, Blish's *Titan's Daughter*, Clarke's *A Fall of Moondust*, Galouye's *Dark Universe*, and Sturgeon's *Some of Your Blood*.

But the outstanding book of the year, he says, was Merril's sixth annual anthology, including Aldiss's "Old Hundredth" from *New Worlds*.

Some of the guest editorials are by writers who appeared in the magazine this year—they are discussed above along with the writers' fiction—but others are not. These are wildly uneven. Edward Mackin, a writer who has not previously appeared in *New Worlds* at all (his Hek Belov stories were exclusively in *Science Fantasy* after *Authentic* folded), contributes "Anything Is Possible" (**123**), which rambles on about the supposed possibilities of SF while keeping one foot firmly fixed in cliché and the other in equivocation. Samples: "The quality of the writing, and the techniques employed, have improved tremendously over the years; but something of the old magic seems to have vanished along with that first innocence." "I'm all for the balanced, if superficial, view when it comes to sex in s-f; for pulchritude rather than pornography." And: "when the estimable Mr. Ballard talks about s-f becoming abstract and 'cool' he is obviously stretching a hand towards the intelligentsia."

Mackin has the *New Worlds* Profile in the issue, and it is revealed that he has worked as a press-tool setter (with hobby of repairing, or wrecking, radios, TVs, and tape recorders), postman, salesman, painter, "but more recently he has settled down to being the central Editor of a small circulation literary review paper which reaches most parts of the world"—studiously not named.

William F. Temple takes up sex and gender in "That Impossible She" (**115**), with results that are depressingly familiar and ought to be left to speak for themselves, e.g.: "For the most part, women are interested in new scientific ideas only to the extent of being unreasoningly afraid of them...." "Man doesn't reason as much as he likes to think he does, but woman reasons hardly at all. She thinks with her glands, including glands which men don't possess." "Man reasons and explores. Woman reacts and stays at home." "Any soldier going into battle with a woman on his sword-arm or his mind will be handicapped. Similarly, so will a s-f narrative." But on the other hand:

> Clearly something is unsatisfactory about the male characters as depicted. Something is lacking.
>
> One feels this about the famed *Starship Troopers*.... Where are all the new little Starship Troopers to come from? The general impression is that of a troop of perennial boy scouts.... But these Peter Pans feel compelled to prove that they aren't just a bunch of fairies from the Never-Never-Land. Sometimes they perilously approach what Robertson Davies describes as "the false and excessive manliness of the tough homosexual" in their attempts to show that they are not only men but, in fact, *homo superior*.[43]
>
> Confine s-f to male characters and they remain emotional dwarfs.
>
> Bring women into it, and they gum up the works.
>
> The solution, as I see it, is to try one's best to leave women, as characters, out of the plot if possible. But also try not to ignore their influence on men. Aim at depicting men who have some knowledge of women—not just carnal knowledge, either—who, indeed, have learnt something of life from their womenfolk.
>
> Then maybe we'll have spacemen who are complete human beings.... Women fit into s-f by reflection, not presence.

Temple gets the *New Worlds* Profile this issue. It notes his distinguished SF pedigree.

---

43. Here Temple anticipates the argument made at greater length by Thomas M. Disch, which concluded: "A friend of mine has assured me he knew several enlistments directly inspired by a reading of *Starship Troopers*. How much simpler it would have been for those lads just to go and have their ears pierced." Disch, "The Embarrassments of Science Fiction," in Peter Nicholls (ed.), *Science Fiction at Large* (Harper & Row, 1976), pp. 154-55.

Arthur Sellings responds to Temple in "Postmortem" in **118**, equally direly: "...there is currently far too much emphasis on [sex]—a decadent, almost morbid preoccupation with sexual functions.... It is an imbalance found in much of the best contemporary serious literature, and I do not believe that s-f suffers by comparison." And more: "Personally, I find that women come naturally into s-f. Just because of their illogical 'feminine' attitudes, they make good foils for s-f argument. One can overdo it, of course, so that you finish up, as *Galaxy* did, with too many cosy stories of things happening to a family when they should rightly have happened to individuals." Huh?

Groff Conklin, in "The Third Level" (**119**), provides his take on what's wrong with SF: too much rehashed semi-scientific extrapolation, too little attention to people (i.e., "the life and thinking of the human (or, for Pete's sake, non-humans too!) who are the hand-puppets in these pseudoscientific marionette shows"). This takes four pages for no discernible reason. In **122**, N.J. Patterson takes issue with Conklin's statement that "it would be difficult if not impossible, for example, to write a thrilling melodrama about the recent discoveries in ATP and DNA in biochemistry." "Why should it be impossible?" Patterson asks. Why indeed. Conklin has the *New Worlds* Profile in **119**, nattily dressed with bow-tie looking like he just lost a part in a 1940s movie to Cary Grant. It is revealed that his 29th anthology is about to appear from Dell, but this is a weekend occupation: he spends four days a week as Senior Writer with the American Diabetes Association, and is otherwise occupied collaborating with Noah Fabricant, M.D., on *Colds, Cures, and Complications*.

Robert Silverberg contributes "S-F and Escape Literature" in **121**; Carnell's blurb says "Although he no longer writes science fiction stories Guest Editor Robert Silverberg still retains a close interest in the genre...." This piece is a trifle stiff and stuffy coming from the author of large piles of capable adventure fiction and the smooth and graceful essays we've seen more recently in *Asimov's* and elsewhere, but the point is clear enough—all literature is escape literature, it's just a matter of where you're escaping, and how well the escape is executed. "Escape is necessary. We escape from the city on weekends, we escape from our livelihoods for weeks at a time. The human organism, if it is to grow and prosper, needs change, refreshment, periodic escape."

One of the livelier of these pieces is John Baxter's "View from the Underground" (122). The *New Worlds* Profile in that issue, complete with neotenous photo, says: "This month we take the unprecedented step of offering the Guest Editorial chair to a reader instead of one of the well-known authors in the field." Baxter starts out effusively praising the previous guest editorials as interesting and well-written, but then dismisses them as "short-sighted, illogical, and inconclusive," failing to offer any solutions to the "troubles of contemporary science fiction," obviously because the authors can't be objective about what they make their money from. Their false premise: that SF can be assessed separately from the rest of literature, and that unlike the rest of literature it has a purpose, as social critic and predictor. (Baxter seems to have read different guest editorials from those discussed above.) SF can't compete with such erudite characters as Lewis Mumford and Will Durant (!); "we don't stand a chance in the extrapolation business."

Anyway, SF writers have to mute their social criticism to avoid offending the audience (this, amusingly, in the same issue as Harrison's "The Streets of Ashkalon"). SF also doesn't do too well with science either; Baxter says that *Analog* has abandoned its audience of four or five years previously and is now published for "the young technologists, supplying them with scientific amusettes and light reading for hours spent out of the lab,"[44] a conclusion he bases on its letter column.

And SF can't do fiction either, since while it has tarried with social speculation, everybody else has been perfecting their

---

44. Many years later, Baxter would marry a French woman and now, a devoted Francophile, lives in Paris. So this choice of word "amusettes" might itself be a successful extrapolation.

use of language and experimenting with technique. "The kind of over-plotted narrative story that makes up the bulk of short and middle-length s-f these days is almost unknown in modern literature.... The short story is for mood and emotion. It catches the brief moment of insight and then stops while it is ahead." On the other hand: "Novels are used for the exhaustive delineation of character," but nobody in SF is good enough for that and none of them could have written *The Catcher in the Rye*. And SF's characters are pretty lousy too. Baxter allows for some bright spots—Ballard and Aldiss ("occasionally shows signs of intriguing individuality")—but "in general, science fiction produces the most old-fashioned writing in the world today."

So what's the answer? "We can give *imagination*. No, not the old 'sense of wonder' cliché (which nobody has ever actually explained to the satisfaction of anybody *I* know)." "We can see in science a new kind of beauty"—citing as examples, in addition to *Mission of Gravity* and *More Than Human*—Bester's novels. Say what?

> We should trim our plots of the outdated thinking
> that motivates them. Stop worrying whether our sto-
> ries "mean" anything. The beauty of art is "meaning"
> enough. Stop worrying if the characters "stand up and
> cast a shadow"—stop worrying about character devel-
> opment at all if you like; a number of young writers,
> John Updike for instance, get along fine without strong
> characters, relying on the beauty and skill of their writ-
> ing. Abandon the thinking that demands a beginning, a
> middle and an end for every story, and concentrate on
> writing logical, craftsmanlike prose.

Do that, and SF may have a chance to join the main body of literature, get rid of the stigma, and get rid of the large quantity of dumb SF. Baxter concludes by saying that everybody in fandom doesn't agree with him, but almost every fan he knows is widely read both inside and outside SF, and "There is a growing contempt for the literary quality of what is being served up to us today by many of the science fiction magazines."

As I've noted before, Baxter's own first SF story, "Vendetta's End," appears almost simultaneously with this editorial (*Science Fiction Adventures* **29**, dated November 1962), and it's a heavy character study absolutely chockfull of stock plot.

In **124**'s "Postmortem," Arthur Sellings complains of Baxter's "Little Englander attitude to s-f," which rather confusedly seems to imply that Baxter is proposing that sf writers cling to their narrow ghetto. Sellings wants SF to "re-examine its purpose, cut out the rank growth of vulgarisation, find—all right—*new* roots." (This reminds me of that John Sayles line, "It isn't easy to invent a tradition.") "I, in brief, want s-f to step into its inheritance." (I.e., to be taken seriously by the swells and the gallery.)

The cover of **124** features a beaming Arthur C. Clarke shaking hands with a person alleged to be Yuri Gagarin, viewed from behind in uniform and cap and holding one of Clarke's books in his other hand. Clarke's "guest editorial" is his acceptance speech upon receiving in Delhi the Kalinga Prize (or Award as the magazine has it) for the popularization of science, previously given to the likes of Julian Huxley and Bertrand Russell. It is a nice piece of PR for SF: sense of wonder motivates all true scientists as well as artists, cultural impact of SF is large and unacknowledged, it's helped change the world by promoting space flight, promotes the cosmic viewpoint, is the literature of change—nothing we haven't heard before, but a more pleasant set of clichés than many, and asserted by one who's entitled.

But the clouds move in only a month later, heralding the malign presence of Lan Wright.

He has the *New Worlds* Profile in **125**, which explains his nearly four-year absence from the magazine: he's been spending his spare time as a radio commentator for Watford Football Club on their private broadcasts to the local hospitals. His editorial, "Getting the Message," is a drearily familiar farrago of anti-intellectual clichés. He accuses the other editorial writers of implying that "Science Fiction has a message for the world at large." He says. "All this semi-pathological pap" ignores that most SF writers are semi-amateurs, the public "reads what it wants to read whether it be westerns, thrillers, romances, who-dun-its—or s-f," and the proportionate size of the SF readership has remained more or less constant. This notion is elaborated in terms that might be described as semi-pathological hostility: "I am sick of critics who try and interpret the work of authors, and I am sick of authors who sit back and smirk their self-satisfaction over motives attributed to them which they never intended." None of either are named.

Wright notes the controversy over Heinlein's *Starship Troopers*, and says the book "is an entertainment, and a rattling good adventure story. It is not, cannot be (and was probably never intended to carry) any sort of philosophical message. Any message has been grafted on by a semi-intellectual hysteria emanating from pseudo-intellectual morons who batten on the ideas of others under the grossly misused heading of 'criticism.'" Words fail me, thought fails him. Further: "A side effect of all this is the trumpeting that greets a new author who shows a new style. I recall the eulogies that greeted Jimmy Ballard and Colin Kapp—both authors whom I admire—but I'll wager that neither of them wrote his first few stories with any idea of passing on his own personal testament." If he were lucky, he might break even on that bet—but maybe not.

§

The letter column "Postmortem" appears in five of the 12 1962 issues, and much of its contents is devoted to hashing over the guest editorials, often tediously. I've quoted some of the less tedious above. In **114** there is a very long letter from John Baxter, who trashes covers, praises Lewis's surrealism, complains about SF published in slicks and compares Heinlein's *Saturday Evening Post* stories ("weak, limp, and unappetising") to his "*good* novels" like *The Day After Tomorrow* (a.k.a. *Sixth Column*) (!) or *Stranger In A Strange Land*. *No Blade of Grass* and *Day Of The Triffids* are "blood-and thunder with some sex and sadism thrown in as a make-weight." He's tired of Sector General, disappointed in "Storm-Wind," tired of Brit disaster novels.

Much of "Postmortem"'s contents comes from the magazine's professional writers, who can be as tedious as anyone else. In **114**, Edward Mackin argues with John Rackham: no, the scientists wouldn't fix everything if in charge. Meanwhile Brian Aldiss trashes Rackham's claim that SF is more realistic than other forms; Rackham compared SF to thrillers and cowboy stories, and Aldiss asks, "Why always set this lowly standard?" Donald Malcolm responds to Lee Harding's blaming the writers for the decline in SF quality—it doesn't pay, quality defers to quantity—why not have bonus payments for the most popular stories?

In **116**, John Rackham is back polemically arguing with people who argued with his guest editorial ("I expected to catch some of the airy-fairy minded with that editorial of mine, but never hoped to snare such big fish as I did.") John Baxter takes issue with Arthur Sellings' editorial of the previous year, asking why SF need to change its image—does it really need to be more popular? And he suggests that the search for SF's roots is a blind alley since there are so many of them. Keith Otter agrees with Lee Harding that SF is in a rut, and suggests that interplanetary stories have about been exhausted, but thinks the fault may be with the audience: "Perhaps the fans have built up an immunity to wonder." He wants extrapolation of "new ideals, inventions, trends, and sciences (psionics?)"

In **118**, Edward Mackin continues to argue with Rackham: the scientifically minded are no better than the worst of us and won't do a better job than politicians. He also praises Konstantin Tsiokovski and his predecessor Kibalchich. Lee Harding argues with Donald Malcolm arguing with him: SF ought to be a community venture, success didn't kill it but stunted its growth. The voluble Rackham has two letters: as Rackham, he touts John Langdon-Davies' *Man: The Known and the Unknown*, and under his own name of John T. Phillifent, recounts a Czech psychologist's experiments in bibliotherapy: he gave psychotic patients selected books, found reading was especially good for depression, and "popular scientific literature" (local s-f) "yielded the best results since it made the greatest demand on the patient, but did not arouse pathological distortions." So SF makes you saner, not crazy.

In **122**, Edward Mackin is back, praising Ballard's editorial with its original and intriguing ideas, but disagreeing with his attitude about space fiction. Ballard is right that the space opera readers form the backbone of the readership, and you know what happens when you remove the backbone from something. James Inglis of Ayreshire (author of two stories in *Nebula* previously, and two more in *New Worlds* a little later) also finds Ballard's ideas interesting, but he too defends space fiction—the problem is the writers should do a better job of it. Archie Potts—also soon to appear with a story—says he's been reading since the 1940s, and what's all this fuss about the lost sense of wonder? He likes the best of the old and the best of the new—J. G. Ballard is his favorite, followed by Bulmer, Brunner, and Aldiss among others. One Colin Daly takes up relativity. He should have left it alone.

In **124**, Donald Malcolm thinks the guest editorials are "the best idea that has hit science fiction for many a long day." (He'll get his shot next year, in **128**.)

M. Birch finds it "disconcerting" that so many writers want SF to become an "accepted" literature. "Surely this would be the worst fate that could overcome a form of writing which is exploring the possibilities of science and philosophy with imagination and skill. (I am thinking of J. G. Ballard particularly.)" Whether he is thinking of Ballard as promoting a terrible fate, or as exploring science and philosophy with imagination and skill, is not clear. And, closing out the year in correspondence, Mrs. Judith McLaughlin of Epping, NSW, Australia, announces: "I'm a housewife, ordinary variety, with one strange quirk according to my friends. I actually *like* s-f!" And why does it always have to be credible and scientific? "Being a woman (and it *does* make a tremendous difference), I thoroughly enjoy a well-written fantasy story." Paging William Temple!

§

Leslie Flood continues as regular book reviewer, appearing in eight of the 12 issues, with his usual nice judgments succinctly expressed, and a few unexpected ones. He says of Aldiss's *Hothouse* (**123**): "Basically it is an extension of the Burroughs' type of fantastic adventures and heroics, translated into the remote future of Earth. It's a lot more readable, of course, and a mite more subtle, but just as tedious in its repetitious violence, casual wonder, and the contrived terminology of the sentient vegetable creatures proliferating the green undergrowth covering all the Earth's landmass." And then: "By contrast Zenna Henderson's stories of 'The People' are coolly refreshing...." He has high praise for Damon Knight's *Far Out* in **116**, thinks even more of Budrys' *The Unexpected Dimension* in **118**—Budrys is an "even better writer" than Knight, he says. He waxes impatient with faint praise concerning some big names following familiar grooves. "One could almost feel a tri-di projection of the Grey Lensman telepathically approving over one's shoulder whilst reading Mark Clifton's *Eight Keys to Eden*.... It is superficially slick, highly derivative in ideas, and not susceptible of close analysis, but it *is* extremely readable, and that baited hook is in...."

He likes *The Great Explosion* by "Liverpool's gift to *Analog*" (i.e. Eric Frank Russell): "an uproarious series of deep space adventures, although the sharp edge of his sallies against obtuse authority is becoming blunted somewhat by repetition" (**118**). Simak's *Time Is the Simplest Thing* is "strictly for the dyed-in-the-wool reader to whom the more esoteric principles of the suspension of disbelief come easily, but which may prove a little too glib and uneven for some" (**119**). Flood joins the gender wars in **124**, praising Naomi Mitchison's *Memoirs of a Spacewoman*, noting its "feminine slant on the moral problems involved" in alien contact and "an attention to physical details often eyebrow-raising to a mere male (and at times positively distasteful)."

Flood displays his usual exasperation with Charles Eric Maine, saying of *The Darkest of Nights*, "I am desperately hoping that Mr. Maine will some day capitalize his undoubted and expert talents for a journalistic presentation of modern science, and write the great English science fiction novel" (**124**). Then there are the books I've never heard of, the way led by Olga Hesky's *The Purple Armchair*, in which an alien who looks like the eponymous item of furniture is to report on whether to take over Earth; "a subtly chilling indictment of humanity not surviving as it has done in the past, without aggressive spirit" (**115**). And, distressingly, he has news: "History has been made again—the Penguin edition of John Wyndham and Lucas Parkes' *The Outward Urge* (3/-) went into the top ten bestseller paperbacks for August in the UK, the first time a science fiction book has been in this category" (**124**).

Carnell joins Flood in several issues, mostly contributing one-liners, usually about American paperbacks. In **117** he drives by Leiber's *The Silver Eggheads* ("the ingredients take on the appearance of a mess of mental porridge") and delivers death by faint praise to Ballard's *The Wind from Nowhere* ("Good for a 'disaster' novel.")

§

Advertising continues at a low level. There is no publishers' advertising. The SF Book Club takes a page in **116** and **120**, the BSFA takes half a page in **114**, **118** and **125** (latter two on the inside back cover). There are a couple of half pages each for *Industrial and Commercial Photographer* and *Film User*, two magazines published from the same address; and a quarter page in **117** for *Bloodhound Detective Story Magazine*. There are small ads in almost every issue, of little interest except that John Brunner "requires" copies of some magazines containing his stories in **125**, and in **119** "A copy of '*Last Men In London*' [is] urgently required." Stapledon always seemed to me to transcend urgency. And there are ads for the *Out of This World* TV show in **120** which actually push the house advertising off the inside and outside back covers.

§

So what's memorable in these issues? Unfortunately, not a lot. Kapp's "Lambda 1" and Ballard's "The Cage of Sand" are really the only first-rate pieces of fiction this year, though Aldiss's "Basis for Negotiation" looks like one until the end. Harrison's "The Streets of Ashka(e)lon" remains well known more for (what passed for) its iconoclasm at the time than for any outstanding merit, though it's a perfectly competent story. There are some near misses among Lee Harding's stories, and David Rome's "Meaning" almost makes the cut as well. At the less pretentious end of things, Alan Burns' "Pixy Planet" and Richard Graham's "Schizophrenic" are clever and well done. But overall the magazine remains unsatisfying. Its minimum level of competence was raised significantly in 1958 and 1959 and has stayed raised. But there's entirely too much room at the top, and nobody much is filling it.

4: APPROACHING THE
TERMINAL (1963-64)

New Worlds enters 1963 with issue **126** in the same drab garb as late 1962: covers with monochrome background. Small author photographs not too well reproduced. Story titles and authors' names in black type. Not very interesting abstract designs down the right margin. It gets grimmer. With **130**, the May issue, the photos disappear, leaving only titles, authors, and blurbs, not arranged very well, the result thoroughly cheap-looking.

Here we come to a nadir of sorts: Carnell's always shaky proofreading is foregrounded in the most embarrassing way on **130**, which announces in big letters Aldiss's story "The Under-Priveleged" (sic), with no pictures to distract the reader who can spell. And the next issue is cheap-looking in a special way: a scene from the film of *The Day of the Triffids* is murkily reproduced in black and white, except that the cover background is a dark orange rather than white, and black on dark orange is *really* hard to make out. If I hadn't read the book I'd have no idea what I was looking at. I may or may not know art, but I think I can recognize extremely bad judgment, or indifference.[45]

Things do rebound a bit. In August (**133**), the long-established rhomboidal *New Worlds* logo disappears, replaced by a title running down the left margin of the cover, with story titles and authors dominating the center, over a monochrome stylized

---

45. See these covers at http://www.sfcovers.net/mainnav.htm or http://www.philsp.com/mags/newworlds.html.

sketch of a Lunar surface, credited to Gerard Quinn. There's an attractive new set of typefaces too. This is the least shabby-looking cover style since Carnell abandoned painted covers, but it lasts only until the end of the year. The first four months of 1964—the last Nova issues—retain the arrangement of magazine title and contents listing, but there are no graphics at all, though at least there is some sense of arrangement if not, God forbid, graphic design. So the magazine goes out looking decent if not much more.[46]

And that is it for Carnell's *New Worlds*, not with a bang—not a visual one, anyway. Size and shape remain the same until the end. The price goes from 2/6 to 3/- with **134** and stays there.

The end, unusually for a magazine's demise, was announced months in advance—though not in the magazine itself. The actual decision was made on September 19, 1963, according to Mike Ashley's *Transformations*. It was reported in *Skyrack* 60 (November 12, 1963) based on a press release from Carnell, which said: "It is with regret that I announce that with the March published issues of *New Worlds Science Fiction* and *Science Fantasy*, these two publications will be discontinued and Nova Publications Ltd. will cease to exist. This decision has been forced upon us by a steady decline in sales during the past few years which stems directly from the lifting of the Import Ban and the subsequent intense competition with the paperback market, both home-produced and foreign-imported." (Carnell is not always consistent in talking about the supposed steady decline in circulation. In "Postmortem" in **128**, Lee Harding surmises that circulation has increased since the new covers started, and Carnell interpolates "You are quite right.")

Even more unusually, Carnell said he still needs material for the last few issues and authors should continue to submit until December 31. As a business matter one wonders why they didn't just pull the plug immediately and sink no more money into a doomed venture. I suppose the stakeholders in Nova did

46. Broderick, a sometime-layout designer, finds the last few issues better than that; quite elegant, in their clean, well-balanced, minimalist way.

not consider it just a business matter. They were fans.

Nothing is said in the magazine about the impending doom until the last issue, where there is a certain amount of muted fanfare. In a "Farewell Editorial," Carnell notes that he's writing on Friday the 13th and has been thinking for six months about how to announce the end of the magazine. There's also a half-page black-bordered box headed "The Editor Regrets," announcing that this is the last Nova issue but Roberts & Vinter will pick the magazine up. The reason for the transition is that magazine sales are declining while paperback sales are rising, and Nova can't change format (why this is impossible is not explained), but Roberts & Vinter will make the change to a format more closely resembling standard paperbacks.

Carnell announces the editorship of Michael Moorcock, to everyone's astonishment, and of Kyril Bonfiglioli at *Science Fantasy*, and assures the readership about Moorcock: "Despite his success as a *fantasy* writer, he is unlikely to allow this to influence his judgment on *science fiction* stories." Carnell thanks everybody and says "Let us not look upon this as the end of the line, but merely a natural stage of metamorphosis in the development of science fiction."

His own metamorphosis is announced a few pages earlier, in a full-page notice stating "You will want to know that John Carnell is at present working on an entirely new series to be called *New Writings in S-F.* Four new collections will appear each year." Hardcovers will be by Dennis Dobson, paperbacks by Corgi Books, first volume in the coming summer.[47] "Postmortem" contains a couple of pages' worth of valedictory letters from familiar and unfamiliar names, the former being Moorcock and Jim Cawthorn.

Carnell continues as the absentee landlord, his editorial pres-

---

47. As it happens, Broderick (aged 19) submitted a novella to *New Worlds* just in time to learn that Carnell was shutting it down, but in compensation the story was accepted for the premier issue of *New Writings in SF.* That story attracted a review in Australia awarding it the wooden spoon (or booby prize), justly.

ence manifesting only infrequently. All but two of the issues have guest editorials, and those two are the final issues. In **140** (the March 1964 issue), Carnell provides the classically titled "1964—A Dull Year," and in **141**, his last editorial fling—"Survey Report 1963" and, as already noted, the "Farewell Editorial." Actually the "Dull Year" editorial is about 1963, when to hear Carnell tell it, the only SF novels worth remembering were Vonnegut's *Cat's Cradle*, Ballard's *The Drowned World*, and Gunn's *The Joymakers*. The Trieste film festival was a bust (see below); but he allows that 1964 looks more promising, with Aldiss's *Greybeard* and Galouye's *Counterfeit World* coming up. Interestingly, he still does not mention the scheduled demise of *New Worlds* itself.

The "Survey Report 1963" (based on a reader survey published in **138**, the January 1964 issue) appears in the editorial slot and reports on 350 responses received in five weeks. The most striking findings are that the average age has dropped by nearly 5 percentage points (to 30.8 years) from the previous survey in 1958. Correspondingly, the proportion married has plummeted, and the number with no income has increased (though those who do have an income are making more than in 1958). Technical employment is down and non-technical employment up by 7 percentage points, but that seems to be accounted for by a 9-point increase in students, who are listed under non-technical for some reason. Carnell infers that the older readers are switching to paperbacks in droves, and notes their increasing number and sales figures.

He contributes several other non-fiction items in earlier issues, not in the editorial slot. In **127** there is the "Survey Report of 1962," not about a reader survey, but his Year That Was: he recounts his pleasure with the ABC TV series *Out of This World*, which didn't rate highly enough to be continued, and his displeasure with the "dismal and cheerless" year on the BBC, with a mediocre sequel to *A for Andromeda* and a third-rate serial, *The Monsters*.

In print, he notes the stability of the US SF magazine

scene, the slowly increasing number of books, and the lack of outstanding titles. In the UK, he says, things are looking up, mainly as a result of the Gollancz series. There's news of the Worldcon, the Hugos, and SF publishing elsewhere in Europe. His gripping preoccupation with media SF surfaces repeatedly, in articles in **132** and **134** on the Trieste First International SF Film Festival, in a half-page notice for the Festival of SF Films of the Eyeview Film Group of Bayswater Road, and in **131**, with the nearly undecipherable black and orange cover mentioned above, a near-paroxysm of boosterism for *The Day of the Triffids* film.

Scenes from it appear on the cover, back cover, and inside back cover, the latter two being only slightly less murky than the cover. The cover blurb declares it "The greatest science fiction film ever made!" Inside, Carnell has a three-page review, which is almost a short story in itself. The scene is set: "a great aura of mystery" has surrounded the film, odd things happened like the budget being cut (that's odd?), everything was "under wraps while the special effects were put in." Even when the stills were shown privately, Carnell remained apprehensive and "was prepared to write it off as a bad third-rate science fiction film." But he and Wyndham finally were able to attend a screening, and... "Ninety-five minutes later, it was with a great feeling of relief that we walked out into the Spring sunshine of Wardour Street.... Mere words, however, cannot convey the excellence of the drama or even the plot—it has to be seen to be believed!"

The first of the Trieste festival articles is in the same vein, an anticipatory puff piece describing the festival-to-come as "one of the most exciting and important events in the history of science fiction," to be accompanied by an exhibition of SF books and magazines. In the event, however, in a two-page piece titled "The Mystery of the 'Mare Trieste'" (**134**), Carnell records his disappointment: "...eight days of rather dull fantasies and off-beat movies one could hardly call science fiction.... Of the British entries, the less said the better, for they were appalling." He does praise the "last-minute French entry, *L'Jettie* [sic], a brilliantly contrived time-travel story made entirely from still photographs."

§

Though "The Literary Line-Up" remains regular, the magazine's other features show weakly in these issues. The *New Worlds* Profiles disappear after **134**, replaced by advertising. "Postmortem," the letter column, appears only four times, twice at the beginning of 1963, and then in the last two issues. I mention a number of the letters later, in connection with the stories or authors they comment on. Among the more notable generic items is the letter in **140** from Frank Michaels of Papatoetoe, NZ, who announces that he has been reading SF since 1930 and *New Worlds* since issue **4**, and says: "I've followed your series of editorials by guests with interest and with growing disbelief. Do they really believe the guff they write about s-f having a purpose, an art form? Let's be honest—the purpose of the s-f author is to earn money by writing." He also apologizes for writing his letter with a sprained wrist.

Mr. Michael's ire was no doubt fueled further by the letter from Mike (sic) Moorcock in **128**, agreeing with John Baxter's guest editorial that SF writers are too parochial, but not agreeing that plots are old-fashioned and novels should be concerned solely with character delineation. He adds:

> Certainly there is lots of scope for stylistic experiment in the s-f field and for experiment in story-telling technique—witness Aldiss, my favourite s-f stylist. Also favourites of mine are Beckett, [Anthony] Powell and [William] Golding. On the other hand I enjoy Iris Murdoch who tends to use the traditional plotting techniques. I'm all for innovation—Firbank is by far my favourite innovator—but the fact is that most s-f writers need the traditional means of story-telling since they aren't skilled or talented enough to dispense

with them without seriously spoiling their stories. If 'experimental' efforts are encouraged (a la *F&SF*, for instance) we get an abhortive [sic] apeing [sic] of mainstream experimentation where the author seems to think (and fools editor and reader into thinking) that a diffuse style, lack of plot and characters endowed with characteristics rather than personalities are sufficient, that coherent ideas, objective extrapolation and the rest are no longer necessary ingredients.

In fact this kind of story is the lazy writer's dream. On the other hand take the quoted *Tiger, Tiger* which, for all its experimentation, used a tried and trusty plot as a basis for the experiments.

He goes on to praise Aldiss some more as the only writer capable of rising to Baxter's occasion, and even Aldiss is uneven. "For God's sake don't encourage good craftsmen (s-f abounds with these, at least) to produce pretentious prose poems and vague mists of precise-sounding words instead of the good, solid stuff they are producing now. We might lose the one without gaining anything to take its place." He ends with *pro forma* praise for Carnell's magazines. In retrospect, this seems a truly startling manifesto from the soon-to-be editor of the flagship of the New Wave—although it applies quite well to most of Moorcock's own future *oeuvre*.

Baxter himself is back in **130**, where he gets nearly three pages—the whole of "Postmortem"—wrestling with Lan Wright's guest editorial of the previous year, starting politely but eventually pinning Wright to the mat, but why bother? Baxter actually drops a clanger as loud as some of Wright's, disputing Wright's claim that Orwell was only a political satirist and stating that several books including *Homage to Catalonia* have "no noticeable political bias."

As noted, the guest editorials continue until a couple of issues from the end. Most of them are by active *New Worlds* authors, so I mention them along with their fiction. However, in late 1963 they take a turn towards the academic, even though Carnell had certainly not run out of fiction authors. Did F. G. Rayer, E. R. James, and Colin Kapp decline their invitations? I'm sure we'll never know. Meanwhile, Dr. I. F. Clarke contributes "The Ragnarok Theme" in **134**. Clarke has the *New Worlds* Profile: he is head of the General Studies Department in the Royal College of Science and Technology, where he is known as the "Culture Vulture," and describes himself as "the missionary they failed to eat in five years." Starting in SF with *The War of the Worlds* rather than *Amazing*, he is two years past publishing his bibliography *The Tale of the Future*. His testament, as an Englishman migrated to Scotland: "I now find the heather and haggis a little difficult to endure and prefer cooking exotic meals, enjoy good wines and would rather drink beer in an English pub—above all, I detest stuffed-shirt academics."

The theme of Clarke's editorial: The more things change, the more they remain the same:

> Once all life was a single emergency, when the first communities lived always on the edge of disaster, through the many natural catastrophes [sic] of drought, pestilence, storm, flood, winter cold and failure of crops. To this extent we are different: we know that our control of nature is incomparably greater. Yet we are no more certain of ourselves than any primitive man; we still suffer the same anxieties, the same doubts about mankind's capacity to survive on this planet. And at all periods of major crises these deep, inner anxieties erupt into variations on the Ragnarok theme.... In fact, if all the variations on the Ragnarok theme are plotted on a graph, it will be seen that there is a strict correlation between publication and periods of marked national or international anxiety.

He doesn't present the chart, nor does he identify any periods when there *wasn't* "marked national or international anxiety."

He continues: Works on the theme go in one of two directions: "They are either straightforward destructive images of the end of humanity; or, like *Nordenholt's Million* and *The Day of the Triffids* they show the remnants of mankind finally triumphing over the most terrible catastrophies [sic again]." Why the difference? "...[T]hose who fear or dislike the state of civilization in their time write it off completely in their versions of Ragnarok." Otherwise, we get cosy catastrophes, though of course he does not use that term, invention of which is some years away. Much respect is given to Wyndham and George R. Stewart.

G. H. Doherty contributes the next guest editorial in **135**, "S.x, S-F, and C.........p." There is no clue here as to Doherty's identity. The *New Worlds* Profiles have bitten the dust with this issue, and Carnell does not introduce him in his blurb. However, Harry Harrison identified him in *his* guest editorial in **120** as editor of an early school anthology of SF, *Aspects of Science Fiction*, which Harrison praised as "subversive." (Not too dire, either, nor are his two later anthologies.[48]) Doherty recounts Harrison's convention talk about having a story "torn to shreds by the Medusa-type censor in the editorial offices of a well-known American s-f magazine," expresses his disapproval of censorship without authors' consent, and rambles on for a while to no particularly incisive end ("Sex has long been felt, and is now seen to be a major source of social and personal maladjustment.") If you want to write for adults, he says, you have to deal with sex, and the SF readership really is grown up enough to take it (synopsizing very generously here), then he segues back into the evils of editing writers without notice or consent.

Another and more extensive account of Harrison's talk appears in *Skyrack* 53:[49]

48. William G. Contento, *Index to Science Fiction Anthologies and Collections*, Combined Edition, http://www.philsp.com/homeville/ISFAC/t38.htm#A810 (visited 9/10/11).

49. http://www.gostak.co.uk/skyrack/skyrack53.htm (visited 9/10/11).

HARRY HARRISON presented some new slants on the old theme of Sex & Censorship in Science Fiction. He spoke first on profanity. The hero of his story *Deathworld* struggled and clawed his way through 70,000 words yet the word "damn" was cut from the *Analog* version of the story. Harrison said that Campbell was not aware of this, and mentioned the sub-editing rules and taboos of that magazine. He spoke of the now-famous example of over-riding this censorship when George O. Smith wrote of the original ballbearing mousetrap machine. He held up a cover from the Regency paperback *Damn It* which appeared on all newsstands. Children can read this word, but readers of *Analog* can't. He quoted further examples from the British and American editions of Aldiss' *Non-Stop*, which dealt differently with a reference to some near-innocent sex-play.

Harrison then went on to talk of chamber pots. As he showed a mention of this utensil is widely accepted in Danish advertisements, but when he attempted to refer to a pot in mature, adult S.F. he again met with this ridiculous censorship. His conclusion, he said, was that although SF was trying to present a mature image it had not as yet thoroughly grown away from the old taboos of its pulp origins.

Ted Carnell said that he himself publishes the word "bastard" which offends him personally but deletes other references which offend him. He said that we were entering a world of sickness and quoted as an example the TV programme That Was The Week That Was which depended basically upon sick humour and yet which still receives good reviews. He said that 20% of the stories received by Nova from new or unknown authors were in the "sick" category.

Tom Boardman agreed with Ted Carnell that a publisher has to have a set of rules and mentioned that he always changes the profanity "Jesus Christ!" to "God!" in order to sell a book in Ireland.

John Ashton's guest editorial "Satellite Hunters" (**136**) appears to be another trophy of Carnell's visit to Italy. Ashton, a former fiction contributor (three stories in 1958 in *New Worlds* and *Science Fiction Adventures*) is now the Rome correspondent of "one of our national newspaper groups." The editorial is a slightly breathless account of circumstantial evidence from a couple of radio astronomers about a secret Soviet space mission in mid-1961 that went wrong and killed its crew.[50] Ashton draws the moral that Russian space ventures lack "the human touch" because they don't publicize them enough.

Roberta Rambelli, Italian translator and editor of SF magazine *Galassia*, contributes "S-f and Mythology" (**137**), which observes not very interestingly that if mythology is divided into teratomorphical, theriomorphical, and anthromorphical categories (i.e., gods and demons are respectively monstrous, like animals, or like people), you can find SF that corresponds to each category.

The last of the guest editorials is, according to Carnell, by a person who discovered SF five years previously when he bought a used car and found a pile of magazines in the boot. He is L. H. Barnes, who describes himself as a psychiatrist or as a psychologist depending on which paragraph you are reading. His essay "Possible Worlds of the Mind" (**139**) says that SF helps people mediate the impact of social forces by visualizing the possible

---

50. US space authority James Oberg cites such rumors as "Early in April 1961 Russian pilot Vladimir Ilyushin circled the earth three times but was badly injured on his return. In mid-May 1961 weak calls for help were picked up in Europe, evidently from an orbiting spacecraft with two cosmonauts aboard." He concludes: "But my 1972 study was entirely negative. After considering their sources and their details in the hindsight of subsequent space activities, I concluded that all such stories dealing with alleged flight fatalities were baseless." Oberg, *Uncovering Soviet Disasters*, ch. 10, http://www.jamesoberg.com/usd10.htm (visited 9/10/11).

futures they may engender (though he doesn't quite put it that way). "As a psychologist," Barnes is particularly fond of psionic futures, and thinks the mind won't forever be shackled by the body.

He is captivated by Wiener's suggestion that people could be sent by telegraph like a photographic image, though he wonders if it would be possible to leave things out—"such as the id, the super-ego and a few assorted vestigial instincts." Such speculations are "parallel to the free association technique in psychiatry.... The result is not gibberish.... The unexplored 'antipodes of the mind'—might they not be identical with 'parallel worlds'?" Well, no. After a disparaging aside about the Bat Durston school of SF (again, he doesn't put it that way): "The mainstream of science fiction seems to me a contribution to the effort of modern man to survive mentally, and keep some kind of grip, in a world in flux." Overall, not bad given the author's modest beginnings in the car boot. Not surprisingly, this is his only credit in the SF magazines.

§

Leslie Flood soldiers on with the book review column, appearing 11 times in these 16 issues; his regularity seems to be a function more of the number of books published than his stamina or lack of it. As usual, he displays his flair for succinct and gracious, if sometimes measured, praise, and occasionally displays other kinds of flair. Of Ballard's *The Drowned World*, he says in **129**:

> It is pleasant to be able to record an instance of "local boy makes good"... [Ballard's] early promise has almost matured.... I say "almost" for despite considerable critical acclaim—and I join the concensus [sic] of opinion that this is one of the best s-f novels to appear for many years—*The Drowned World* shows some lack of discipline in its wordiness, vague character

motivations and discrepancies in physical details. Yet these detract little from the vividly imagined overall picture of a world reverted to the Triassic age.... It is not often that the genre is rewarded by a writer of such obvious talent and I look forward to his next book with much anticipation.

There follows in **133** a more idiosyncratic comment on Ballard's first story collection *The Four-Dimensional Nightmare*: "To read them (and they must be read carefully and attentively) is an experience akin to reading Beaudelaire [sic sic sic!] after a diet of the romantics, a whiff of marijuana after plain virginia."

Flood shows considerable partiality towards satire. Of Mark Clifton's *When They Come from Space*, he says (rather incredibly) in **130** that it is "a wonderfully witty send-up of American military bureaucracy.... Gifted writer Clifton has penned a first-rate novel, warm, moving, at times exciting, always deliciously funny and sometimes uncomfortably and bitingly satirical." Sheckley's *Journey Beyond Tomorrow* (**141**) is described as "Ingeniously conceived... as savage and funny a satire as I have ever had the sadistic pleasure of enjoying." Vonnegut's *Cat's Cradle* (**135**) displays "extraordinarily high literary standards."

Flood's highest praise goes to Brian Aldiss, whose "potentiality as a major novelist in the modern science fiction idiom is fully realized in his new story *The Dark Light Years*.... at best as savage as any Swiftian satire, at worst a highly amusing lampoonery, this is a brilliantly painted picture of conflict of divergent life-forms.... It is a cry from the heart of an intellectual at the outrages of philistinism... courageous and inventive novel of an alien culture and the inevitability of non-communication" (**139**).

But Flood acknowledges guilty pleasures as well: "... *After Doomsday* by Poul Anderson is pure space-opera on a galactic scale, with all the effrontery of pseudo-science and cultural inter-relations that it implies.... Thoroughly enjoyable, non-cerebral entertainment" (**129**). Simak's *Way Station* is "a similar piece of wish-fulfillment.... This is the kind of nonsense I simply cannot resist, and Simak does it so well" (**140**). And he retains his skill at putting the boot in, usually to books that are by now completely obscure and for good reason: "Finally, of all the post-atomic holocaust novels that I have read, Derek Ingrey's *Pig on a Lead...* is surely the strangest and most sickeningly desolate, both spiritually and physically." The characters "live off tinned food, practice unnatural sex, and their deranged speech is a vile mockery of the English language" (**135**).

Carnell also appears with some frequency in the book review section, usually with very brief notes on US publications. In **130** he reviews Bloch's *The Eighth Stage of Fandom*, praising it highly but unable to utter the word "fanzine"—it's "amateur s-f publications."

The advertising continues stable as before, with *Film User* and *Industrial & Commercial Photographer* generally sharing the back cover, the BSFA taking half a page or half the inside front cover fairly frequently, the SFBC taking its full page in **130**. Fantast (Medway) also taking a number of half pages, advertising either Cockcroft's *Index to the Weird Fiction Magazines* or *SF Review*, with a few ads for the Newport Book Store and a small notice for the Cambridge SF Society. There are small ads in almost every issue, and **131** (the *Day of the Triffids* issue) has ads for the movie on inside front and back covers.

§

As for the fiction... One of the readers wrote, shortly into the post-Carnell Moorcock regime: "The Nova magazines published some stories that were unsurpassed by American writers, but the average stories which make up the bulk of most magazines were particularly weary and unoriginal in *New Worlds* and even *Science Fantasy*."—P. Johnson of Orpington, in Letters in **144**. That's a bit overstated but there's a kernel of truth in it. There are a few good stories here and a number of reasonably competent ones, but overall, there's a stale and unavailing quality about the whole presentation. The magazine has essentially gone almost nowhere after the great leap forward of 1958-59.

Part of the problem is that *New Worlds* was not able to keep its best contributors. Ballard, Aldiss, Brunner and James White were fading from the magazine, selling their best work to the US market (a complaint of Carnell's from the beginning, even though he was often the one selling it for them) or writing novels or both, and no one of their stature was replacing them. Colin Kapp didn't produce much after his initial burst, and Moorcock, though dominating *Science Fantasy*, only established a presence in *New Worlds* midway through 1963. The most prolific contributors are the likes of John Rackham, a fairly unabashed hack, and Philip E. High, who seems to be writing in his sleep these days. The emerging writers are at best comparatively minor (Lee Harding, Robert Presslie, R. W. Mackelworth), and at worst seem to strive for the routine and conventional (Steve Hall). Reading these issues, my main reaction was "Enough! I'm ready for something new." It is perhaps no accident that others felt the same at the time, and responded with... the New Wave.

§

New Worlds is even more chock-full of serials than usual, with five three-part items in these 16 issues, all by veterans of the magazine, and mostly cause for exasperation.

First up is Lan Wright with "Dawn's Left Hand" (**126-28**), in which Regan, a commercial traveler, is on board a spaceship when it blows up. He is rescued by aliens and reconstructed, better than new if you don't care what you look like. He was rescued with some property of his cabin-mate, Manuel Cabrera, gets mis-identified as Cabrera, and can't prove otherwise. He unwillingly casts his lot with the enormously powerful Cabrera family, after convincing *them* he isn't Manuel, since it's clear he will be killed if he doesn't accept their protection—after all, somebody blew up a spaceship to get Manuel, though it's not clear why. He is taken back to the Cabreras' mountain redoubt—Xanadu, no less—on a grossly overcrowded Earth (he "turned away to gaze in revulsion at the spawning horror of an over-populated world that was spread like some malignant growth over the land beneath").

At Xanadu he masquerades as Cabrera, the truth known only to a few family members. From there, he tries to escape, inspired by an anonymous note telling him how, is captured by another faction which also is in possession of Cabrera's "carrier" (brief-case?) which supposedly contains some galaxy-shaking secret but can't be opened, escapes from *them*, and is rescued by the Cabreras. He is then informed by his beautiful nominal sister (who rides up on a big black horse, and allows that she isn't that put off by Regan's weird reengineered appearance) that Manuel once mentioned a man named Plender on a planet named Cleomon. Naturally, Regan proposes to the Cabrera patriarch that he go there.

So the family spaceship is placed at his disposal and he heads off, only to learn that cousin Carlo, whom he does not trust, has slipped aboard. On arrival, they are informed by the planetary police chief that this Plender was murdered 16 months ago. But wait! Here's Plender's lawyer, in the next office, and he tells them that Plender was involved with Manuel in negotiating a deal for two Earth-type planets in a system occupied by an alien species that really can't use them. These planets would provide *lebensraum* for bursting-at-the-seams Earth and relieve the growing tension between it and the colony planets who are hard pressed by Earth's economic demands.

Off they go to these planets, only to find that the Cabreras, including the patriarch, are going there too, and there's some-body in residence. It's Manuel, who engineered his own fake death, and the real deaths of 68 other people. Though he talks of relieving Earth's population pressure with the two empty planets, clearly he has gone into business for himself and is waiting for Earth and the colonies to destroy each other, leaving him in power. Manuel attacks Regan, who crushes him with his alien-made prosthetic arms. The Cabrera patriarch, after witnessing his son's violent death, declares that this man wasn't really his son, Regan is, and Regan is wondering how he can marry someone whom everyone thinks is his sister.

As is often the case with Wright, the essential plotting principle here is One Damn Thing After Another, with seemingly significant plot devices (the aliens who patched Regan up, the "carrier" with the big secret in it) appearing and then being forgotten, and new rabbits pulled out of the hat as needed when the action starts to flag (the beautiful sister appearing on her horse and whispering the names of a planet and a man is the best example). This is not a big problem, at least on the level at which this story was written to be read (i.e., on autopilot), since Wright has developed a reasonable facility for keeping things moving. Of course if you stop and pay attention, the clichés—of plot, character, and style—become overwhelming. Here's a trifecta: "The fever of the unknown was in his blood; action for the sake of action was his goal; danger for the sake of danger tingled his nerves with eager delight." The previously quoted "spawning horror"—the run of humanity as Lovecraftian monster—is characteristic, too. In fact, there is a fundamental sort of incompetence here at the word-and-sentence level. Consider this passage:

> The sun of Alpha Regis burned upon Regan's head. It was the one concrete thing on to which he could latch in a world that had suddenly exploded around him. Vaguely, he knew that he should be feeling all the emotions that had been pent up within him for so long, yet all he was aware of was a cold wonder that he had not considered the possibility earlier. At one stroke, above the mental numbness that he felt, all questions were answered; each and every portion of the great panorama fell into perspective with a clarity that was blinding in its simplicity.

So here we have the burning sun, which is concrete, and you can latch onto it. (Or "on to which he could latch"—consider that stilted construction in the same sentence where the world is exploding.) In the burning sun he experiences a cold wonder, also mental numbness—in fact, they seem to be the same thing. And we've got a panorama falling into perspective with clarity, blinding, simplicity. Want to pick maybe any two of those?

There's nothing *terribly* wrong with any of this—most of them are probably not technically mixed metaphors or other identifiable gaffes of a sort that anyone has put a name to. But one would think a writer would want his language and imagery to add up, preferably in a way that doesn't call attention to itself, rather than pushing and shoving and stumbling over itself, in ways that are hard to miss if the reader is paying *any* attention. Of course there's your answer: he is writing for people who are *not* paying attention, and indeed he is hostile to the idea that attention should be paid—see his guest editorial only a few issues before. Reading Wright is sometimes the literary equivalent of the experience described in C.S. Lewis's "The Shoddy Lands"—nothing is sharp, nothing is used with precision, the author doesn't really know his tools and doesn't much care about them anyway.

The basic science fictional logic is shoddy, too. The McGuffin here—the mainspring that is revealed to be driving all this plot—is Manuel's ostensible plan to get control of the two empty planets and relieve all the tensions of interstellar politics by dividing the population of Earth—said to be 40 billion—three ways. That is, about 26 billion people are going to be transported by spaceship from Earth across the galaxy. Got a lot of spaceships, have we? Big ones? Admittedly Wright is far from the only SF writer to present interstellar colonization as a population control measure, but this is an especially fatuous example of an unexamined absurdity, given the facts Wright himself has foregrounded.

In making these comments I am standing on the shoulders of giants, or their midden-heap. Brian Aldiss memorably let fly on this writer and this story in the second (Winter 1965) issue of *SF Horizons*, in his article "British Science Fiction Now," the section titled "The Knitter of Socks: Lan Wright." This, we recall, is an allusion to Wright's *New Worlds* Profile remark about one of his stories being like "a person knitting a sock who cannot turn a heel." Aldiss's indictment of Wright is even longer than mine, and of course more sophisticated and attentive: "To write a novel, which after all is an immense and unnatural labour, we must be recreating some ideal that we have within us, an ideal (perhaps of a way of living) that cannot be achieved in any other way.... James Joyce parades his debt to Homer. Lan Wright parades his debt to a hundred forgotten detective stories."

Aldiss points out that Wright presents Regan as cool and ruthless, then undermines his portrait by presenting him as vacillating and feeble, and in any case he is remarkably unpleasant at all times, often for no particular reason. (And don't forget that "The fever of the unknown was in his blood; action for the sake of action was his goal; danger for the sake of danger tingled his nerves with eager delight." In addition to its other vices, this sentence presents yet another version of Regan with not much connection to any of the others.) Aldiss says Wright is "his own claque"—that is, he or his characters are always commenting on the action, either directly or by Wright's description of their reactions (Regan's "cold wonder" is one of his examples), as if he is uncertain whether his audience will get the point otherwise. As to the denouement, Aldiss reflects on the fact that Regan is rhetorically adopted by the elder Cabrera as the brutally murdered corpse of Cabrera's real son lies between them: "Authors like Ian Fleming and Spillane have sometimes been castigated for morally offensive scenes in their novels, but they have never produced anything like this."

The best that can be said for "Dawn's Left Hand" is that it is a competent idle read that goes down smoothly enough if you don't think about it. In the UK, it had a hardcover edition the next year from Herbert Jenkins titled *Space Born*. In the US, it went straight to Ace Doublehood as *Exile from Xanadu*. All these titles are about equally inapt; "Dawn's Left Hand" is a phrase of Omar Khayyam's from a quatrain which boils down to "seize the day."

§

The next serial is E. C. Tubb's "Window on the Moon" (129-131), which follows the same track as its predecessor: hardcover publication by Herbert Jenkins in the UK and paperback by Ace (this time standalone) in the US, both titled *Moon Base*. It's no more impressive than "Dawn's Left Hand," but its deficiencies are considerably less interesting.

As the title suggests, it's set on the Moon, where UK, US and USSR have bases, but only the UK base has a window, or women. It starts out in semi-documentary mode looking like an international politics/spy thriller. A commission of inquiry arrives at the UK base, along with a supposed technician—the viewpoint character, Larsen—who is there to install laser weapons, but who isn't what he seems. We get a tour of base activities, which include growing a brain from raw materials. Why this is being done on the Moon is not really explained, and the brain doesn't seem to be doing anything. Others are occupied in developing an infectious biological agent that has the effect of a nerve gas. One can understand why *that* is done on the Moon, but not why the gas is trotted out and used to kill a rabbit in a plastic box for the entertainment of the visiting delegation, or why the delegation stays in the same room during this demonstration, rather than fleeing from the insane risk to which they are being subjected.

Larsen goes outside with some of the station personnel, has a freak accident and falls down a cliff in his spacesuit, and even more freakishly survives. While in the infirmary, he sneaks into the room next door and finds Seldon, the agent he is supposed to have been meeting up with, who is not very coherent. He is also missing all his limbs, we learn later, but Larsen manages not to notice that on this first encounter. A party from the American base shows up, having observed that mysterious secret signals are emanating from the UK base. They leave their detector with the British, who profess no knowledge of the signals, and head back home; later they are found dead with their vehicle wrecked. The commission of inquiry gets in their spaceship and heads home. Their spaceship explodes.

The time of these disasters and other seeming accidents corresponds to the peaks of the mysterious signals, which seem to be emanating from Abic, the potted brain. Larsen decides he has to stop Abic's depredations, but when he tries to shoot it, the bullet doesn't explode when the firing pin hits it, and then the metal bar he tries to smash its case with breaks off in his hands. Everybody in the station is chasing him, and he runs around pointlessly for a while, but finally surrenders and explains what he has discovered about the brain. In turn, it's explained that Abic has harnessed luck, which is a natural force like gravity or magnetism, and knows what to do because he's wired into the station's electrical system. Abic also contains a symbiotic virus which has now spread to the station crew and to Larsen; since it infects them with luck, they can't be killed accidentally. Now they know it has bred true in Larsen, they can try to spread it to all of Earth, thereby saving humanity. Why it was necessary for Abic the lucky to kill two spaceships-full of people remains obscure and unexplained.

There's more, plenty more, and it connects some of the foregoing rather widely spaced dots, without making the book overall any more plausible, or any less boring for its implausibility. Leslie Flood reviews the Jenkins hardcover in **141**, mentioning that the series "apparently intends to aim its sights no higher than a competent level of action-slanted science fiction," but calls Tubb's novel "an exciting adventure novel," too generous by half.

Tubb's photo is featured on the cover of **129**, and a slightly peculiar one it is: he's sitting at a table or standing at a dais, and what appear to be a couple of disembodied hands (presumably belonging to a shorter person standing behind him) are either putting on or taking off a set of headphones from his ears. Tubb's guest editorial, "Let's Build a Bridge," appears in **132**, and like a lot of these editorials, it takes several pages to convey a few sentences of content: All fiction needs to entertain, most SF is too esoteric to entertain most people, can't ignore the wider public, must entertain, communicate, educate, and enchant. "There should, I feel, be a way to bridge the gap between the outsider and the addict so that both can read and enjoy the same story even if they do it in different ways." He cites *1984* as an example but doesn't say what he thinks *1984* does to accomplish this end.

In passing, he says his argument about the need to address a wider public "points out the fallacy of those who advocate stories without beginning, middle, or end, and demand that science fiction should be so avant garde that it reaches a point beyond sense or reason. Stories—if they can be so called—that are nothing but a frothing jumble of words can be pleasant nonsense but that is really all they are... non-sense." Disappointingly, he names no names and identifies no frothing jumbles. Within a few years, with the advent of the New Wave, he'd have had no shortage of candidates.

§

John Brunner's "To Conquer Chaos" (**133-135**) is as agreeably readable a shuffling of stock elements as his last serial, "Crack of Doom," was not. Carnell says in "The Literary Line-up" (**132**) that it is written with Brunner's "exceptional talent for word-picturisation." Well, yes. There's a primitive and sparsely populated feudal Earth, clearly the aftermath of some comprehensive disaster. From the feared Barrenlands, *things* (sic) periodically emerge and wreak havoc. A young social outcast has visions no one understands of a more populous and luxurious world. In a parallel plot, an isolated and dwindling human community inside the Barrenlands lives in and around a strange domed structure, whose people think their mission is to keep it operating and to kill the *things* as they emerge.

The plots come together at the end, and the young outcast saves everybody's bacon, and of course he gets a girlfriend out of the deal too. The revelation at the end is fortunately more original than the setup. Occasionally the bad guys are a bit too Snivelyish ("That man standing behind Idris there, with a sneer on his face, now lifting a hand to twist his fine black mustachios....") but otherwise it's a very smooth potboiler, essentially a pretty good YA novel, but in no way as incisive as Brunner's material in *Science Fantasy*. P. Schuyler Miller said (*Analog*, April 1965): "John Brunner doggedly—it sounds more British than consistently—maintains his ability to write superior SF adventure yarns with original settings and gimmicks.... Nice job, all through." Of course it went straight to Ace, though as a standalone volume rather than a Double, and doesn't seem to have had a UK edition.

Brunner also has his second guest editorial in **138**—he's the only double dipper in the group—called "On Political Attitudes in S-F," in which he rambles more intelligently than most of his colleagues. His points: political thinking in SF has been getting smarter as the Cold War has waned, good writers aren't wedded in their work to any particular political system (citing himself and Heinlein), it's usually in the background and often seen "through the distorting mirror of a violent action yarn." Just about anything can be politics, but a lot of established writers have a hard time seeing it that way, since they are heavily influenced by an engineering tradition, which is suspicious of democracy, and/or the "pulp magazine tradition in which there were certain conventions about villains and heroes which led to sharp black-versus-white principles being implied in the plots...."

But things are getting better, as illustrated by Chad Oliver, Robert Abernathy, and Poul Anderson, and "This is an area in which I find myself naturally doing most of my work." It's tempting to apply all of this to "To Conquer Chaos," the political lessons of which seem to be that power corrupts and leads to twisting of mustachios, everything falls apart without strong leaders (a piece of the plot I didn't recount—the man with charisma died), and in this vacuum, ordinary suckers with courage and vision are everyone's salvation even if they are regarded as hopeless geeks. Could be worse—in fact, it's *been* worse.

§

The next serial comes well advertised. In "The Literary Line-Up" in **134**, Carnell says that upon returning from Italy (the Trieste film festival), one of his first acts was to read Colin Kapp's first novel, so far untitled. "It turned out to be brilliant and is probably the greatest story since Alfred Bester's *The Stars My Destination*." The next month's "Literary Line-Up" says this "magnificent new novel" is now titled "The Dark Mind" (later *Transfinite Man* in its US paperback edition) and is "one of the most powerful stories we have ever published."

Unfortunately, in the event, the usually more imaginative Kapp begins by living up to Aldiss's remark about Lan Wright, and "parades his debt to a hundred forgotten detective stories." Ivan Dalroi is a private investigator working for the Cronstadt Committee against Failway Terminal, a seemingly all-powerful corporation which has its brutalist headquarters athwart a slum district in a nameless city. Failway (perhaps a pun on "railway," the British form of "railroad," weirdly and antonymically spliced with Safeway, the supermarket chain[51]) has a monopoly on the technology of "space-time lattices," which amount to a means of access to parallel worlds, on which Failway engages in Mall-marketing as well as nefarious and lucrative activities

---

51. If this seems fanciful, it's worth noting that the long-established and powerful US chain Safeway entered the UK market in 1962, around the time Kapp was writing *The Dark Mind*. See "Not the weakest link in the chain," http://www.thenorthernecho.co.uk/archive/2003/10/04/The+North+East+Archive/7013570.Not_the_weakest_link_in_the_chain/ (visited 9/10/11).

beyond the reach of Earth law and order (of which there doesn't seem to be much anyway). The Cronstadts would like to know what happened to several of their representatives who entered Failway and never emerged. To Dalroi, it's a personal mission, since his girlfriend was tempted by Failway many years ago and has not been seen since.

Kapp seems determined to collect the set of PI clichés in the first few chapters. A bomb goes off in the bar Dalroi has just vacated. An agent of Failway waits to ambush him in his office, but Dalroi, the master of disguise, gets in unrecognized and clobbers the agent. He tries to fire his secretary because things are going to get dangerous, but she refuses to leave. He calls the cops about the Failway agent and gets a lecture about not knowing what's good for him, or them. ("Sorry, Dalroi! You'd scarcely expect me to risk my pension trying to make out a case for you against Failway. You know which way the world turns.") The language is often over the top, as usual for Kapp, but at this point to no very interesting end. ("Dalroi therefore turned back to the wall. It was twelve feet of unrelenting brick, capped with the sordid spite of broken bottles trapped in cement.")

As matters progress, the thriller maneuvers continue. At one point Dalroi is knocked out by a blow to the head and awakens strapped to a chair in the citadel of his enemy for some dialogue with their chief of security, who then leaves Dalroi alone so a mysterious figure can arrive and cut his bonds, allowing him to escape. Gradually these devices give way to hints that everyone is watching Dalroi, indeed has been watching him for a long time, because he is *a very special person*, as Carnell puts it in "The Literary Line-Up" (**135**).

It is ventured by the Cronstadt biggie that "The dark side of Dalroi's mind is a region of activity such as we have never met before. His breakthrough will be a mental Hiroshima." Later we learn that Dalroi was earlier convicted of murder but survived electrocution three times, finally released at the direction of the Black Knights, a secret police agency that seems to be fond of leaving chess pieces around as mementoes of its activities.

Of course, it turns out Dalroi was innocent of the murder all the while. Meanwhile, recaptured in the Failway building, Dalroi is tossed through the matrix polariser without benefit of vehicle, passing through a certain amount of overwritten metaphysical torment into transfinite space and fetching up at a sort of cosmic spiderweb. More particularly: "Trapped on a web of crazy, discontinuous geometry, Dalroi cursed and wept like a mad thing."

But when the going gets tough, the superhuman get going, in boldface type in ever-larger fonts:

ACTION! REACTION! ACTION! REACTION! ACT!...

TOOTH! NAIL! WILL! SPITE! HATE! FIGHT!...

HATE! HATE! HATE!

Universe upended, gravity sideways, entropy turned inside-out.

CONCEPTION! DECEPTION!
TRANSCRIPTION! ABSTRACTION!
HATE! HATE! HATE!

Apparently all you need is hate, and hate will find a way:

> Then he rose up, and by sheer indomitable force, he smashed the dimension back into the miniscule [sic] quanta of energy from which all things are made.
> Transfinity shuddered. Strange new nebulae leaped into existence, and others paled and were extinguished.

Now Dalroi is back on Earth, by means not exactly explained, wrecking the joint, bombing a bank and then damaging Failway itself by contriving... a train wreck. Back through the matrix polariser he goes, for some havoc tourism in Failway's "levels," coming across in passing a large field of *cepi*, the narcotic on which much of Failway's power depends, in a peculiar artificial landscape: "Outside the sphere of light from the ungodly moon a vast, dark plain lurked in black bewilderment." He figures out how to destroy it, at considerable risk to himself ("Dying radiation sauntered in.") He runs into his former girlfriend, now a high-class prostitute, who invites him to stick around. Before he can get out, they are joined by his old friend, the Failway chief of security, but Dalroi manages to escape to another and sleazier level:

> This was the place where the cold-eyed thirsting could find its slaking and where the sleepless agonies of wanting found a little brief relief.
> The women were painted with a lavish imprecision which stamped them for what they were.

Dalroi is picked up by one such, who turns out to be an agent of the Ombudsmand (don't ask, too many moving parts already), who sticks around only long enough to inject herself with the staggeringly deadly and contagious Venusian small-pox, so Failway will have to evacuate and abandon this level. After the evacuation, Failway saturates the place with some strange radiation that disintegrates buildings, clothing, etc., leaving only Dalroi, naked in a sea of burning dust, from which he teleports away. Next he is being seeded subcutaneously with molecules of sodium and set on fire, just like Alfred Bester's Gully Foyle in *The Stars My Destination*. But wait—it doesn't any longer seem to be Failway he is fighting. Instead, it's "enti-ties," and at first they seem to have the upper hand, here in this hellish chaos of twisted geometries (as Kapp might have put it), where "Entropy moaned with anguish."

But they reckon not with Dalroi and his bold-face capital letters: it's "**TOOTH! NAIL! WILL! SPITE! HATE! FIGHT!**" again, and the kid rocks out: "He had knocked a complete dimensional level straight into a transfinite loop, the absurd mathematical shriek from which no undistorted form had ever returned." He translates himself back to Earth, still burning from the sodium, and invades the headquarters of the Black Knights, who hold a number of the principals (Cronstadt, the Ombudsmand, etc.); Dalroi is content to rescue his secretary. But wait—things are not what they seem, including his secretary, who ambushes him with "white fire."

And when he wakes up, he gets the scoop: We humans are not quite property, but we're in quarantine, held in check by the civilized races of the universe, who refer to us as the Destroyers because that's what we've done to them repeatedly. ("You carry the ever-pregnant seeds of Hell in your souls.") Too civilized to wipe us out, they've sent us to "far exile in a corner of transfinity, and built by genetic engineering a blockage whereby all the inherited knowledge in the racial brain was locked down out of reach." (My favorite, racial memory again.)

Now the blocks are weakening, and Dalroi is the throwback, too dangerous to live. So they engage in psychosurgery to remove the block completely so he can see everything in the dark side of his mind, because they think it will kill him. (Why don't they just shoot him and then cut him into pieces to be sure? Oh, they're too civilized.) He does see his dark side ("Malice was a note on a gigantic organ thrust deep into the inner ear. Hatred was a shaft of illumination so bright that it blinded through sixty feet of concrete."), but instead of dying, he defeats it in some fashion. But this triumph avails him nothing: the alien wardens leave and the humans come in, and *they* shoot him—though (I know you'll be surprised) there's some hint that he might not really be dead.

Whew! Be warned that the foregoing long synopsis grossly oversimplifies the plot, which suggests van Vogt and Alfred Bester on steroids (the style just suggests the steroids). But there are big differences from *The Stars My Destination*. Bester's novel was ultimately an optimistic book: humanity's got a pretty interesting future, and the damaged character at its center does big deeds and wins a victory (however ceremonial and maybe Pyrrhic, no half-pun intended) for the ordinary folk. This one is a thoroughgoing bummer of a conceptual breakthrough: humanity is irredeemably evil and destructive, and the upshot of the protagonist's triumphant unmasking of reality is to reveal our universe as a claustrophobic dead end with no future except more of the same.

The only professional review this book got (in its Corgi paperback original edition) was by Moorcock, under his James Colvin pseudonym, in *New Worlds* **154** (September 1965), which says: "Billed as 'an exciting new science fiction discovery,' Kapp is heavily in debt to Alfred Bester's *Tiger! Tiger!* in this novel. His visual imagination is above average but his handling of character and dialogue is poor in the extreme and his technique, where it is his own, does not match his imagination or his ability to come up with convincing scientific ideas. One is inclined to feel that the author should spend much more time studying his craft before attempting his next novel." He's right as far as he goes, although he doesn't give Kapp credit for at least trying to push the genre machinery a bit and produce something a little more incisive than another rehash of the tiresome Man Called Destiny routine. But the novel is dragged down by its parodically overwrought style, plus—and this is what bothers me most about it—this world is *thin*. About all we see of it is the Failway Terminal and its transfinite levels, and cameos of the various heavies. How anything works or how anybody lives is barely hinted at.

§

The Carnell era closes out, reasonably fittingly, with a serial by James White, so long a mainstay of the magazine. "Open Prison" (**139-141**), later booked as *The Escape Orbit* and reviewed by no one.[52] is another sober and well-meaning (but

52. That is, there is no entry for it in H. W. Hall, *Science Fiction Book Review Index, 1923-1973* (Gale Research Co., 1975). It may have been

good-natured, not humorless at all) gnaw at the bone of White's preoccupation with war. In the future, starfaring humanity has been at war with the Bugs for 60 years or so, after the mutual loathing of the majority overcame the efforts of the more enlightened to keep the peace. It's not total war. There's an agreement to protect prisoners of war; and the Bugs are doing this by dumping their prisoners on a habitable planet, without spaceships at the bottom of a gravity well, and guarded by watchers in orbit (an idea White auditioned some years earlier in "Dogfight" (**81**)). Now there are thousands of human military personnel on this planet, some of them imprisoned for as long as 23 years, and they are sharply divided between the still gung-ho who are planning the impossible escape, and the Civilians who have, in effect, dropped out and taken up farming and family life. Sector Marshal Warren arrives to find himself the ranking officer on the planet, and he of course takes up with the Escape Committee.

The story quickly turns into a romance of logistics, with considerable sexual politics as well, since this is a highly gender-integrated military. The Escape faction doesn't trust the women: "Their basic drives—the maternal instinct, the need for security and so on—predisposed them towards the Civilian philosophy," so most of them join the Civilians, and those who have no husbands by then are always trying to entice the Committeemen. Also, one of the women's preoccupations is that the available uniforms aren't too smart-looking.

Believe it or not, this is really not a misogynist presentation. However burdened he may be with the sex role assumptions of the 1950s, White is actually trying to think about a problem that most writers of the time would just handwave aside or make dogmatic proclamations about, with sympathy and respect towards both views.

In any case, Warren arrives, scopes things out, takes command, defuses the rapidly worsening factional conflict, and

reviewed in un-indexed fan periodicals.

sets a direction and gets everybody working together actually to realize the far-fetched escape plan, which involves faking a crashed Bug ship and then hijacking the rescue vessel that is sent for it. Essentially it is a study in military command, which may seem an odd thing for White to engage in, given his sympathies, but of course he has some rug-pulling up his sleeve, if you can tolerate such a metaphor.

As Warren explains to the commanding officer who will be left behind when the successful Escape Committee heads off in their captured vessel: we won't be back for you. Under the strain of this endless war, not just the military, but the whole of interstellar civilization is falling apart. With a crew of fanatically dedicated and competent military officers, Warren will take over a chunk of that civilization and stave off the collapse into barbarism. Meanwhile, those left behind on the former prison planet will keep alive the science of the interstellar culture and, in a few hundred years, re-achieve space travel and go forth to pick up the pieces.

The impact of the novel is blunted by White's style, which remains pedestrian, even pedantic. Here's the opening sentence, lucid but leaden, and absolutely representative of the whole:

> When Warren had been extricated along with the other survivors of the erroneously named *Victorious* and made a prisoner of war he had thought that he knew what to expect, his expectations being based on the knowledge of how enemy POWs were handled by his own side.

It's also a bit facile, and more than a bit self-defeating, to have Warren's grand scheme revealed only in an info-dump in the last chapter. Though we see what Warren does, and it's interesting enough, we don't see the development of his understanding and his intentions, which would have been much more interesting. White has created a heroic figure of a quintessentially science fictional sort, a competent military officer whose practical struggle with his duties leads him to a vision and a plan that transcends his military role and perspective entirely, and then has made the least of him dramatically.

Still, the story grapples with large issues with great ingenuity; certainly it's the best thing White has produced to date, and probably the best ever of the indigenous serials in the Carnell *New Worlds*. And of course it went straight to Ace and UK paperback (Four Square), and now it's totally forgotten—last UK edition Corgi 1970, last US edition Ace 1983.

White has his turn as guest editorialist in **127** with the plaintive "The Oppressed Minority," which starts out in a gently comical vein recounting all the competing demands made on SF writers in guest editorials and elsewhere, and ends up:

> ...s-f writers are a misunderstood and oppressed minority, and... they should be encouraged more and jumped on less if the field is to improve. A writer honestly wants to produce good science fiction full of the Sense of Wonder and all of the other essential qualities, and the science fiction readership is in the position of being his artistic conscience. But a conscience is supposed to prick him from time to time, not stick dirty great knives in his back.

It seems excessive. White has been criticized a few times in "Postmortem," mainly for the growing repetitiveness of the Sector General stories—but knives? Is he hypersensitive or has he been subject to scurrilous attack in some other quarter? White has the *New Worlds* Profile in this issue, along with photos both with the profile and on the front cover. It is revealed that he has a new child, a new work room in the attic, a new book (*Hospital Station* in the US), and a Hugo nomination for "Second Ending," and hangs out with Gerard Quinn among others.

§

In the absence of Brunner and White, the biggest names among the short fiction contributors are J. G. Ballard, Brian Aldiss, and Michael Moorcock. Ballard has three stories in these issues, meanwhile continuing to sell heavily in the US: he had eight stories in *Amazing, Fantastic, Fantasy & Science Fiction*, and *If* during the comparable period, plus two in *Science Fantasy* and one in the UK *Argosy*. His *New Worlds* stories include two of his best and best-known. "The Subliminal Man" (**126**), beloved of anthologists (nine appearances in the first 15 years after its magazine publication) and Marxist critics, is, with "Billennium," one of his most conventional SF stories, a straightforward hyper-extrapolated dystopia. This one foregrounds advertising, conspicuous consumption, and planned obsolescence. It's interesting that he couldn't sell it in the US— too strident, I guess the editors thought.

If it were funnier it would be the perfect *Galaxy* story, but you get the sense that Ballard isn't kidding, and anyway *Galaxy* had moved on by then. Or maybe editor Pohl recognized it as the story "The Midas Plague" could have been, and didn't like being shown up. "The Subliminal Man" features one of Ballard's traveling players, the slightly unhinged young obsessive whom we met as Kaldren in "The Voices of Time," and who for that matter is a wilder-eyed version of the protagonists of "Build-Up" and "Chronopolis." We will deepen our acquaintance with him in *The Atrocity Exhibition*.

Here, called Hathaway, he is accosting the psychiatrist Dr. Franklin: "The signs, Doctor! Have you seen the signs?" Hathaway is convinced that gigantic signboards being erected around London are intended to emit subliminal advertising to speed up the consumer market even more. It is revealed during the first few pages that Dr. Franklin commonly works 12-hour days and has a consultancy on Saturday to pay for it all, and trades in his car for a new one every three months or so. On his way home from work, he realizes he needs some cigarettes, so he stops and buys a carton—which he puts in the "dashboard locker" (glove compartment) with three unopened ones.

Hathaway is right, of course, and is ultimately shot trying to sabotage one of the signs.

This story is not only Ballard's first notable engagement with consumerism, it also contains the first appearance of one of his other large preoccupations:

> But at least the roads were magnificent. Whatever other criticisms might be levelled at the present society, it certainly knew how to build roads. Eight, ten and twelve-lane expressways interlaced across the continent, plunging from overhead causeways into the giant car parks in the centre of the cities, or dividing into the great suburban arteries with their multi-acre parking aprons around the marketing centres. Together the roadways and car parks covered more than a third of the country's entire area, and in the neighbourhood of the cities the proportion was higher. The old cities were surrounded by the vast, dazzling abstract sculptures of the clover-leaves and flyovers, but even so the congestion was unremitting.

Ballard said of this story in his introduction to it in *The Best Science Fiction of J. G. Ballard* (Futura, 1977):

> Given the voracious needs of the modern consumer goods society, who can blame the merchandisers for doing their best to keep up with us? The kind of psychological force-feeding that I describe in "The Subliminal Man" isn't that different from the efforts I was making at the time cramming large amounts of what seemed to be up-market pet-foods down the throats of my three infants. Even the most extreme stratagem was, after all, for their own good. I mention this because I don't see the central character of this story as entirely a victim.

Ballard's "End-Game" appears a few months later in **131**. It is an ingeniously contrived head-piece, so quintessentially Ballardian that it's hard to know whether to call it a masterpiece or a self-parody. Maybe the two are not incompatible. It begins:

> After his trial they gave Constantin a villa, an allowance and an executioner. The villa was small and high-walled, and had obviously been used for the purpose before. The allowance was adequate to Constantin's needs—he was never permitted to go out and his meals were prepared for him by a police orderly. The executioner was his own. Most of the time they sat on the enclosed veranda overlooking the narrow stone garden, playing chess with a set of large well-worn pieces.

The larger chess game is, of course, Constantin's game with the executioner Malek, first trying to learn what Malek's orders are so he can find a way to save himself, later on—after an hysterical and futile effort to break out of the house—trying to enlist Malek as an ally in communicating with the authorities in this generic Eastern European dictatorship and obtaining a retrial. In these latter stages, he convinces himself, and tries to convince Malek, of his innocence (of exactly what we are never told), leading to the final scene, in which the execution is clearly imminent and Malek says, "Of course, Mr. Constantin.... I understand. When you know you are innocent, then you are guilty."

The homage to Kafka is explicit; early on he writes, "This ironic inversion of the classical Kafkaesque situation, by which, instead of admitting his guilt to a non-existent crime, he was forced to connive in a farce maintaining his innocence of offences he knew full well he had committed, was preserved in his present situation in the execution villa." The story conveys an impression of being one of Ballard's most carefully written stories, but in fact Ballard said it "was written in two days, straight on to the machine. No revision whatever, except for the odd word here and there. I was in the right mood, my mind was working the right way...."[53] It is largely held to a flat and mundane documentary style calculated to wring out the tension of the situation, though Ballard is unable to resist the occasional characteristic rimshot ("Around him a thousand invisible clocks raced onwards toward their beckoning zeros, a soundless thunder like the drumming of apocalyptic hoof-irons").

Many of the *New Worlds* readers must have been puzzled by "End-Game," since it contains not a shred of the science fictional, nothing at all to suggest that the events occurred at any other time and place than a generic Eastern European 1963 or 1957. In fact Harold Mead, author of *Bright Phoenix*, calls Ballard on it in "Postmortem" in **140**, praising Carnell's apparent campaign to get pseudo-science out of the magazine, but suggesting he may be "leaning too far the other way.... 'End-Game' could have taken place in Russia or any of the totalitarian states." Carnell makes no attempt to rationalize it as SF in his blurb, which states only "A psychological chiller about a man sentenced to death—and with no indication to him of the day, hour and minute of his execution, only the place." In the preceding issue's "The Literary Line-Up" he tried a little harder: "Jim Ballard produces a fine 'inner space' story titled 'End Game,' which is very much in the tradition of his work in *The Drowned World.*"

"End-Game" was reprinted in Harry Harrison's 1968 anthology *SF: Author's Choice* (*A Backdrop of Stars* in the UK). Harrison stated his parameters in the Introduction: "This volume has been fashioned by the writers whose stories it contains, chosen by them despite the barriers and restrictions I placed in their way. I wanted only stories that they liked, that had not been anthologized before, that they had a particular reason for writing, that were of a certain length—and I still reserved the editorial prerogative of rejection, which I exercised freely."

53. Interview conducted by Peter Linnett (Feb. 1973), on file with David Pringle.

Ballard supplied a two-page-plus commentary which continues to indulge the charade that "End-Game" is an SF story:

> The psychology of guilt and rebellion is barely looked at by science fiction. By and large a literature of optimism, and much the worse for it, science fiction assumes that the chief obstacles in the way of human liberty and progress are faults in social and political institutions, and that once these have been corrected a millennial age will dawn. Of course, nothing could be further from the truth. At the best (and worst) of times it is difficult to know which side of the bars we are, for the simple reason that we can never be sure which side we want to be.
>
> These inversions, one of which "End-Game" illustrates, can take place within a society, an institution, or even a marriage.

And he recounts some of the peculiar role-reversal moments he experienced during his internment in China. He continues:

> The situation in "End-Game" reflects ambiguities and motives of a similar kind, although in a more domestic and confined context. Here questions of guilt and responsibility complicate matters....
>
> Constantin, the convicted hero of "End-Game," begins by accepting the fact of his guilt.... At first his plans to escape are concerned with his own physical survival, but later he conceives of the moral notion of his own "innocence." Imperceptibly the failed political opportunist transforms himself into a martyr to his own innocence, a credo which he erects into a cathedral. Constantin is now an internal escapee.
>
> It is Constantin's absolute conviction of his innocence for which Malek, his executioner, is waiting. "Only a truly innocent man can know the meaning of

guilt," Constantin remarks, but Malek knows full well that the reverse is true. Only a truly guilty man can conceive of the concept of innocence at all, or hold it with such ferocity.

Perhaps I have misread my own story, and its real significance, if any, may lie in another direction altogether. Nonetheless it seems to me that a significant moral and psychological distance now separates us from Kafka's heroes, who succumbed in the end to their own unconscious feelings of guilt and inferiority. We, by contrast, in an age of optimism and promise, may fall equal victims to our notions of freedom, sanity and self-sufficiency.

So what did the *New Worlds* readers make of all this? They placed it dead in the middle of the issue's contents, after the Tubb serial and the Joseph Green novelette, and before the David Rome and Robert Presslie short stories.

Ten months later, in **140** (the next to last Carnell issue), we have Ballard's consensus masterpiece "The Terminal Beach." Even Ballard seems to agree. He wrote (again in the 1977 Futura paperback *The Best Science Fiction of J. G. Ballard*) that it "is for me the most important story I have written. It marks the link between the science fiction of my first ten years, and the next phase of my writings that led to 'The Atrocity Exhibition' and 'Crash.'" Just so. And here's his more contemporaneous comment, quoted by Judith Merril in *10th Annual Edition: The Year's Best SF* (Delacorte Press, 1965), where the story was anthologized: "'Terminal Beach' represents the most extreme expression to date of what I have called 'inner space'— that area where the outer world of reality and the inner world of the psyche meet and fuse. Only in this area can one find the true subject matter for a mature science fiction." This story essentially capped Ballard's long run as a prolific contributor of short fiction to the SF magazines. After this, for roughly two years, there was only "The Illuminated Man" in the May 1964

Fantasy & Science Fiction and an excerpt from *The Drought* in Moorcock's *New Worlds* plus review articles on William Burroughs and Wyndham Lewis. Then, the pieces collected in *The Atrocity Exhibition* began to appear.

"The Terminal Beach" was heralded by Carnell in the previous issue's "Literary Line-Up" as "a fascinating short novelette with an 'inner space' background by J. G. Ballard [...] which has all the ingredients of what Kingsley Amis recently quoted as 'Ballard-land.' Basically, the overwhelming craving of a bomber pilot to return to the scene where he dropped an H-bomb." The same proposition appears in the story blurb. One wonders if Carnell actually read the story or just leafed through it counting the words. (Michael Moorcock reports that he and Barry Bayley had to persuade Carnell to publish it.[54]) In any case, the protagonist Traven is a former military pilot who may or may not have participated in bombing Osaka, and whose wife and child have been killed in an automobile accident. He has sneaked onto the island of Eniwetok, the scene of many H-bomb tests, but there's nothing in the story to indicate that Traven dropped any of them, or had any part at Hiroshima or Nagasaki either. Claude Eatherly is mentioned in passing, but Traven isn't he.

What is really going on? I have always found this story as elusive as it is compelling, and spending more time with it doesn't lessen either impression. Traven, who used to drop bombs on Japan, sneaks on to Eniwetok, where he slowly starves, has hallucinations of his dead wife and child, and has a delusional conversation with the nearly mummified corpse of a Japanese man, in which he is absolved for the death of the man's relatives in Osaka in 1944.

So here is a man haunted by death: the death he has caused and the death that has destroyed his family. He is also trying to escape from time, and the physical features of the island (at this point a mostly artificial landscape—the beach of the title is

---

54. http://www.ballardian.com/angry-old-men-michael-moorcock-on-jg-ballard (visited 11/6/11).

made of concrete), chiefly the vast array of regularly arranged concrete blockhouses, promise that escape, as Ballard says repeatedly in various ways ("He had entered a zone devoid of time"). He also seems to be escaping from life, since there's not much to eat on this abandoned island, and he is starving to death. When he gets inside the area of blockhouses, he often can't get out—ostensibly he gets lost, but there seems something else at work too. After his hallucinatory conversation with the dead Japanese man (simultaneously grim, hilarious, and cryptic), he drags the body to a point between the blocks and the bunker where he sleeps, and ties it upright in a chair. The story then ends with this splendidly incantatory passage:

> As the next days passed into weeks, the dignified figure of the Japanese sat in his chair fifty yards from him, guarding Traven from the blocks. Their magic still filled Traven's reveries, but he now had sufficient strength to rouse himself and forage for food. In the hot sunlight the skin of the Japanese became more and more bleached, and sometimes Traven would wake at night to find the white sepulchral figure sitting there, arms resting at its sides, in the shadows that crossed the concrete floor. At these moments he would often see his wife and son watching him from the dunes. As time passed they came closer, and he would sometimes turn to find them only a few yards behind him.
>
> Patiently Traven waited for them to speak to him, thinking of the great blocks whose entrance was guarded by the seated figure of the dead archangel, as the waves broke on the distant shore and the burning bombers fell through his dreams.

So, at the end of the story, Traven has been expelled from the Garden of Eden, which was actually death, and *he* has put the archangel at the gate to protect himself from it (sorry, no flaming sword), and he's actually getting some food to sustain his life; but his dead wife and child are still appearing and getting closer to him.

That is a grossly inadequate account of the story, but the more I look at "The Terminal Beach" the more daunting it gets. As with Traven and the blocks, I'm afraid if I spend much more time in it I won't be able to leave. It is so packed with suggestion and allusion that reading it is like stumbling through a jungle at nightfall, worrying that something significant could be lurking behind any trunk or frond. (Or, as Ballard puts it in the first paragraph: "The landscape of the island was covered by strange ciphers.") It is simultaneously obscure and explicit. While much is mysterious, there are things that Ballard wants you to know and he says them right out.

For example, if you couldn't figure out the Garden of Eden reference at the end on your own, that's okay—the dead Japanese man says, a page earlier, during the hallucinatory dialogue, "This island is an ontological Garden of Eden." On the other hand, Traven's wife and child manifest themselves as he becomes more captivated by the blocks, seeming to be a harbinger of his escape from time, i.e., death. But when he leaves the blocks and starts returning to life (sort of), they come even closer. What sense does that make? Ask me in a few years, because that's how long it would take to get to the bottom of this baffling and captivating story. (If it even has a bottom.)

"The Terminal Beach" is one of Ballard's best-written and best-visualized stories. The hellish environment of the abandoned island and its installations is described with oppressive precision, and for good reason: it maps the psychic landscape of his character. (Again, Ballard tells you if you can't figure it out: "'This island is a state of mind,' Osborne, one of the biologists working in the old submarine pens, was later to remark to Traven. The truth of this became obvious to Traven within two or three weeks of his arrival.") It is simultaneously grandiose and mundane, deeply serious and blackly and scabrously funny. The building walls bear shadow outlines of the plastic dummies that were arranged in "inoffensive domestic postures" for the bomb tests. When a naval party comes ashore to search unsuccessfully for Traven, they bring some beer and make a party of it. "On the walls of the recording towers Traven later found balloons of obscene dialogue chalked into the mouths of the shadow figures, giving their postures the priapic gaiety of the dancers in cave drawings."

I've done no more than scratch the surface of this dense and intricate work, which, more than the *Atrocity Exhibition* stories, merits the term "condensed novel." But it's worth saying a bit more about the surface. "The Terminal Beach" is organized into mini-chapters of around 100 to several hundred words, each with its italicized title ("The Blocks," "The Synthetic Landscape," etc.). Most of it is told from a viewpoint near, if not quite inside, Traven's head. But Ballard shifts viewpoint abruptly several times. The section "The Blocks (III)" backs away from Traven, and the author is speaking directly to the reader: "To grasp something of the vast number and oppressive size of the blocks, and their impact upon Traven, one must try to visualize sitting in the shade of one of these concrete monsters...." One brief section, "Traven: In Parenthesis," reads like the author's note to himself, and possibly is just that:

> Elements in a quantal world:
> The terminal beach
> The terminal bunker
> the blocks

> * * *

> The landscape is coded.
> Entry points into the future = Levels in a spinal landscape = zones of significant time.

Another section is in theatrical dialogue, between Traven and the Japanese corpse. And there's an epigraph, a quotation from *War, Sadism, and Pacifism* by Edward Glover (a real book—Allen & Unwin, 1947), which appears several pages into the story, rather than at the beginning as is more common. So the story has a bit of the feel of a collage to it, and the author's presence is more obtrusive than usual, in addition to the story's consisting in large part of the delusions of a madman. One wonders what the readers of this SF magazine thought about a story that pushed the stylistic and substantive envelope as much as this one did. Unlike anything else Ballard published in the Nova magazines (or the US SF magazines for that matter), this one overtly tosses aside received notions of story-telling.

We have only a few inexplicit clues about how "The Terminal Beach" was received. The "Literary Line-Up" section of *New Worlds* survives the Moorcock transition, prosaically retitled "Story Ratings," and in **144** we see that "The Terminal Beach" was rated first in its issue, ahead of the James White serial. Letters to the editor do not seem to have made it from Carnell to Moorcock, though one reader (a J. S. Torr of Orpington) advises another in Carnell's last "Postmortem" (**141**), with specific reference to "The Terminal Beach": "If Mr. Michaels is puzzled by some of Ballard's stories, I suggest that he read them slowly, as 'literature,' and not in hurried snatches as he would read a thriller. Ballard does not only communicate by factual exploration, but also the inventiveness of his language. In this he is a poet, and should be read as such." How widespread such enlightened sentiments were is unknown. We do know (because Aldiss tells us in his "British Science Fiction Now" article in *SF Horizons* 2 (1965)) that Donald Malcolm described it in some other venue as "tripe" and "codswallop." Would E. C. Tubb have called it a frothing jumble? The answer is lost to history.

Ballard's own regard for "The Terminal Beach" is indicated by the fact that he revised it extensively for publication in his collection of the same name, though the original magazine text continued to be used in some US reprintings, including Ballard's 1971 collection *Chronopolis* and Robert Silverberg's 1970 anthology *Alpha One*. The revised text is used in the 1977

Futura *Best Science Fiction of J. G. Ballard*, the later *Best Short Stories of J. G. Ballard* (Holt, Rinehart & Winston 1978), and, of course, *The Complete Short Stories* (Flamingo 2001).

Almost every page has several revisions, and many pages have quite a number. Most of them are fussy line edits, and a few move around the elements of a sentence or paragraph, usually making matters slightly more explicit (e.g., "The young woman drove over by jeep that afternoon with a small camp bed and a canvas awning" becomes "Later that afternoon the young woman drove over to the blocks by jeep and unloaded a small camp bed and a canvas awning."). A few are more substantive. In the paragraph quoted above that begins "As the next days passed into weeks, the dignified figure of the Japanese sat in his chair fifty yards from him, guarding Traven from the blocks. Their magic still filled Traven's reveries, but he now had sufficient strength to rouse himself and forage for food." Ballard rightly eliminated the phrase "Their magic still filled Traven's reveries"—magic is definitely not *le mot juste* here.

The most substantial revision is to the first paragraph of the story, with text added to the *New Worlds* version shown in bold and text omitted from it in square brackets:

> At night, as he lay asleep on the floor of the ruined bunker, Traven heard the waves breaking along the shore of the lagoon, **like the sounds of giant aircraft warming up at the ends of their runways. This memory of the great night raids against the Japanese mainland had filled his first months on the island with images of burning bombers falling through the air around him. Later, with the attacks of beri-beri, the nightmares passed and the waves began to** remind[ing] him of the deep [long] Atlantic rollers on the beach at Dakar, where he had been born, and of **watching from the window** [listening] in the evenings for his parents to drive home along the corniche road from the airport. Overcome by this long

forgotten memory, he woke uncertainly from the bed of old magazines on which he slept and **went out to** [hurried towards] the dunes that screened the lagoon.

One wonders if this revision was not prompted in part by Carnell's misreading that Traven had dropped an H-bomb on Eniwetok—now the correct reading is front and center.

§

Brian Aldiss's contribution to these issues is reduced both in quantity and in quality from prior years. The first of his three stories is "The Under-Privileged" (**130**), an off-handedly razor-sharp parable for our time about a couple of illegal immigrants. Unsurprisingly, he did not sell it in the US. Safton and Corbish, from Istinogurzibeshilaha, are members of a long-lost offshoot species, descendants of a spaceship-full of humans who crash-landed on a relatively barren planet and over generations became cold-blooded. They are legally migrating to a main-stream human planet but get scared and skip the official intake regime, slipping into the big city on their own.

There they encounter a human who offers to show them around, buys them a drink since they don't have any money, takes them sightseeing in the nearby museum/zoo run by the Infectious Diseases Preservation Association, where they take in the Virus Hall, the Bacteria House, Protozoa House, etc. On the way out the human gets them vaccinated (a requirement to exit the building, he says) and offers to escort them where they want to go, Little Istino, which proves to be a large red building. En route he admits that he is an immigration officer and that the shot was really to inoculate them against unhappiness; they will never go back home: "You'll be too happy to leave." "Arm in arm, they turned and hurried into the big scarlet-painted cage."[55]

Aldiss has the *New Worlds* Profile in **130**, but it consists

55. The immigration officer is recursively named Slen Kater, a play on the name of the UK sf fan Ken Slater.

mostly of several photos of him mugging in a ski cap. It does say that he is "hard at work on a new monumental epic novel which we hope to see in the near future," but doesn't identify it. I suppose *Greybeard* is an epic of sorts; the word hardly fits *The Dark Light-Years*.

Aldiss reappears in **139** with two stories, both inconsequential, blurbed as "a pair of paradoxes." "Counter-Feat" is a cartoonishly contrived story about an Earth businessman trying to get off an alien planet despite the connivance of the corrupt local police. "One-Way Strait" is less cartoonish but equally contrived: a crash-landed space traveler has to figure out whether the aliens he encounters are telling the truth about the way to safety, in a variation on an age-old logic puzzle.

§

Michael Moorcock, who has been prolific in *Science Fantasy* and a presence in *Science Fiction Adventures*, but has not appeared in *New Worlds* except for a minor collaboration in 1959, has three stories in these issues. But first he has his turn as guest editorialist in **129** with "Play with Feeling," which cites the absence from SF of "originality of style or characterization," and says "that any serious treatment of human affairs will not be attempted." He notes his predecessors' argument that "it's just entertainment" and responds:

> ...Yet what seems to be forgotten is that fiction can entertain on many levels—that there is serious entertainment as well as the lighter variety, that s-f is one of the most potentially flexible media for the presentation of the human drama there has been and that only lazy writers or bad writers or downright stupid writers find it impossible to stimulate the mind and the emotions at the same time.

Further:

Let's have a quick look at what a lot of science fiction lacks. Briefly, these are some of the qualities I miss on the whole—passion, subtlety, irony, original characterisation, original and good style, a sense of involvement in human affairs, colour, density, depth and, on the whole, real feeling from the writer.

He's looking for writers "who will want to appeal to *all* the reader's senses, to strip away as much illusion as possible, to show things as they really are and to do so masterfully, with passion and craftsmanship. This is the science fiction writer I am interested in—but as yet he hardly exists."

Those who come close include J. G. Ballard, E. C. Tubb, Brian Aldiss ("in short stories particularly, looks as if he's going somewhere"), and John Brunner. New writers make the mistake of "imitat[ing] slavishly what has gone before." That's not what's wanted. But things are looking up. Standards are rising. "Occasionally a novel appears which can be judged by all but the most rigorous criticism—*Stars My Destination, A Case of Conscience, More Than Human, Canticle for Leibowitz, The Drowned World* all contain qualities of good writing, good characterization, good themes and interesting ideas. But they still contain flaws which, elsewhere, would be remarked upon, yet are overlooked by readers who have grown to expect flaws as being apparently symptomatic of science fiction." And his credo: "It is my contention that a mixture of the fabulous and the familiar can produce art which comes closer to defining Truth than anything else—so long, of course, as a good artist is in control of his material." Finally he notes that mainstream writers are starting to move in on SF themes (citing Angus Wilson's *The Old Men at the Zoo* and Anthony Burgess's *A Clockwork Orange*), so SF writers had better get cracking.

Moorcock also has the *New Worlds* Profile in **129**, which notes he's 23 and just married, recounts his now familiar history (*Tarzan Adventures*, Sexton Blake, writer for the Liberal Party), and says: "One of his favourite pastimes is the reading and study of Man's early cultural activities and many of the background settings to some of his long stories are placed against possible extrapolations of our own early civilization."

It's probably unfair to hold up Moorcock's fiction against his prescription, so I won't try too hard.[56] "Flux" (132) is a very readable story that is also very peculiar if you stop and think about it. It begins with Max File, Marshall-in-Chief of the European Defensive Nuclear Striking Force, being brought by robot limousine to the chamber where the Government of the European Economic Community is waiting for him. It seems that Europe is on the verge of civil war, and they can't get a handle on things. One of the government men says: "As an industrial economy, Europe passes comprehension!... We are the first government in history which is aware, and will admit, that it does not know how to control events.... Europe suffers from compression.... Everything is so pressurized, energies and processes abut so solidly on one another, that the whole system has massed together in a solid plenum."

Or maybe Europe is just choked on its own metaphors. Anyway, they've decided the solution is to send Marshall File ten years into the future to report back, and by the way he's leaving right now. So File finds himself first in a fragmented Europe where there is a sex war featuring cannibalism in Northern Europe, and in Greece, social breakdown and mass psychosis occasioned by putting three-quarters of the population in suspended animation. Then he gets back in his time machine, which seems to malfunction and deposits him in a far future where gallant lizard-men with spears, airships, and automatic language-teaching devices face doom from a deteriorating atmosphere and menacing "mineral intelligences"—but they can fix his time machine ("'Our science is very ancient and very wise,' the chief said, 'though these days we know it only by rote.'")

---

56. Moorcock himself said of these stories, "I had had a few stories in *New Worlds*, but none of these was remarkable." Introduction to Moorcock (ed.), *New Worlds: An Anthology* (Flamingo, 1983), p. 13.

The chief also tells him he'll never get home, nobody can understand time. Sure enough, he winds up first in a sort of metaphysical kaleidoscope, then in a "lush world of lustrous vegetation" (also giant armadillos), and so arbitrarily forth, until File is beset by revelation: *"It was totally random. The universe was bereft of logic"* (emphasis his). It's all flux, and File has become a disembodied intelligence, who then gradually accumulates a body, and then figures out that he can create things. Then why not recreate the European Economic Community? Sure thing, works just like the old one, except it turns out they are all speaking the lizard-men's language. The story is clever and well visualized, and Carnell put it in his anthology *Lambda I and Other Stories*.

"Not by Mind Alone" (**134**) is a peculiarly Gernsbackian story (or maybe a belated F. Orlin Tremaine Thought Variant) which proposes, through a 16-page sitting-room conversation, that humanity's natural state is one of individual private cosmoses, uncoordinated in time with one another, with no dimension of shared experience. One of the characters learns how to reinstate this micro-autarkic Eden, thereby achieving "True Freedom," and never mind how we're all going to survive under this compartmentation.

"The Time Dwellers" (**139**) combines offbeat conceptualization with overripe but amusing *Science Fantasy*-ish props. The Scar-Faced Brooder (son of the Sleepy-Eyed Smiler and the Pinch-Cheeked Worrier) is galumphing down a beach, in a *Fin-du-Monde* future where everything is covered with salt, on his seal-beast. (I think I'd rather walk.) He lives in Lanjis Liho, a place where they relate to time as if it were real estate, and he has left town to seek his fortune because the Chronarch won't give him a piece of Past or Future for his own.

After an encounter with his old acquaintance the Hooknosed Wanderer, he comes to the town of Barbart (home of the Barbartians!), on the way encountering a stranger riding "a heavy old walrus," and quickly gets in a pile of trouble, since the Barbartians experience time the way we do, and he has dared to eat his lunch when it wasn't lunch-time. But the judge, after sentencing him to a year in jail, recalls that in Lanjis Liho they know about machines, and wonders if the Scar-Faced Brooder can repair their Great Regulator (apparently, their clock). He quickly sees that the life-core (take a guess) is about to go critical, so he combines his native and his newly learned conceptions of time, and "With an effort of will he reduced the temporal coordinates to zero. It could not progress through time." (So how is it going to power the Great Regulator now?) Now that he has learned that one can recycle the same period of time, he's heading for home to tell the Chronarch about it, though not without another encounter and philosophical discussion with the Hooknosed Wanderer. Judith Merril gave it an Honorable Mention.

§

After the marquee names, there is a great deal of business as usual from the middling *New Worlds* regulars, the all-too-familiars one might call them. The most prolific writer in these issues is John Rackham, with seven stories, mostly pretty clichéd and boring. All but one of them are part of his "X People" series. These are based on the less than captivating premise that after World War II, the growth and development of IQ testing eventually resulted in the identification of "individuals so far above the norm as to be unmeasurable."

The first of these stories, "Dossier" (129), concerns one Gavin Strike, X-Person, who solves the problem of rescuing a kidnapped savant by sending his captor a booby-trapped book, while demonstrating his superiority to the other characters, whose respective admiration and resentment comprise much of the story. Strike is not without weaknesses, however—demonstrating his superiority is very demanding emotionally and he virtually collapses after such a performance. For no apparent reason, Judith Merril gave this rather ordinary story an Honorable Mention.

In "Confession" **(130)**, Ward the X-Person has covertly shipped out on a military expedition, and a piece of equipment is lost. The tough-guy commanding officer has put all ten soldiers who might have been responsible in the stockade until someone confesses. Ward tells them that the guilty party should confess, and the worst that will happen is that they get sent back to Earth and discharged. So they all confess, and the CO flies off the handle and puts Ward in irons to be shipped home. During these proceedings we hear a lot about Ward's parlous and ambivalent emotional state. But the story reads like a retelling of a campfire tale from World War II, if not earlier. The SF elements are almost superfluous; and it's overlong (22 pages) and boring to boot.

"The Last Salamander" **(132)** is considerably better within its limits, a sort of Morlock rendition of Clarke's "Out from the Sun." In an electrical generating plant, in one of the furnaces, suddenly there's a big ember that won't go out, and when poked with metal, it absorbs the metal and gets bigger. How to kill it? The solution is not especially imaginative, but the difficult and risky business of getting it done with tools at hand is well told and visualized. Carnell thought enough of this story that he put it in the anthology *Lambda I*, and he's right—within limits.

The question that isn't pursued at all is *Why* kill it? Why not try to figure out some way to contain it, study it, maybe communicate with it? (The protagonist has had a sort of inarticulate telepathic contact with it.) Call in the boffins from the uni, at least? The lack of thought is especially surprising since the protagonist is "one of the rare and precious 'X' people," who is making a tour of various power generation facilities. In fact, the "X people" gimmick makes so little difference it could easily go unnoticed.

"Deep Freeze" **(134)** is aridly geekish though fortunately short. It posits a mystery: why is Modelite, a substance that expands tenfold exposed to water, suddenly selling by the thousand tons rather than the pound? Because bad guys are dumping it into the ocean to make barriers to block the Gulf Stream and freeze out Europe. The X-Person comes up with the solution: start packaging it in very strong bags so they will explode after a while underwater and wreck the barriers.

"Crux" (**136**) seems determined to make more of the "X people" motif and winds up reading like a Null-A comic book. Dr. Arthur Sixsmith, bored with his profession and his patients, gets a midnight call to come or else his female friend (relationship ambiguous) will meet a bad end. He finds Leng, a wounded gangster, who lives over the Nadir Club, and whom he treats. He has to stay at the gangster's place until Leng has recuperated. There ensues a philosophical discussion:

> "You're quite good," Sixsmith admitted, gently. "I suspect you were, at one time, a gentleman. In the widest sense of that term. However, in adopting the argot of violence, you have fallen into some of the habit patterns of that class. You are still thinking in grooves."
>
> Leng's face darkened, swiftly, and his weapon came up, seemingly a part of his right hand. "Clue me, doctor," he ordered. "All the time, you've been acting weird and talking like a book. What are you, anyway, some kind of screw-loose fanatic? Come on, now, talk it out plain. I don't like playing games."
>
> "You think in grooves," Sixsmith repeated. "You have an obsession. To you, no-one ever does anything except under compulsion of some kind. You seek, always, to find some sort of lever to apply; fear, pain, violence—and now cupidity. You may be right, of course."
>
> "You bet I'm right. Levers, eh? I like that idea."

Etc. Suffice it to say that the doctor is not having any, indeed he is the one manipulating the situation, because he has been told at the Institute that it will take extreme pressure to develop his X talent, and now he's got it. Shortly he causes a vial of essential medication to materialize in his hand, then heals the gangster definitively by telekinesis and teleports himself and girlfriend back to his apartment, where he calls a cab for her, since he doesn't need any help now. So there you are, from gangster melodrama to the ripest *Analog*-style psionic wish-fulfillment, in only a few pages. It gets points for audacity if little else.

"Die and Grow Rich" (**139**) is another SF insurance story, evidently a thriving subgenre. Hird tries to show his stuffed shirt boss the virtues of computerised insurance computations, but his apparatus blows up and he's in the doghouse big time. His friend Broome the X-Person discovers that the problem was large numbers of duplicate entries in the insurance company's files (i.e., "Does not compute!" though of course they don't put it that way), and that's because somebody is running a resurrection business—folks are dying of the sinister Dunn's disease, their life insurance is paid, and then they are alive and insured again, and *driving up everyone else's premiums.* Upon further investigation, Hird and Broome wind up tied to chairs in the basement of an altruist who has been conducting this resurrection scam to raise money to perfect his cure for Dunn's. Naturally they join to facilitate his scheme, and Hird gets the girl, in this piece of extruded product.

"Man-Hunt" (**135**) is not an X-People story, but it might as well be—it's a G-Prime story! And one that reads as if it were rejected by *Thrills Incorporated*[57] as too clichéd. Will Reece is a Galactopol man—a G-man, first class—and he's teamed up with Krager to take interstellar criminal Buller ("Bully") Hawkins alive! Krager is a G-Prime: "The G-Primes were living legend. No-one outside of the select few of the hierarchy, the governing council, knew exactly how many there were, or who or where they all were at any given time." Etc. To cut to the chase, literally in this case, Reece and Krager crash-land on the jungle planet where Bully is holed up, Krager acts like a conde-scending jerk towards Reece, who tells him off and repudiates

57. A particularly incompetent Australian pulp SF magazine of the early 1950s.

the whole Galactopol enterprise. Krager goes after Bully and gets cornered, Reece single-handedly cleans Bully's clock and brings him back. But it was all a set-up! Bully is a real enough criminal, but he's got an implanted tracking device, and Krager was testing Reece to see if he could become the next G-Prime. Fade to black in the thrill of belonging. En route we are blessed by pulp-rhetorical knee-jerks at every turn, e.g.: "Reece, at twenty-eight was large, lean, and as fit as constant and rigorous discipline could make him. He filled his Galactopol-grey uniform snugly and none of the content was fat." "But Kruger, twenty years older than Reece, was forty-eight and on his breast-pocket blazed a single sun-burst in gold." Approaching the moment of truth:

> "Give up, Bully," he said, "I'm taking you in, alive."
> "Not you, nor six like you," Hawkins spat. "Go on, lawman, shoot. You won't get me otherwise."
> "Give up, damn you. You haven't a chance!"
> "You or me, lawman. You'll have to kill me..." Hawkins came steadily on. "Why the hell don't you shoot?" [Etc.]

§

Philip E. High is back—not that he ever left—with four stories, also mostly lackluster. "The Big Tin God" (126) is the usual sort of slapdash goods he has been producing all too frequently. The sketched-in backstory is that a series of world governments has become more and more intrusive, forcing nations to break up into individual cities as a cure for nationalism. But now they've got cityism, and the current world government, Interlaw, has turned into a parasitic bully. Towards the end, however, there's a reference to how the story's menace could "threaten the Empire." Apparently High has forgotten his starting premise and isn't doing much rereading and revising.

The Interlaw forces are invading an unidentified city for some equally unidentified reason, and they discover a whole other city underneath, and beneath that there's a secret installation protected by powerful defenses. It's a giant computer, referred to as Dopey, that is manufacturing items for its defense; what could they be? Turns out it's manufacturing human beings. This is a setup and a punchline but not much of a story in between.

"Bottomless Pit" (128) is a rambling and overlong number about an expeditionary force whose goal is to swipe some high tech from mysterious incommunicado planet Shrule. After some excitement with fast-growing thorn bushes and psychotropic fog and the like, they wake up to learn that they have turned into web-fingered, silver-furred Shrulians. Why? The Shrulian doctor explains, "This planet is unique in the known universe because its chief characteristic is biological conversion." And further: "No, it is not subtle differences in the atmosphere alone, there are countless other factors, biological factors such as air and water-borne bacteria subtleties in solar and natural radioactives. All these affect the alien body in different ways...." OK, now I've got it. This one, by the way, starts out with a pre-Newtonian observation by a character who finds a warning buoy in orbit: "Just how they could get a device as small as this to orbit an entire sun system at such a distance is completely beyond me."

These stories are the work of a writer who seems to have become indifferent and inattentive. Matters improve a bit in "Point of No Return" (132). Tamossin, an interstellar peace-keeper, arrives on an unnamed colony planet, accusing the regime of using forbidden weapons, either "warrior robots" or machines guided with pieces of human brain, against the local insurgency. He gets a demo from their deviser, and that's not it at all—pilots' personalities are telepathically transferred into these eight-foot flying gun platforms, which are operated by an artificial brain. Trouble is, the pilots don't come back too effectively and there's a ward full of psycho cases to prove it. Tamossin's suspicion is confirmed when a rebel missile lands on the home base and kills the whole roomful of telepathic pilots, and the flying cylinders are *still flying*. Tamossin orders the planet evacuated, noting that there are going to be several hundred pretty pissed-off minds packing a lot of weaponry when they discover they no longer have bodies to return to, and "what does it feel like to know *you've created an alien race*." This one is at least professionally made, direct and to its modestly original point.

"Relative Genius" (**137**), High's last for Carnell, is actually pretty good, back up to standard: the protagonist wakes up with his memory wiped in a sort of benign prison camp run by aliens who have conquered humanity (or so he's told by a fellow inmate who has escaped the wipe), and of course he turns his thoughts to planning an escape under the watchful cameras and robotic eyes of his captors. Upon succeeding, he and his confederate find out that something else entirely is going on. This one is succinct and energetic, and if the end is a bit familiar, getting there is mildly ingenious.

§

Steve Hall continues to strive towards the ordinary, though less prolifically than before. He has only three stories in these 16 issues, compared to seven in 1962's 12 issues. "Inductive Reaction" (**128**) is another under the Russ Markham pseudonym in the Galactic Survey series, the one about the two married couples exploring the galaxy. This time the authorities want to keep the womenfolk home because the mission is too dangerous, but they're having none of it, so the four of them are dispatched to Oris IV, where the treacherous natives, after behaving with the utmost servility, rose up and slaughtered a bunch of Earthpeople for no apparent reason. The planet's star is "a blue-white, high-energy star radiating well into the shorter wavebands," and Oris IV has impregnable Heaviside and Appleton layers.

When our characters arrive, the natives are obsequious again, and the men accept their invitation to a ceremony, and everything is fine until they get benignly drunk, at which point the attack starts and the women, who have tailed them unnoticed, jump out of the underbrush and knock everybody else out with what Hall describes as "nerve gas." The connect-the-dots explanation: the natives are empaths, but they've got their polarity reversed, so the more benign our attitudes are, the nastier the natives get, and they receive the feeble radiations of brain activity easily because the planet has "a perfect 'radio mirror'" around it so nothing like cosmic radiation gets through to confuse the issue.

This dreary contrivance is followed by "The Jaywalkers" (**130**), which among other things is a disharmonic convergence of Hall's stylistic infelicities, e.g.: "Grace [the Director's secretary] knew with an accuracy of better than 99% which matters would interest the dapper man whose vitality and sheer, all-encompassing judgment ensured that the right man or woman or the appropriate combination of both sexes was found for the problem under review." Or: "Four pairs of eyebrows lifted enquiringly at Conte's provocative opening sentence and eight ears were on the qui vive not to miss a single item of information." We're only two pages into the story and things don't get better. The Special Survey Team is dispatched to Orontes, accounts of which are so implausible that the Director doesn't tell them *anything* about it, so they will form an unbiased impression. They start feeling funny when they enter the atmosphere, the ground looks translucent, and when they land, they sink into it and it permeates the spaceship. Or, as Hall puts it:

> The vessel moved towards *and into the ground, its own fabric and the flesh of its occupants intermingling with the substance of the planet like two miscible fluids....*
>
> *Waving gently, as if under the influence of an intangible breeze, were the green needles and splotches of lucent colour which were the plantlife of Orontes II!*
>
> With a dream-like disbelief the five humans stared wide-eyed at the planetary surface *which ran,*

apparently unmarred, throughout the cabin's length and breadth. [Emphasis Hall's, throughout.]

The answer, presented by the women via info-dump, is that we've got a new kind of matter here: rotate everything by 180 degrees and you get antimatter and blow yourself up, but rotate it 90 degrees and you just become mutually intangible. So... er... why did the ship stop a bit under the planetary surface, rather than just sinking to the center of the planet? There's no answer that I can find.

Hall concludes his SF magazine career, and almost his SF career (he had one more story in *New Writings in SF 2*), with "Now Is the Time" (**141**). The good news is that it's more competently written than its predecessors, the bad news that its substance is trivially clever at best. It's election time in Euthanasia, the Rabidist Party is using a computer to formulate its platform and is leaping ahead in the polls, but the otherwise unnamed Opposition rents its own computer, which tells them to reveal to the public that the Rabidists are using a computer, so the Opposition wins in a landslide. Perhaps this was thrillingly futuristic in 1964, or 1946.

§

The benignly exasperating Donald Malcolm is present with three stories, all in the Matthew Brady planet exploration series that began with "Yorick" in 1962, and with a guest editorial. In "Twice Bitten" (**127**), Brady et al. have found a splendid planet, except for the bees, which stung one of their company, Paul, leaving him paralyzed for four days. Now they all go around swaddled in protective clothing and clouds of bees follow them everywhere they go. They figure out it's Paul the bees are following, so he submits to being stung again, and this completes the process. Now he can communicate with the (beg pardon) hive mind, and the bees are intelligent, friendly, and happy to share their world (well, maybe they're not really that intelligent after all). It's pleasant enough, and Malcolm manages to refrain from name-checking God this time, but it's amateurishly overwritten in a way that I don't remember from his earlier stories. E.g.:

> The fateful day dawned as the warming star breathed life into the heady, exhilarating air. The sleepy land, a-glitter with a profusion of star-bright dew drops, rolled with the assuredness of all eternity to the horizons. The trees reached politely for the first, tentative caressing fingers of sunlight, while the flowers, of all the subtle hues on nature's palette, prepared to receive their humble share....
>
> The yellow star had cleared the horizon, and it continued to prise loose the grip of the paling night with a wash of faintest rose-gold light.

And other portions have a peculiar and equally amateurish boys'-book jocularity to them:

> Paul nodded sagely, causing Alan to hide a grin, and remarked, "The gist of your cerebral meanderings boils down to this: we aren't asking the right question."
>
> "The magnitude of your profundity astonishes me!" Gordon mocked with gentle irony, seeking to deflate Paul's smugness.
>
> "I didn't know it showed that much," Paul came back at him, laughing.

Unaccountably, Judith Merril gave this an Honorable Mention.

In "Dilemma with Three Horns" (**138**), the Brady bunch are on a high-gravity planet, and do they have problems (hence the title). All of a sudden, the planet's star is emitting more radiation and they're worried it's a variable and they're going to get fried. There's now such a radiation layer around the planet that they can't leave; and the heavier members of the expedition are beginning to fall prey to syringomyelia, a serious spinal condition[58] as a result of the double-Earth gravity. What to do? Take off, and enter hyperspace before hitting the radiation belt, of course. Doing so that close to a planet is usually not recommended, since it's dangerous ("They'd be reduced to spacedust in an instant, sir."). But it works, except that they don't just get past the radiation, they wind up in the middle of the following week, and observe that the planet has been stripped of air and water by the stellar activity. Like "Twice Bitten," this one contains a number of ill-advised rhetorical flights, e.g.: "Dawn boiled up out of a cloud-shrouded horizon with an angry yellow-white radiance. The star, sprouting prominences and flares like horns, bounced into a clear sky like the Devil's handball, bright and venemous [sic]. Breakfast was an apprehensive meal." (The gustatory fallacy! Don't think I've seen that one before.)

And God is back, after a brief absence in "Twice Bitten." For no particular reason, since he plays no further part in the story, we are introduced to Chaplain Macauley,

> a servant of God, space-age style.... By advanced hypno-teaching methods, he had been instructed in the esoteric fundamentals of every major religion on Earth. He could administer to each man according to his spiritual needs with knowledge, sincerity and conviction and was as adept at celebrating mass as he was at finding, unerringly, the direction of Mecca. Macauley was puissant in his pursuit of the atheist, the backslider and the downright un-Godly. Macauley never gave up.

And here's his *modus operandi*: "Ultimately, when a man came face to face with realities which he couldn't rationalize

---

58. Look it up: http://en.wikipedia.org/wiki/Syringomyelia (visited 9/11/11).

or otherwise wish away, it was comforting to have something bigger than himself to run to. That was Macauley's ace in the hole."

But nothing comes of this diversion. The ace is not played. Maybe next story. This one ends with a shameless set-up:

> And ahead?
>
> The spiral arm which nurtured the Sun was tapering off into the almost endless darkness. There waited reality in its starkest aspect. There, however briefly, man might approach and begin to comprehend the mystery of creation and set his philosophy on a practical footing....
>
> What, he wondered, lay out there, beyond the reach of storms?

So, of course, the next story—the money shot—is "Beyond the Reach of Storms" (**141**), a phrase Malcolm borrowed from Arthur C. Clarke.[59] "Out at the edge of the Milky Way, where stars are lonely beachcombers on the shore of an unimaginable sea of space stretching two million light years to the next island of light, they found the strange sun." Strange because it has a hole in the middle, with a field of stars visible through the hole, which is oscillating and slowly closing. Brady says they've got to go through before it closes. Obviously there is intelligence in there, since their test probes have been sent back. Two small ships go through the hole and that's when things get metaphysical and dualistic, or do I mean Manichaean?

Aboard Brady's ship, everything is black (no stars outside the portholes), and they all start feeling like hell—literally. "Brady's mind was a maelstrom of evil desires, thoughts and incidents. All the bad things he had ever done in his life crowded in upon

---

59. Specifically, from Clarke's short story "The Other Side of the Sky." Malcolm, "Reminiscences of a Science Fiction Writer; or, 'I knew the Late, Great Bob Shaw,'" *Relapse* 15 (Autumn 2009), p. 9 (http://www.efanzines.com/Prolapse/Relapse15.pdf) (visited September 7, 2011).

him, each event fighting for premier place. His mind was like a hole, oozing with thick, suffocating mud, which threatened to submerge his consciousness." Etc. And then they arrive:

> Something demoniacal swelled and glowed within him as he gazed out on the face of the planet. The all-pervading colour was a deep smoky crimson. The ground immediately surrounding the ship was flat and rocky; a few hundred yards off, on the port side, lay what appeared to be the edge of a gully, with pale, roseate steam or smoke eddying lazily from the fissure. Behind the gully rose a forest of gnarled, leafless trees, like fingers grasping for paper money floating in a breeze.

And what's with the other ship? Everything's light! Including the passengers! "Despite themselves, the other men were drawn into the trance and soon the seven knelt in a ring, holding hands, while their minds meshed in a purity and a goodness so absolute that it threatened to destroy them." Soon enough, they, too, land: "It had come down on [a] field of flowers whose colours might have been scooped from the hearts of the stars themselves. The field was like a palette, covered with soft saffron yellow, strange amber-gold, salmon, honey-streaked pink, deep cerise flared with silver, bright, glowing black and dull bronze." Etc.

Both parties walk out their airlocks into their respective landscapes and fetch up in the same place, a shimmering building where they are expected: "Greetings, men of Earth," says a scintillating column. Here are the caretakers of the universe, and they are looking for a few good species to become Guardians of a galaxy: "To be a servant of the Creator—for that is the function of the Guardians—a race must have humility and deep faith. Its members must be a mixture of good and evil, lest they suffer because of the lack of this mental balance." (Our heroes passed.) It's going to be hard work, but we'll have help: the caretakers give the humans a box that contains the sum total of knowledge. Hey! Sounds like the forbidden fruit to me! But I don't think that's what Malcolm had in mind. Exactly what a galaxy needs to be Guarded from, or who if anybody has been doing this job for the caretakers for the previous millions of years, is not discussed.[60]

Now that Malcolm has brought God almost on stage, it's not clear what he would dare do as an encore. Carnell's blurb says this is the final story in the series, and it is. Although Malcolm published five more stories in *New Writings in SF* under Carnell's and then Bulmer's editorship, Matthew Brady is no more. Carnell put this story in the US version of his anthology *Lambda I*, but not in the British version. Maybe that's because the readers voted it into fourth place in the issue, according to "Story Ratings" in **144**.

Brian Aldiss selected Malcolm as one of his exhibits in "British Science Fiction Now" in *SF Horizons 2*, the section tantalizingly titled "Donald Malcolm: Beyond the Reach of Criticism," but unfortunately he has almost nothing interesting to say about him, focusing mainly on how Malcolm's characters talk and talk, and how much attention is paid to such matters as drinking coffee and smoking cigars—quite true, but a bit beside the point to my taste. He does note that Malcolm described Ballard's "The Terminal Beach" as "tripe" and "codswallop" (though he expressed admiration for other Ballard stories) and he "can generally [as of 1965, that is] be found conducting a jovial-pugnacious correspondence with the robuster type of fan in the correspondence columns of 'Vector,' the BSFA journal."

Malcolm has the guest editorial, "Fallacies in Science Fiction," in **128**, which is actually more methodical and better thought out than a lot of these, whatever one thinks of the substance of Malcolm's opinions. He discredits Kingsley Amis's notion that social satire is the role of science fiction. After all, he says, hardly anybody has heard of Frederik Pohl,

60. Broadly speaking, this is the same plot as in J. T. McIntosh's "Relay Race" in **22** (1954), discussed in volume 1, *Building New Worlds*.

apotheosized by Amis. It's hard to hold up a mirror to society if nobody's looking. SF would have to be read by lots more people. but that won't happen—"Change is the life-blood of science-fiction" and they're not interested in change. (Not like us: "Contemporary society scorns science fiction and its adherents, while we laugh up our sleeves.") If the run of society tried to read *New Worlds* they couldn't understand it, the magazine would have to be full of footnotes, parenthetical explanations, and a glossary, and it would "no longer help to bind together writers, editors and convinced readers who have a deep, abiding interest in, and love of, science fiction...."

So SF will never become popular in its present form. It "offers both too much and too little"—too much in that it demands that the reader think, too little in that it doesn't provide "Spillane-like violence, Greene-like maudlin religion, sex/strip-tease/animated foundation garment sagas—fill this one in yourself—and Waugh/Delaney-like homosexuality. It seems to be smart to have practitioners of the latter perversion littering modern novels." (This is not Samuel R. Delany he's referring to, but Shelagh Delaney, mainstream playwright of working-class angst, mostly notably *A Taste of Honey.*) "Television, the Sunday press, and many modern novels (and some not so modern reprints) have gone noisily hysterical over crime and vice, and no opportunity is lost to drag the whole sordid mess out for our questionable benefit. (One Scottish newspaper recently published a strip cartoon about a mass murderer, convicted and hanged for his crimes.)" SF, however, ignores this stuff "to its everlasting credit." SF can't be effective satire because "(a), it reaches too small an audience, and (b), it considers beneath notice a lot of the aspects that need satirizing."

Malcolm says in passing that trying to define science fiction is a waste of time, and agrees with John Rackham that all stories have a message, then trashes Arthur Sellings' notion of a tyros' SF magazine—Carnell is already busy, and such a magazine would give license to inept writers rather than requiring them to learn the hard way, by getting rejected from a magazine that publishes the professionals. "We made it, or we wouldn't be writing guest editorials!" And here's the anthem: "Writing isn't a game for faint hearts who need molly-coddling." What's the answer then? "More quality, combined with a planned expansion of science fiction into the outside markets. Quality first." And how? "Sorry I can't come up with a route map to the treasure of quality." But here's a hint: "A trivial theme will almost certainly result in a trivial story." And expansion? "Those British writers with a regular and successful output should try work with the mainstream magazines, thus creating a taste for science fiction right on the uninitiated readers' doorsteps."

Malcolm has the *New Worlds* Profile in this issue, with brash and wholesome photo; there's also a photo of him instructing his kid at the typewriter on the cover of **127**. He took a course in astronomy some years ago and now belongs to the British Interplanetary Society (Scottish secretary, no less) and three astronomical societies, and his interests include philately, archaeology, art, and records. He also produces a lot of science articles, which appear "regularly in seven journals" (unnamed). Interestingly, it doesn't say what he does for a living, though it does say that much of his writing is "planned during off-work hours" and he writes rough drafts during his lunch break. Carnell refers to Malcolm as "a fairly new writer" in the blurb to his guest editorial, even though Malcolm has been publishing fiction since 1957.

§

Barrington J. Bayley makes several appearances as P. F. Woods, the first being "Natural Defence" (**133**), presenting the not very interesting gimmick of a living planet with an immune system that it can't control and that hence attacks the arriving Earthfolk space explorers, a problem resolved by the equally uninteresting expedient of the planet's committing suicide. "Return Visit" (**136**) is, if anything, less interesting: an alien manifests itself to warn that humanity's ancient enemy Lussfer is coming back. Lussfer appears in the guise of a yard-long scorpion and repels the best the Army can throw at it, then Lussfer is attacked by ants and vanquished. The point is elusive.

"The Countenance" (**138**) is an improvement: the idea is just as geeky a dead end as the others (why do spaceships not have windows? Because if you look outside it will kill you), but the build-up is superior. It's a quite good sketch of a smart fellow who never quite connects with society and can't leave well enough alone. (Sounds a bit like Bayley's fiction, but never mind.) Oh, and why does looking at space kill you? "We think it is because he sees the universe too nakedly, too incomprehensibly vast. He loses himself in it, and his consciousness is whisked away into space like a fly would be if we opened the main port."

"Farewell, Dear Brother" (**141**) is a ponderous and peculiar epic about a man whose twin brother is always passive-aggressively abusing and exploiting him, and doing stupid things that require rescuing. On the Planet of No Temperature, which has interesting properties such as superconductivity, the evil twin gets in the way of some circulating voltage and impresses his personality on it, and the protagonist carries a version of it in a piece of rock he brings home, where it causes him marital trouble until he goes back and dumps the rock where he got it. This one is turgid, boring, and twice as long as needed even for its uninteresting purpose.

§

Fortunately, some of the regulars provide more interesting material. Robert Presslie's renascence continues, with four stories and a guest editorial. Most of Presslie's stories are fundamentally silly—some trivially silly, others magnificently so. "Ecdysiac" (**126**) is one of the latter. It proposes that there are aliens, or something, in our midst, which take over the bodies of humans and make everyone see them as different people, who assume influential positions but whom nobody can remember when they're gone. Our protagonist, Pike, mysteriously learns to see them as they are, and of course tries to figure out how to kill them:

> "This was the victim.
> "This was the man he had killed three times already."

A homemade sodium-filled bullet doesn't kill the being either. The usurped body reappears (a middle-aged woman, not the man it had appeared to be) with a big hole in its chest. And afterwards? "It was the same as it had been after the other killings. Always he felt the same needs. The need for a drink and the need for a woman." Off he goes to a bar and conveniently finds a woman sitting alone, and she conveniently agrees to get drunk and sleep with him. The police show up, and he's taken in for an interrogation which becomes less harrowing when the police captain reveals that he, too, sees the body-snatchers, and they've been tracing Pike and his proximity to bizarre murders, and in fact they planted his woman friend when they saw which bar he was headed to.

The story then heads towards a "Don't Look Now"-style denouement, but not before we get a flashback to Pike's revelation, during his early life in Germany, that Eva Braun was really a middle-aged man who was pulling Hitler's strings. (But wait—we *remember* Eva Braun! What happened?) The plot is quite similar to the kind of story Francis G. Rayer has been writing recently, but Presslie is a much more vigorous and vivid writer—there's lots of good local color about Warsaw, where this story takes place—and he pushes his ideas to the bizarre limit with deadpan conviction.

"Till Life Do Us Part" (**127**) goes even further in the same vein, at least until the end. It's tempting to quote at length, and I won't resist:

Spence Logan never gave a dull party in his life. One glance as I entered the spacious room told me his latest death party was unlikely to spoil his record.

The room was tightly packed with guests but I was just that few inches taller than most of them and I was able to catch a glimpse of him at the far side of the room.

Anyone not knowing the set-up would have called me a liar if I had told them Spence Logan had been dead for two centuries....

...Between the heads of the guests and the high domed ceiling there was a cloud that reeked of every prurient narcotic smoke I had ever heard of. The tobacco tube in my mouth practically branded me as a saint among sinners.

There was an overtone to the smoke that I could not quite place at first. Then I was squeezing my way between two women and I recognized the sickly smell of carbon tetrachloride and I wondered just how much depravity they had been through if they had to resort to inhaling carbontet before they could even begin to get a sex kick.

This party is taking place underneath the Atlantic Ocean, and the guests are deathmembers and liferenters: there's a drug called Limbothene that puts one into suspended animation, and a technology of personality transference ("an astonishingly simple combination of VHF radio and encephalo-electrics"). So the swells put their bodies on ice (becoming deathmembers) after finding less fortunate persons willing to rent their bodies for personality transfer (liferenters). When the liferenters start getting along in years, they get paid off and traded in on younger models, and with their new riches they, too, can find someone to rent. Sounds a bit like a Ponzi scheme, what?

Charles van Beer has come all the way from Venus to confront Mr. Spence Logan about his decadent ways, and he does so after a couple of stagey and catty conversations with Logan's, er, female associates. Logan takes him into a big room with an instrument panel, explains that being a deathmember isn't actually as great as the women were making it out to be, since it's really very uncomfortable being in somebody else's body and they have to revert to their own bodies for a day once a month to discharge the agony. But look, what does that instrument panel remind you of?

That's right: "'The stars, Charles,' he said. 'We've got to get to the stars. What do you say?'" And of course Charles falls right in with the plan, though it's not made clear whether this instrument panel is just going to tear the underwater redoubt away from Earth, or whether the whole planet is going walkabout. This rug-pulling reversion from the depths of decadence to the most conventional sentiment of SF, like a smiley face in the abattoir, might seem to rob the story of all point and intensity, but in context it's the most bizarre touch of all.

"Dipso Facto" (131) is one of the trivially silly ones: Ragg goes to the planet Snox, where he is obliged to engage in an eating contest with one of the locals. The Snoxians cheat by teleporting the swallowed food from their stomachs and dumping it on Umba, which as a result is garbage-strewn and smelly. But Ragg has his own dodge, pills that speed up his metabolism so he digests as fast as he eats. Prevailing in that contest, he sets up another one involving the large quantity of Scotch he has brought in his spaceship. Et cetera.

Presslie winds up his *New Worlds* career, and his SF magazine career (he did have a couple of stories in *New Writings in SF*, but that was it for him), with "No Brother of Mine" (137), which shockingly is not silly at all: a sensitive kid oppressed by coarse and stupid parents finds a little man, obviously extraterrestrial, cowering downstairs in the family fallout shelter, and they react coarsely and stupidly as he tries to communicate and then dies. The kid responds by getting less sensitive. It's incisive and not just oppressive because Presslie keeps it brief, yielding one of this forgotten author's best stories, recognized as such by

Judith Merril, who gave it an Honorable Mention.

Presslie's guest editorial, "Speaking for Myself" (**133**), is a considerable disappointment compared to his fiction. He wrestles first with "What does Joe Public want?" and concludes that SF generally isn't it, since there was recently more publicity about an athlete's back troubles than the launch of a communications satellite. And what's happened to the sense of wonder? Nothing—there's a first time for everything, and after that it's hard to get so excited, so "you cannot have the marvellous old stories more than once." But SF is developing, except in the area of Love Interest (sic). "Today we find writers looking at things with a finer focus. Instead of the galactic background he pins himself to one planet, even to one street of one town thereon." And: "The cardboard hero is beginning to breathe. It won't be long before he wants company. Female company." Presslie has the *New Worlds* Profile in this issue, with lean and hungry-looking photo. He's a manager for a "firm of multiple chemists" (pharmaceutical ones), and has not much of interest to say that's any different from what's in his editorial.

§

Lee Harding has a couple of stories and a guest editorial. "Quest" (**129**) is a sort of thematic museum piece, which starts out heavily echoing Ballard's "Build-Up." Mr. Johnston tells the Divisional Controller that he wants to see something *real*, instead of the unrelieved urb-scape that stretches away "like the carapace of some gigantic crustacean. He stared bleakly at the towering confections of steel and plastic...." OK, it's a lobster and a cake all in one. After this conversation has gone on fruitlessly for some time, the Divisional Controller suddenly freezes and smoke begins to rise from him. He's not real either. So Mr. Johnston goes off on his quest through the endless city, and after a brief attempt to get to the bottom of things by descending to the lowest level, he takes an aircar and flies around, finally finding a large park, deserted except for an elderly codger of a custodian with whom he has some pleasant conversation before learning that the custodian, too, is a robot, and for that matter all of the plants are manufactured, and as for Mr. Johnston himself, you can fill in the blank. It's readable enough, if overwritten, but like much of Harding's work reads like a sort of YA rehearsal of standard SF themes. Carnell put it in his anthology *Lambda I*.

"The Lonely City" (**133**) is in the same general vein but scales greater rhetorical heights: Kerril is canoeing down the river and comes across a city, in good repair unlike the rest of them. "Decaying Xanadus squatting like cavernous cheeses upon the crust of the world"—End Time as Ploughman's Lunch? Never mind. So he makes an unscheduled stop. "The canoe drew abreast of the grotesque ramparts." He feels a fresh breeze, and it turns out the city is alive, and levitates him around town, marveling at his existence "'Yes,' he said. 'I am man.'...And all over the city rose a simultaneous echo of the word, a gigantic *ah*! of exhultation [sic] that grew and thundered in his ears. The entire city shook with terrifying emotion."

Kerril is wafted to City Hall, where the Mayor (a "cyber unit," of course) explains why this city didn't crumble like the others: "When we foresaw the doom approaching our deserted streets we knew that unless we worked quickly, time might over-run us. We developed a technique whereby we could deflect the winds of time. Continue to exist outside of the regular continuum. Cast off the yoke of entropy. Protect our city until such time as mankind had need of us again." But Kerril explains that it ain't us, babe: "We can never come back to you, we have *outgrown* you." This does not compute for the city, which entreats Kerril to remain, even for a while, but he refuses: "I am oppressed by your towering buildings." The city, scorned, declares that Kerril will stay whether he likes it or not.

After this tantrum, the city calms down, realizes it is obsolete, and decides to end it all. Unfortunately, it can't activate the necessary processes itself, and presents Kerril with a big black switch, which he obligingly pulls. Then he gets back in his canoe and rides off, but quickly realizes that he's exercised his body enough, so he dematerializes and flies off. "Something indefinable soared and was gone, like an eagle, towards the setting sun." I probably shouldn't mock these primary-colored renditions of some of the great themes of the genre—on some level, Harding's work would make a great one-stop theme park exhibit of "that was science fiction" when the whole show is over—but I am too cynical and decadent to stop.

Harding's May 1963 guest editorial "From the Edge of the Pond" (**130**) is a bit unfocused, but like his stories is enthusiastic if overwritten. He slags his predecessors, describing the earlier editorials as "in turn, introspective, belligerent, and, in the case of John Rackham and Brian Aldiss, personally prejudiced and blandly indifferent." Nobody was objective, he says, until John Baxter came along and showed them the way. Harding condemns the haste of SF types to seize upon works by main-stream writers and slap the SF label on them, as well as the obsession with SF as a vehicle for social satire, "a garden liter-ally overgrown with a multitude of Pohlianish [sic] weeds that have all but strangled the life and imagination out of contempo-rary science fiction." Exercise your imaginations, don't worry if somebody calls it space opera, bring "pulsating life" back into the SF magazines.

SF, Harding explains, is ineptly written compared even with the mediocre mainstream; van Vogt's *Players of Null-A* "reads like a first draft of some ambitious hack," and Heinlein and Asimov's early works aren't much better—but he admires Stewart's *Earth Abides.* "In all its thirty-odd years of existence as a genre, science fiction hasn't yet produced a novelist compa-rable to, say, John Dickson Carr, Christopher Blake, Edmund Crispin or even somebody as outré as Ian Fleming"—they can "produce good novels *consistently,* and deserve the position they have won," compared to the likes of Clarke with his handful of novels. Wyndham and Christopher have done OK, and "we'd better not let Charles Eric Maine out of our calculations either." Hmm. At this point Wyndham had published the four novels on which his reputation rests; Clarke had published *Childhood's*

End, The City and The Stars, The Deep Range, and *A Fall of Moondust*, among others. And they're not competitive with Ian Fleming?

He proceeds: "One has to look no further than James Blish, himself dreadfully alone in the task of adapting the technique and traditions of magazine science fiction and, applying them with what is perhaps the highest concentration of literary skill and integrity to be seen in science fiction today, has managed to turn out a succession of highly successful novels," citing four. Heinlein is ambitious and might get better, Aldiss is good but a prophet without honour in SF (presumably this was written before his 1962 Hugo for the "Hothouse" stories).

The point of all this has become elusive, but Harding reminds us: these are exceptions he's been talking about, and SF writers generally "prefer to cling to the out-moded intricacy of plot." He advises comparing *A Case of Conscience* to del Rey's *The Eleventh Commandment*. "The crucial point is, of course, that the majority of science fiction writers are incapable of writing anything above the level of the standardised action-adventure plot, so if there is to be an overnight revolution in the style of magazine science fiction writing, I for one would certainly like to know just *where* it is going to come from." Those who can, are moving on to write mainstream novels: Bradbury, de Camp, Vance, Pangborn, Bester, and Budrys. (Budrys? It never happened, or he couldn't get it published.)

He acknowledges Baxter's call for more "mood and emotion," but he can't imagine Rackham or Bulmer turning out work in an "advanced style," or Philip E. High or Steve Hall writing a "penetrating, stream of consciousness narrative." There are only a few real SF milestones, and he gives "short shrift to such pretentious twaddle as Zenna Henderson's *Pilgrimage*, Sheckley's *Status Civilization* and del Rey's *Eleventh Commandment*, while retaining a good word for the more impressive failures the field has produced, novels like *Venus Plus X, Starship Troopers, Stranger in a Strange Land*, Aldiss's *Hothouse* and particularly *Minor Operation*, with its brave attempt to put 'normal' human beings into s-f and not the 'knotted pine' stereotype.... It seems strangely out of place that science fiction, of all forms of imaginative literature, should not be sorely in need of a sense of importance, but more necessarily, a sense of proportion."

§

Joseph Green continues his Loafer series in the established born-to-be-mild style with "The-Old-Man-in-the-Mountain" (**131**), in which the Loafers start to attend human schools and there's about to be hell to pay from the bigots. Cut to Brian Jacobs, a large and maladjusted individual who has fled into the wilderness and subsists as a mountain man (vegetarian, no less), and feels twinges of the Loafers' talent for controlling animals, but the Loafers won't help him develop it. So he snatches Micka, one of the Loafers' little girls, hoping she'll help him out, and high-tails it back to his cave. Loafer/human search party in pursuit, and before the inevitable brawl is over, Micka has displayed psi talents previously unheard of. What's more, while she was slamming Jacobs against the cave wall, she shook loose his talent and now he is a Controller too, ready to rejoin society. They're going to fix him up with the spinster schoolmarm. Oh, and the movement to kick the Loafers out of the schools fizzles out.

Matters become more incisive in "Refuge" (**132**), partly because Green has become a smoother and more confident writer in the course of this series. Timmy the Loafer, about to marry one of the humans, decides instead that he wants to go off on *havasid*, the Loafers' *Wanderjahr*, a traditional year's hike around Loafer territory and an institution which has kept Loafer society more or less unified. He's worried that the old ways are dying and the Loafers are being seduced by the Earthfolks' lifestyle, and that's mostly what he finds, up to and including a Loafer village which has pioneered natural teledildonics: they use the psi powers that permit them to control animals to transmit pornographic dreams to humans, and some of them serve as prostitutes as well for those humans who aren't content with dreams. But no one is being taught Control.

Timmy returns from his journey a changed Loafer, and also by heredity the leader of his tribe, and announces his intention to take those who will join him and withdraw into the forest away from the humans. There they'll continue to cultivate the psi talents they now know can be developed far beyond controlling animals. And he's going to marry one of his own kind. The sentiments are still conventional but the presentation is sharper. One crucial question isn't asked. After the humans have learned (from the Loafers' intelligent trees) how to transmit living things without killing them, people have started pouring in from the crowded and impoverished Earth at the rate of 250 a week, with no end in sight. Why don't the Loafers ask that they be stopped and the planet left for its natives? Why don't any of the humans even entertain the thought? *Ad astra* knows no second thoughts even in this otherwise intelligent series, and everybody else just better get out of the way.

§

John Baxter, whose first stories appeared in 1962, bids to become a regular, here at the end of (some) things. The first of his four stories is "Eviction" (**128**), in which he seems to chew more than he bites off. His propensity for scene-setting is on full display:

> The Director's office was a good one, as director's offices go; blonde wood and royal blue carpet, Swedish glass and American lighting, French abstracts on the wall and through one wide window a view of the Scottish highlands that most Southerners would have given their arms for. A surer sign of influence was the decanter of whisky displayed in a prominent position on a side cabinet along with a set of glasses. No furtive

bottle in the bottom drawer for the director of Loch
Carran Research Establishment.

It was rather good whisky too, Paul Antman thought
admiringly as he took another sip, though hardly worth
coming all the way to Scotland to sample.

After such windup, what delivery? Antman, a lawyer, has
been summoned because aliens have landed and claimed the
planet is theirs and we have to leave. We are descendants of
colonists with whom they made a deal that they would periodically provide machines and the colonists would mine minerals
for them, but the colonists never did, so now they have to strip-
mine the planet and make it uninhabitable. But the relics of the
ancient machines prove to be so old as to show that the aliens
didn't keep their side of the bargain, so the contract is void. One
might write an interesting story beginning at that point, but this
one ends there, with a gimmick. (Judith Merril disagreed, giving it, but none of the others, an Honorable Mention.)

"Interlude" (**136**) is more tendentious, and clichéd to boot,
if well enough rendered: Terran Space Forces Major Payne is
recuperating in solitude from a leg wound on a tropical planet
with simple happy natives when an enemy pilot crash-lands.
On examination, she proves to be a Girl, as one put it in those
days. They strike up an idyllic relationship and he shows her
the remains of the natives' great civilization, which they have
abandoned. A message informs him that things are heating up
and the Space Forces are coming to pick him up, so he lets the
Girl steal his spaceship and get away. The story ends with a
conversation between Major Payne and one of the natives and
the proclamation that "There was no point in living if, like Tagi,
you did not realize that happiness is not enough."

With "Toys" (**138**) it's back to overblown scene-setting:

The address I was looking for was somewhere down
in the maze of ancient buildings and twisting lanes that
huddles at the Sydney end of the bridge, overshadowed

by the disdainful pylons. It's called The Rocks—I've never discovered why. The historians probably have a neat explanation, complete with footnotes and old references, but I doubt that it is the right one. Even a young country must have its secret places, and The Rocks is ours. If there are explanations and histories, they won't be found in the records of any university, but in the minds of the old men who sun themselves before the crumbling terrace houses and the cats that roam through the shabby lanes.

The narrator is looking for the shop of a toymaker, whose sign most prominently says "Bootmaker," but below it: "'Toys also,' it read, almost apologetically...." After braving the disdainful pylons and the near-apologetic sign, we come to... the door.

The door, of the ordinary panelled kind, had been painted in robin's egg blue, and the harsh sun had crackled the surface like the glaze on an old Chinese vase. It was the sort of door that one expected to see in a glossy magazine, with a gaunt model leaning languidly against it. It had... character, if that is the word. With a certain diffidence—the feeling I have when touching a painting to feel the texture—I knocked, then pushed the door open.

Emerging to get to the point, we learn that "J. Kraus, prop." (as identified on the almost apologetic sign) does make toys, and they are quite splendid ("Every item was a masterpiece of workmanship"), and there's a discussion of how toys influence the children who play with them, and of J. Kraus's brother Wilhelm back in the old country, who unlike the rest of the family insisted on making war toys. A few weeks later the narrator is window-shopping ("I was walking through the more elegant part of the city, browsing among the big department stores with their Americanised facades and chic merchandising") when what does he see but... war toys, imported, impeccably made, obviously the handiwork of Wilhelm, and the narrator pretentiously muses about their baleful influence ("...each bringing with it a tiny increment of death, planting in every child a dark and evil seed. Accident or design? We would find out soon enough....").

"The Traps of Time" (140) is much better and less irritating. It begins with the same overdone set-up, the beginning of the day of a swell in some far-future Asian society, checking out the crystal roses on his balcony for a paragraph, then dressing for another, etc. But this is certainly more interesting than the texture of the door in "Toys," and things get moving quickly enough. We are in the presence of the Primus of Time, who is caught out in some unspecified misdeed and flees in his bootleg time machine, wreaking havoc with the continuum and requiring the attention of the Monitor of Time City, and coming to a very bad end indeed in a dangerous area of time. There's a nice twist at the end as well. It's time travel hokum as usual, of course, but concise and well turned, so that's all right.

§

Bill Spencer, who has contributed on and off for several years, speeds up his production with four stories just in time for the end. In "The Nothing" (132), stock plot meets psychedelia: pilot Delgado is saying goodbye to his family, getting a send-off speech by the President, just before he blasts off to... the Zero, where the zero-field eats away like boiling black acid at the outer walls of his capsule, and an enormous spiral forms itself in what is left of Space, and there's something whimpering soundlessly in the blackness (that's Delgado): "Indefinite things with no specific shape or purpose moved round it." Then: "There was only a quantum of awareness, which had no name. Without description, absolved from any reckoning." A couple of drops of clear fluid shimmer with their own translucency and coalesce and vanish. Delgado is now somehow linked with his counterpart, sitting in another cabin somewhere. Somebody opens the cabin hatch and leads him out, and it turns out he's on the wrong world. Maybe the drops of clear fluid got switched. The President starts up again. "He wanted to release the man from this absurd, limiting emotion. To free him from his mental straight [sic] jacket. To show him that everything that surrounded him—the world, the people in it, the entire solar system—was part of the same huge pattern, the same living organism. Was linked in one identity. But it would take too long. Now there was so much to do." To wit, announcing: *"My brother, too, is safe...."*

"Project 13013" (**135**) is another out of the stockroom: scientists are testing an immortality serum on mice, and are about to test it on Carlson, one of their own. When they shoot him up, he is swept away into the future to experience a few brief moments of his long and full life, borne on a distinctly Ballardian tide ("Ocean-like, the time wave engulfed him, and swept him along on its swiftly moving crest") to fetch up at some prematurely hippiesque sentiments: "There was a fullness, a completion, in what Carlson saw which swelled up and enveloped him in warm flames of emotion. Beyond emotion, the music and the sight blended into a texture of total symphony in which Carlson was both the creator and the absorbed listener." And: "A sense of the total significance of existence hovered tremulously at the edge of his mind. Gently he moved his mind up towards it, to envelop it, but it escaped edgeways. Yet when he did not look at it directly, the intuition, the total meaning was there." But as far as the spectators are concerned, Carlson just dropped dead after a few seconds.

For "Jetway 75" (**140**), Bill Spencer is reinvented as William Spencer. This story is another in the familiar genre of Traffic Dystopia. A psychologist watches a kid make model human figures and then destroy them with his model jetcar. Then the psychologist puts on his jetsuit, goes out into the jetway right outside his door (they're everywhere), and tries to get to his own jetcar despite the drivers who are trying to kill him. Of course, when he gets behind the wheel himself he loses no time in going after a pedestrian (that is, "A snivelling, abject, defenceless pedestrian!") who has had the temerity to get in his way. Spencer is rarely subtle, but this one reads like an anvil dropped down a flight of stairs.

Almost the same is true of "Megapolitan Underground" (141), a Mass Transit Dystopia about a man on a crowded subway of the future in which the passengers are kept entertained by slice-of-life scenes as they pass, but the protagonist realizes he can't remember where he's going, and his ticket proves to be illegible, and the idea is broached either that this is a population control subway, destined for the center of the earth, or else sitting still underground while the slice-of-life scenes are moving. Or maybe the protagonist has just gone nuts.

Spencer has become a reasonably capable writer. These stories probably read a lot better back when their attitude was newer. Oddly, this is Spencer's last story in *New Worlds*—he did not appear during Moorcock's tenure, and never in *Science Fantasy* under Bonfiglioli, though he would have been at home in either. Instead, he disappeared from the SF magazines for three decades, though he had four stories in *New Writings in SF* from 1964 to 1971, and then he surfaced again with a few stories in *Interzone* from 1993 to 1997.

David Rome has a couple of stories, but his first contribution of 1963 is the guest editorial in **126**, "I Like It Here," an insubstantial piece that lives up to its title, starting with the funny looks he got on the bus reading bound volumes of *Thrilling Wonder Stories*, continuing with how he understands the writers can't get paid more, and anyway *"The s-f writer doesn't claim to be a figure of real literary standing!"* (Emphasis his). Besides, if SF writers got paid mainstream rates, soon enough they'd be elbowed aside by more popular types wanting the higher rates, so better we all forget literary virtue and stay *"Bold."* "As far from high-cocked-little-finger *literature* as we can get."

He reappears in **131** with "Occupation Force," which reads as if he were paying precociously close attention to Vietnam.

Soldiers on patrol on an occupied planet are pushing the civilians (kids, no less) around for no apparent reason. They return to base, but one of the kids provokes them through the fence and a soldier gives chase, catching him briefly before he escapes. But what's that thing stuck to the back of his neck? "The adhesion bomb was small, but it blew the airlock apart and detonated the ultimate weapon.... The explosion was visible all the way back to Earth." It's brief and incisive and would be very effective if that last line didn't so clearly echo Philip K. Dick's "Impostor."

"Foreign Body" (133) is one for the recursive file, but not much else. An SF writer isn't getting any checks, but that's because an extradimensional alien is intercepting his mail, and demands money before it will transmit. Transmit what? Some sort of alien, of course, which bursts into gray specks that fly away. The editor of course rejects the writer's account.

Some of the familiar names have only a single story in these issues. Francis G. Rayer and E. R. James have a story each, their last bows in *New Worlds*, and as graceful as could be expected from them. This is it permanently for Rayer in the SF magazines, and for 24 years for James. Rayer's "Aqueduct" (128) is well-meaning and labored business as usual for him. On an unnamed planet, it *never* rains, but there's a nice big river and the Earthfolks are building an aqueduct so they can irrigate 500 square miles for crops. Nobody has bothered to find out what feeds this river. The most notable life form on the planet is a beetle, which flies all over the place in swarms of millions or more, and its transparent larvae clog the river and have to be filtered out. The beetles are a big nuisance, so the Major wants to kill 'em all, but the aqueduct-builders have this nagging reluctance. Might the beetles have something to do with the river flow? Ya think? It's a pleasant commercial for the balance of nature.

James' "Forty Years On" (135) features Dormer, a space pilot who has just been found after four decades of suspended animation following his heroic diversion of a shipful of near-critical uranium from the immediate neighborhood of Ceres.

But his story doesn't add up, even though he believes it, and he's suspected of caching the unexploded uranium cargo in an orbit where only he can find and retrieve it. A couple of twists later, all is revealed and everybody is happy. It's innocuously clever, which is about the top of James' range.

Clifford C. Reed makes another of his sporadic SF magazine appearances (the first in four years, with only a few more to go) with "Unfinished Business" (**140**), a curious and heavy-handed melding of ordinary conventional sentimentality and SF-style conventional sentimentality. Eric Summers' wife is killed in an accident going to visit their friends for whose unborn child they are to be godparents. So he emigrates to Star 93, carrying his big load of rage and resentment. Seventeen years later, Summers comes back for a visit, still full of rage, and ambivalent about having anything to do with the people and especially their daughter who in some sense were responsible for his wife's death. When the 17-year-old daughter meets him at the spaceport she's like his wife reborn, and just itching to go back to Star 93 with him.

Jonathan Burke, a once prolific contributor to *Authentic* as well as to Carnell's magazines, reappears with his first SF magazine story in five years, and his last ever, "When I Come Back" (**137**), an accomplished horror story about a couple whose child falls unconscious and wakes up two days later with memories of somewhere else, and then becomes an apparent tool of alien invasion by personality transfer. Judith Merril gave it an Honorable Mention, deservedly.

Edward Mackin appears for the first time in *New Worlds* with the very strange "The Unremembered" (**140**), which is utterly unlike the Hek Belov stories that ran regularly for years in *Science Fantasy*. In a dystopian urbanized and automated future, everybody lives for centuries by virtue of the Rejuvenation Clinics, but now the birthrate is falling and the kids are killing themselves off in high-speed accidents, the substance that keeps everybody alive is running out, and people are starting to queue up for euthanasia at the Clinics. Many apparitions of people appear and disappear arbitrarily. The superannuated protagonist theorizes that these are people who, after their Rejuvenation treatments are stopped, deviate too far from the modulations of the Life Force, which are a speech pattern—"A single word spoken by the Almighty."

Sure enough, a few pages later he has become one of them, and things only get more metaphysical from there: "Sometimes he was aware of being outside the solar system altogether, journeying through the galaxy with the ice-cold radiance of the blinking stars his only company, and this was worse. His personality was reduced to shards and then to dust, and the dust scattered over the cosmic wastes, and along the star trails." Etc. Shortly thereafter, he is on his way to join "the Word before it became flesh... the healing Word... the world's end, and a new beginning..." It's tempting to try to fix him up with Donald Malcolm, but in fairness this is a much more readable and atmospheric story than I am making it sound, with both the pervasive decay of the society and the escape from the flesh effectively conveyed. Donald Wollheim and Terry Carr picked it up for the first volume of their annual "world's best SF" anthology.

By the way, Mackin gets prophet points for this vision of factory farming:

"Hens? Get up to date, woman, for heaven's sake! You know what? I saw an egg production unit once. It's just a damn great automated hell! There were three-thousand hens there; but you couldn't see a single one. Not one. They were de-squawked and built in. Machines of flesh. Just parts with measured quantities of food through the neck. What does a hen want with head or eyes? It doesn't need to peck grit either. The soft eggs drop into neat, little plastic containers, which are whipped away by the belt to be sealed and stamped.

"When the production figures decline for any unit it is automatically replaced, and still you don't see the hen. Just a metal box, wired and tubed, and inside is a legless, featherless, headless creature: a bit of equipment that wore out...."

We're not quite there yet, but certainly on the way.

John Ashcroft is another returning veteran, sort of. He had a smattering of stories in *Science Fantasy* and *Authentic* 1954-57, one in *New Worlds* and a few in *Science Fiction Adventures* in 1961, and now he's back, but doesn't stay. "The Shtarman" (**133**) is his last appearance in the SF magazines. Ashcroft also has the guest editorial in **131**, "Beer in the Wine Bottle," which acknowledges the literary defects of older SF but says it still has its virtues, and criticizes the routinized quality of a lot of current production ("Too much is taken for granted by stale writers in staler stories"), and in a hundred-odd-page magazine, "there should be at least one idea, event, situation, scene or character that remain vividly in the mind, and too often there isn't." People in the future won't "be all white, English or American, named George and Bill, uttering 1960 slang, smoking cigarettes, drinking coffee, spending shillings or dollars, and in all ways indistinguishable from the neighbors of some of our witless scribes."

He goes on to mock transplanted Westerns ("Jim Donovan gazed soberly through the port into endless black gulfs beyond the Galactic rim," etc.) and "bureaucracy duplicated—triplicated?—nay, googolplexicated—on Galactic scope" ("Supreme Galactic Co-Ordinator Hugo Schrilheim shoved some documents aside, lit a cigar," etc.). He denigrates Russell's *Wasp* ("I enjoyed it, but not as s-f"), praises some unspecified fresher stories by amateurs or newcomers, and says, "To me, many such stories have offered the tang of wine after Russell's pleasant but prosaic beer. Now, I like beer—but not when I find it in a wine bottle!"

Unfortunately, his own story "The Shtarman" may be wine, but if so it's heavily watered. An Irish farm worker has recurrent impossible dreams of space, and of course they are real and he is in telepathic contact with aliens, and it goes on and on and bloody on—almost 27 pages (but Judith Merril Honorably Mentioned it in her annual anthology).

§

There are a few new writers in these final issues. The most notable ingénue is R. W. Mackelworth (1930-2000), whose first story "The Statue" appears in **126** (January 1963) and who has five more in these issues, then seven more in *New Worlds* and *Science Fantasy* under the post-Carnell regimes in 1965-66, and then is gone from the SF magazines, though he had five more stories in *New Writings in SF* and one in *New Writings in Horror and the Supernatural*, all by 1972. Mackelworth published a few novels, a couple seemingly adapted from his magazine stories, the last in 1981.

"The Statue" is an extremely amateurish story about space explorers who find themselves marooned on a desert planet in the company of a statue that one of them, Trudi, telepathically determines is a malicious robot that wants nothing more than to be taken back to Earth to work its evil will there. Obviously they can't do that, so they'll stay on this world and make the best of it. It is revealed that this is all a set-up by which explorers are recruited and then entrapped into becoming colonists. The moral ramifications of this policy are not explored, and the story also features king-size lapses of logic, not least that this band of colonists consists of three men and one woman—not a high-percentage strategy, one would think. This is all rendered in prose sometimes so clumsy as to support the view that Carnell by this point is hardly paying attention. (E.g.: "Her words came as if punctured with too much care and seemed to hang in the air between them.")

But Mackelworth's next, "I, the Judge" (**130**), is a considerable improvement in its over-the-top way:

This is to be a Show Trial.

I dislike them because Justice, like the age, has become theatrical enough, even the New Justice. There were certain rhetorical passions in my young days but they had restraint and poise.

The Trial will be very short. The screening companies have a tight timetable to meet. More to the point, the authorities prefer a demonstration that is short and useful.

The People heed the crack of the whip.

Behind all this attitude, not to mention use of the present tense before it became fashionable, the story is a bit murky, but it seems that the defendant in this trial gave a Martian slave his freedom, a no-no in this future regimented society. Judges are human but guided by a computer (the "Aid to Justice") which has the ultimate authority. This judge has about had it, and contrives to have revealed in this trial that the Martians are actually intelligent. Having done that, instead of excusing the defendant (the swells' preferred verdict), the judge sentences him to death. As the story ends he is sabotaging the computer with a knife so it can't overrule him, and so maximum discredit will fall on the regime from his cruel decision. Carnell blurbs observantly: "Mr. Mackelworth's second story for us is considerably different to any we have recently published. Although it is outwardly a robot story, there is a very big difference in the manner of the telling."

Next is "Pattern of Risk" (132), also a nice try, though a bit more sedate than "I, the Judge." A business executive gets a call from an executive of his insurance company, who tells him that there is a pattern in his company's accident claims indicating that someone is sabotaging things for the insurance money. Their predictive methodology shows that one of the company's spaceships, with crew, is next to go (nice film they have of this future event, too). The implication is that the protagonist is the villain but it's never stated, and it seems to be contradicted by his firing one employee, cancelling his trips, and repairing the defective heater in his office. The story is entirely dialogue-driven and suggests that Mackelworth's closet ambition is to be a playwright (an impression consistent with some of his stories in *Science Fantasy*). I'm not sure this story ultimately makes any sense, but it's much livelier than 90% of its company, and it's the second example in these issues of the subgenre of Insurance SF (the other, in case you've forgotten, being Rackham's "Die and Grow Rich" in **139**).

"Rotten Borough" (**134**) returns to the over-the-top black comedy of "I, the Judge," this time taking on the legislative branch. In an unspecified country of the future, there is only one opposition MP, elected by the West, but he is enthusiastically rumbling with the ancient and corrupt Prime Minister over a plan to extend the central government's TV coverage to the West and thereby subliminally brainwash the last hold-outs into voting for the majority. All this is presided over by the robot Speaker, who is designed to be incorruptible and who keeps order with a shock device. The Prime Minister is eventually provoked to pull a gun and is killed after shooting the Opposition, who proves to be a robot and is merely dented. It is revealed that there is only one family left in the West, a fact concealed from the public by the mass manufacture of robots. The whole sequence of events has been orchestrated by the Minister of State, a representative of the sole remaining family. All of this is recounted in a smooth and cynical voice by the narrator, a journalist. Thus, the first paragraph:

> One wit described the Parliament building as "the most enduring comedy of all." For all that, it's quite a showplace and the people love it. They respect the old fashioned pile of glass and metal as if it were more than a mockery and perhaps I can't blame them, everyone likes to support a long run.

"The Cliff-Hangers" (**137**) is a tastily sardonic tale of corporate malfeasance, beginning:

There were five men in the room. Four sat in plush, executive chairs and the fifth was a projection on a tele-screen. The room was stamped with the set, ancient pattern of such places. In the room, secrets were whispered by earnest mouths into open ears and bold, hypocritical speeches bored dull holes into tired ideals. It was a Boardroom. Its brown and polished aspect betrayed it and the filter-cleaned safety of modern cigars mingled with the still potent fumes of old brandy giving it a special atmosphere.

Today's agenda is to sabotage the computer of a rival corporation so it can't bid against the Company for a lucrative contract. They've hired an agent to do this and are following the action through an audiovisual link, seeing through his eyes. Of course things come to a spectacularly bad end, enthusiastically rendered, and concluding with a variation of the device later featured in David Langford's Hugo-winning "Different Kinds of Darkness" (*Fantasy & Science Fiction*, 2000).

"The Unexpected Martyr" (**139**) is a sort of companion piece to "Rotten Borough." Here another unspecified future nation is governed by sequential revolutions, and the story consists of several aristos, including the Recorder—150 years old, apparently a brain in a box, who is supposed to take all this turmoil down, but in fact keeps two sets of books, one sanitized—sitting around talking and watching while the current revolution gets out of hand and maybe brings the whole system down. This one is mostly attitude with not much interesting happening, and becomes tedious at 18 pages. But Mackelworth seems to have discovered the same liberating truth as Ballard. Once you show Carnell that you can perform at a certain level of competence, he will publish almost any damn thing you submit, so why not make the most of the opportunity?

The eccentric Ernest Hill makes his first appearance in the SF magazines with "The Last Generation" (**138**), an annoying contrivance in which a bunch of sentient entities, origins unspecified but seemingly artificial, know they are living in the last of the 100,000 years of their existence; what to do? Galgan, last of the Penultimate generation, goes off to consult God, a giant computer that speaks in riddles until pressed, then explains: "the galaxies of anti-matter are approaching the galaxies of matter." The story eventually dissolves into metaphysical gibberish about how "The End became the Beginning, and the Beginning, the End," but not before there is a lot more capitalization under the bridge, e.g.: "As the years descended, we accepted the Ultimate, its inevitability, pre-orientated the Communal Contemplative. Now individual fear has destroyed the faculty in you, the Last Generation. Without the Contemplative you are ill-equipped for the Reasoning. Do not try, my friends!" Hill will have half a dozen more very uneven appearances in the post-Carnell *New Worlds* and *Science Fantasy*.

Hilary Bailey's first appearance in the SF magazines, "Breakdown" (**135**), is solidly in *Galaxy* territory. In the future, perfection has been achieved under the Automated Government, and atavistic urges are bled off with the "neurodram," which allows submerged personalities to emerge and raise cathartic hell—under supervision of course. Those with milder problems go watch them in Neurodram Park. But the barroom brawl the characters are watching goes out of control.

John Garforth appears for the first and only time in the SF magazines with "Lack of Experience" (**134**), an amusing and well written if completely ridiculous satire about a robot who is bored with his life working in a library ("Some leisure class reader would come up to me and ask where she could find a book on how to sleep twenty-five hours a day—the dynamic approach to killing time."). Naturally he pursues romance and meaning, having various picaresque adventures on the way, such as being accosted by yobs as he promenades with his female acquaintance:

"Hey, look, it's a bleedin' shiner!"
"Knocking it off with our women!"...

"Can you fight, tin pot?"

"Sorry. I don't need to. Come round and get beaten up when we're testing metal fatigue."

And so on. Garforth is a pseudonym for Anthony Hussey, of whom there have been several in recorded history.[61]

Carnell says Pino Puggioni's "Yutzy Brown" (135) is a fruit of his trip to Trieste—while in Italy, he said, "we are always prepared to consider science fiction stories by continental writers." This is Mr. Puggioni's only appearance in the UK or US SF magazines, but he is credited with a couple of dozen stories from the '60s through the '90s in a Web guide to Italian SF, and it looks as if he had a collection published, insofar as I can infer from a language I can't read.[62] A man living on a colony planet wins a literary contest and travels to Earth to get his book published. The director of Intergalaxy, the big publisher, proves to be a machine, and rejects his ms. in a matter of seconds, having reduced it to algebraic equations and found it insufficiently logical to interest the public. Next day the aspiring author comes back and proposes that if books can be reduced to equations, equations can be expanded into books, and here are three series of them. This leads to his arrest: his equations were copied from a book for the mentally deficient. The outcome of the court case is to put him in charge of Intergalaxy, since he has now demonstrated the "incongruity and grossly illogical logic" of the incumbent. It is hard to tell if this loosely Sheckleyesque nonsense was translated (there's no credit) or if English is the author's second language. A sample: "I began to speak with extreme decision to that half-rusted

61. Indefatigable bibliographer Phil Stephensen-Payne tracked Mr. Hussey down and (abetted by Steve Holland) determined that he (b. 1934) is also the author of several Avengers novels, a Pallisers novel, and four Paul Temple novels ghosted for Francis Durbridge. "Lack of Experience" was his first professional sale.

62. http://www.fantascienza.com/catalogo/A0667.htm#4327 (visited 9/11/11).

mass of wheels whose reasoning was that which only a human element could give."

H. A. Hargreaves' first SF magazine story (and only one, until a couple of items in *On Spec* in 1989 and 1990, per Miller/ Contento) is "Tee Vee Man" (**137**) ("The Tee Vee Man" on the Table of Contents). A communications repair man in orbit doesn't get much respect, even though his job is hard and dangerous, and even when he fixes a communication satellite in time for a suspicious mob in an unnamed Central African country to be shown that their beloved leader is alive and well and addressing the United Nations, thereby avoiding a bloody uprising. This post-colonial patronization is reasonably well turned. H(enry) A. Hargreaves (b. 1928) had several stories in Carnell's *New Writings in SF* anthologies, and is reported ("The Literary Line-Up," **136**) to be a professor at the University of Alberta. Some four decades later, we are told, "H. A. Hargreaves is one of Canada's remarkable, one might even say legendary, speculative fiction writers. He is a retired professor of English, formerly at the University of Alberta (Edmonton), and was twice nominated (1982 and 1983) for the Lifetime Contributions category in the Prix Auroras. His collection of short stories, *North by 2000*, in its time received wide critical acclaim from both peers and periodicals." Or so says his publisher, which also specializes in glasswork and cooperage.[63]

Roy Robinson, who collaborated on a story four years previously in *New Worlds* with one J. A. Sones, is back on his own with "Adaptation" (**129**), a hard-working alien contact novelette in which human explorers land on a planet and discover it's earthlike except there's only one significant animal form, rodent-like, which they call ratoids. The ratoids shortly develop the ability to eat the humans' crops, and when the humans try to stop them, larger and more dangerous forms begin to appear, until suddenly there are humanoids attacking their robots and burning down their outbuildings. Everybody off the planet!

63.　http://5riversnews.blogspot.com/2011/05/ha-hargreaves-work-to-be-published-by.html (visited 9/11/11).

What's behind all this? Kinlay the zoologist isolates a virus from the brains and nervous systems of the animals, whips up a vaccine, and under its influence their captive humanoids become docile and friendly. It's a bit clumsy and amateurish but with a rewrite could have appeared in *Analog*. Robinson seems to have given up after this—he has no more credits in the SF magazines.

James Inglis is not a new byline or writer, having placed a couple of stories in *Nebula* shortly before its demise in 1959. He has a couple more stories in these *New Worlds* issues, which are his last appearances in the SF magazines. "Compensation" (**129**) is a pleasant and reasonably competently written alien contact story bearing conventionally unconventional sentiments. Humans land, find the alien and planetbound Thorm, who prove to be telepathic, and after some deliberation the Thorm decide they'll share their world with humans. The protagonist is pitying them for not having achieved space flight when their Thorm contact spreads his wings and flies off, and the human realizes he's the one who is pitiable. "The Game" (**134**) has an axe to grind too: the characters are dolphins trained by humans in the Game, which is to track that strange creature the Submarine and report back. Then they actually see a Submarine, quickly figure out what they're being used for, and hastily depart the scene of their treacherous exploitation.

§

We come to the last of the dregs. Peter Vaughan's first published SF story is "Live Test" (**127**). He had one more in the next month's issue of *Science Fiction Adventures*, which I described above as "fatuous," and this one is not much better. A spaceship crew discovers that they're badly off course, the generators and the regulators are rubbished, and communications are screwed up too; but we know from the title that it's all a set-up, and indeed the people in charge admit as much when the crew improvises a way home.

Gordon Walters is also a new byline, but not quite a new writer—it's a pseudonym for George Locke, who had one previous story in *Authentic* in 1957. "Pet Name for a World" (**127**) presents an interstellar exterminator—actually a forensic something or other, but he is engaged to poison the vampire that is terrorizing the potential colony planet Angstrom Veema. That's right, one vampire. It's hard to tell if Locke is purposefully writing parody or playing it straight, but it doesn't matter since neither would do him credit. It's a very silly story *and* not especially funny.

B(rian) N. Ball makes his second and last contribution to *New Worlds* with "The Postlethwaite Effect" (**136**). A nebbishy scientist makes a major discovery in physics as a result of a sadistic chance remark by the man who used to torment him in school, and names the discovery after him. It's really about the scientist's wife, who has taken over his life and managed his discovery so as to make him (and her) rich, and Ball's main agenda seems to be to skewer his caricature of an unpleasant woman. Not much of interest here.

David Busby's "No Ending" (**136**) acts out its title, going on for 22 interminable pages. It's a tiresomely overwritten and pretentious story about a man living in the last human settlement outside the City, who is crazy and thinks he is God. When somebody from the City appears and tries to preach to him and "God"'s followers (at least he thinks they are his followers), he takes exception and kills the visitor. It turns out that the City folks are getting ready to leave Earth, and they're taking the country folks with them, but they'll leave God behind by himself as punishment.

David Jay, who has no other credits in the SF magazines, contributes "Burden of Proof" (**126**), a not very interesting story about a man who is convicted of murder and executed for killing another member of the Space Exploration Service. Later the natural phenomenon that set up the circumstantial evidence against him is revealed.

And here (in **128**) is Walter Gillings (1912-79), founding editor of the pre-Carnell *Science Fantasy*, with his second published piece of fiction in the SF magazines. (The first was "The Midget from Mars" as by Thomas Sheridan in a 1938 *Tales of Wonder*). It's also his last, and just as well. In "Too Good To Be True," the editor of an SF magazine is receiving manuscripts from a writer who obviously knows whereof he writes (an extraterrestrial this time). Either Carnell was being nice to Gillings after all these years by publishing it, or Gillings was helping Carnell out by filling a last-minute hole in the magazine.

David Alexander, who according to Miller/Contento has one prior SF publication in *Fantasy Fiction* in 1953, contributes "The Disposal Unit Man" (**133**), a heavy-handed satire. In the future, population will be controlled and the food supply kept up by selecting neighborhoods and killing everybody in them, by means of gas, robotic disposal units, and robotic snipers.

§

So, the final reckoning: what's immortal here? Not a lot. This transitional year and the end of Carnell's reign produced one unquestionable classic, Ballard's "The Terminal Beach," the cuckoo's egg that almost by itself justifies Carnell's 17 years of effort. Not far behind are Ballard's "The Subliminal Man" and, with some reservations, "End-Game," and Aldiss's "The Under-Privileged."

Still, there are quite a few near misses, sharp or solid or vivid or ingenious, including Rackham's "The Last Salamander," Presslie's "No Brother of Mine," Mackin's "The Unremembered," Moorcock's "The Time Dwellers" and "Flux," High's "Relative Genius," Green's "Refuge," Baxter's "The Traps of Time," Rome's "Occupation Force," Mackelworth's "Rotten Borough" and "The Cliff-Hangers," Burke's "When I Come Back," and Garforth's "Lack of Experience." Even Harding's near-museum pieces "Quest" and "The Lonely City" would still read well in an anthology if surrounded by good company.

§

Here, then, is the legacy of the Carnell *New Worlds*:

The fiction is a decidedly mixed bag, some of it excellent, some of it (concentrated in the early years) abysmal, and a great deal of it unremarkably competent—or unremarkably less than competent. The majority of the serialized novels by the regular contributors whom Carnell developed achieved only the lowest rung of book publication, mostly for good reason, and most are forgotten today (even some that deserve much better, like James White's "Open Prison" a.k.a. *The Escape Orbit*). The *New Worlds* novel that has survived the best, Philip K. Dick's *Time Out of Joint*, appeared there only by happenstance, after the demise of the US magazine that was to publish it. The magazine also provided a first UK publication for a number of novels that had previously appeared in the US, ranging from the capable to the mediocre; the most distinguished of these was probably Theodore Sturgeon's interesting and readable failure, *Venus Plus X*.

New Worlds's record is more impressive with respect to short fiction. J. G. Ballard contributed a remarkable string of striking and original stories, most especially "The Terminal Beach," closely followed by "The Voices of Time," "The Waiting Grounds," "The Overloaded Man," "Chronopolis," "Billennium," "The Cage of Sand," "The Subliminal Man," and "End-Game." Brian Aldiss's best stories did not appear in *New Worlds*, but his second best are impressive enough: "Outside," "Gesture of Farewell," "Blighted Profile," "Incentive," "Segregation," "The Pit My Parish," "Moon of Delight," "Soldiers Running," "Old Hundredth," "Under an English Heaven," and "The Under-Privileged." None of the magazine's other writers made such notable contributions, but throughout its history it published a scattering of excellent and memorable short stories and novelettes, including Arthur C. Clarke's "Inheritance," Peter Phillips' "Plagiarist," John Christopher's "Balance," J. T. McIntosh's "Bluebird World" and "Report on

Earth," John Brunner's "Host Age," James White's "Tableau," Colin Kapp's "Breaking Point" and "Lambda I," and Robert Presslie's "Another Word for Man." Many more, by these authors and others including Arthur Sellings, Harry Harrison, Wynne Whiteford, Lee Harding, John Rackham, Michael Moorcock, Joseph Green, R. W. Mackelworth, John Baxter, and Jonathan Burke, were intelligent and capable, and still read well today.

It must be acknowledged that some of the successes of *New Worlds* and its companion magazines were likely accidental. As noted repeatedly in the text of these volumes, Carnell's story blurbs indicate that sometimes he had little understanding of what he was publishing. He was reluctant to publish some of the best and/or edgiest stories in the magazines—Aldiss's "The Failed Men" and Moorcock's "The Deep Fix" in *Science Fantasy* and Harrison's "The Streets of Ashkalon" and Ballard's "The Terminal Beach" in *New Worlds*.

On the evidence of the magazines and the statements of some of those who knew him, Carnell was a man of limited gifts and vision, but one who accomplished more than have many more talented people by virtue of sheer effort, persistence, and good will. Brian Aldiss said bluntly, "He had no literary taste."[64] But even if he didn't know literature, he knew the difference between competent and incompetent commercial fiction (even if he perforce published a few examples of the latter in *New Worlds*' early and difficult years), and strove consistently to maintain and improve his magazines' standards, despite the numerous examples of publishers who appeared to prosper with no standards at all, at least for a time.[65]

---

64. Aldiss, "The Glass Forest," http://www.solaris-books.co.uk/aldiss/html/glass_forest_4.html (visited 10/19/11).

65. As Gordon Landsborough, veteran of UK publishing, put it: "John Carnell wouldn't lower his standards at a time when the commercial interests were destroying the market with their rubbish; all those years—and how long they seemed—he kept his patience, struggled on a shoestring and strove for better writing." (Philip Harbottle, *Vultures of the Void: The Legacy*, p. 262.)

Further, Aldiss's "no taste" remark came only after he said, "Carnell was honest down to the last half penny, and brought his magazines out regularly." And that statement points toward Carnell's significance to British science fiction. He was an institution-builder. He helped put a roof over the head of British SF. After several years of erratic schedules, he entered an arrangement with a larger publisher that allowed the establishment of a reliable monthly schedule, filling out the magazine with US reprints for a time until he was able to develop a stable of writers who were capable of producing enough professional copy—and, conversely, who knew that they had a reliable market for what they produced.[66] He diligently publicized events in the SF community, such as conventions (and he served as chair of the first World SF Convention to be held in the UK) and the International Fantasy Award, and conducted an ongoing conversation in his editorials and letter columns about the state of SF publishing and other aspects of the genre. He relentlessly promoted SF in the visual media, as long as he thought it was worthy—and when it wasn't, he seemed to take it almost as a personal betrayal. His influence was felt far beyond his magazines, from his work as agent, as judge from the beginning of the UK Science Fiction Book Club, as editor of at least one publisher's SF line, and as informal advisor to SF publishing generally.

In the end his dedication flagged, and the results were visible in the magazine. Aldiss again: "...[T]here is no doubt that towards the end of his long and successful reign his interests lay elsewhere, and he let less interesting writers have too

66. Carnell was not entirely alone in this endeavor. *Authentic Science Fiction* maintained a monthly schedule beginning in 1951. However, it was never sufficiently well budgeted to attract the best material, and few stories it published are remembered today. It ceased publication in 1957. Gordon Landsborough, who helped establish it, said bluntly, "It was starved to death." (Harbottle, *Vultures of the Void: The Legacy*, p. 138.) *Nebula Science Fiction*, started in 1952, paid its writers better, but did not manage a regular schedule until 1957, and ceased publication in 1959. Like *Authentic*, it published few stories that made a lasting impression.

great a say."[67] But the building was done. Carnell had set the stage for the next major development in UK science fiction. the New Wave adventures of *New Worlds* itself. and had himself moved on to the next mode of SF publishing as editor of the *New Writings in SF* anthology series.

67. Aldiss, "British Science Fiction Now." *SF Horizons* No. 2 (Winter 1965).

ABOUT THE AUTHORS

JOHN BOSTON is Director of the Prisoners' Rights Project of the New York City Legal Aid Society, where he has worked for many years, and is co-author of the *Prisoners' Self-Help Litigation Manual*.

DAMIEN BRODERICK is an Australian science fiction writer, editor and critical theorist, with a Ph.D. from Deakin University. Formerly a senior fellow in the School of Culture and Communication at the University of Melbourne, he currently lives in San Antonio, Texas. He has written or edited some 60 books, including *Reading by Starlight*, *x, y, z, t: Dimensions of Science Fiction*, and *Unleashing the Strange*. *The Spike* was the first full-length treatment of the technological Singularity, and *Outside the Gates of Science* is a study of parapsychology. His 1980 novel *The Dreaming Dragons* (revised in 2009 as *The Dreaming*) is listed in David Pringle's *Science Fiction: The 100 Best Novels*—and with Paul Di Filippo, he has written a sequel to Pringle's book, *Science Fiction: The 101 Best Novels, 1985-2010*. His recent short story collections are *Uncle Bones*, *The Qualia Engine*, and *Adrift in the Noösphere*.

INDEX OF NAMES

Gollancz, 110-11, 196, 213, 230, 245, 269
Graham, Richard, 87, 190, 202, 249, 263
Green, Joseph, 193, 245, 302, 338, 360
Gunn, James, 268
Guthrie, Alan (E. C. Tubb), 18, 58
Hall, H. W., 293
Hall, Steve, 195-96, 242, 244, 279, 320, 337
Haller, F., 22
Hamilton, Edmond, 134
Hansen, Rob, 13
Harbottle, Philip, 117, 238, 360-61
Harding, Lee, 19, 23, 50, 83, 123, 189, 202, 220, 239, 241-42, 259, 263, 266, 279, 334-37, 358, 360
Hargreaves, H. A., 355
Harmon, Jim, 174
Harrison, Harry, 102-03, 120, 133, 139, 198, 227-30, 255, 263, 273-74, 300, 360
Hart, Dale, 175
Hasse, Henry, 135
Hawkins, Peter, 78-79
Healy, Raymond J., 135
Heath, Phillip, 98
Heinlein, Robert A., 40, 96, 113, 163, 258, 336-37
Hemming, Norma, 149
Henderson, Zenna, 261, 337
Hesky, Olga, 262
Hickey, P., 238
Higgins, H., 238
High, Philip E., 18, 62-63, 190, 236, 238, 279, 318, 320, 337, 358
Hill, Ernest, 352
Hodgson, William Hope, 134
Horne, Lance, 99
Horton, Rich, 132, 147, 189
Hoskins, Robert, 97, 174
Hoyle, Fred, 121

Hutchinson, Joyce Carstairs, 91, 249
Hynam, John, 16, 31, 75-76, 99
Inglis, James, 260, 356
Ingrey, Derek, 278
Irwin, Mark, 31
James, E. R., 17, 19, 80, 138, 150, 230-32, 272, 345
James, Kathleen (Joyce Carstairs Hutchinson), 91, 249
Jardine, Jack, 98
Jarr, 14, 152
Jay, David, 357
Jesus, 275
Johns, Kenneth, 13, 28, 100, 137, 140, 151
Johnson, Leslie, 117
Johnson, P., 278
Jones, Langdon, 186
Jordan, Sydney, 14, 15
Jorgenson, Ivar (Robert Silverberg), 94, 131
Kapp, Colin, 16-17, 19, 60-61, 102, 203, 216-18, 258, 263, 272, 279, 288-89, 291, 293, 360
Karloff, Boris, 203-04, 206
Kemp, Earl, 27, 103
Kippax, John, 16, 31, 75-76, 170, 173
Knight, Damon, 50, 101, 106, 261
Knox, Calvin M. (Robert Silverberg), 130-31, 146
Kornbluth, C.M., 128-29, 133
Kuttner, Henry, 104, 229
Kyle, David, 117
Landsborough, Gordon, 360-61
Lane, Derek, 98
Langdon-Davies, John, 259
Langelaan, George, 89, 90
Langford, David, 143, 352
Laumer, Keith, 93
Leiber, Fritz, 242, 262
Leinster, Murray, 102
Leslie, Desmond, 120

INDEX OF TITLES

9 781479 400041